LOCKED in LIES

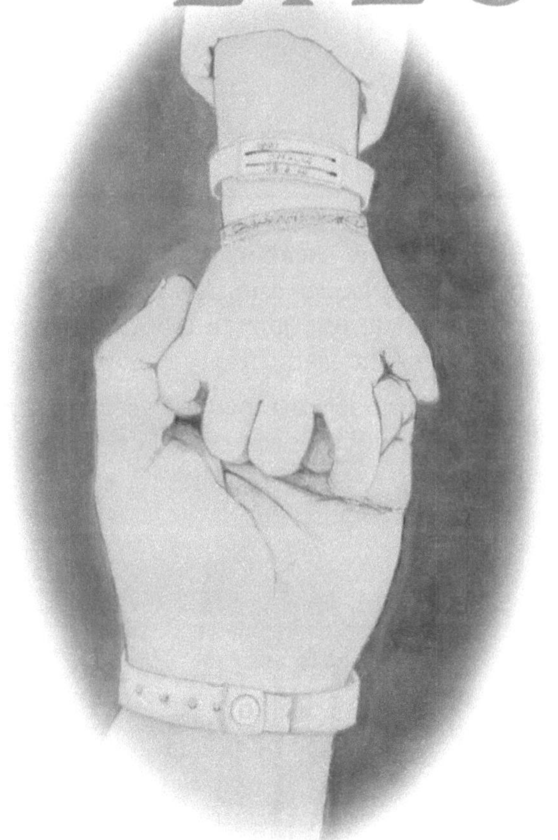

MEREDITH REECE

To find out more about this author's
upcoming releases and free giveaways
visit the website and join the community at:
www.meredithreece.com

Or, come chat with me on Facebook at:
Meredith Reece – Author

LOCKHEART MYSTERIES

LOCKED
in LIES

LOVE OR LOYALTY
- CAN TIME
REALLY HEAL
OLD WOUNDS?

MEREDITH REECE

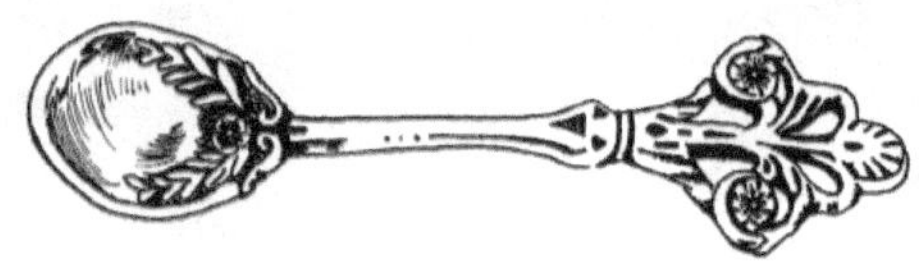

This is a work of fiction.
Names, Characters, places and incidents either are the
product of the author's imagination or are used fictitiously.
Any resemblance to actual persons, living or dead, business
establishments, events, or locales is entirely coincidental.

For my Grandmother, Shirley
and my sister, Karlene.

Forever friends - Forever loved

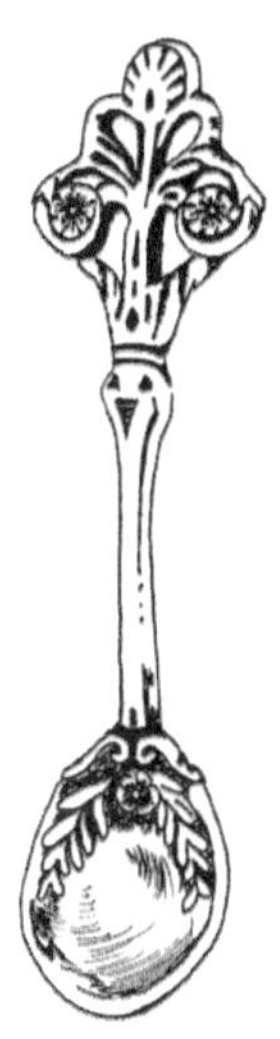

LOCKHEART MYSTERIES

Contents

PROLOGUE

Scotland

Wednesday 13th September 2017

Jess

B LING-BLING'

Jess fumbled in the dark, swiped her phone, and held it close to her face. Rubbing the dust loose from the corners of her eyes, she blinked to a semi-coherent state. What notification was so important it could wake her at 4:00 am? Trying to focus on the blurred screen took a few seconds. It was a message from Facebook - from a person she'd never heard of before.

Chloe Spencer. And who might she be?

Jess had become accustomed to receiving messages from people she didn't know. Ever since taking Mrs Jenkins' advice to set up a Lockheart family Facebook group, she'd had a flood of inquiries. Regrettably, this meant she was now the admin for every known Lockheart descendant across the globe. Even though it was difficult to determine if a contact was trustworthy or even related, she made every effort to keep herself safe online. A quick search of a person's profile would reveal necessary information she'd need to decide if they were a genuine person, a troll, or a fake.

Jess tapped on Chloe's name and was taken to her profile page. Chloe's privacy settings were adequate enough and only revealed what was necessary.

Chloe Spencer: Age twenty-two, lives in Wellington, New Zealand. Not in a relationship.

A profile picture showed a bright eyed sandy blonde girl with her arms wrapped around a brunette friend or sister. Both girls looked ready for a night on the town, but which one was actually Chloe? Jess couldn't quite pick. A quick preview of her friends list pointed to the brunette being Danielle Spencer - who was engaged.

So they're sisters then... or maybe even cousins, like me and Ella.

Jumping back to Chloe's profile she perused her public photos. Scrutinising them with care, checking every tagged friend against those that were in her friends list. Jess trawled the web of Chloe's Facebook life and eventually concluded that her profile was genuine.

Jess jumped back to her inbox, finally opening Chloe's message to read it.

'My name is Chloe Spencer and I think your grandmother, Marta Lockheart, might be my Grandmother too. Can we meet?'

Jess did a double take - checking that she had read the message correctly.

Grandma Marta was Chloe's grandma too? How could that be possible?

Well this just got weird. Ella is gonna FREAK!

Could Uncle Max have another child? What about Mum? Or, maybe Grandma had more secrets she'd rather stay buried.

She didn't even want to entertain the idea she might have an older brother or sister living somewhere out there. Having Brody as a brother was bad enough, but at least she was the eldest and could lord it over him.

If I had to have an older sibling, an older sister might be all right.

Jess tossed in bed - her mind flicking through different scenarios. She couldn't reply to Chloe's message just yet.

Ella will know what to do.

PART ONE

2017

Palmerston North - New Zealand

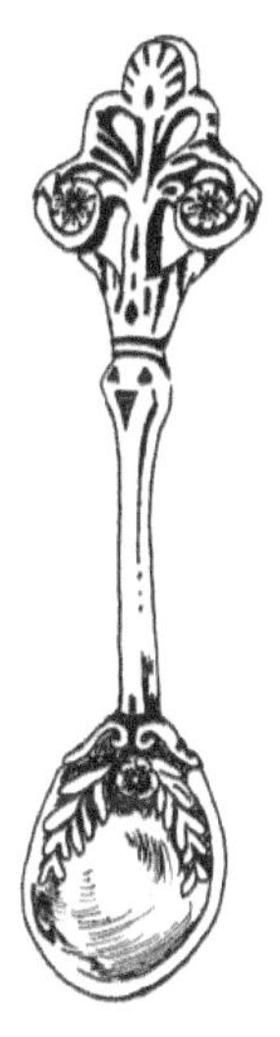

CHAPTER ONE

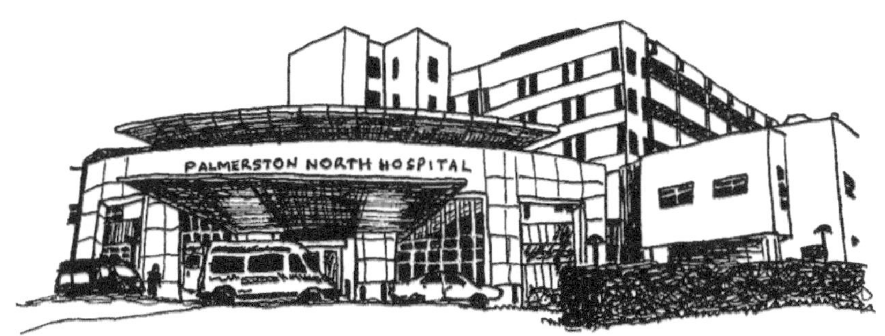

Saturday 29th July 2017

Chloe

IF CHLOE WEREN'T so devastated, she'd have strangled the doctor then and there on the spot. His words, delivered in monotone precision, drained the blood from her heart and pressed what little air remained from her lungs.

"There's nothing more we can do. I'm sorry."

Tears threatened. She inhaled in shudders and her heart thumped harder.

This can't be happening - it's not fair. Mum was fine this morning. In fact - she was better than fine - she looked radiant.

The doctor cleared his throat, its sound muted by the hospital room walls.

What could he possibly have to add to that?

"Elizabeth, Jack. It's time you looked at making an end of life plan."

Dad, sitting in a chair next the Mum's bed, leaned his elbows to his knees and flattened both palms over his face. His shoulders slumped.

Then, like a computer on reboot, he sat back up. "No. No. What about more chemo? It's got to be worth a try - surely."

A sickening feeling clogged Chloe's throat. He must be insane - why else would he ask for more poison to be pumped into Mum? The side effects from previous rounds of chemotherapy were horrendous, and Dad had suffered too.

Tears pooled. She swiped them away before Mum noticed.

Her heart thumped, thicker, faster, her face flushing with heat. Was it selfish to consider siding with Dad?

"Unfortunately it's metastasized. It's spread to the liver and throughout her entire lymph system. There's no way for us to treat it effectively anymore." The doctor locked his eye on Mum until she met his gaze. "Another round would likely kill you."

His words cut deep, the artery of hope now severed for good. Mum's life would end - sooner rather than later.

Tears fell. Chloe wanted to scream - to yell at him until he changed his mind. But that's not what grown adults do. They nod and paste a feeble smile of resignation on their face, bowing in acceptance of whatever verdict the medical professional tells them.

The miracle of medicine! What miracle? There was nothing miraculous here. Just her family being ripped apart by a monstrous disease. Medicine's mortal limits were finally reached, its chemicals no more useful than a placebo.

Now what - prayer? Perhaps, it too, was as naïve a treatment as the chemotherapy, but at least the side effects weren't so lethal.

Please God. Please. Just a bit longer.

During her first year of teacher training she'd offered many such tiny prayers. Why she ever thought God listened seemed incomprehensible, but Mum believed and that's really what mattered. If healing was not to be granted, more time seemed a reasonable request. Mum's remission had only lasted two years, falling well short of what was expected.

"We'll do everything we can to keep you as comfortable as possible over the coming months. But, we have no real way of knowing just how many you may get. It could be six - maybe even twelve - if you're lucky."

Mum dipped her eyes before linking them to Dad's. Chloe watched their silent exchange, a mix of devastation, resignation, and fear. But, amongst it all, there was hope and strength too.

Mum turned to her. "It's all right, sweetheart. We always knew this could happen." Mum twisted the plastic band around her slender wrist.

"I know, but..." Chloe wrenched her eyes from Mum's so she wouldn't have to watch them pool with despair. Instead Chloe sought comfort in the distant Tararua ranges to the southeast. Today their outline, often shrouded in grey tufts, was uncannily clear and a blue expanse seemed to float above their shoulders. How serene and light the air was. Nothing like the stuffy ward they sat in on the fourth floor.

How dare the sun continue to shine? And on today of all days.

The promise and hope of the morning's sunshine, prayerfully requested for the benefit of her parents' 30th anniversary vow renewal, had been welcomed and praised only hours ago. Now it seemed to mock them. Hospital windows, sealed shut like a containment facility, were a tangible force field between a sparkling life outside and the dimness of death within. Chloe shivered despite the warming glow casting shadow lines about the room. A chiffon shawl dipped between her arms behind her back and she clutched her bare skin in a hug. Today should have been a joyous day, a celebration shared with family and friends. Her arms ached for a hug. Had the guests all gone home yet? Three hours was more than enough time for them to realise the ceremony wouldn't take place. Not today anyway.

Danielle, her older sister by two and a half years - AKA - the good daughter, took care of Mum when Dad couldn't or had to travel. Always there - always willing. Chloe tried her best, but no matter how many hours she spent helping with celebration plans, or travelling home to visit on weekends, it never seemed to be enough. What made it worse was Danielle had a knack of twisting the knife of guilt deeper just by looking at her.

The rapid clicking of heels hearkened said sister's arrival, and they pulled to a halt near the door. Her brown sheath of ironed hair jutted itself inside the doorway.

"Found you. Sorry it took so long. I had to convince the guests to stay and eat the food. There's no point wasting it - especially since it's all been paid for." Danielle bent to give Mum a hug and, on release, corrected her wig - which sat slightly askew.

She took Mum's hand and squeezed it. "How are you feeling? What did the doctor say? I knew I shouldn't have let you have that champagne this morning." She shook her head.

Before Danielle's questions could be given answers, a large arrangement of flowers pegged by Grandma Iris' panty-hosed legs trotted through the doorway. A smile as wide as the bright pink Gerberas below it, beamed at everyone in the room.

Mum nodded sombrely at Danielle. "Later. Okay." Danielle lowered her head before stepping aside.

Chloe wished she could be as unfazed and undaunted by her mother's sudden collapse as Danielle and Grandma seemed to be. Iris' spritely disposition carried a source of great calm much needed at the moment. Chloe admired her grandmother's tenacity and wished she could boast half as much of it.

"Here you are," Grandma said, setting the flowers on the bedside table. "Dad will be here soon, Lizzy. He's just chatting up the nurse to see if he can get you a few more pillows. You can never have too many pillows according to him. The day's not a complete loss, you can still enjoy these" - she fingered the petals - "and the Reverend is on his way."

"Oh, I don't think we're quite there yet." The doctor replied without lifting his eyes from his iPad - his tone as serious as his frown

Grandma made a face. "Heavens, I should think not, Doctor! Lizzy's strong, she'll be fine - you'll see."

The doctor clamped a tight smirk between his lips and winked at Mum.

Grandma, more confident of her own diagnosis, and indignant towards the doctor, went on. "Reverend Wilson has agreed to conduct the ceremony here at the hospital. Would you like that?" She stroked Mum's cheek, then held her hand.

It was the first time Mum had been asked what *she'd* like since arriving at the hospital and her response was awaited by all.

"Thanks, Mum. That would be lovely. I'm sure I don't look half as good as I did this morning though."

Dad, now perched on the bed next to Mum, brushed a slip of hair off her face. "It doesn't matter, sweetheart, I'd marry you again even if all your hair fell out."

Everyone laughed at Dad's cheek. Mum's hair had already fallen out from chemotherapy two years ago, and it had only just now reached a length worth styling. Chloe loved the pixie-cut look. It made Mum look more modern, even a little younger, despite her sallow skin. Danielle, however, mourned the loss of Mum's ash-blonde locks and insisted she wear the wig she'd bought to match her old style for the special occasion.

Agonizing over the decision for days, Mum went with the wig. Judging by the look on her face now, and the amount of patting she was doing, she possibly wished she hadn't.

Danielle, with a painted smile, moved to help Mum reset her hair. Grandma went to the door and popped just her head outside in search of Granddad - or perhaps the Reverend.

Chloe dabbed her eyes, feeling wretched for not helping with something…anything. Mum looked at her and seemed to read her thoughts. With eyes on the cusp of a trickle, Mum spoke. "It's all right. I'll be okay." She turned and looked up at Danielle, taking hold of her hand. Danielle paused but her composure remained intact. Her sister had staunch super powers in that regard. She never cried. Not even when their first cat died - they were only eight and six. Chloe was special that way (at least that's how Mum put it). Chloe had a friend called Misery, and Misery seemed to visit at the most inconvenient times. Chloe swallowed hard and the arteries of her heart yanked apart like the stretchy limbs on an action figurine. Every time her mother cried, her eyes watered too, even if she had no problem of her own to cry about. They shared a bond much deeper than most and Chloe wondered if it bothered Danielle sometimes. All Chloe wanted was to wrap Mum tightly in her arms - and never let go.

"Hello, Reverend." Grandma opened the door wide and ushered him in. Reverend Wilson followed meekly, clasping his hands together, he stood at the foot of the hospital bed. His thinning grey hair matched his thinning grey jumper which already sported patches on the elbows.

"Well, Lizzy, Jack. It's not the ceremony you had planned, but if you're ready, shall we proceed?"

Granddad Tom entered the room with an armload of pillows. "Let's get the show on the road, Reverend." He off-loaded the pillows, propping Mum into an upright position. He nodded at Reverend Wilson to continue.

"Well then, shall we begin?"

"Wait. Where's Mark?" Danielle squeaked before the Reverend barely had a word out.

Chloe rolled her eyes. They were always waiting for that man. What Danielle saw in him was a mystery to Chloe. She'd rather have to sit through one of Danielle's childhood violin recitals than have to listen to her sister's fiancé, Dr Mark Hughes, waffle on about the latest cancer survival statistics.

"I'm here." Mark glided into the room, his whole body moving like a cruise ship parking itself at the wharf. Backwards then forwards, edging himself closer until positioned squarely behind Danielle. Chloe watched his arm snake around her sister's waist. Her stomach shrunk. Jeremy never did that to her anymore. She folded her arms across her middle to fill the void and huffed. *He better have a damn good excuse for leaving me here on my own.*

For the few minutes it lasted, Mum and Dad's vow renewal ceremony took them all to a happier plane of existence. The love in her parents eyes, despite all the hardships they'd faced (and the ones still to come), was a love like no other. With promises remade, and love renewed, everything was right. And she'd do anything to keep it that way.

The Reverend excused himself - as did Mark, each leaving the girls respectively with a comforting hug and Dad with a hand shake. Mum's eyes opened and closed, growing wearier by the minute. Grandma nodded to Granddad and he moved to give Mum a kiss on her forehead. Grandma did the same but also with a hug. "Sleep now, my love. We'll see you again soon."

"I think we should head home now too, girls. Let Mum get some rest." Dad leaned over Mum to kiss her goodbye, her hand still clamped in his, a hold they struggled to break until the last second. Dad smiled. "I'll pop back in a while and make sure they're looking after you. Okay?" Mum nodded. He kissed her again and pulled away, allowing Chloe and Danielle to say their own good-byes.

Danielle went first, lingering her ear a moment by Mum's lips as she whispered something to her. She nodded. Chloe was about to do the same when her mother spoke instead.

"Chloe, would you stay for a bit. I'd like to speak to you alone."

"Of course," She replied, looking to Dad and Danielle for approval.

Dad nodded. "It's fine, Chloe. You can take our car home." He handed her his keys. "We'll catch a ride with Tom and Iris."

Dad placed his hand on Danielle's back and motioned her towards the door.

Twenty minutes later Chloe left the deathly silent corridors of the hospital with her mother's words playing on repeat - looping without start or ending inside her mind. Strangely, and a little frighteningly, it had little to do with her mother's sickness and felt more like her last thoughts and wishes.

"You'll find your way, Chloe. Life's a funny game. I've played my turn and now it's yours. My only regret is that I never got the chance to meet my birth-mother. I'll never truly know why she gave me up, but I'm glad she did. My life might not have turned out so well if she hadn't. I'm so grateful to have had two beautiful girls of my own. Giving me up can't have been an easy decision for her. I only wish I could thank her properly and give you and Danielle the chance to know where I came from. Maybe you two could try and find her for me - together. That would make me so happy. And, if I never get the chance, say thanks for me."

Say thanks?! The sentiment seemed absurd. Surely she could do better than that for her mother - couldn't she?

If it was Mum's greatest wish to meet her birth-mother, then no matter what it took, Chloe would do anything and everything in her power to make it happen. Even if it meant swallowing her tongue and pride when inevitably Danielle took over. The more Chloe thought about it, the more she realised that Mum's request wasn't just about herself - but rather a desire for her daughters to get along better - when she was no longer around to bridge the gap.

The task was no small petition, and would require every last ounce of will-power. Based on the events of last week, it would take multiple miracles to get her sister on board. Heck! She might even have to agree to wear the hideous mint meringue bridesmaid's dress Danielle wanted for her own wedding. Let's not get ahead of ourselves though - that ghastly excuse of a dress has far more use as a shower puff than as tender for blackmail.

For you Mum - I'll do anything for you.

Unsure of how she came to be at her family home, Chloe turned the handle on the old wooden front door and walked inside, all the while searching the catacombs of her mind for evidence she'd actually driven herself there. The hallway, with its kauri floorboards scarred by childhood races and pointy umbrella ends, was always dim and sombre no matter what time of day or season it was. The house harboured memories and secrets of bygone generations, each with its own troubles and triumphs. Every chipped bit of paint and squeak in the floor reminded Chloe that the house now embodied her own history too. The hallway, always cool and slightly musty, was Chloe's favourite part of the house as it carried the promise of warmth from the fireplace in the living room. Ornamental pine cones, balanced neatly in the fire's hearth by her mother when the chimney was boarded off, were the only hint the fireplace ever had a former life. Four years ago during a particularly bad winter Dad got really sick. So Mum, being the family's healthy home advocate, insisted they install an air conditioning unit - like so many others already had in the street. She'd touted some nonsense about it reducing their carbon footprint and Dad had decided it wasn't worth fighting her logic behind it. Mum now kept it running ten out of twelve months, regardless of the temperature outside, and Chloe loved sitting in the heated waves of air. Twinkle, the family cat, liked it too, and they would often curl up together on the window seat and look out over the foggy back garden in winter.

"Is that you Chloe? We're in here," came the velvet voice of her father from the kitchen.

We? Who else is here? She should have guessed, but with her mind preoccupied by her mother's request all rational thoughts had evaporated.

Chloe poked her head around the door.

"Come have a cup of tea with us, Chloe." Danielle's unusually courteous offer was no doubt given with an ulterior motive. "What did Mum say to you?" *There it was.*

Her sister's need to know everything was barely masked by that familiar half smile. Chloe knew it well and if Dad weren't in the room she would have replied, 'None of your business'.

As parental supervision was, in fact, present, she dare not give her sister opportunity to argue. They would no doubt do that when he left. Chloe hated their sisterly spats. She thought by now, since they were older (and supposedly wiser), that their childish behaviours would have subsided. Much to their parents' dismay, it seemed they had both inherited their Grandmother's stubbornness and neither would relent.

Danielle poured a cup of earl grey from the tomato red teapot and handed it to Chloe, her eyes a little kinder than usual.

She did love Danielle. Despite all her annoying 'perfect-ness' she was the only other person who truly understood how she was feeling. They'd both made a considerable effort these last few months for the sake of their parents' celebration, but not without a healthy dose of verbal frustration on both their parts.

"Uh, Mum just wanted me to keep looking for her birth-mother. I think it's the missing piece of the puzzle that's keeping her hopes up. She wanted me to thank her birth-mother, if" - she locked eyes with Danielle - "*we* - found her."

"What a strange thing to say," responded Danielle clinking her cup down on her saucer and piercing a stare into Chloe opposite her. Chloe couldn't think what she'd said to win such a glare but ignored it.

"That's what I thought," Chloe replied. She couldn't fathom why, but it always made her uncomfortable when Danielle agreed with her. "Dad do you know anything more about Mum's adoption? I mean - specifics?"

Dad crunched his brows together as if attempting to retrieve a file about the topic. He always considered his words carefully - a trait that occasionally bugged her. Wasn't the best response the one that came naturally? Not so with Dad. Every reply seemed to be filtered first before being given. She'd never noticed it as a child, but now his pauses and considerations tested her patience.

"Your mother only found out she was adopted by accident. The day before she told you girls, she had been to see Grandma Iris. An old friend of your grandmother's was visiting from Auckland. The woman... Pearl I think her name was...didn't realise Lizzy didn't know the truth. She unintentionally spilled the beans. Lizzy was pretty upset."

Chloe looked at her father. It dawned on her that as a child she had rarely ever seen either of her parents very upset. It wasn't until Mum's cancer diagnosis that the family felt like it actually had a collective heart-beat and tear ducts. Searching her memories, a low set fog seemed to lift from an image in her mind.

"I remember that day. Mum was crying in her bedroom. I'd never seen her cry like that before." Chloe's chest ached once more.

"Really? When did that happen? I don't remember Mum crying." Danielle pulled her head back into her neck. The idea that she'd somehow been excluded from the event appeared to bother her more than the news of their mother's grief.

"It happened the day she found out." Chloe's frosty words matched her baltic glare. Even her father rubbed his hands together.

"Well, where was I?" Danielle seemed immune to the sudden drop in temperature, more concerned about finding an answer from which she could defend her absence.

"How should I know? Maybe you were at a lesson or something." Chloe noted her volume had escalated and she paused mentally to dial it down. "Anyway, Mum grabbed me in a hug so tight that I could barely breathe. She said something to me. What was it?" Chloe grew impatient to recall her exact words. She nodded when they came. "She said, 'I could never give you away, Chloe. I would never let someone take you away from me'. It was weird and it kind of freaked me out."

Dad turned to look directly at her, his eyebrows raised. He scratched the side of his face - like he did when he read the newspaper. Chloe fiddled with her fingertips, and frowned. "I didn't understand what Mum meant. I was only about five I think. I remember thinking I was going be taken away from her and given to someone else."

"Ahh," Dad sighed, eluding he'd struck some clarity. "That explains a few things. Lizzy had such a hard time convincing you to stay at school when you started. You'd kick and scream in a teary mess whenever she left." He tilted his head towards her. "You really thought you would never see us again?"

Chloe loved the fact that Dad had included himself in the situation and she decided there was no reason to make him think otherwise. "Yeah. It was only when Mum hounded me with questions that she finally understood. I told her I was scared I'd never see her again. I think it's why I feel so close to her - and you," She added, placing her hand over Dad's on the table. He cupped his other hand over it, smiling. "You and Mum do share a special bond."

Danielle cast her eyes to the table and could no longer look at Chloe. She knew Danielle didn't share the same type of relationship with their mother as she did. It wasn't something she'd ever tried to rub in her sister's face but Danielle seemed to take it that way regardless.

Danielle cleared her throat and shrugged. "Well, I only remember Mum announcing it at dinner. At first I thought she was joking. But when she started going on about Uncle Matthew and Aunty Susan not being her biological brother and sister - I thought she'd gone mad. She seemed happy about being adopted though." She paused to take a sip of tea and flattened her hands, one on top of the other on the table. She leaned forward. "I always assumed she wasn't interested in finding her birth-parents."
Chloe could tell Danielle was hurt. It wasn't the first time she'd been unknowingly kept out of the loop.

Dad's peace-maker resolve kicked in and his tone softened. "It was hard for Mum to explain it. You were both still quite young. But she insisted you know the truth. Keeping her adoption secret from you, the way Iris had kept it from her, wasn't the sort of thing Lizzy could do. She doesn't like secrets. The truth is really important to her - even if it might hurt."

"I think the truth of her adoption hurt her more than we realise." Chloe cast her gaze out the window. Grey shards of cloud now cut across the sky. The sun was losing the battle on the glorious day's forecast.

Twinkle rose from her now shaded spot on the deck and retreated inside. Danielle, unable to do likewise with her tongue, felt it necessary to chatter on. "Do you really believe Mum's still upset with Grandma, Chloe? She seems fine to me. But...maybe," Danielle appeared to be considering something deeper and Chloe thought she caught a glimpse of pain in her sister's eyes. "Maybe I've just been too busy to notice." Danielle clutched her tea cup as if it were her own heart. "I just don't understand why she didn't tell *me* she wanted to find her birth-parents? I'm much more likely to know where to look than Chloe." Danielle's protest, although heard, went unappreciated and unanswered. Chloe understood how she felt. Disappointment in one's self was a feeling she was well acquainted with. It was only when she took a class in college on child psychology that she could recognise the signs when it manifested. Her sense of empathy, though well-developed already, grew even further towards those who suffered from it. Was Danielle really unaware just how much Chloe desired her acceptance?

"Well if Mum truly wanted to find her birth-parents she *would* have asked me, so she can't be that desperate. Chloe finds it difficult enough locating her car keys - let alone a decent boyfriend." Danielle's laughter cut short when she found herself alone in the joke. Chloe tossed her previously compassionate feelings aside. Yup there she was, Danielle, perfect as ever and able to explain the unexplainable regardless of who might be hurt.

Dad, diplomatic as ever, tried to steer the girls away from conflict and back towards Mum.

"Danielle. Have you considered that maybe Mum asked Chloe to find her birth-parents because she thought it might help the two of you keep working together on something? Your mother has been so happy these past few months - seeing you girls working on our anniversary celebration. She told me you've been getting along really well. She's so proud. I think she'd like it if you girls made an effort to continue this way - instead of butting heads all the time."

Chloe tempted a glance at Danielle to gauge her response. It was blank and Chloe wondered if her sister would ever truly get it.

"I think it's important you girls really understand why it's essential you get along. Mum might not have as much time left with us as we'd like. I want whatever time we do have, to be meaningful and happy. Your mother deserves to see the positive things she's accomplished during all her years of raising you both. Please, for her sake, try to work together on this. I know you're both very different, but try to use that to help one another, not tear each other down." Dad looked at each of them waiting until they both finally eyed each other. Danielle blushed a little and Chloe smiled back. Dad reached for Danielle's hand and cupped it on the table. "You are right, Danielle. Mum wasn't upset about being adopted. She's very happy with her family." Then he reached his other hand to Chloe's again. "But, Chloe you're right too. She was upset. She was upset because her parents had lied to her all her life. Lizzy knows that her birth-mother wanted to keep her, but it just wasn't possible. She wasn't married, and in those days an unmarried woman was encouraged to adopt the baby out. That way, the child would have two parents and be part of a family. Who knows where Lizzy might have ended up if her birth-mother had tried to keep her."

"I suppose so." Chloe nodded.

Danielle nodded too. "She might never have met you, Dad, if she hadn't been adopted. And then we might never have even existed!" Danielle's suggestion was just as unsettling to Chloe as the prospect of having never met their mother was to their father.

He breathed deeply, withdrawing his hands from both girls. "Well she *was* adopted and I *did* meet her and everything is the way it was meant to be."

"And I'm glad of it," Danielle added, quickly sipping her tea before she could blurt anything else out that might be considered offensive.

Chloe padded her fingers on the side of the tea cup. "Well not everything is as it should be."

"No," her sister agreed. "But Mum wouldn't want us to sit around and mourn her when she is still very much alive, would she?" Danielle looked at them, waiting for a reply.

Dad cupped his hands together. "So, when do you head off, Chloe?"

Chloe thought she caught a glimmer of a tear in Danielle's eyes, but she dabbed a finger to their corners before any moisture had a chance to escape. Danielle buried her nose back in her tea cup, and when she was done her half-smile had returned. Chloe marvelled at her sister's ability to control her emotions. She had never been able to master her own the way Danielle did. How deep did her sister have to bury the thoughts before they were no longer a threat? Exposure of inner turmoil lay far closer to the surface for Chloe, and like a loose thread on a bedspread, she picked at it often.

"I had planned to head back tomorrow, but I haven't heard anything from Jeremy. So I might stay another night."

"Mark could give you a ride back if you like. He has surgery in Wellington tomorrow afternoon. He was lucky he could get today off, but he knew it meant a lot to me."

Pain stabbed into Chloe's ribs. How could such a simple string of words cut her like that?

"That's okay, I wouldn't want to be an imposition."

Danielle looked as if she was about to say something and then thought better of it. "Well... Mark won't be back from the hospital for a few more hours. He said he wanted to check in with a few colleagues there. Are you going to go back to see Mum tonight, Dad?"

"I'll pop up there for dinner, and I'll stay for as long as they'll let me."

"Sure. Chloe? Wanna order some pizza?" Danielle's words were left hanging there for Chloe to find but she was lost in her own head again.

"Chloe? You in there?" Danielle waved her head side to side.

Chloe twisted a tress of hair between her fingers and tossed it behind her with a flick of the wrist. "Oh, what? Sorry. I just don't get it. Why would Granddad and Grandma keep it a secret from Mum? I knew a girl at school who was adopted and her parents told her. She's known her whole life."

Danielle huffed like it was up to her to respond. "Well it's different these days. For starters there are very few people who opt for a closed adoption. People are more open to staying connected to the birth-parents. Sometimes it's the only way an adoption can take place. It's healthier for the child too...or so they say. Mum was born in the sixties. What is now socially acceptable certainly wasn't back then. Can you imagine if you or I got pregnant when we were in high school? Nowadays you barely even hear of it because most girls our age would get an abortion. It's sad I know, but it's true. I knew a girl at school who had one and her parents never even knew about it. It really messed her up though."

"Really? Who?" Chloe sat up and leaned in. An unknown tit-bit of gossip was rare these days.

"Uh...Candice - but just keep it to yourself, please."

"Oh, sure." Chloe frowned and nodded. "She was such a pretty girl. I always admired her, but she kinda just faded into the background her final year of school. Do you really think Mum's birth-mother might have been in high school when she got pregnant?"

"Maybe. It's possible," Danielle said.

Dad's face turned stern and stiff, his jaw locked and his eyes narrowed, an echo of his job as a high school Principal. Chloe recognised the look instantly and knew a lecture would soon follow. She sensed his discomfort of the topic at hand - his inability to step off the moral high ground. He couldn't say nothing. To him, silence was as good as approval.

"Well we taught you girls from a very young age that your actions have consequences. Your mother and I prayed every day that that particular lesson didn't have to be learned the hard way. Sadly, a few kids weren't so wise. Over the years there have been a number of accounts from around the school district. I did my best to drum it into my boys. If they thought they were ready to indulge their desires - they had also better be prepared for the consequences and responsibilities that resulted from their actions."

Chloe remembered well the many lectures they'd endured over the dinner table about her and Danielle keeping themselves 'pure'. Often given detailed accounts about raising a baby as deterrents. But it never occurred to her that her father was drumming the same speech into the boys at his high school. Realising now that he had reasonable knowledge about what went on in the other schools in the district, she couldn't help but wonder just *how* much he knew about her own escapades. A lump caught in her throat and she felt her face warm. She dare not look at him - fearing he'd take the discussion further. Chloe looked at Danielle who was staring straight back at her with a grin that screamed, '*I know*'.

Chloe darted her eyes elsewhere, frantically searching for the words to divert attention away from further inadvertent revelations. "Well, I'm just grateful I won't have to deal with any of that. Teaching Primary kids has got to be much less of a mine field than teaching teenagers. I appreciate that it can't have been easy for you, Dad. But I think you and Mum did a great job. We turned out all right, don't you think?"

Danielle straightened, rocking her shoulder to sit up tall. "One daughter engaged to be married and one about to graduate teachers college. I'd say we turned out better than all right, Chloe. I'd say Mum and Dad hit the jackpot with us!" She giggled, and Dad smiled at her quip.

"The jackpot, aye? Well, maybe. I think that might only come when we meet our first grandchild." The twinkle in Dad's eye had Danielle a little unnerved and Chloe loved it. Watching her sister squirm was well worth the slight discomfort she'd felt herself only seconds ago.

Danielle stammered and blushed. "Well, Mark and I don't want to start a family too quickly. Sorry Dad, you'll just have to wait a bit longer for grandchildren."

"For heaven's sake, don't let your mother hear you say that."

Danielle's smile vanished.

Dad's tone was serious, but Chloe knew he had only said it to tease her. Danielle stood and started to clear the cups from the table. She often mistook comments made in jest, even though she handed out plenty of her own.

Chloe struggled to conjure some sympathy for her. "She'll just be happy to make it to your wedding day, Danielle. It's unlikely she'll ever get to see me married."

Before Danielle could rebut her claim, Chloe's phone rang and she swiped to pick it up.

"Jeremy. Oh, um, let me just find somewhere private." Chloe wandered off to her bedroom, flopped down on the bed and stared up at the ceiling. Plastic glow in the dark stars dotted the roof and reminded her of her eighth birthday when she was obsessed by everything space related. That obsession ended the moment she watched a documentary about the Apollo 13 mission. But right now she was happy for a bit of space - preferably for a few hours at least.

"Shall we order the pizza now?" Danielle asked when Chloe finally returned to the kitchen. "Dad's gone already. Chloe... What's the matter?"

Chloe slumped into the couch and stared into space, numb to the conversation she had just had with Jeremy over the phone. "He's not coming," her tone vacant. Chloe pulled the end of her sleeve over her hand and wiped a knuckle near her eyes. Tears were a sign of emotional weakness and though she could do nothing to prevent them falling, she knew Danielle would likely mock her for them.

"Who's not coming?" Danielle asked. "Jeremy? Don't worry, Mark will give you a ride back to Wellington tomorrow if you like. You'll have to be ready on time though."

Chloe sobbed in great heaves. Drawing her knees to her chest, she planted her face on top and hugged them tight. Her voice, confined to the small cavity, mumbled, "You don't understand. He's not coming ever!" More sobs followed, their drips leaving spots on her pyjamas.

"What do you mean, Chloe? Who's not coming?"

Chloe lifted her streaked face. "JEREMY! He's decided that we need a break and that I should go to the U.K on my own. What will I do, Danielle? I've booked the tickets and everything. I can't just cancel my trip, we've been planning it for ages. How can he do this to me? It's because I'm too needy, isn't it? I know I'm overly sensitive sometimes, but we were good. I thought everything was good. I don't get it. I wish Mum was here. I wish everything was better. I hate that Mum's sick and there's nothing I can do to help her. What should I do, Danielle?"

Why she would ask her sister for advice now when she usually shrugged off anything Danielle suggested, was beyond good reasoning.

But right now she just needed something to make sense and to have a perfectly right answer. She could always rely on Danielle to have one.

"I don't know."

Great. Now what?

"Tell me what's happened and let's see if we can work it out together, shall we?" Danielle's concern and empathy was as much of a shock as it was a relief. Maybe this might be the catalyst to sever their stubborn ways.

After a lengthy chat that drew into the wee hours of the next morning, both girls lay on their parents' bed beside one another. "Does this mean we are friends now?" asked Danielle.

"I hope so," Chloe felt for her sister's hand and held it. "I'm tired of fighting with you, you're a pretty tough opponent."

"You know, I only fight with you because I want your approval."

Chloe let her sister's hand go and rolled to her side. "My approval?! But that's all I wanted from you."

'Well from now on you have it. And if Jeremy thinks he can mess with my little sister again, he's got another thing coming."

"Thanks, Danielle."

"You know what, Chloe. I think you should still go on your trip. You don't need a guy to go with you. Go on your own. Remember my friend Joy? She lives over there. How about I message her and see if she'd let you stay for a bit? At least until you get settled in your job. I'd feel much better if I knew you had someone looking out for you over there, and so would Mum."

"I'll think about it. I think what I'd rather do is focus on finding Mum's birth-mother for her. I just know it would help put her mind at ease."

"Okay. Tomorrow I was going to go and help Granddad and Grandma get started on their packing. They move into the village in two weeks. How about we see if we can get some answers there?"

"Agreed. And I'm not leaving until we do."

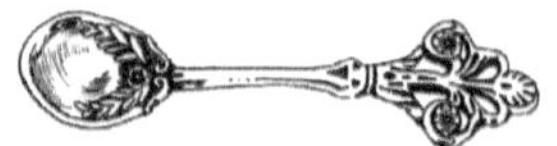

CHAPTER TWO

Saturday 5th August 2017

CHLOE PERCHED ON the armrest of her Grandmother's red velveteen couch. She held in her hands one of the many photo albums stacked beneath the wooden coffee table. Some of them she'd looked through many times before, others looked so deteriorated she feared they may fall apart. But this one - this was her favourite. It contained page after page of her family holidays at Ohope beach.

Warm fuzzies filled her heart as she trailed a finger through the pages - each snapshot commemorating a treasured moment. Her favourite image in the whole album was the giant sand castle she and Danielle built with the help of their father. All three grinned like mad sculpting geniuses, and every time she saw it, she giggled. The top tier of the castle almost reached to her seven year old belly button, which protruded shamelessly between the layers of her pink bikini. She could still hear the echo of giggling squeals when their father tickled them as soon as Mum had taken the picture.

Her childhood was one to be envied by today's standards. Her parents still loved each other and were committed to honouring their wedding vows. They'd promised to love each other through sickness and health, and although the last year had tested that promise, Chloe knew her parents could easily last another thirty years - if only her mother lived that long.

"Look at this one, Danielle." Chloe held the album out to her sister. "Remember when you and I dressed up for that New Year's party at Sasha's?"

Danielle giggled at the memory and tried to strike the same pose she had in the photograph - hand in the air making a V with a scrunched up face, and her tongue poking out.

Since the album was now commandeered by her sister, Chloe searched for another from the pile. A dark grey one sitting on the bottom was not one she'd seen before and instinctively she felt the need to retrieve.

"What's in this one, Grandma?" Chloe held it up for Iris to see. Her grandmother shuffled past boxes sitting about the room to take a closer look.

"Oh that's just some informal photos from our wedding and our first house in Palmerston North. There's some pictures of your Mum in there as a baby too, I think."

Chloe smiled, the thrill of finding something in her grandparents' house she'd never seen before was rarer these days. She settled the album closely on her lap. "Cool… I've seen pictures of Mum when she was little - but none of her as a baby. Where have you been hiding these all this time?"

"I found them in the back of the wardrobe the other day when I was clearing it out. I thought it was time they joined the rest. I hope you girls don't mind helping with all this." Iris gestured to the piles of her life's collections scattered all about the floor. "It's a lot I know, but I'm so grateful for the help."

"It's not a problem, Grandma. We're pleased to do it, aren't we, Chloe?"

Chloe was now too engrossed in the grey album to answer her sister's question.

"Chloe?"

"What? Oh yes, not a problem at all, Grandma." She looked up to see her grandmother's face wrinkle with joy. Chloe smiled back. She loved how simple it was to make her Grandmother smile.

A buzzer sounded from the kitchen. Grandma threw her hands in the air, and scurried from the room. "Morning tea won't be long, girls," her voice trailed off.

Chloe looked around the room. Although Iris and Thomas had lived here ever since she could remember, their lives before she existed was shrouded in mystery. Now that they were moving, the piles of paraphernalia they had acquired over the years was in desperate need of a culling. As items of novelty and normality were found, collected, questioned, and sorted, the girls gleaned much insight into the lives of their grandparents. The whole process painted a vibrant picture of Thomas and Iris Johnson's life thus far. And perhaps the album would shed even further light in that regard.

Chloe was determined to remember it all and offered to document the decluttering for her grandparents in a photo book. Things might have to be discarded - the memory of those things, however, could be held onto forever.

"Whoa! Now that's just creepy!" Chloe breathed, pulling the album closer to her face.

"What? What is?!" asked Danielle.

"Look at this picture and tell me that's not weird," Chloe said drawing her brows even closer than they already were.

Danielle took the album and stared at the wedding photo. It took her a moment but then she spotted it. In the background, standing outside the church with other attending well-wishers, was a woman wearing a plain baby doll dress staring right at the camera. The fact that she was pregnant was not the main reason for Chloe's interest. It was the fact the girl's face was almost an identical match to her own.

"So you have a doppelganger from the 60's. Cool! You should try that look with your hair next time you have a costume party to go to." Danielle squinted her eyes between the photo and Chloe - as if trying to picture the hairstyle on Chloe's head.

The enormity of the woman's presence at their grandparents' wedding had obviously eluded Danielle.

Chloe huffed, pointing at the photo. "It's me! But how? It's spooky, don't you think? I wonder if Grandma knows who she is?"

Danielle shrugged, handed the album back to her, and continued turning the pages of their holiday album.

"Danielle! I'm serious. Don't you get it?"

"Get what?"

"This woman in this picture. Do you think it could be Mum's birth-mother? Look she's pregnant!"

"Oh," said Danielle, quietly inhaling the shock of her suggestion. "I suppose it could be. Let's ask Grandma, shall we?"

"Do you think she'll mind?"

"No, why would she? She's always tried to be open and honest about it since mum found out. It's Granddad who's more likely to get edgy about it. Just ask when he's not around."

"When who's not around?" asked the deep gravelly voice entering the room. "My eyesight might be fading girls, but my hearing's not," Thomas said, raking his hands through his thick salt and pepper hair. Granddad was still a very handsome man given his age. His physique was excellent and not a lick of fat clung to him. Cricket-seasoned leather skin covered his forearms and what little amount of muscle did remain on his bones was taut and toned. His sleeves were rolled to the elbow. He still wore a shirt and tie even though his days at the law firm were well in the past by twenty years or more.

Rolling his shoulder, followed by his whole arm, Thomas bowled a screwed up ball of newspaper towards Danielle - just as they'd witnessed him do hundreds of times during family cricket matches at the beach.

Danielle, with the reflexes of a cat, flicked the album into a bat and fended off the flying newsprint sending it soaring towards Grandma's prized vase. With milliseconds before it stuck, Granddad stretched out his arm, catching the ball before it did any possible damage, and just in time for Grandma to see him do it. If it had taken place outside, Granddad would surely have chucked the ball in the air and given himself a round of applause. But with Grandma's stern eye fixed on him, he quickly tucked the ball of paper behind his back and gave her a cheeky grin, "Mmmm, looking good luv…and those scones aren't half bad either. If there's any extra whipped cream - I'll take it!"

"Whipped cream indeed!" Iris scolded. "I'll give you whipped cream!" With her finger, Iris swiped a dollop of cream from one of the scones and smeared it on Thomas' nose. Ignoring him, she placed the tea tray on the dining table and unloaded its contents. Only then did she turn around to catch his response.

Granddad's sly grin morphed into shock and then returned - spreading wider across his face, "I was hoping you'd say that!" Grinning cheekily at his wife of fifty seven years, he took her in for a creamed nose kiss.

"Thomas!" she blushed when he finally released her.

Despite Grandma trying to dismiss her embarrassment, both Chloe and Danielle giggled at the fact that she couldn't seem to wipe the pleased look off her face even if she could wipe off the cream.

Chloe loved the fact that her grandparents were still in love and occasionally acted like a couple of teenagers. She'd seen her grandmother chased along the beach by her grandfather often enough to know that although they may look old they were still very much young at heart. She only hoped that one day she too would find someone who would love her as much as Thomas and Iris loved each other. Chloe sighed. It certainly wouldn't be Jeremy though.

Granddad always said, 'If you love someone - show them. Words are cheap and easily forgotten but actions are like a fog horn - sure to blast all doubts away.'

She'd taken those words to heart, ending a relationship, after discovering the guy's actions weren't all that loving after all.

Granddad had an answer for that too. 'His loss, Chloe. He didn't deserve you. You are more precious than gold and if he wants to treat you like shit, he's only got himself to blame if he ends up smelling of it.'

Taking a similar tone to that of her grandmother, she replied, "Granddad!" She'd never heard him swear before.

"Come on! You know what I mean. It doesn't have the same impact if I say manure, 'shit' just has a better ring to it - and that boy sure is some, I'd say."

Chloe was amused and a little disturbed but then, what else did she expect? Granddad was the epitome of tongue in cheek. If there was ever a smart quip to be had - then he had it. It's one of the things she loved most about him. He wasn't like most other old people. Granddad had the kindest heart and the happiest demeanour of any senior citizen she'd ever met. He'd re-enact senior moments of forgetfulness, he'd fumble clumsily with the dinnerware and furniture like he was losing his agility, but it was all an act - meant merely to entertain. He was as nimble as the days he'd caught a cricket ball off the wicket or a six'er headed for the boundary. The hardest part had been watching him slowly decline due to his eyesight. Cataract operations on both eyes had kept him going for the last twenty years but those too were slowly beginning to fail.

"Now what's this secret you girls are keeping from me?" asked Thomas, now seated at the small round dining table, wiping the last bit of cream from his nose and licking it off his finger. Iris, who sat next to him, was pouring the tea into four Royal Dalton porcelain rose tea cups leaving one to spare.

"Your father shouldn't be too far away. What secret?"

Both Chloe and Danielle rose from the sitting room to join their grandparents at the dining table. Morning tea was always a 'sit at the table' occasion in the Johnson household and Grandma never failed to deliver a morning tea worthy of the Queen herself.

Sitting in a neat circle on the matching Royal Dalton rose serving plate, were five of Grandma's freshly baked buttery scones - smeared in strawberry jam and topped with a modest dollop of cream. Steam rose from the cups of tea set on saucers and plates beneath. A silver teaspoon perched to one side held an image at its top of some place their grandparents had visited. A pair of gumboots from Taihape, a steam train from Kingston, and a Pahutakawa tree from the Coromandel. Iris was very proud of her teaspoon collection, and the more special ones hung on a wooden display board on the wall.

Passing a rattling set of tea ware to each of the girls, Iris tried her best to keep her hands steady. Chloe and Danielle politely took the cups and set them down in front of them. Both immediately reached for the sugar bowl. Chloe relented, allowing Danielle the customary older sister rights to go first.

The girls cherished their tea parties at Grandma's house. The etiquette and manners taught and practiced during such occasions had seen the two girls commended by the parents of their peers whenever they had visited or stayed over.

Danielle finished dumping a third teaspoon of sugar into her cup.

"I don't see how you can drink it with that much sugar," Chloe said, her voice sticky with sarcasm.

"It's because I'm so sweet, isn't it Granddad?" Danielle replied winking at Thomas. He'd told her that on many occasions and even though the tea was sickly sweet she hadn't the heart to drink it without sugar now. It was their thing - their special saying together.

Thomas smiled back at Danielle - his warm eyes giving no hint as to his true thoughts.

"Is someone going to tell?" Thomas asked finally when he couldn't take the silent slurping of tea any longer.

"Tell what?" asked Chloe, flapping her eyelids like butterflies.

Thomas cleared his throat, "Oh I get it. It's about my birthday party next month isn't it? Well I'll save you the trouble girls, I already know all about it. A little bird just couldn't keep quiet and sang like a Tui in a Kowhai tree when I caught her trying to lie about it!" His infectious chuckle accompanied his hand as he moved it under the table. Grandma twitched in her seat, spilling her tea and turning a lovely shade of beet red. Both girls giggled.

Iris straightened herself, took her napkin from her lap and dabbed her chin dry. "No, Thomas, I'm sure it has nothing to do with your birthday. We've already discussed that this morning and you can just keep your sticky nose out of it in future or you'll not have any party to go to at all." She turned to face Chloe, "So what's the secret, girls?" She looked from one to the other.

Danielle got up from the table and retrieved the grey album. "Well, we were just wondering who the girl in this picture was?" She held it out to her grandmother and pointed. "She looks the spitting image of Chloe, don't you think? I wonder if I have a doppelganger out there somewhere?" Danielle trailed off bemused by the thought.

Iris pulled down her reading glasses, perched atop her neatly set white hair, and rested them on the end of her nose. Pushing her chair back to make room she took the large album from Danielle. "Let's have a look."

Holding the album wide, Iris moved it back and forth until her vision was satisfied.

Chloe, sitting beside Iris, leaned in and pointed. "There, see!"

Thomas also leaned in, looking over his wife's shoulder to see what they were all staring at. When he saw it, he quickly sat back upright in his chair and buried himself in his cup of tea. Reaching for a newspaper folded neatly in a pile on the side table, he fumbled to open it and turn it the right way up.

Meanwhile, Iris was studying the photograph, looking down and then up multiple times - peering over the red rims of her reading glasses to stare at her youngest granddaughter.

Danielle who was standing behind the two women grabbed her sister's hair and played it into a similar bouffant looking style like that of the girl in the photo. "See? Now can you see it? Do you know who she is, Grandma?"

"Oh my goodness, yes there is a striking resemblance." Iris pointed to some of the other faces in the photograph. "That's Uncle George and Aunty Peg, Mary; her cousin, with her husband Henry and little Georgie." Iris looked at Chloe again and squinted. "Sorry - but I haven't a clue who this girl is or who she might have come with. I've never noticed her before. "I wonder who she is and why she was at our wedding?

Thomas. Do you recognise who that is?" Iris shoved the album in her husband's direction. He shook a fold of newspaper down on the corner to glance momentarily at it and promptly flicked it back up. "No, not a clue."

"Really are you sure? It's not one of my relatives, nor any of our friends. It must be someone from your side." Iris shoved the album towards him harder, insisting he take another look.

Granddad huffed, closed his newspaper, and took another look. Chloe soon realised he only did so to satisfy his wife's curiosity rather than to actually look at the woman.

"You know who she is, don't you, Thomas?" Grandma said with astonished confidence. She was the only person that could read Granddad when he was using his poker face. Chloe knew then that Granddad knew exactly who the girl in the photo was, but it seemed he wasn't about to tell any of them.

Granddad's prompt retreat to the garage, after morning tea, was made even more suspicious when he asked not to be disturbed. Grandma didn't bat an eyelid at his request and joked that he was probably trying to get rid of his 'Girly' posters from 'way-back-when'. But Chloe wasn't buying it. His comment about clearing out a specific cupboard didn't quite sound right and she was determined to find out why. Chloe waited a moment until she thought he'd feel more confident no one had followed or would see what he was up to. After a few minutes had passed she told Grandma and Danielle she had to use the bathroom, but instead made a quiet approach towards the garage.

Granddad was busy with his head buried in a box and when he finally found what he'd been looking for he held it up in the light to take a better look at it. Chloe cleared her throat and the item took a startled tumble to the ground and rolled across the garage floor. Chloe dove for it before it disappeared between two shelves stacked beside each other against the wall. Taking a quick glance at the silver object before she handed it back to him, Chloe noted it was a baby's bracelet. She had worn one herself as a baby and Mum now kept both hers and Danielle's in a jewellery box on her dressing table at home. Chloe occasionally took it out and marvelled at how she could have ever once fit the tiny silver band.

"Uh, Th-thank-you, Chloe. Did you - ah, need something?" Granddad's face had lost some colour and he looked like a cat caught on the kitchen bench seeking any escape possible.

Chloe's cheeks flushed red, "Um," She looked around the pile-laden floor of the garage, "Sorry to startle you, Granddad. I just wanted to ask you some questions." It wasn't her presence that seemed to worry him - but the fact that Chloe had seen and handled the very object he'd obviously been trying to hide. He tucked it into his pocket.

"So whose was it?" She pointed.

"It was your mother's." He turned back to his box and repacked some of the papers and old records he'd removed.

"Really? Can I see it?" Chloe held out her hand. Granddad turned back to her and planted both fists in his trouser pockets firmly.

"I saw mum's baby picture in the photo album before and noticed her wearing a bracelet - I wondered where it was. It's not in her jewellery box where she keeps ours."

Granddad cleared his throat as if to speak but said nothing.

"Pleeease, Granddad. Mum asked me to keep looking for her birth-mother. I think it might help bring her some peace."

Granddad's face softened and he shrugged. "We adopted her before we came to Palmerston North. We thought it was best if she didn't know. Lizzy is our daughter. My little girl. What does she hope to gain by stirring up the past? She doesn't know what she's asking. Better to leave the past in the past and move forward, Chloe."

"I understand Granddad, you did what you thought was best for Mum and I know she loves you both very much. I think all Mum wants to do is set her birth-mother's mind at ease. She knows it must have been a difficult decision for her and I think she just wants to offer her some forgiveness."

Granddad mulled over her words for a moment and then pulled the bracelet from his pocket and handed it to Chloe. She grinned as she picked it up and twirled it between her fingers.

"It's beautiful! So ornately engraved. Mine and Danielle's are much plainer than this. Why doesn't it have her initials though? M - I is it? Or is that a J? & P - M." Chloe changed her expression as the answer dawned on her, "Is this from her real parents?" Chloe blurted and then stopped immediately once she realised what she'd said. "Sorry that's not what I meant, you're her real parents. Do you think these are the initials of her birth-parents? What did you know about them, Granddad?"

"I only really know for certain who P.M. is. The mother's a different story. You mustn't tell your Grandmother about any of this. Promise?" The urgency for Chloe to agree told her that this was information that not even her grandmother knew. Why did everyone insist on keeping everything secret. Wouldn't it just be easier to get everything out in the open so no one was kept in the dark? Chloe knew that if she had any hope of getting her grandfather's help she had better agree to his terms.

"Sure, Granddad. I won't say anything. So who was P.M.?" She offered the bracelet back to him but he shook his hand allowing her to keep hold of it for now.

"P.M. was my best friend - in fact he was my best man at our wedding. Peter McGreggor. Gosh - I haven't talked to him in years." Granddad grinned quite cheekily and was obviously reminiscing some fond memories of the man.

"You knew him! You knew Mum's birth-father?"

Granddad furrowed his brow and bobbed an open hand to the ground at her. "Keep it down, will you. Yes. He was a good mate of mine from university days. We played in the first fifteen cricket team together." He looked at Chloe as if trying to weigh whether or not he should tell her. Did he think she was still too young to know some things? Granddad usually always watched his tongue around herself and Danielle. It was only as they'd gotten older that he'd relaxed in that area. Chloe stood tall and tried not to feel like a little girl who was eager to learn some sort of playground gossip.

"Peter was what you'd probably call a playboy of sorts. He was always flirting with the girls. The mothers too." He raised an eyebrow at her to make her realise how unusual that was. "He was very charming and he always seemed to get away with it - the cheeky sod. There wasn't a mother in town that didn't want her daughter to date him. He had a beguiling smile and a way with his words. I couldn't believe his nerve sometimes. Lizzy got his smile for sure."

"So. What happened?"

"Well, Peter got a girl pregnant during one of our away tournaments and she came looking for him at our wedding."

"So that woman in the photograph - it really is Mum's birth-mother?"

Granddad folded his arms across his chest and nodded, casting his eyes to the ground.

"I knew it!"

Granddad's prompt, "Shhh!" sounded like a hard sweep of a stiff bristled broom on a concrete floor. His eyes widened and Chloe could tell she had better obey. She reduced her tone to barely above a whisper. "So Grandma never knew that Peter was the father?"

"No. And I'd like to keep it that way. She and Peter didn't really get along, you see, and I worried that if she found out Lizzy was his child she might not agree to adopt her. As far as Iris knows, Lizzy was a baby born out of wedlock that needed a family. I asked my sister to tell her about the baby, and Iris asked me on our honeymoon if I thought we should adopt her. Of course I said yes - it was the plan all along. I don't want Iris looking at Lizzy any differently than she has all her life. It took months for Lizzy to forgive your grandmother. It was Iris' decision to keep Lizzy's adoption a secret from her and when we moved to Palmerston North it was just too easy to not tell anyone that she was adopted. I just went along with whatever she wanted. I didn't want Iris to ask any more questions about Lizzy's birth-parents than was necessary. Iris and Lizzy are in a good place now. Can't we just leave it alone?"

Chloe took a deep breath and took it all in. "I see your situation, Granddad. But this is about Mum, and if Mum wants to know, then I'm going to try and find her birth-mother for her. You and Grandma have had Mum all your life. Her birth-mother has missed all the years that you have enjoyed with her. Don't you think it's worth trying - for Mum's sake? It's not about you guys anymore. We have no idea how much longer Mum might be here with us, and I, for one, am going to try and fulfil her last wishes."

"Okay, Chloe. You win. I'll do my best to smooth the waters if things start to get choppy. And if it all turns to custard - I'm blaming you." His grin belied he truly would and Chloe joined his game.

"Sure Granddad it's all on me. But so is the credit." Chloe took the last laugh knowing Granddad liked taking credit for things he barely had a hand in. "So this guy, Peter. Where is he now? And do you have any clue as to the mother's name?"

"Marta. The girl's name was Marta. But I haven't a clue what her surname is. Peter, on the other hand, I think moved to Australia. We lost touch fairly quickly once we left Auckland. He did come visit us here once to ask if I'd come play on a tour in Australia - Lizzy was about three at the time. I was so worried, but he didn't say anything about Lizzy to Iris. He understood. He gave your mum a small teddy bear and left. I haven't seen or heard anything from him since that tour."

CHAPTER THREE

Jess

WHEN CHLOE RETURNED to the living room, it appeared her presence had only been missed by one: Danielle. Her sister's 'where have you been' look, was best ignored for the time being. She would rather not draw any further unnecessary attention. Dad had arrived and was fingering through a rather large pile of newspapers.

"Iris. Do you really need to keep all these?"

"No. I suppose not. They just always come in handy. It's an old habit I guess, collecting newspapers for the fireplace, but ever since we had that air-conditioning unit installed we've hardly lit the fire. To tell you the truth I do miss it. It was always so comforting to have the fire going. The kids would sit around, drinking their hot chocolates before bed. Do you remember girls?" Iris crinkled her nose at them. "It was a lovely tradition. It's just not the same anymore. Sitting around a plastic rectangle on the wall hasn't an ounce of charm to it at all!"

"No. But at least Thomas no longer needs to cut the firewood and he gets to keep his fingers too." Dad winked at Granddad, who had just returned from the garage.

Chloe looked at Danielle. She was busy wrapping Grandma's china from the glass cabinet with tissue paper.

"Danielle can use them, Dad. It'll help cushion the china in the boxes."

Iris jumped her brow at him, wiping her hands down the skirt of her apron. "See, Jack. I knew they would come in handy someday."

Dad chuckled and dumped the stack on the floor beside Danielle.

It wasn't until later when the girls were out in the garden that Chloe was able to pull her sister aside and explain what she'd been up to.

"Granddad knows. He's known all along. He knows who Mum's birth-parents are. But he made me promise not to tell Grandma. For now I think it's best we just keep it between ourselves and see if we can track down the father, Peter McGreggor. I mean, how many could there be in New Zealand, right?"

"You'd be surprised." Danielle raised an eyebrow.

"Granddad said he might have moved to Aussie."

"Well if that's the case, then it could be a lot harder to find him than you think. Did he say anything else about him?"

"Yes. They studied Law together at Uni and played on the same cricket team - the first fifteen I think."

"Well that's a start. I have a training course to attend in Auckland next week. How about I visit the university and see what I can find out."

"You really think you can find something there? What about just looking on the National database at your work?"

"Chloe! You know I can't do that, that's not the sort of thing I'm allowed to do. If I were to get caught, I might lose my job. Besides don't you think I would have looked for Mum already if I could have?"

"Well if you change your mind, Granddad said the girl in the photograph's name was Marta. He didn't know the girls' surname. But Marta can't be all that common. If we can find Peter - he might be able to tell us her full name - surely he'd remember. Granddad said that Grandma didn't like Peter very much so 'Mum's' the word."

"What's this about your mother, girls?" bustled Iris as she joined the two girls chatting by the pink camellias.

"Oh, uh, I was just saying to Chloe that we should pop up to the hospital soon to see Mum - before Chloe has to head back to Wellington."

"Oh yes, She'd love that. Could I come with you?"

Chloe tensioned a glare at her sister.

Danielle reached and took Grandma's hand - patting the top of it with the other. "Uh, if you don't mind, we'd like to see mum - just the two of us. I'm not due back in Wellington till tomorrow. So, how about you and I visit her together before I go?" Danielle warmed a full smile and waited for Grandma's consent. Chloe wasn't accustomed to seeing Danielle this way and she wondered if she would ever get used to it. Chloe let her shoulders drop a little.

Grandma placed her other hand on top of Danielle's like a game of snap. "All right. Tell the truth I'm exhausted. I'm going to sleep like a doll tonight. The house feels so empty with everything stacked in boxes. I'm so grateful to the both of you for all your help, girls. Give Lizzy my love and a big hug and a kiss from me." Grandma planted the affectionate gesture on Danielle who stood closest. Chloe giggled. Then Grandma stretched out her arms to include her, kissing her cheek also.

"Travel safe my dear. And give my love to Jeremy. I'm sorry that he couldn't make it today."

"That's okay, Grandma. He's a little busy with work at the moment. I'll pass on your regards." Chloe was in no frame of mind to go into the emotional details of her recent breakup, and judging by the look on Danielle's face she'd made the right decision.

With farewells given and a look from Granddad that hinted she keep her lips tight, Danielle and Chloe left with arms waving out the car window.

Mum was sleeping when they arrived but awoke as if emerging from a memory, not a dream.

"Chloe, you're a star sweetheart. Thanks so much for helping dad with the gardens. Could you please pour me a glass of water?"

Danielle nodded towards the pitcher of water on the bed table, while she dragged a second chair over to the bed. "They must have given her a dose of the drowsy meds she usually asks for."

Chloe poured the water and passed it to her. "Here you are. How are you feeling?"

Mum propped herself up into a seated position and rubbed her hand over her head to flatten her hair. After rearranging her nightgown into something which looked vaguely adequate for visitors she replied, "Oh, um all right I suppose." Her face screwed at the surroundings.

"You know you're in the hospital, aye Mum?" Danielle sat in the chair and placed her hand on mum's arm.

"Yes, I've gathered that, Danielle. The doctor prescribed me some sleeping tablets as I didn't sleep much last night. What time is it?"

"It's two. Mum, I have some news." Chloe jumped straight to it without acknowledging her mother's mental state - spouting all the gossip she'd learned from Granddad. She may have overestimated her mother's ability to follow the string of words she hastily assembled, but her excitement couldn't be restrained. "We've finally got a clue. I found a picture of me in one of Grandma's photo albums. I was at her and Granddad's wedding. Well it wasn't me of course but it was a girl who looked exactly like me. Granddad was really troubled when we pointed her out in the photo and obviously knew more about her than he was ready to divulge. So, I followed him to the garage and asked him who she was. You wouldn't believe it Mum, but he knows who your real father is and the name of your birth-mother." Chloe waited for the words to sink in - testing the strength of her patience. When their mother finally did speak it was not at all the thrilled sound Chloe had expected to hear.

"Oh, I see." Mum's eyes watered and she appeared to shrink before Chloe's eyes.

"Did you hear what I said, Mum? I think we have a solid lead now. Granddad said that your father was his best-man at their wedding. I never would have guessed that in a million years. It's strange isn't it?" Chloe jabbered enthralled by the mystery of it all.

"I suppose it is," Mum said barely audible.

"Danielle's gonna go to the University in Auckland next week and see what information she can find on this - Peter McGreggor."

"Peter. Was that his name?" She said, her words barely leaving an imprint on the airwaves.

"Yes and he was a lawyer - just like Granddad. He also played cricket. In fact I think that's how he met Marta, your birth-mother, it was during one of their away games. I'm not exactly sure where she came from yet or where she is now, but if we can track down Peter maybe he can tell us more about her."

"What?" Mum looked completely baffled and Chloe knew she'd not done her explanation justice in the excitement of sharing it all.

"Sorry, Mum. It's been a very long day, and Chloe's not explaining it very well. You deserve to know the whole truth."

"It's all right, Danielle. I heard her. I think I understand. I'm just...well, sad."

"Sad? Why? Isn't this what you wanted, Mum?" Chloe lowered her brow.

"Yes. I know what I told you. But honestly, I didn't think you'd have any luck finding answers. Dad knew? All this time - he knew. I don't understand. Why didn't he say anything when I found out about being adopted? He just let Mum and I fight. Why would he do that?" Tears trickled down Mum's slightly flushed cheeks.

"I don't know. Granddad made me promise not to say anything about Peter to Grandma - there's some bad blood there I think. Grandma doesn't know Peter is your real father and Granddad said that if she had known - she might not have wanted to adopt you. I think he was trying to protect you. He really wanted you - they both did. You know they love you very much. Don't be mad at Granddad." Chloe touched Mum's other arm and briefly shook her head.

Mum pursed her lips. "No, all right. No good comes from holding a grudge anyway. Mum and I proved that, and I don't have time to waste on bitterness." Mum's spirits rallied and she seemed to comprehend what it might all mean. "So this Peter. You say he went to university with Dad?"

"Yes. That's what he said." Chloe nodded.

"And he played cricket?"

"Yes."

"And where did you say you saw a picture of this woman Dad thinks is my birth-mother?"

"Marta. She was in one of Granddad and Grandma's wedding photos in the background... She was pregnant."

"You should have seen it, Mum. Chloe looks just like her." Danielle blurted, then looked at Chloe. She scrunched one cheek. "I should have asked if I could borrow the album. Then we could've shown Mum. Why didn't I think of that before we came?"

Chloe was certain the thought would bug her sister for the rest of the afternoon, but she didn't want Danielle retrieving it. "We don't want Grandma finding out the truth just yet. Let's not stir until we're a bit more sure about Peter and the information first."

"Okay. I suppose you're right." Danielle squeezed Mum's arm. "But if I can find it when we unpack at their new place I'll bring it over for you to see, Mum."

"Thank you, sweetheart, that would be wonderful." A warm pink returned to Mum's lips as she smiled and Chloe felt a glimmer of hope that maybe, just maybe, it was the kind of medicine she had needed all along.

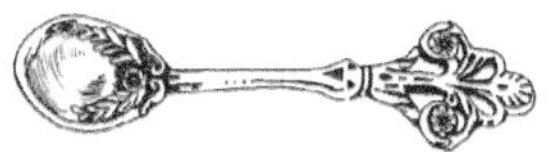

Thursday 10th August 2017

Chloe pressed the phone to her ear and listened to the voice-mail Danielle had left her.

"Hi Chloe. Good news. I've managed to track down Peter - well, sort of. Granddad was right he's living in Australia - in Sydney to be exact. I don't know his address yet, but I've got a phone number which should link us to his sister, who apparently lives in Christchurch now. I've been on such a wild goose chase. I've got a wonderful idea. Give me a call when you're free and I'll tell you all about it."

Chloe couldn't decide if she was up to calling her sister back right now. Jeremy had just been around to her flat and apologised for his poor choice of timing with his break up call last week. Keen to remedy his mistake he'd pleaded with her to understand his position. "It's just temporary - a break," he said. "It's for your sake as much as mine."

Echoes from her chat with Danielle enabled her to read between his words - boosting her confidence. She wasn't being needy. He hadn't even asked how her mother was, and his stand-off body language revealed far more truth than his tender lips ever would. She would definitely miss those. The way he'd brush them against her eyelids, down her nose and tease her lips - making her melt like chocolate in its wrapper.

This is gonna be tougher than I thought.

All it took was a replay of his last remark to snap her back to reality. "I thought you loved me, Chloe. You said you'd love me forever. You're just the same as your sister you know." She'd tried not to read too much into that - but what did he mean? The way he'd said it with that impish grin had left her with an ache in her gut and a deep sense of dread. Was there any truth to her suspicion? Had he and Danielle known each other in the past? Danielle never said anything. Maybe that's why she had tried to warn her off him. Danielle said he was a waste of time, and all he would ever want was to keep her like a fish on his line. Chloe could see now she'd been a convenience for him. Always there when he needed to talk things over about what he was going through. After the week apart, she'd come to the conclusion that he actually needed her more than she needed him - just as Danielle said. How did she know? She felt strangely liberated and yet slightly disturbed. At least Jeremy's ego took a long overdue hit. Asking Danielle outright if she'd had a thing in the past with her now ex-boyfriend was not something Chloe wanted to hear let alone face right now.

Her stomach moaned and she realised she hadn't eaten since lunch. Hunger was the perfect reason to put off calling her sister back. Chloe grabbed the first thing she saw in the pantry. Two slices of wholegrain bread. Her mind already wandering, she stood in a daze contemplating what options there were to fill it. Natural reflexes picked peanut butter and she imagined Jeremy's face as she wiped the bread with her knife smearing the nutty-ness all over it. Chloe giggled.

Jamming the sandwich into her mouth, she spied the phone on the table in the exact position it had been on a previous date. A moment of déjà vu struck - instantly transporting her to a conversation she'd had with Danielle during one of their calls about the vow renewal plans. She'd been eating the same sandwich for dinner and been mocked for such a terrible choice. Even Mum would think it wasn't a suitable meal. Pushing the self-inflicted judgment aside she took another bite and nudged the phone with her foot to a different position. Danielle can wait. Reaching a slightly greasy finger to hit the TV remote button, the phone sounded and she huffed, rolled her eyes and answered between sticky bites. "Hello?"

Danielle's bubbly voice greeted her on the other end and Chloe put the phone on speaker, keeping her mouth as far from the receiver as possible.

"Hi Chloe. I'm glad I've caught you. I tried a couple of times and finally gave up and left a message. Did you get it?"

"Ah, No. I've only just got in." Lying to Danielle was easy when she wasn't standing in front of her.

"Where have you been? Are you eating? Just a minute..."

Keen to avoid Danielle's questions she was happy to wait and give her as many minute's as she wanted. Chloe stuffed in another mouthful while Danielle finished up a conversation with a work colleague.

"You still there, Chloe?"

"Yes. I'm here," she mumbled through the macerated bread.

"What are you doing?" Danielle mused.

"I'm eating dinner."

"But it's not even five o'clock yet. I wish it was though."

"I know, but I was starving. It's just a snack really. Hard day is it?" Chloe attempted to change the subject.

"You could say that. Never mind. I've got some news that I think you're gonna like."

"Cool. What did you find out?"

"Well, I went to the University and they couldn't tell me a whole lot except to say that Granddad did complete his degree in Law and so did

Peter McGreggor. They couldn't tell me much else about Peter, but suggested I try the cricket club when I mentioned that they had both played in the first fifteen. I had much better luck there as I ran into the club's historian, who just happened to be uploading some of the old club photos onto the website."

"That's great. Did you find one with Peter in it?"

"Judith was most helpful. Her husband, Malcolm, is one of the older members of the club and since she helped organise the centennial celebrations ten years ago she has been in charge of the archives ever since. Some of the clubs really old documents and photos were destroyed in a couple of fires. But we did manage to find a team photograph. Granddad was in it and so was Peter." Her sister's glee could not be masked, even over the phone, and Chloe couldn't help but smile - picturing her at the other end. Chloe's questions about her sister and Jeremy faded to the back of her mind. Maybe she wouldn't even bring it up. Would it really help anyone if she did?

"Fantastic. So did you manage to find an address for him?"

"Well no. But then Judith made a few calls, and before I knew it, we were off to see Allen - one of their other teammates."

"How did you manage that?"

"I dunno, it was pretty lucky that I even got to meet Judith. She only goes into the club once a month. Anyway, we got to Seawood Views and I was just praying that the guy would have some recollection of Peter. Judith wasn't really sure if Allen would be able to remember Peter or not but one of the other men she had called had said to ask Allen as he was kinda the glue that kept in touch with everyone. He said he thought Allen and Peter had stayed in touch since they were both from Auckland."

"So, did he?" Chloe reached for her laptop, awaiting at least a hint of useful information - not just a complete history of all of the University's cricket team members.

"Yes, he did. In fact Allen was most informative about Granddad's teammates. You should have been there, Chloe. It was hilarious. Granddad is going to be so mad when he finds out that I know all of his team's secrets."

"Sounds like you're gonna make sure he knows." Chloe snuffed. "That ought to come in useful when he tries to pull one on you in future."

"I hope so." Danielle giggled and then sighed. "You wouldn't believe it, Chloe, but Granddad had a nickname amongst his team-mates and you'll never guess what it was."

"Fine, I won't. Tell me."

"Bond - Bail Bond." Danielle said it in a deep voice, the way they say it in the Bond movies. "Allen said they called him that because Tom was always bailing them out whenever they got arrested for drinking too much. Bail-Bond Tom they called him."

"No way! That's hilarious. Wonder if Grandma knows?"

"I doubt it. Peter had a nickname too and it says it all really - Playboy Pete. Allen reckoned every girl who ever laid eyes on him would chase after him. According to Allen, Pete always had a girl by his side and never left a dance without a pretty one on his arm."

"If that's true, Mum might have other half-brothers or sisters that nobody knows about. That's just weird." Chloe screwed her face up at the thought. Danielle continued seemingly without absorbing Chloe's random suggestion.

"When I asked him about whether he knew where Peter was, he said that he had been in touch with him a couple times by phone after he moved to Sydney, but he hadn't heard from him in a while. He gave me his phone number - I haven't tried calling it yet. Allen said his younger sister, April, knew Peter's younger sister, Christine, quite well as they went to Diocesan Girls' High together. Allen gave me his sister's phone number to call and said she would be able to put me in touch with Christine. She goes by the name Christine Goodwin now and she should have an address for Peter in Sydney. It's the best information I could find, Chloe. What do you want to do? Should we call the number Allen gave me and see if Peter answers. Or should I track down his sister and try to get his address first?"

Chloe thought for a second pitching her eyes to the ceiling. "Well, I don't know. Did you ask Mum?"

"I haven't spoken to her about any of it yet. I thought we could work on this together. Find Peter first, and then go from there."

"Don't call him yet. I don't want to lose this lead. What's Peter's sister's name again?"

"Christine Goodwin. Allen thought she lived in Christchurch."

"Okay. Give her a call and see if you can get Peter's address. I think that's probably our best option for now. But what will you say? We need a story so that Christine will give us Peter's address."

"I know, I've been racking my brain and haven't been able to come up with anything remotely plausible."

"Really? I would have thought you had to make up random reasons for calling people at your work all the time." Chloe half-joked.

"No, Chloe. When I call someone I usually have a reason for doing so." Danielle's sarcasm gave Chloe a subtle reminder that their recent collusion was still a work in progress. She didn't want to jinx their new 'friends' status by getting into an argument with her, so she dropped it. "Well, let me think... I know. Why don't I call posing as the secretary at Granddad's old law firm? I'll say that we need to update our records for Peter McGreggor as he's listed as one of the beneficiaries in a recent will that's being reviewed. That should be convincing enough. I can do that. I know it's been a while since I worked there, but I know exactly what to say. I'll even use their secretary Maria's name. That way if this, Christine Goodwin, calls the firm back to confirm anything she'll think it's legit."

"Chloe, that's genius. Are you sure you want to be a teacher? I think you'd make a much better blueberry... I mean actress."

"Ha, Ha - not funny. You're never gonna let me live that down are you?" Chloe tried to ignore her sister's bait. When Chloe was eight years old she had played Violet Beauregarde in the school's production of Charlie and the Chocolate Factory. For months afterward, Danielle called her Blueberry and giggled every time. Chloe hated blueberries, and when she had to wear the sumo-like costume, she was so embarrassed she blushed like a peach every time the word was mentioned.

"Sorry. Old habits die hard I guess." Danielle sniggered. "So, shall I call Allen's sister for you and get Christine's number? That shouldn't be too hard. I'll just tell her I'm tracking down some of Granddad's old cricket buddies to invite them to his birthday party."

"For heaven's sake, Danielle, why didn't you just suggest that in the first place? Can't we just say that to Christine?!" Chloe bit her tongue. *Old habits indeed.*

Danielle tapped her forehead. "Oh! Woops" - she nodded - "I guess that could work too."

Chloe rolled her eyes and was glad Danielle couldn't see her do so. At that moment she honestly wondered if she was in fact really younger than her sister. "Right. You make the call and let me know how you get on then."

"Sure, Chloe. Sorry I didn't mean to make this seem difficult. I'm just... well honestly I'm just excited about it all. Getting to work on this with you is really… well, special. When will you next be home? We should probably tell Mum about all this."

"I'm not sure. But you're probably right, Danielle. Mum perked up a lot when we gave her the news about Peter last time. I really hope we can deliver her some more good news, and soon."

"Me too."

"Now what's the wonderful idea you mentioned?" Chloe opened a Google tab and was about to punch in a search for the Auckland University Cricket Club.

"Oh, yeah, that…Hey you did get my message!"

Chloe had busted herself. She slapped a palm to her head as punishment and offered her excuse. "I was just about to call you back but I was gonna wait till I'd finished eating. Does it really matter?" Danielle's response came quick and Chloe knew all was forgiven.

"No. I get it. Well I was just thinking. If we do manage to get an address for Peter in Sydney, why don't you stop in and see him on your way over to London? I don't mind paying any extra fee to change your flights for you. It would be perfect, and I bet if you turned up on his doorstep he wouldn't be able to refuse to speak to you. What do you think?"

"Um, honestly, I'm not sure I can do that. For starters I wouldn't have the first clue what to say. That would be really weird, don't you think?"

"Well it's got to be better than just phoning him. If all we can do is talk to him on the phone he may just hang up. But if you're standing there in person - I doubt he'll be able to turn you away. Any way - it's just a thought. Have a think about it and let me know. We'll have to change your flights soon if we're gonna make it work though."

"Okay. I'll think about it."

"Talk to Mum, see what she says. She's very excited about your trip. She's told all the nurses on the ward that her daughter is off on her OE and she's super proud of you. Please consider doing this for her. Just remember, she's the reason for all of this and what a great gift it would be to find both of her birth-parents."

Chloe felt the strings of manipulation tighten as if being tuned like her sister's violin. She'd grown so accustomed to the way Danielle played her words, that whatever she suggested always seemed like the right thing to do. Danielle once convinced her that if she didn't steal a couple of ice-blocks from the freezer for them, the bird they were nursing outside would die. She hated to admit it, but yes, she was once that gullible. Chloe had since wised up to her sister's manipulative ways, but occasionally still felt trapped by them. Danielle knew all of her weaknesses and insecurities, and seemed to know exactly what to say to get what she wanted.

Chloe decided then and there that, for Mum's sake, she would agree to meet Peter in Sydney - **if** they could get his address that is. Meeting her biological grandfather couldn't be all that bad - could it?

Chloe also decided, more for the fun of it, not to tell Danielle just yet. She'd make her sweat - just a little.

"We'll see. But I'm making no promises."

"I'll call you tomorrow once I've spoken to April, and hopefully Christine too. Maybe then you'll have an answer." Danielle probed.

"Maybe." Chloe smirked on the other end of the line, then hung up.

CHAPTER FOUR

Monday 21st August 2017

"I'M SO NERVOUS, Danielle. What if he doesn't want to speak to me? What will I do if I can't find him when I get there?"

"Don't worry about all that now. Why wouldn't he want to talk to you? He may be a bit shocked when he sees you, with you looking like the spitting image of a girl he got pregnant years ago. But he'll come around - you'll see."

"Oh Thanks. You're a great help. I'd forgotten I look like Marta. He's gonna get the shock of his life. I hope I don't give him a heart attack or something. Mum would never forgive me." Both girls reserved their laughter to a short burst.

"Flight 309 to Sydney, Australia is now boarding through gate two. All remaining passengers should now board the aircraft."

"Well this is it. Wish me luck." Chloe pulled her bag over her shoulder and yanked on her hair trapped beneath the strap. Danielle grabbed her for a hug as soon as she had her bags sorted and Chloe's heart swelled with a love for her sister she hadn't felt for a very long time. Her eyes glassed and as soon as Danielle pulled herself away from their embrace Chloe saw the feeling was mutual.

"Be good and call me as soon as you can."

"I will." Tears dripped without restraint from Chloe's eyes.

"You can do this, Chloe. I know you can. You're my sister and I believe in you."

Chloe wished her sister hadn't said it as soon as the words hit her ears. A new stream of tears effortlessly slipped out and she fumbled for the tissues in her bag.

"Right, now off you go and have the best adventure. I love you." Danielle hugged her one last time before Chloe turned and walked towards the gate. Looking back before she stepped through the door of the snaking corridor, she gave a timid low wave at Danielle.

This was it. This was *it*. The moment she feared most of all.

She was alone. All alone and no one would be there by her side to talk to, or ask... well, anything really.

Chloe lifted her head and positioned it a little straighter on her shoulders.

Right. It's time to put my big girl boots on and do this thing.

I can do this. I can do this. I'm sure I can do this... At least I hope I can do this.

Chloe's internal pep talk took her all the way to the door of the airplane, where people seemed to be sucked inside without a moment's hesitation. Anxiety gripped her bladder and gave it something to worry about.

Oh God, not now... At least let me make it inside.

Chloe placed a hand on her stomach and mumbled to herself, "You can do this. You'll be fine. It's completely normal. Everyone's doing it. See."

"Are you all right, Miss?" asked an elderly lady of about the same era as her grandmother. She was walking in front of Chloe and had paused at her allocated seat. "Did you say something, honey? I'm a little hard of hearing so you'll have to speak up. I'm Sally, nice to meet ya!"

"Oh, no. Sorry. I was just muttering to myself."

"That's all right, honey. I do it all the time. Gives one confidence when it's lacking. Sorry for the hold up, I'm a little slower these days."

Chloe then noticed the woman's legs were tightly bound and that she hadn't been wobbling down the aisle due to the restricted space, like the rest of them were. She was struggling just to walk, full stop. "That's all right, I'm over here anyway." Chloe pointed to the seat across the aisle from where the woman stood. "Can I help you with that?" Chloe opened her hands. The woman turned, smiled and allowed Chloe to lift her hand luggage into the overhead compartment for her.

"Oh thank you, honey. You're a dear. You from here?"

Chloe tucked her own bag into the above compartment alongside the woman's and dropped into her seat - clearing the aisle for other passengers to pass. "Yes. I'm from Wellington. You?"

"Oh honey, if you can't tell where I'm from then I can tell you ain't much travelled."

"No, you could say that. But you're American by the sounds of it and from the south if I'm not mistaken. I loved watching reruns of Dallas with my Grandmother. You remind me a little of them."

"Your Grandmother's got good taste, honey. You know I once got to play one of the extras on the show. I'll never forget it. That 'Bobby' was such a dreamboat. That's how we came to be in Noo Zee-land, you see. My late husband was a Kiwi and I met him at a rally in North Dakota. I was so smitten by his accent that we got married within a week. My parents were mortified when I told them. But once they met Bob, they couldn't have been happier with him if they tried. Now that Bob's gone, I've decided to take one last trip back home before I retire from traveling all together. It ain't easy getting old, honey. I don't recommend it." Chloe smiled. Her Grandmother had said exactly the same thing almost word for word and it made her feel a little homesick already. At least Sally seemed nice and was happy to converse with her.

"So where are ya heading…ah, what's ya name, honey?"

"Chloe. I'm Chloe Spencer." She held her hand out over the aisle momentarily so she could shake hands with Sally. "I'm going to London, I have a teaching job there. I start in September but I planned to take a short tour around Europe before I start. I'm not so sure I'll be doing that now though."

"Really, why not? That sounds wonderful. You really should do it, Chloe. You never know when you might get the chance again - if at all. I wish I'd been able to travel when I was younger. It would have been much more enjoyable than with the limitations I have now. You have the rest of your life to knuckle down and work or have kids or whatever it is you think you want to do. But to have the opportunity to travel in your twenties - that's not a thing to sneeze at. Grab it by the horns and ride the bull wherever it may take you. Bob took me to Spain when we retired. I'd always dreamed of seeing and perhaps even actually running with the bulls. But there's no way we could do it in our sixties. Maybe there's more sense about doing that sort of thing when you're older. But I really do feel like I missed out on a lot of what some of my friends got up to. I used to write to my good friend Georgia after I moved to New Zealand. She always told me I was so brave to move so far away to such a small island. But to tell you the truth I envied her as much as she did me. I thought she was the lucky one getting to travel through Europe with her family and then down into South America. Her letters were such a source of thrill and excitement for me as we lived way down here in the back hills of Martinborough. Life on a sheep farm, as wonderful as it was, is nothing like being chased by bulls down a city street by any stretch of the imagination. Although there was that one time when the ram did charge at Bob and I when we'd given him a fright. Poor old girls.

I did feel for the ewes when Sam the Ram was let in on their paddocks. Makes me wonder what on earth their conversations were like, you know, like that movie - BABE, where the sheep talk. God, what I wouldn't give to have been in amongst the flock to hear all the gossip about Sam. He was a stud all right. Didn't mess around either. Only had him in the paddocks for two days usually and he'd be done - the dirty dag. Made Bob stand on end too - if ya catch my drift." Sally winked.

Chloe bit her tongue. If she had been anywhere else she would have exploded with laughter. Fortunately Sally's little tale had distracted her to the point that she hadn't even realised they'd taken off. She liked Sally and couldn't wait to hear more stories about life on the farm in Martinborough. Sally had promised her at least a dozen or so more good ones, to help 'pass the time' she said. They were so good that Chloe never even bothered to check what movies might be showing.

By the time the captain announced their descent into Sydney, Chloe was feeling much more relaxed and calm about the whole idea of meeting Peter. Sally had been a wonderful coach about having courage and being brave when Chloe knew deep down all she wanted to do was stay put at the airport and catch her next flight. Sally had even offered to come with her. Even though Chloe knew she should be brave and do it on her own she had graciously accepted Sally's offer to accompany her.

As they pulled out of the airport in the rental car Sally suggested, instead of taking an expensive taxi, Chloe felt so relieved she had company. Her stomach didn't have time to flip itself in knots as simply navigating their way to Little Bay consumed all of her mental resources. But as soon as they pulled into Peter's driveway, things got very real, very fast. Not only was her stomach writhing like a freshly caught eel, but her brain had turned to slush, and her palms felt as clammy as a wet swimsuit.

Once Chloe had engaged the hand brake, Sally rested a hand on her shoulder. "No thinking. Just doing."

Chloe twisted her brow, bit the corner of her lower lip, and nodded once.

Sally's encouraging words were exactly what she needed to hear. But sadly, they did little to convince her feet to follow through.

She held her hand on the lever of the car door - every muscle in her arm frozen to actually pulling it.

Like a childish game of statues, the rest of her seemed stuck too. Her feet lodged in concrete gumboots, and her heart pumping with the dread of Handel's Sarabande suite No.4. To this day, she could still hear Danielle's whiny rendition of it from the weeks of torment she'd put them all through.

"Go on, honey. You can do it. I know you can. He's gonna be fine, and you are too."

Chloe looked at Sally's big blue eyes. Taking as much courage from them as she could, she pulled the handle. "That's it, off you go. I'll be here waitin' for ya." Sally gave further encouragement in the form of a shove to the shoulder. Chloe wasn't sure what to make of that. She'd only known Sally for the length of the flight from Wellington to Sydney and now that she thought about it, she wondered if she really could trust Sally to wait for her with all their bags in the boot of the rental car she'd insisted they get. She dismissed the thought instantly citing the absurdity of her random musings. She'd been watching too many detective crime shows on Netflix and now her mind always seemed to question even the most genuine people or circumstances. Chloe stopped in the driveway to look back at Sally through the car window. An edgeless smile beamed, with popping eyes as if verbally saying, 'Go on - off you go.' How did she do that?

It must be an American thing. Their voices are typically louder - so it stands to reason that their eyes would be too.

Chloe nodded, advancing towards the front door with as much courage as a Girl Guide ready to sell biscuits.

She pressed the doorbell and waited for the chime to sound. When she heard nothing, Chloe tapped the door three times with the back of a knuckle, then clasped her hands behind her back. She and Sally had talked about this happening during the flight, and Sally's advice seemed completely sound at the time. 'Just wait. Give it some time. They may be indisposed or out in the garden. Hold your ground and be patient.'

The door showed no signs of opening anytime soon and Chloe was having trouble with the 'hold your ground' bit. All she wanted to do was turn and run as fast as she could down the street...or maybe she could hide behind that bush over there. She eyed its leafy foliage and decided it wouldn't offer the camouflage she needed to cover her growing red face. Was it getting hotter?

Chloe's heart buzzed like a honey hive and all she could do was count to ten with fluffy marshmallows in between. That was another one of Sally's suggestions.

One fluffy marshmallow, two fluffy marshmallow, three fluffy marshmallow...

They'd had so much fun acting out the possible scenarios, seated comfortably in the air. But now standing outside in the heat of the day, counting to ten after knocking three times (four was decided to seem too demanding), it only just dawned on her that they hadn't practiced what she would say if someone actually answered. Sally had convinced her somehow that that was the easy part. 'It's the getting to the door, knocking and waiting - that's the hard part.'

Chloe now disagreed. Sally had made that part seem like fun - a game even. But now, standing there waiting, Chloe realised she had no idea what she was going to say. Too late.

The door whinnied on its hinges as it swung open, and a woman stood there blinking back.

Chloe straightened. "Hello. Is this the residence of Peter McGreggor?" She asked, fearing it was.

"Yes. But Peter isn't here at the moment. Is there something I can help you with?" The lady's eyes were kind but her apprehension as to why Chloe was asking was obvious when she hugged herself closer to the door.

"Umm. No. I mean, Yes - maybe. You see, I was hoping I could speak with Peter privately. It's a personal matter and it's really important that I speak with him. I don't have a lot of time. I've got to get back to the airport by seven. Please. If you know where he is could you tell me?"

"I don't even know who you are. I'm not about to tell you where my husband is if I don't even know your name or what you want to speak to him for." The kindness in the woman's eyes had evaporated and Chloe realised she hadn't conveyed her purpose for seeing Peter very well.

"Oh, no, I mean, yes, sorry - you're right. You don't know who I am. My name is Chloe Spencer and I'm Jack Spencer's granddaughter. My grandfather was very good friends with Peter at Auckland university I believe. Peter used to be a very good cricket player - or so my grandfather says anyway." Chloe waited for the woman's response unsure if she would soften at her explanation or close the door on Chloe's face. She breathed a sigh of relief when the woman smiled at her for the first time.

"Oh. Okay, well Chloe, Pete's at the podiatrists at the moment. He shouldn't be much longer. He's been having some trouble with his calves lately so the doctor referred him to the foot man. Would you like to come in and wait for him?"

"Uh sure that would be great. I'll just let my friend in the car know." Chloe backed away from the door, skipped to the passenger door of the car to inform Sally. The woman, who Chloe quickly realised hadn't given her name, called after her, "You're both welcome to wait for him inside." Chloe nodded she understood and spoke briefly to Sally who, at first, didn't want to intrude on Chloe's family meeting.

"Please, Sally. You're so good at making small talk. I could really use your help here. I'm so nervous and I don't know what to say."

"All right, honey. You win." Sally pushed her door open, gathered up her handbag, and followed Chloe to the front door. Chloe acted out the introductions. "Sally this is… um, Sorry I didn't catch your name."

The kind eyes now glinted with a little cheek. "That's because I never told you," smiled the woman. "My name's June. I'm Peter's wife." She held out her hand to Sally, who shook it briefly.

"So, Chloe, what is it you wanted to speak to Peter about. You said it was personal. Is your grandfather all right?"

"Oh, yes, he's fine. His eyes aren't so good but he's still very mobile. I've been learning all sorts of things about him lately that I never even knew."

"Really, like what?"

"Well he once had a job at the cheese factory when he was a teenager. And he went on a cricket tour with his team to Australia when my mum was three, leaving my grandmother at home for four weeks on her own. She was not impressed."

"I wouldn't have been either," June replied.

"She obviously forgave him though because nine months later my Aunt Sue was born." Chloe grinned and Sally burst out laughing.

June's eyes crinkled at the edges. "Peter and I have been married ten years this November - we met on a cruise in the Caribbean. We struck up a conversation at the bar the first night and we just never stopped. He's a well-travelled man and I liked the fact that we had visited so many of the same places. Even some of our favourite spots were the same." June paused, opened the fridge, and withdrew a large pitcher of what looked like iced tea. She eyed them both for a nod and then proceeded to pour three glasses. "He's been married before. We both have. He's got three kids, two girls and a son in Perth. We don't see him much but the girls live nearby." She slid the drinks in their respective directions along the kitchen island. "I have two. A son - Adam. He lives in the UK and works for a big finance company. And then Heather. She lives in Brisbane. She and Nigel have three children. Gareth is fifteen, David is ten and Matilda is just seven. I miss them so much. We're going to them for Christmas this year and I'm so...Oh that sounds like Pete now."

Rumbling sounds of a garage door opening were followed by a vehicle pulling inside. The mercury in Chloe's fear-o-meter spiked to a new high. She wiped what little moisture there was from the side of her glass and smeared it across her forehead. Her stomach knotted and she looked at Sally who was already staring at her. Her eyes were saying something all right, but just what, Chloe couldn't decipher before Peter entered the room.

"I'm home, sweethea..rt." Peter looked at all of them a little bewildered. "Oh, you have visitors. Sorry to interrupt. Hello, I'm Pete, June's better-half." Peter strode towards Chloe with his hand outstretched. His head cocked to one side and one eye cinched at the corner. She took his hand but lost all her words in the flurry of the moment. Sally stepped in and offered her hand to ease the mounting tension. "Hello, Pete. I'm Sally Robson, and this is Chloe Spencer." Peter clasped Sally's hand - turning his attention to her. "Well, welcome. Nice to meet you both." He angled his head back at Chloe, his eyes squinting like he was trying to place her. "And how do you know my lovely wife then?" He returned his gaze to Sally, and then June. His smile was so kind. Chloe didn't want to be the reason to wipe the warmth from it. So she stalled. "Oh we've only really just met. You have a lovely home here."

Peter looked a little confused, and then eyed her with a scrutiny that caused a memory to spring from captivity.

"Oh my god!" Peter's eyes sprang wide like a strangled chicken.

"Chloe. I think it's time you spilled, honey," Sally said with a tone of insistence.

Chloe looked at June. "I know I should have told you when we arrived but I didn't know how to say it." She turned to Peter. "You see, you are my mother's father." She paused for a second to let it sink in. "I've tracked you down because my mother is sick and she would very much like to find her birth-mother before it's too late."

"You...you look just like her! Is she all right. Lizzy. Is she okay?" Peter asked, his hand on his chest.

Chloe was taken aback. Not just because he'd recognised who she looked like, but because of his familiarity with her mother's name.

How should she respond? Tell him everything? Maybe she should hold off until he gave her what she wanted. That didn't seem right though. If she were the one who was sick - her Dad would want to know how and why.

"Yes, she's doing all right for now, but the prognosis isn't great. She has cancer, but she was in remission. It returned a couple of weeks ago. She's on meds but the doctors don't think it's worth putting her through another round of chemo again. It's unlikely to help at this stage."

"Oh, God. How is she? Does she know about me?"

"She's good most days but she's still in the hospital. They're thinking of sending her home soon so she can enjoy the time she has left at home.

She told me she wished she could have met her birth-mother and that she wanted me to thank her for her. She's known that she was adopted since I was four. One of Grandma's friends let it slip during a visit. Mum was devastated. It took her ages for her to forgive Grandma."

"I…I don't know what to say." Peter pulled himself a chair from the dining table and sat down. "I guess I just thought that she would never know. Tom promised he wouldn't tell a soul. I guess he couldn't keep it a secret forever. How is Tom? Is he still alive? I stayed away. I didn't want to cause Tom or Iris any trouble - especially Iris, she never really liked me much after… well it's all water under the bridge now I suppose."

"Granddad said as much. But Grandma still doesn't know you're Mum's real dad. Whoah! I just realised that if you're Mum's real dad then Granddad isn't my biological grandfather. That's weird."

'Don't worry about all that, Chloe. Genes are not what make us connected to another person, it's our relationships that count," offered Sally in the most sombre voice Chloe had ever heard her use since they'd met. Chloe took solace in her eyes and moved the conversation on. "Peter. I know you may not want to talk about it, but I could really use your help."

"Sure, anything."

"I need to know. Who is Mum's birth-mother? I mean, I know her name was Marta - but that's all Granddad could tell me. He didn't have a surname or even where she lived." Chloe kittened her eyes as best as she knew how, "Please, Peter. If you know anything, Mum would be so grateful." Making it Mum's request seemed to help Peter understand the urgency of her plea.

"I'll tell you everything I know, Chloe but please remember, I was young and very foolish and I never really considered what my actions could result in. I truly am very sorry for what happened. I only hope that one day Lizzy can forgive me."

"She has, she will, and you're welcome to tell her in person yourself if you wish. But for the sake of my grandparents, I only ask that you do it privately and preferably without Grandma finding out - if that's even possible. Mum wants to meet you, Peter, and time is not on her side. So if you're going to do so, make it soon."

"I will, Chloe. I can promise you that."

PART TWO

1959

Masterton –

New Zealand

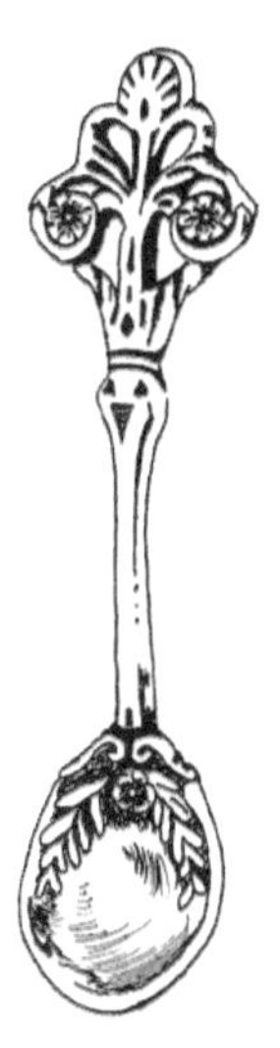

CHAPTER FIVE

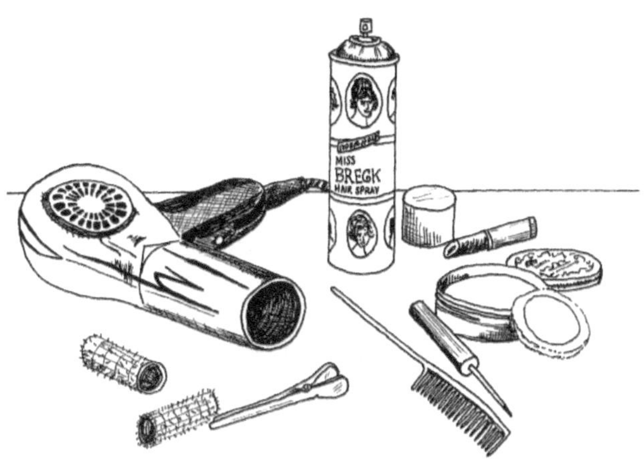

Monday 2nd November 1959

Marta

MARTA INGLES WASN'T a typical picture of beauty like her
mother. But despite a smattering of unwanted freckles across her
nose and cheeks, she often caught people's attention with her cat-like
eyes and oversized bottom lip - which she often bit when she was
nervous. Marta wouldn't believe that her looks had any merit. Her
freckles caused the most frustration and provoked the greatest loss of
tears. Where the freckles came from, no one could explain. The fact that
they gave her the appearance of someone much younger than sixteen
years was yet another cause for grievance. Fortunately her shapely
curves offered much better proof of her maturity than her face ever
would, and she took every advantage of them when choosing her clothes.

Her mother, Margaret Ingles, known to most just as 'Maggie', was beyond beautiful. Likened often to Brigitte Bardot and stared at by women and men alike.

Marta knew exactly why Dad had wanted to marry her before going off to war, much to the envy of all his comrades. She lived in hope that someday, someone might like her as much - so she too would have someone to love and care for.

But more than anything in the world, Marta wished she could look just as beautiful as her mother. Her flawless porcelain skin was prayed for every night before falling asleep, but the good Lord never erased the ugly freckles from her face as she requested.

Mum understood and sometimes offered her the use of her expensive foundation powder. But no amount of baby-skin tinted dust could disguise the spotty mess beneath it completely.

Marta's consolation and encouragement came by the fact that her eyes were quite striking and her hair was golden blonde - both of which people often said were desired. She'd become quite good at applying mascara to her lashes and her mother always tried to draw everyone's attention to them. "Look at those long lashes and gorgeous eyes, they're so soft and warm, you can't help but melt into them!" she'd say. They were hazelnut brown, not green like her mother's, or arctic blue like her father's. Another mystery to her.

Freckles and brown eyes aside, the one thing Marta most loved to do and actually liked about herself was her hair. She could style it in almost any fashion she tried. Her mother had taught her how to pin curl it and she'd spend hours on the weekends practicing new looks. Her favourite lately was the new bouffant style. Back combing it to give it a high back lift with a flicked out curl at the tips. She would comb a portion of hair across her forehead sweeping it to a pin-up at the back, or even tucking it underneath the rest of her hair making it resemble a headband made of hair.

She may not have had the face of an angel - but the hair of such a creature? Most certainly. God himself would likely order all celestial beings to style their tresses just as Marta Ingles did.

"Marta, would you mind styling my hair like yours, darling? I have a faculty meeting with the heads of department at the College this evening and I'd like to try out your latest creation. Evan always compliments me when I wear it done up," her mother gave her a slanted smile - the one she always used to get her own way.

Mr Evan Davidson was the newly appointed English teacher at Rathkeale College and Marta had met him briefly when Mum offered him a ride into town after school one day. She thought he was very handsome and much younger than she expected a teacher could be. Most of her own teachers were at least in their forties and some of the sisters were practically antiques.

Her mother had managed to secure the role of principal's secretary at the newly established private boys' college just on the outskirts of Masterton. Since Mum was often asked to manage the faculties' administration and refreshments for their meetings, Marta likewise, was expected to fill in for her mother's increasing absence from home.

Since Marta had already prepared the dinner, Mum took the opportunity to spend a little more time on her appearance than she usually would. Marta relished the rare moments they had together and was glad to help style her mother's locks however she wanted. Dad didn't like it much when they giggled together. She wasn't sure why. But as he wasn't home yet, Marta would make the most of it.

Marta held the blow dryer in one hand and began brushing her mother's hair in the completely wrong direction - teasing it to a frenzy.

Mum had complete faith in her ability with her hair and even though she was occasionally jabbed with the comb, she never scolded Marta for it.

Vanity kept their lips shut and their eyes batting at their mirror images. Everything that needed to be said was done with occasional hand gestures and eye signals through the noise of the dryer.

"There," said Marta finally, smiling back at her mother's reflection as she tucked and titivated the last few strands of hair into place.

Maggie admired herself in the mirror and pushed the curled ends up with an open palm. "Ooo, Marta! You're a star! I LOVE it!" She squealed back at her now blushing daughter. "Firm it up for me, will you?"

Marta took the expensive can of hairspray and gave it a shake while her mother clasped her hands over her face. After a thorough dousing and a couple of sneezes, Marta patted her mother's shoulders. "There you go, all done."

Mum took the pink powder puff and patted her nose, cheeks and forehead to freshen her makeup. Marta watched intensely as her mother extended and widened each corner lash with her black liquid eyeliner, giving her eyes a more seductive appearance. Marta liked it and would practice it on herself once her mother had left. She felt certain that if she could master the technique it might help detract even more attention away from her horrible freckles.

Mum parted her plump lips and rubbed the depleted cherry red lipstick around them - smacking a kiss into the air for good measure. "Good girl," she smiled at Marta, noticing her daughter's undeniable attention and admiration. "Thanks for getting the dinner ready, darling. Have a go yourself at this later if you like." Mum handed her the eyeliner, and gave a sly wink. "Just don't let your father see you, all right?"

Standing, Mum turned herself from side to side reviewing herself in the full length mirror. With a nod of affirmation she grabbed her black fur coat and strutted towards the back door.

Just as she opened it, there on the step stood Dad, about to enter.

"Wowsers!" - His eyes boggled - "Where are *you* off to?"

"Oh, you know, Lionel, I told you yesterday, I have a meeting at the school tonight."

"Oh that's a relief, I thought maybe I'd forgotten an anniversary or something."

"You did. It was last month," she said curtly.

"Really? Oh I'm sorry, Maggie, how can I make it up to you?"

"Well for starters you can let me go out tonight and if you're lucky I might just be home by nine."

Dad simply shrugged and let her pass.

Dad was used to Mum's domineering ways, he even said he admired her for it. But it never stopped him worrying about her when she went out on her own at night. The liberalisation of women and the Women's Rights movement were not ones he fully agreed with or supported. But with a wife like Maggie, there was hardly anything he could do to stop her. Marta liked that her mother had a mind of her own and almost always used it. One day she hoped to be just like her.

Dad trusted Mum. He had every reason to. She had never let him down. She respected him, looked after him (and us kids), and she never missed a church service unless she was sick. Mum said their relationship certainly had its challenges in the early days after Dad returned from the war. But the joyous news of a baby on the way so soon after he got back made him much happier and more grounded, she said.

Marta knew there was more to the story that her mother wasn't telling her. She'd often been able to sense when things weren't quite right. But she certainly hadn't been able to read the clues and uncover anything new that she didn't already know about her parents and how they'd come to be together.

Marta went and stood by her father on the doorstep and watched as Mum reversed the car in the turning bay and sped off down the dirt drive. Plumes of dust danced into the air, muddying the pink coloured sky for a moment. With the sunset now spoiled along with dad's mood, he huffed, "What's for dinner, Marta?"

"Food," She replied in a jovial tone. She knew she was risking her father's wrath as soon as it slipped out and she desperately wished she could take it back. Spending time with Mum, doing their hair and makeup, always put them both in such a good mood. Marta couldn't help but let her feelings spill over just a little. Dad didn't like it much. She and Mum were such good friends and she wondered if he thought they were conspiring against him. But then Dad had never really shown her much love or even kindness for that matter. As long as she did as she was told and helped out around the house she knew she would be looked after, but other than that, Dad usually just ignored her. Lately she had begun to watch how her mother behaved - learning and gleaning from her brazen ways. Marta started to practice some of those traits at home. Some of which had landed her with a slap across her face from her father or being grounded if her mother was present.

Dad cleared his throat as if to reprimand her but simply said, "Right," and marched off towards the bathroom. Marta darted back to the kitchen to busy herself until Dad had finished washing up. At the dinner table, all four of them sat and lowered their heads as Dad gave a prayer of thanks for the food. Marta's two younger brothers - Harry and Jimmy, screwed up their noses at the casserole before them. "Do we have to eat this?" asked Jimmy.

"Yes." Dad grunted, "Now eat!"

Both boys picked up their utensils and began to eat. Marta hoped her mother wouldn't return home too late. She hated it when Dad was in a mood. There was usually nothing she could do to appease him. So instead, she took herself off to her room after dinner and spent the rest of the evening practicing with the eye-liner and rehearsed all manner of scenarios of what she would say if a boy ever asked her out.

When Mum pulled in the driveway at 9:20 pm, Marta thought she'd done considerably well given her expected time home could vary anywhere from half to two hours late - depending on the mood she left in. And given tonight's departure, Marta assumed Mum wouldn't be home before ten (unless the meeting either went really well or very poorly).

The car door squeaked open, then banged shut, followed by the main door to the house. Mum's heels tapped on the kitchen floor, and soon Marta heard the muffled voices of her parents conversing. Mum's animated pitch confirmed her suspicions of a successful meeting. Dad's grumble tone implied he'd either woken from his nap in his chair or he didn't much care for Mum's chatter. Either way, Marta was desperate to know why Mum seemed so happy. She crept out of bed and placed an ear to her door.

"Why not, Lionel? It would be a great opportunity for Harry to have the boys here - Jimmy too."

Boys? What boys?

"But where will they sleep, Mag's?"

Dad didn't often call her mother by her pet name - that was usually reserved for their bedroom. 'Maggie' was about as causal as her father ever got. Mum hated her actual name - Margaret. Only her grandmother ever called her that and she was a horrid person (or so she said). Marta had no way of verifying that, given her grandmother died when she was very little.

"Harry and Jimmy can share," Mum cooed. "It's only for a week, Lionel. You'll see. We'll make it work. I had to. Please don't make me go back on my promise. I'll make it up to you…I…" Mum's voice petered out and Marta couldn't hear what Dad said back.

Marta tip toed back to bed and drew the covers up to her neck.

Boys - here?

Why on earth would her mother invite boys to stay here? There was barely enough room for the five of them already. Of course it would probably be left up to her to cater for them. Marta frumped her lips.

Mum's news might be good for her brothers - but for her? Not so much. All it meant was more work.

The only benefit she could hope for was that maybe these boys might be closer to her own age than her brothers.

She dare not hope though - it usually only ever resulted in disappointment.

Sunday 22nd November 1959

It was late November and the days were getting longer - warmer too. Dad loved it as it meant he now got to wake up in the daylight to milk the cows. There was talk in town amongst the various committees about reinstating daylight savings time - as they'd done during the war. But Dad was fiercely against it. He said that, 'If the chatter in Wellington isn't silenced soon, us farmers will lose our only bit of respite all year.'

Marta understood. She had occasionally helped Dad with milking during weekends and term breaks, and the bitter darkness before dawn was fraught with creepy squawks and rustling scavengers.

She'd not left the comforts of the house this morning though (except to attend church). Yesterday Mum had given them an arm's length of chores to cross off, and the boys had been enlisted to help too - much to their disgust.

By 6:00 pm Sunday they were all feeling the effects of an arduous weekend's work and were still yet to eat the dinner Marta had prepared earlier.

The bus pulled in to Rathkeale College much later than they were expected, and so did some of the host families.

The Auckland University Cricket club had requested to be hosted by the College while they played a number of one-day matches in the surrounding areas. Mr Phillips, the college Principal, was eager to establish some sporting traditions, and as such, had agreed to the terms without consulting the rest of the heads of departments first. This had put noses out of joint and teachers in a spin over the clashes with their exam schedules.

Mum had come home from her meeting three weeks ago quite excited by all the 'heated discussions.' But as usual she'd made short work of all the faculty's protests. She knew just what to say and how to say it when it came to soothing hot male heads and was especially good at it with Dad too.

As a result, Mum was put in charge of practically everything except umpiring the cricket matches themselves. She'd spent hours sorting out where each visitor would be billeted, what areas would be available for their use within school grounds, and co-ordinating timetables with the Wairarapa Cricket club for the use of the pitch for their practices. It had been a lot of extra work for her over the last three weeks. Which meant Marta had been busy too.

There were perks though. She was the envy of all her friends at school when she told them they were hosting not one - but two boys in their home. Her best friend, Cherie, asked her parents if they could host one too, but they flat out refused. She couldn't understand why they said no, but Marta did. Given Cherie was an only child, she could see how it might not be deemed very appropriate. For the first time Marta was actually grateful to have two younger brothers.

Harry, the oldest brother at fourteen, was a member of the junior cricket team at the local club and was getting quite good at hitting the ball. His bowling needed a lot more work though. Harry was ecstatic when Mum told the family that two of the Auckland boys would be staying with them. Jimmy, on the other hand, was miffed that his room would be commandeered by the strangers.

Harry made a prompt rebuttal - throwing sand on Jimmy's flames. "The boys can give us tips on how to bowl better, Jimmy. Plus - it'll be fun to have you sleep in my room."

Marta knew her older brother would much rather have shared his room with one of the university boys, but he would have to make do with his younger brother if there was to be any sort of resolution. Jimmy came around and from that moment there wasn't a day when Harry didn't talk about the cricket players' visit - peppering Mum with all sorts of questions and suggestions.

For all the excitement about the coming cricket tournament you'd think the boys, who stepped off the bus, would look more like celebrities. But the bewildered bunch of boys looked very tired from the eight hour drive and resembled very little of the hot-shot cricket players Harry had talked about for weeks. Sixteen boys looked like they'd just been dragged from their beds and Marta eyed them all, speculating which ones she thought, or rather hoped, were theirs.

An overly tall boy with ginger hair and long arms looked slightly out of place amongst his other teammates and Marta hoped he wasn't one of their guests. She was relieved when her mother pulled him and another boy, who had thick black wavy hair, aside and called on Mr Forge, who was to host them. The boys walked to where their bags had been unloaded from the bus, picked out theirs and began moving towards Mr Forge's car.

Marta hadn't wanted to go and stand near the bus when it arrived. Even though she'd spent all afternoon since she got home from church freshening up her face and redoing her hair she had no intention of parading herself in front of such a large group of boys. She hadn't the courage for it. Mum did though and Marta watched as she flipped her hair and smiled her cherry lips at the boys and their supporting older club members. She could hear her mother's laugh, even from inside the car, and she practiced how it sounded coming from her own mouth. It sounded strange - but was easy enough to replicate. Whether it elicited the same response from the opposite sex as her mother's often did was, as of yet, still to be to be determined.

Thank God Mum didn't force me to stand outside with the other hosts.

Observing the boys incognito was a gift she hadn't thought so valuable. Now she knew better.

It was then one of the boys spotted her spying on them from the back seat window, Marta's breath stuck in her throat and her heart did a double flip. He didn't look away - just stared back at her. Her eyes were taken captive by his and by some intangible force she couldn't escape them. He was very handsome with a hint of shadow around his jaw. Marta like his sun-kissed golden coloured hair the most. That was until she saw him smile. Marta felt herself melt into the back seat and a warmth heated her through. Their invisibly linked gaze was only broken when his name was called and he was paired with another boy who had golden hair, slightly darker than her own, He stood tall and proud and was holding a green folder. Marta wondered what was in it. Drawings, Poetry, letters? All were unlikely but her romantic side could pretend it held such treasures. In all probability it would be cricket related papers. Marta predicted him as the team's captain.

Both boys walked to get their bags and were introduced to their host, Mr Dawson. Marta's heart sunk with pity. The Dawsons had a five year old son, and twin girls who were seven. The only reason they were even billeting the boys was because Mr Dawson had insisted that someone on staff should at least host a couple of the students. When Mum said she would host two, Mr Dawson said there should be at least one teacher to host as well. Since no one else put up their hand, Mum made up her mind for him and thanked Mr Dawson for offering to volunteer to be the school's faculty liaison. Mum said he was not impressed, but he was also not about to be shown up by her mother.

Marta tracked the boys' movements until she heard her mother say, "Just a moment, Mr Dawson. My apologies, but I have mixed you up with another family. One of the boys is allergic to cats and I believe you have two cats, don't you, Mr Dawson?" The boy holding the green folder looked confused but didn't say anything.

Her mother cleared her throat and looked at the remaining four boys yet to be discharged into the care of their hosts. "Sean Young, and Allen Stoddard?!" The two boys joined the cluster around her mother. Ah... good. Go and get your bags boys, you are going with Mr Dawson."

Marta's heart banged in protest at the lack of oxygen being supplied. It wasn't until Mr Dawson started directing Sean and Allen towards his car that she could exhale and suck in a fresh dose of O_2. The boy who'd locked eyes with her earlier looked over his shoulder to where she sat. He smiled and Marta wondered if he really could see her or if he might have been smiling at something, or someone, situated behind their car. She couldn't tell and had to look and check. Nope, nothing. He was definitely looking at her. But why?

Marta's heart chugged to a quicker pace.

The last remaining pair of boys were ordered into the care of Mr Phillips along with the Auckland team's coach as well. That only left the boy with the green folder and the one who had seen her. Both boys lifted their bags to their shoulders and followed her mother straight towards the car.

Their car. The one she was sitting in.

Her stomach coiled and she couldn't move. Her eyes glued to the smiling boy who seemed to be chatting in a most jovial way to her mother. Whatever he said caused Mum to laugh in her usual flirtatious friendly manner. They were all laughing once they reached the car. Marta turned her attention to her fidgeting hands to avoid any close eye contact with the boy. If she looked at him, she knew she wouldn't be able to stop herself turning red.

Mum unlocked the boot and the boys tucked their bags inside. Doors flung open and Marta couldn't tell who she would end up sitting next to. She only prayed that her heart would stop racing and that if it wouldn't, no one would notice that it was. Without any attention to her presence, all three of them hopped inside.

"Right-o, lads. This is my daughter, Marta. Marta, say hello to your new short-term older brothers."

Mum's joke was laughed at by the boys and Marta's flush could not be tempered.

"Where's your tongue gone then?" Mum turned in the driver's seat to eyeball her. She took Marta's brown-eyed glare as a warning not to push and promptly turned back to start the car.

"Sorry boys, seems the cat's got her tongue."

Everyone laughed except Marta. She did try but all she wanted to do was hide like a turtle in its shell right now.

The best she could do was to tuck her hands between her knees, and pray the steam away from her cheeks. She couldn't be more mortified if she tried. Her mother's next spell of chatter would prove otherwise.

"Right lads. You may not know it - but I've saved you tonight. I couldn't let two handsome young men like yourselves stay with Mr Dawson. I know neither of you are allergic to cats - but could at least one of you pretend to be while you're here. Mr Dawson would never let me hear the end of it if he ever found out. He's got twin girls - they're seven. Each of them have a cat, and - they - are - horrible. Aren't they Marta?" Mum extended her neck so she could eye her in the rear-view mirror. "So I expect you'll be mighty pleased and dreadfully grateful when you hear Sean and Allen tell you all about the terrible Dawson girls. Marta's not normally this shy," she glanced again. "She's the best hairdresser and the best cook in town. You're in for a treat tonight, boys. She's made you a shepherd's pie and a chocolate steamed pudding too. My Marta's just the best young lady you'll ever meet in Masterton. Her eyes are so pretty, don't you think?"

"Mum!" Marta screwed her expression. Her saving grace came from the boy sitting next to her in the back seat - the one with the green folder - which now sat in his lap.

"Really? I love chocolate pudding. Mum used to make it all the time. I've missed it while I've been away at Uni. I'm Thomas by the way. But you can just call me Tom." Tom held out his hand for her to shake. She felt a little awkward but took it and let her hand be bobbed by his. It was cool but firm - a real business-like shake. His smile was gentle and his eyes were a smooth grey with speckles of green like Pounamu treasures amongst stones in the river.

"Nice to meet you, Tom."

She'd done it. She had spoken and she didn't sound ridiculous at all. In fact she quite liked how her voice had sounded. It was solid and sure and portrayed an air of confidence she neither had, nor expected. But here it was and she was going to make the most of it while it lasted. The boy in the front seat whipped around and now faced her with his smile. The same one that had sent a hot knife into her chest earlier.

"Hi, I'm Peter, but my friends all call me Pete." He strained an arm to offer his hand. She shook it feebly. It was warmer than Tom's - softer too. She attempted to let go before the heat from his hand made it all the way to her neck. He gripped it tighter.

Her eyes jumped to his. They were soft blue - like the afternoon sky on a warm summer's day. He gently squeezed her hand before letting it go.

Tom jabbed Peter in the shoulder and butted in. "That's not all they call you."

"Don't listen to him, Marta. He's got it in for me. Reckons he's gonna beat my running record during the tournament. I doubt it though." Peter's smile broadened revealing a stunning set of straight white teeth. Marta wanted to touch them, but she knew that was just weird. Peter's perfect teeth reminded her of her mother's perfect skin and suddenly she felt very aware that her cheeks were freckled and she was not so perfect - in any way at all.

"I like your hair," said Tom.

The sudden compliment came out of nowhere and Marta wasn't sure what to say. She'd never had a boy compliment her about her appearance before.

Marta's cheeks radiated like freshly stirred embers. "Thank you."

"She's a beauty boys, so I expect you to be on your best behaviour and be sure to look out for her."

"Oh, we will, Mrs Ingles. I'll keep an eye on her." Peter winked over his shoulder.

Her eyes slung beneath heavy lashes, and she dragged a corner of her bottom lip with her teeth. Peter remained transfixed until Mum cut in.

"Oh, Peter. Please - just call me Maggie when we're at home. Mrs Ingles makes me feel so old."

Peter pulled his eyes from Marta to focus on her mother. He cocked his head to the side "You shouldn't feel old, Mrs Ingles. You're gorgeous. Why, I thought that Marta here was your younger sister." He stole another glance back at her.

'Oh you're a charmer all right. Watch out for this one, Marta. If anyone knows how to sweet talk, it's me, and this lad's got a ton of sugar up his sleeve - I'd bet money on it."

"He's certainly guilty of that." Tom rested a hand on the back of Mum's seat. "But don't hold it against him, Mrs Ingles... I mean, Maggie. It's a talent so many of us lack. I'm not sure where any of us boys would be if it weren't for ol' Pete here. I certainly wouldn't be engaged to my Iris that's for sure. If he hadn't stuck his oar in and shoved me out to sea, I'd probably still just be dreaming about talking to her." Tom sent his gaze out the car window to the fields beyond, his face soft with a memory he was obviously enjoying.

"You're engaged?!" Mum gushed. 'Wow! But you're so young. You can't be much more than twenty-two! Don't you want to live a little before you settle down? There's plenty of time to get married later." Mum shook her head. Marta knew her mother's sentiment only echoed what she longed for if she could have her time over again. Mum never got the chance to travel or even attend university. She'd married Dad so quickly and so young. It was something Mum cautioned her about on occasion. 'Don't marry too young, Marta. Make sure you've done something for yourself before you have a family. Because once you do - that's it. Your children become your life.'

She'd never said so directly, but Marta always felt her mother wanted to add, 'and my life was over,' but she never did. Mum made up for the loss of her youth by working in paid employment and taking an active role in the community. She was much more confident and brazen than the other mothers Marta knew - most of whom certainly weren't working mothers. Mum had managed a certain amount of independence just by having a job and Marta was adamant that she would too someday.

Turning into the entrance to their farm both boys seemed taken aback as they wobbled down the long dusty driveway.

"Wow, Maggie. This place is amazing! I thought we were heading to town, but those hills and that sunset are simply stunning!" Peter's romantic sentiment and admiration weren't lost on Marta or her mother. They were used to seeing their family home every day and its novelty was not so obvious to them anymore. But now Peter had drawn her attention to it, Marta quickly saw how lucky she was to live somewhere where beauty was on her doorstep - even if it did come with a pile of muddy boots and the smell of fresh manure.

"It sure is beautiful all right," said Tom. "Reminds me of home a little. My parents live in Warkworth - in town though. But it looks a little like this when the sun sets too."

Mum opened the boot of the car. The boys collected their things and followed Marta to the back door.

"Show them their room, Marta. I'll be in shortly." Mum instructed, heading for the open sheds where Dad would be fixing farm machinery or sorting fertilizers.

Marta opened the door and called out to her brothers. There was no reply. They must be out in the sheds with Dad, or possibly checking the rabbit holes for residents. She didn't mind being alone with Peter and

Tom, but she hoped Mum wouldn't be too long. She toured them around the few rooms in the house - skipping her own as they went down the hall.

Both boys leapt on Jimmy's bed as soon as she informed them the room was theirs for the week. The rough and tumble ceased quicker than Harry and Jimmy's bouts did. It made Marta feel comfortable knowing they felt easy around her.

Peter stood and cleared his throat. "I don't mind taking the stretcher, if you give me first dibs on the shower in the morning." He held a rigid hand to Tom.

Tom grabbed it and thumped it once. "You're on. Although I think I got the better deal."

"We'll see."

Marta moved to leave. "Well if you need anything - I'll be in the kitchen. Dinner will be ready in ten or so."

Peter jerked to cut her off from departing.

"Which is your room, Marta?"

Tom grit his teeth. "Peter. You've no need to know that."

Marta tilted her head back and to the left. "I'm up there - next to my parents."

Marta drifted in and out of sleep all night. The excitement of their guests had her a little on edge, especially seeing as she had a little crush on Peter. Tom was nice and all, and very polite, but he was engaged and Marta would never consider entertaining romantic thoughts towards someone who was already taken. Besides, she liked Peter more anyway. He was funny and kind and made her feel like the most important person in the room. She'd never met anyone like him - certainly not amongst the school boys anyway. They all seemed so immature and were always pulling pranks, daring each other to do stupid things.

Marta had fallen victim to one such prank when Joseph Gates had walked up to her in the park one day and asked her to be his girlfriend. She was only twelve at the time and she'd been so enamoured by the fact that anyone would want her as a girlfriend that she had said yes straight away without telling Cherie about it first. If she had, Cherie would have saved her a whole lot of heart ache by informing her that Robert Kirkwood had dared Joseph to ask Marta out and that if he did, Robert would then have to ask Lucy Jenkins out. Lucy Jenkins was barely one notch above feral, by Marta and Cherie's view. She certainly wasn't date-able. Marta on the other hand was considered quite pretty by her peers - even though she disagreed because of her freckles. Marta struggled to accept that she'd been lumped in the same boat as Lucy Jenkins. As it was, Joseph came and sat with her in the park the following weekend and was pretending to be interested in her as his girlfriend. As soon as Robert walked past, Joseph said, "I did it - but only because I wanted to see you ask out Lucy!" and then he laughed at Robert and then at Marta, "I didn't really want to go out with you - it was just a joke," He told her. She was so embarrassed and made up her mind never to be duped by a silly boy again.

But what could she do now? Peter was there - in her house - sleeping in Jimmy's room and in a few short hours he would be up and eating breakfast at her kitchen table. Marta lay on her side, closed her eyes, pictured his face and then planted a kiss into her pillow. She ran her tongue over her lips. What did he taste like? Never had she ever wanted to kiss a boy so badly. Marta lulled herself into a wonderful dream, where Peter was her boyfriend and she turned up to school with him on her arm. Cherie was so jealous.

Completely enveloped by her make believe world Marta barely heard her alarm clock. Mumbling voices and regular door slams spoiled the dream and there was no way she could drift back to sleep. Mum's voice yelled down the hallway, "Breakfast's ready!"

Marta leapt out of bed and hastily began combing her hair into some suitable do-up for breakfast - she'd fix it properly after. Reaching the table she wished she done her hair and face first as Mum was already done. Picture perfect and ready for work. Quickly she grabbed herself a bowl of cereal and excused herself to the bathroom.

Later, Peter came and stood in the bathroom doorway and watched her comb her hair into its final style. She did her best to ignore him but when she saw he was eying her from head to toe, her skin glowed hotter than she thought possible (unless one was ill with fever). Peter's lips curled into a delicious smile and she felt as though he could see right through her cotton dressing gown. Feeling like prey, caught in his gaze, she walked towards him slowly - her eyes rooted on his. She'd observed her mother doing this once and she couldn't quite believe what she was doing or why she felt so fearless given their proximity to one another. He must have felt unnerved by the change in her attention as she noticed the rise of his throat's apple as he swallowed deeply. Seductively she inched herself past him as he stood in the doorway, making sure he felt the presence of her body. Marta drew her face closer towards his cheek - lingering she whispered into his ear, "Good morning." She pulled away with a wide smile across her face, pleased that she'd managed to pull off her act so well and that her greeting had stirred him more than intended.

Peter's grin slammed into his cheeks - turning them pink as if he'd been slapped. He couldn't restrain himself. Reaching, he grabbed Marta's hand and held her warm fingers in his own. He took them to his lips and kissed the backs of them. She giggled softly, her confident act slipping away.

"Wow." He half-whispered, half-groaned. His eyes skimmed her hand and weighed anchor in her gaze. Finally he blinked and pulled himself away, down the hall and disappeared inside Jimmy's room.

Marta's body tensed at the sound of Dad coughing as he entered through the back door without warning. He was back from milking the cows and would be tired and hungry. Just his mere presence reminded Marta of how unholy she'd behaved. A pang of guilt stabbed like a knife to her gut and she sent up a silent prayer for forgiveness immediately as she made her way back to the kitchen.

"Morning, Maggie. How are our guests doing, everyone sleep well?" Dad scooped a slop of cool porridge from the bottom of the pot. He dumped two tablespoons of brown sugar on top and then drowned it in fresh milk from the morning's takings.

"They sure did, Dad," Jimmy squirmed in his chair, excited to tell the morning's news.

Harry beat him to it. "Pete ate six Weetbix! I'm gonna try eating six tomorrow."

Jimmy's face soured. "Hey, I was going to say that!" He crossed his arms with a humph.

"Whatever keeps you full and fit to work on the farm is fine with me, son."

Dad's dream had always been for the boys to work on the farm with him. He'd never mentioned any dreams that he had for Marta. So she presumed he didn't have any. As long as she was a good girl, found a suitable husband and committed herself to service in the church, Marta figured he'd be happy for her and probably relieved to have one less mouth to feed too.

Mum's voice hollered its last instruction for the morning. "Right-o lads, you're with me. The rest of you better get to the gate before the bus gets here."

Marta watched as Mum, Tom and Peter drove out the driveway and down the road. She couldn't wait to get to school and spill all the details to Cherie about her and Peter's bathroom greetings this morning. Come to think of it, she couldn't wait for school to be over so she could watch Peter some more. She could only fantasize that he might feel the same way about her as she did about him.

CHAPTER SIX

Friday 27th November 1959

IT WASN'T JUST Harry who was greatly disappointed by how busy Peter and Tom were over the next four days. Marta's disappointment was starting to affect the evening meals. Pots banged harder on the stove and cupboard doors were slammed and then abused if they didn't stay shut. Even Mum had inquired if anything was the matter - which she couldn't answer of course. If Pete and Tom weren't playing a game at Rathkeale College or in one of the surrounding towns, they were at the college practicing for a game. Tired and hungry whenever they'd returned home, they hadn't had much time to spend with the family.

Now it was Friday, that would all change, much to Marta's relief. All the visiting boys were to be in town at the Queen Elizabeth Park Oval for their last practice - so they could test out the ground before the big game tomorrow.

Since the boys would be free to roam the streets for the afternoon, Marta had offered to meet them at the State Milk Bar for a milkshake after school. Peter and Tom agreed.

If she could manage, Marta thought she might also try and sneak out at the lunch break and go watch the boys practice at the oval. The problem was, she hadn't quite figured out how yet.

The whole town was abuzz about the one-day match between the Wairarapa Seniors and the Auckland boys. It was the first time any university had sent a sports team to the rural town. It was all Mum's doing of course.

Once she told Mayor Marchbank that the college was hosting the students, he'd insisted that they also play the district's senior cricket team too. The old boys hardly ever got the chance to play up-and-coming candidates for the International Cricket team. Naturally his proposal was spun as an opportunity to raise money for the Town Hall. The severely damaged building had been beautifully rebuilt after the earthquake, but it had also put the town into substantial debt.

Poor Mayor Coddington had retired early due to all the stress and deputy Bill Marchbank took over.

Dad liked Mr Marchbank and thought his campaign to reduce debt was very admirable. After all the election fuss, Dad felt vindicated when his suggestion to have the votes recounted was accepted. Mayor Marchbank was reinstated, and Dad said the town had dodged a bullet in Norm Tankersley.

Marchbank was a well-respected man and Dad was sure he would keep his promises. So, when Constance Marchbank, the Mayor's wife, heard of the boys' visit, she suggested to the Ladies Aid Society (L.A.S.) that they hold a dance after the game - to celebrate whoever won of course. Her husband had given his support and Constance was certain they'd be honouring their local team. So there wasn't to be a snippet of gossip otherwise (at least not amongst the L.A.S. members).

Since Mum was on the L.A.S. events committee, she'd been called in to help with organizing that too.

When Dad went to the Empire last night, as he did on occasion (but only to keep his ear to the ground, he said), he'd heard Councillor Robinson propose a wager on the game amongst the farmers and townsmen to help bolster the fundraiser as well. He said the Ranfurly Club were backing the wager and that every bet placed would benefit the Town Hall fund regardless of who won. Dad came home very upset about all the betting and told Mum all about how gambling was the devil's work and that it was just, 'Not right! I don't believe the Lord or Bill Marchbank would endorse such a wager. It doesn't bode well for the town's integrity and Greg Robinson should know better. The man's new position on the council has gone to his head! Who does he think he is - the Prime Minister?!'

Marta, listening carefully through the bedroom wall, heard everything her mother said to sooth Dad's self-righteous anger.

"It couldn't hurt, if it helps pay off the hall sooner, can it? Doesn't it say in the Bible to, 'Owe no one anything?' And just last week, Father Wilson spoke from Psalm 37 about how 'The wicked borrow and do not pay back, but the righteous are gracious and give'. It's all for a good cause, Lionel. And the Ladies Aid Society is selling raffle tickets at the game for a meat and cheese pack. Is that the devil's work too? We sell raffle tickets at the church fair - it can't all be bad." Then a few seconds later Mum said confidently, "Well - I've bet ten shillings on the Auckland boys. I don't think the old boys will be able to keep up with them. The boys have won every game they've played so far and I reckon they're going to win on Saturday too."

"Heavens, Maggie! What on earth possessed you to do that?"

"Instinct, Lionel. Are you going to come to the game?"

Marta held her breath and waited for Dad's answer. When it never came she was disappointed, but soon knew why when the sound of her mother giggling promptly ended her time glued to the wall.

The next morning, Marta felt more determined to skip school altogether when Peter caught hold of her hand in the hallway and invited her into Jimmy's room.

"Tom's in the loo. Quick - there's something I want to show you."

Once Marta was inside her brother's room she suddenly became hot and very aware that they were alone - *together*. The whole predicament felt risky but too exciting to leave. The thrill of doing something questionable made her heart flip on itself. Even more so when Peter grabbed the tops of her shoulders and pulled her towards him, locking her in against his chest. She hadn't had time to react and stood awkwardly with her arms tucked to her sides. Peter let her go but she didn't move. She couldn't. She was lost in his blue eyes which were hungrily eying her lips. Peter leant his face to hers and she closed her eyes. His lips pressed gently on her forehead, and then on her nose, and then her cheek, his breath hitching in hesitation above her parted lips. Before Marta's mind could think, she flickered her eyes and lunged for his lips with her own. His mouth received hers, encasing her as a glove would a ball. A current pulsed through her whole body like a shock wave after a bomb exploded. She'd never felt anything like it before and all she could do was yield to the devastation.

The sound of the toilet flushing snapped Peter out of their lovely bubble. Marta quickly realised what she'd done and although she was happy, she couldn't seem to make her lips move into a smile. Instead she cleared her throat and smoothed her school dress. *Ugh, I don't want Peter seeing me like this.*

She bolted from the room before Tom opened the bathroom door.

Marta grabbed her red Capri pants and her favourite sleeveless white shirt. She stuffed them in her bag along with a dark rose red lipstick and two sparkly hair pins from the top of her mother's dresser. Exiting the house she jumped into the front passenger seat of the car so she wouldn't have to look at Peter on the way to school. Marta felt unsure of herself - a trail of questions all led to dead ends. Had she done it right? Did he like their kiss? He hadn't said anything, but neither had she. She had no words. She felt silly and shy.

Since Mum was dropping the boys into town to the Oval she'd offered to drop Marta at school instead of taking the bus. Marta wondered if it was such a good idea after all when no one spoke and the awkward silence started to feel almost palpable. Mum pulled to the kerb outside St. Brides and Marta went to hop out. Peter's voice almost echoed when he broke the silence, "Can't wait to see you later, at the milk bar I mean." Marta looked over her shoulder and caught his subtle wink. She knew then that he wanted to see her much sooner than that.

Marta waited until the car had vanished around the corner. What should she do? If she went into school then she might never find a way to escape. But if she stayed out here on the street someone might spot her in uniform and report her absence. The rebel in her was silenced when too many obstacles presented themselves. She wasn't used to coming up with ways to hide or get away with things.

She was good. She'd always been good. If not for her own sake, then for her father, who would certainly make sure any punishment was administered if she wasn't *good*.

But she liked it - this inner rebel. Marta felt more alive than ever when she was around Peter and she liked how he made her feel - so special and pretty. He'd told her on Tuesday night before bed that she was the prettiest girl he had ever seen. Surely he must have meant it. He would have seen lots of girls up in Auckland. So for him to say such a thing made her feel almost as beautiful as her mother.

Marta sighed and entered the main door of the school's white weatherboard buildings. At least she could ask Cherie what she should do. Maybe she might even help her come up with a plan of how to escape.

By the time morning tea break arrived Marta was anxious to get their plan underway. She and Cherie had passed too many notes to count during maths class and then all through biology too. Marta asked to be excused from class just before the lunch bell rang in order to get changed into her capris and shirt. Once she was changed she would cover them with her dress over the top. Cherie suggested that Marta climb over the fence behind the maintenance sheds next to the playing fields. She agreed it was a good spot, but was still anxious that someone might see her. Cherie wanted to come along too but wisely insisted that two absent girls from the same class would be much more out of the ordinary than just one. At least this way, if Marta's absence was noticed or questioned, Cherie would cover for her.

Marta made it over the fence all right, but executing the manoeuvre tore a tiny hole in the back of her dress. She lifted the uniform's long mass of green fabric over her head and stuffed it inside her bag. Annoyed she'd not considered her red capris might stand out like a nose on a clown, she tied her school jumper around her waist in a bid to conceal her fiery legs as she walked down the road.

Walking casually had been Cherie's idea. "Don't run," she said, "You'll only draw more attention to yourself. Walk as if you are meant to be there. And don't stop to answer anyone's questions. If someone asks why you're not in school just tell them you have a doctor's appointment. People never ask why you need to see the doctor, it's impolite, so you should be safe." Cherie's advice proved invaluable when she passed Mrs

Grady standing out in her garden. The nosy woman couldn't help asking where Marta was off to.

"I have a doctor's appointment." Marta pitched her voice slightly higher than usual. Mrs Grady's hearing was as bad as a sheep shearer's. The contradiction of saying a prayer that she wouldn't need to repeat the lie was not lost on her and Marta lowered her gaze to the pavement.

"Oh, right." Mrs Grady nodded and continued pruning her roses.

Cherie was right. People didn't like to talk about the doctors. It was as good as a free pass if you didn't want people knowing your business. She did her best to walk with her eyes forward and assurance in her step. If it weren't for all the gardens starting to bloom with their honeysuckle scents she might have arrived at the Oval much sooner. Bees hovered over colourful bulbs, and everyone else with a job to do was too busy to notice Marta's unusual presence wandering the roadside, or so she wanted to believe.

Nearing the town park she spotted through the trees an occasional white player out in the field, awaiting a ball to fall in his vicinity. She ducked between trees until finally she was close enough to hear some of them talking. It took her a few minutes to figure out which one was Peter. They all looked the same in their white trousers, white shirts and cream sweater vests. It was only Peter's golden haystack of hair that distinguished him. He was in the outfield on the opposite side to where she stood.

Scampering from one tree to the next she wondered if she may have been better disguised if she had just remained in her school uniform. When she made it behind the third tree she retrieved her dress and slipped it on. At least it would hide her red legs while she tree hopped to the other side of the field.

As she got closer Marta heard the sound of a whistle and all the boys started walking in towards the pitch in the middle.

Great. Now what?

She paused, but needn't have worried. A couple minutes later the boys were headed back out into the field. Only it wasn't Peter who walked in her direction now, but one of the other boys.

Where did he go?

A movement in front of the grandstand caught her eye. It was definitely him.

Without hesitating she ran, hopping between trees as if she were a rabbit, back towards the grandstand. Deep breaths combined with excitement made her chest heave. She placed a hand on it to still the pounding. Inhaling and exhaling she leant her back against the rear weather-boards of the grandstand until she had recovered her breath completely.

Skimming her back along the side of the building's wall she inched forward and peered up the stairs to see if Peter was there.

No.

Maybe he's out front?

She was about to crawl under the stairs to take a look when she felt a tap on her left shoulder.

Marta spun around, dreading she'd been caught by a local who'd recognised her. Instead, Peter's pool blue eyes surrounded her, and if he didn't blink soon she'd need a lifesaver to pull her out their whirlpool.

His grin widened, and he brushed her cheek with the backs of his fingers, swiping free a strand of hair caught in her lashes.

"What are you doing?" He leant an arm against the wall above her.

Her ears burned first, and then her freckled cheeks felt as hot as her red capris looked. Stunned to silence and trying to be coy, she bit the corner of her bottom lip and hovered her eyes under the hood of her brow.

"Ahh..."

"I was wondering when you'd show up," his words slid out like chocolate sauce, and his eyes wandered south of her neck.

She turned to gaze at the players on the field. "I was just going for a walk and..."

Peter put a finger beneath her chin and directed her stare back to him. His thumb lingered at her lips, and he traced them softly. Her lips tingled and her tongue went limp. How did he do that?

"Now what's this you're wearing? I was sure I spotted you in red." Peter's warm hand dropped from her lips to the mismatched top button on her dress. The proximity of his hand so close to her racing heart made her stop breathing and she couldn't take her eyes off his fingers. She went to reply but her tongue wouldn't move. Her breath shallowed, making her a little light-headed. Her voice when it came was barely a whisper. "You did..." She sucked her bottom lip into her mouth to moisten it and swallowed before continuing to explain. "I thought I might be a bit obvious so I put my dress back on over the top."

"Well. I prefer you in the red." Peter said, his eyes trying to undress her.

She looked down at her half buttoned dress and began removing it in haste. Peter placed his hands over hers and she stopped. Slowly he slid the last two remaining buttons undone.

He's no novice - that's for sure.

She didn't care. She slipped off her dress, smoothed her shirt and unbuttoned it from the bottom to her waist. Taking the two front ends she tied them into a knot just above her belly button, leaving a tiny slit of her waist exposed. She'd worn it that way last summer and noted how well it emphasised her figure.

"There. That's better." Peter took both her hands in his and swung them open to view her whole figure. "You look gorgeous, Marta."

She pulled her shoulders towards her ears and laughed, unsure if she should be embarrassed or proud, the latter feeling bizarre. Peter's attention spurred a sudden shot of confidence and she squeezed her shoulder blades tighter together.

Marta pulled her hand from his and smoothed her hair. It had likely become a little out of sorts from her sprints through the trees. She pulled a single green leaf from among her locks and Peter laughed. He took it from her, and twirled the leaf between his finger and thumb before releasing it into the air.

"Come sit up here with me, out of the sun. I'm out for ten, for a drink. It's hot out there today." He led her up the stairs into the shade. Sitting beside each other on the long wooden bench, Peter slid his arm around her waist to pull her closer, but she squealed and leapt a little from his ticklish touch. She giggled to recover and grabbed hold of his hand and placed it back around her waist where she wanted it forever. Never before had she felt so wanted, so lovable. Peter's hands were like a drug and she didn't ever want to be parted from them.

He offered her a drink from one of the bottles on the bench next to them. She took a polite sip and handed it back to Peter. The cool water was refreshing and she wished she had taken more. Her twenty minute midday walk from St. Brides to the Oval had made her thirstier than she'd wanted to admit, not to mention all the additional running about the trees too. Peter took a swig of water and placed the bottle back on the bench. Marta gestured for another sip. Peter chuckled and obliged. Taking another sip she looked at everyone out on the field for the first time. She'd forgotten they were all there and wondered if any of them had seen her take her dress off, or heard her squeal when Peter put his arm around her. They seemed as unchanged in position and demeanour as any group of cricket players on a field were. Aside from the occasional cheer, you'd hardly believe any sort of game was actually being played at all.

Not wanting to seem like just a silly school girl, Marta recalled a bit of advice her mother once told her. 'All men like you to ask them questions - just as long as it's something they know the answer to. Don't waste your breath asking how they feel. Stick to what they already know. Men like to feel like they know more than you do. It feeds their ego. That's important Marta. You'll understand one day darling.'

So rather than just stare at Peter, admiring his lightly stubbled jaw and fine smile lines at the corner of his eyes, she looked out to the field and let him begin her lesson. "So what part do you play?" She asked.

"You mean, what position?" His correction was kind and pleased.

"Yes, your position, what is it?"

"Well I'm usually in the outfield but sometimes the coach will put me in closer if I'm needed. Otherwise we all take our turn with batting and I bowl a pretty fast ball when my arm's feeling good."

"Right. I don't know much about cricket really. I mean, Harry plays but I've never been to one of his games." Marta prayed her admission wouldn't displease him. Peter took his gaze from the outfield and placed it back on Marta.

"Really?"

Marta sensed he was a little disappointed, but not enough to remove the smile from his lips. She wanted to kiss them again but she couldn't tell when was the right time. Obviously it wasn't now as Peter seemed away with other thoughts as he gazed at the field dotted with his teammates. Then, turning his whole upper body to face her squarely, he gathered her eyes to his own, and reached to hold both her hands.

"Marta. You know I'm quite a few years older than you are and you know I'm just visiting, don't you?" All Marta could do was nod. "I can't stay here in Masterton, even if I wanted to. We head back to Auckland on

Monday." Peter's words ploughed lines of disappointment across her forehead. Her whole body internally screaming, 'NO!'

Peter's thumbs rubbed the tops of her hands, but he never broke contact with her eyes. "I really like you - a lot, and I hope we can at least enjoy our last few days together. Will you come to the game tomorrow?" All Marta heard was that Peter liked her and wanted them to spend time together. She would just have to forget about the 'last few days' bit and do anything she could to reassure him she would be there for him.

"Of course I'm coming. I wouldn't miss it for the world. Everyone in town's coming! They're all very excited you know. There's a wager going amongst the men in town... and some of the women too." Marta added remembering her mother's bet. "It's five to one you lose to the senior team tomorrow.'

"Really?"

This new information seemed to peak Peter's interest far more than Marta expected.

"And what are the odds if we win?" The glint in his eyes gave away his desire to place a bet of his own.

"I think I heard Mum say, ten to one if you win. Mum's bet five dollars on you boys. Please say you'll win. I know they're only betting against you because they want to raise money for the Town Hall. But who cares! I'm sure you'll win!"

"Don't be so sure, Marta. I've heard of some of your senior players before and some of them were pretty good back in their prime. I don't know. It's hard to say really. But I think we have a pretty good shot at winning as long as Allen gets his head on straight. Those Dawson twins have been playing a number on him every night. He hasn't had much sleep the whole time we've been here."

"Oh, I'm sorry to hear tha..." Marta stopped when she saw Peter stand up.

"Well, I'm back in. Will you stay and watch?"

"Yes, but I'd better get back before school ends. Ms Kitrew will not be convinced that I had a doctor's appointment for three hours unless I produce an actual doctor's certificate. I haven't a clue how to fake one of those, so I better get back to class."

"All right, suit yourself. I know I'll play better knowing that you're watching me." Peter kissed her on the forehead as she gazed up at him. He turned and followed the stairs back to ground level, tossing his cricket ball into the air as he went. Out on the grass in front of the grandstand he glanced back at her, smiled and waved and then ran out onto the pitch. Marta sighed. How had she fallen for someone so hard so quickly? And for someone who was soon to leave town no less. Life really was cruel sometimes.

Out on the field Peter cupped the ball between his four fingers and thumb. With a deep breath he began a steady take off, lifting his legs off the ground, each step more powerful than the last. With a roll of his arm he wound the ball into position for maximum velocity and released it just as he reached the line. The ball whizzed so fast that Marta found it difficult to follow and before she knew it, all the boys cheered when a crack rang out from the wickets, now sitting askew. Peter held his arms spread wide in the air with a grin just as wide to match.

He was good then. Very good by the looks of it, Marta surmised. Boys came running from the outfield to congratulate his achievement.

Marta realised it was time to go when they all started to head for the grandstand. Peter had seen her leaving and parted from the group, running to catch up with her. "Marta, wait!" She spun around to his call and continued to walk backwards till he arrived. When he planted an overly confident kiss hard on her lips, she immediately looked to the boys who now stood in a group watching them.

Marta felt her cheeks turn the colour of her pants again and Peter smiled, pleased to have made a spectacle of them both.

"You're good luck to have on the sidelines. That one was for you." He winked. Skipping backwards he pulled away saying, "I'll come pick you up from school soon." He turned and ran back to his teammates now ambling towards the grandstand.

Marta moved away as quickly as she could with her head tucked down, as if doing so would hide her embarrassment or even existence. She could tell the moment Peter reached the other players when she heard them all laugh and jeer at him. She even heard a few of their comments.

"Hey! Playboy Pete. Who's the lucky one this time?"

"She's a pretty thing ain't she? I'd say Pete's the lucky one!"

Marta knew Peter liked her, but she couldn't quite tell if she was little more than a fancy for him. It was the first time anyone had looked at her in that way and he made her feel more like a woman than a silly young school girl with a crush. Her thoughts on the matter consumed the entire walk back to school and before she even realised it, she was sitting back in the classroom.

When the final bell rang at three o'clock. Marta ditched her dress once again - having placed it over the top of her clothes when she'd returned. Would Peter really be there to pick her up? She prayed all afternoon that he would.

Entering the sunny footpath in front of the school buildings Marta gazed up and down the street for any sign of Peter. As she did, a wolf-whistle grabbed her attention and both Peter and Tom removed themselves from behind a tall bush.

"What are you doing hiding in there?" She asked, "Did all the girls scare you off?" Marta giggled.

Peter touched her elbow. "No. I just wanted to surprise you. God you're beautiful." He smiled, clutched her head in his palms, and kissed her full on the lips. His words seemed a little slurred. And as soon as he had kissed her she knew exactly why.

He was drunk.

Marta blushed when she saw that Suzy Thomas and her group of friends had seen them kiss. They were the popular girls and if they thought you were cool, then you were. Marta saw them exchange whispers and knew Peter's kiss would be their newest hot topic.

Peter continued, "Me and Tom and a few of the boys had a wee drink at the Empire. I think they might have been trying to get us drunk so we'd have a hangover for the game tomorrow, but we showed them, aye Tom!" Peter reached to slap Tom on the back but missed and bumped into Tom's shoulder with his eye. Peter masked the mishap with a side hug and then slapped Tom's back once he'd found his bearings. Peter then seemed to sober up pretty quickly. Marta followed his haunted gaze and spotted Sister Fletcher, her school Principal, moving quickly towards them.

Pointing a thumb over her shoulder, Marta urged them to follow. "Let's get going, shall we? No point hanging round here to get in trouble." She turned and double stepped in the direction of town.

"Marta! Marta!" the elderly Sister called. She couldn't risk stopping now or the woman would quiz not only her appearance, but also where she was going with the two young men. Having Peter and Tom by her side, gave Marta a sort of arrogant confidence that she need answer to no one, let alone Sister Fletcher. She could only pray that her Principal hadn't noticed Peter's state of inebriation. For now all she wanted to think about was getting as far away from school as possible so she could mull over the phrase Peter had spoken.

'God you're Beautiful.'

Did he really believe that?

She hoped so.

Once they'd filled themselves on milkshakes and hot chips, Peter sobered enough to avoid disapproving stares. A quick nap before dinner and he was right as rain. Later that evening after dinner Peter asked her to sit with him on the porch and watch the sunset.

"Are you nervous about tomorrow?" She asked.

"Not really. We plan to win. That's what counts."

"Well you're pretty sure of yourself."

"Am I? Well when you have a good coach, a good captain, and a great strategy - nothing beats that."

"Strategy? Don't you just hit the ball and run. I thought whoever gets the most runs wins."

"Yes. Well that's the simple version. But Coach would tell you there are far better ways to win a match than just hit and run. Like for instance, it's better to bowl first, and bat last. That way most of your team is on the field in the morning when it's cooler, and not standing out in the field running all afternoon." He paused, letting his lips curl crookedly at the edges. "But I have a secret." He leaned close to her ear, and whispered, "I bowl much better in the afternoon. That's when I've really warmed up." His breath rustled strands of her hair sending tingles up and down her neck. Marta nodded, gulping back the buzz in her throat.

"Plus, whoever bats last has the advantage. Knowing exactly how many runs you need to beat is a pretty good motivator. Batting first, you're setting the bar for the other team. All they have to do is get one more than that and they win."

Peter made the game seem infinitely more interesting when he took her hand and drew on it with his finger to explain how the infield and outfield positions were chosen.

"See, if the ball goes high, we have more time to get under it - and hopefully catch the batter out. Tom's good at that. He has longer arms than me."

"Well you certainly caught me out today. If I'd known you were going to kiss me in front of all those people - I'd, I'd...well I don't know. Mum was right. You sure know what you're doing. Is it true you have lots of girlfriends?"

"Who told you that?"

"No one. It's just...boys like you tend to have lots of girlfriends, so I just assumed you would."

"No. I don't. The boys just like to think I do. I just like talking to people. And it's not my fault if they happen to be attractive. Besides, why wouldn't anyone want to be friends with you? You're about the most interesting person I've met so far on this trip."

"Me?"

"Yes. You."

"But, why?"

"Well. I don't know. You're mysterious, and I like that. You don't fawn all over me like some others. You're more reserved and that's...well, that's interesting. Plus you've got this whole vibe thing going on."

"Vibe? What vibe?"

"You're captivating. Irresistibly captivating. You look at me with those eyes, and I'm gone. Thing is, you don't even know you're doing it. And that just drives me nuts."

"I drive you nuts?"

"Yes. But in a good way." He stood up and pulled her up too so their noses were inches apart. Peter's eyes slunk backwards and rolled to the side. "See. You're doing it again."

"What?" She blinked. "I'm not doing anything."

"Yes you are, with your eyes. It makes me want to just kiss you so badly."

"Well. Why don't you then?"

Peter dragged himself away and picked up his cricket bat. He turned his head towards the house, searching for anyone who might be spying on them.

"I would. But you know I can't. Not here. Not now."

Marta crossed her arms and pouted momentarily.

Peter kicked his toe on the end of the bat. "Come here and I'll show you how to hold the bat." Marta did as he asked. Taking the offered bat, she clutched it like a golf club. She'd watched the boys play long enough to gather the stance was similar.

"Not like that. Here. I'll show you." Peter draped over her like a full length cardigan, his body warm against her back. He guided her hands and bent her forward, chopping the end of the bat into the lawn. He imitated the motion of a follow through, and then stood back. "Now you try."

She practiced the motion on her own a few times.

"Now let's give it a real go, with the ball." Peter backtracked a short distance.

"Not too fast though." She stood up, and jutted a hip to the left, unaware she'd now changed her trajectory.

"Ready?"

Marta set her position, keeping her fingers and thumbs in place. She chopped the bat twice and nodded. Peter took a much slower run up than usual. His shoulder didn't roll over, instead it undercut like a softball pitch. Marta smacked the ball with relative ease, and sent it sailing past the washing line, narrowly missing the corner of the house and the windows nearby. Marta dropped the bat and placed her hands over her cheeks.

"Nice shot!" Peter called.

Within seconds her brothers ran outside, followed by her mother.

"Can I have a turn?!" asked Harry.

"Sure. Just give me a second." Peter moved in, back towards the porch on the side of the house. "She's a great shot, Maggie. At least she cleared the house."

"Uh-huh. Well maybe you could take it a little further away. And not too long. The boys will be headed for bed soon."

Both brothers moaned.

"Uh. Sure. Just one other thing. I was wondering if it would be all right with you if I take Marta to the dance tomorrow night?"

Marta was as surprised as her mother looked pleased. Then Mum's face changed to one that wasn't so sure.

"That's a very kind of you. You have my consent. Getting Lionel's on the other hand, may prove more of a challenge. But I'm sure you'll think of something." Mum's laugh made Marta's stomach knot. *Would he?* Could he convince Dad to let her go?

Dad walked out to the porch. "Someone say my name?"

Mum wrapped an arm around his waist. "Peter here wants to take Marta to the dance tomorrow."

"Does he now?"

Tom came outside then too. "What's this?" He exchanged a mix of glares with Peter.

"Peter's asked Marta to the Dance," Mum replied.

"Has he." His tone was flat with zero encouragement.

Peter moved towards her father and took his hands out from his trouser pockets. "How about this, Mr Ingles..." - he stretched his hand forward.

Marta shook her head. *No.No No. Don't make it a bet - Dad hates bets. And if you lose then so do I!*

"...If we win the game tomorrow, you let me take Marta to the dance. If we lose, then you can decide if she still gets to go."

Gosh he was clever.

Mum's taut grin lifted her earrings a little. She loved Peter's offer. Dad just looked at Peter's hand with contempt.

Mum nudged him in the ribs. "Oh go on, Lionel. It can't do any harm. We'll be there. And Tom here will keep his eye on them. Won't you Tom?"

"I most certainly will, Maggie." Tom's lack of smile gave Dad further reason to withhold his approval. But with Mum convinced it was fine he could hardly refuse.

He took Peter's hand and crunched it in his grip. "Aye, all right. But only if you win."

As soon as Dad let go, Peter shook his hand out, stretched it twice and blew on it. Jimmy had retrieved the ball Marta hit, and threw it to Peter. He caught it, tossing it back in the air as he jogged away from their invisible pitch in the lawn. He rolled his shoulder in preparation to bowl it towards Harry, who was already waiting in front of the wickets. Tension mounted as he chopped at the grass. Peter held nothing back. The ball whizzed and smacked the wicket so hard that it went flying out of the ground like a javelin. Harry looked dumbstruck into the air and the cat went scampering for cover.

Peter now had all the motivation he needed to win tomorrow's game. And if by some act of God they didn't, Marta knew he would find a way to dance with her wherever they were.

Saturday 28th November 1959

The one-day match between the Auckland boys and the Wairarapa Seniors started off quite well - given the Seniors won the toss and chose to bat last. As tiresome and boring as cricket had seemed previously, Marta now found herself watching every ball that was bowled and every bat that hit the ball, counting the runs herself and following the scoreboard closely.

As the last ball of the day left Peter's hand with as much force as the first day's ball had from Greg Larsen's (a local who once played for New Zealand's national team), Marta held her breath. The ball flew past Mr Harrow's bat and straight through the wickets. The resulting chorus of cheers from the visiting boys echoed about the field. The grandstand erupted in courteous applause and cheering, although a collective sigh of disappointment also swept through the spectators in a silent realisation of their loss. For some, the loss was more costly than for others. Mayor Marchbank seemed unaffected by the final score and made his way over to the Auckland team to congratulate them and to shake the coach's hand. But others found it hard to offer little more than a frown, seemingly more upset about their own financial loss than that of the Wairarapa Senior's pride.

Sitting snugly in the car with Mum and Dad in front, sandwiched between Tom Sand Peter in the rear, Marta felt safe and sure that the evening would be a wonderful experience. One she hoped she'd cherish for the rest of her life.

What she hadn't bargained for was just how memorable it would be. That night would never leave her thoughts, not for one single day and nor did she ever want it to. But eventually it would fade and time would conceal all that happened on the night of November the 28th 1959.

CHAPTER SEVEN

Saturday 28th November 1959

MUSIC THUMPED FROM the Town Hall when they pulled into the parking lot. 'The Signatures' were already booked out of town for the date of the dance, so Freda Goldburn, chair of the Ladies Aid Society events committee, said they had little choice but to call in an unknown band from Wellington. Without having heard the band first, Maggie warned the committee about the ramifications of such a hasty decision. But as they had so few bands to choose from at short notice, they simply went with the cheapest. 'The Harpers' were set up centre stage and although they could carry the beat and play the melody all right, some of the lead singer's notes were a little off-tune. It caused nearly all to respond in one of two ways: cringe at it unbearably, or embrace the off-tune merriment by singing along. Punch was being served and the Mayor had allowed a temporary license for beer to be sold, but with the strictest instructions that anyone found to be intoxicated would be removed from the premises and fined five pounds (or so a man said when we entered). Since the senior constable was a friend of Mayor Marchbank, they had agreed to have two officers on patrol who would see to the safety of the public and arrest anyone who became disorderly. Marta looked around the hall and spotted only two other girls she knew from school. Suzy Thomas, who had seen Peter kiss her at school yesterday, and Suzy's best friend, Gigi Richmond. Gigi didn't like Marta much and was often teasing her about her freckles. But tonight Gigi didn't appear to be bothered by Marta's presence at all, and Suzy seemed very eager to talk to her.

"Marta!" Suzy waved across the hall, gesturing for her to join them.

Marta was reluctant to let go of Peter's arm in fear that she would lose him in the crowd or worse, to another girl who wanted to dance with him. Marta looked at him and Peter let her go but stopped her to whisper in her ear. "Don't leave me all alone for too long. I want to dance with you all night if I can. I'll get us some drinks and bring them over."

Marta smiled. "Thank you. Come save me from them soon." She hinted. Marta moved around the few who were dancing and greeted Suzy and Gigi with as much politeness as she could muster. "Evening, Suzy. Gigi. Looks like it's going to be a fun night. Did you girls bring a date?" Marta only asked because she had and knew it was possible they hadn't. But then Suzy pointed out a boy standing in the corner near the front, his eyes glued to the bass guitarist's every move. "That's Nathaniel. He's from Rathkeale. He asked me out two weeks ago." Suzy smiled, clearly pleased with herself, seemingly more than she was with Nathaniel. She offered him a pitiful wave in return to his eager smile.

"Oh. That's nice. What about you, Gigi? Here with anyone special?" Marta hoped she wasn't but only so she could rub it in her face like she had done about her freckles.

"Yeah. Nathaniel had a mate who needed a date. I only agreed so I could come see the band. Jack's not really the kind of guy I go for." Just as she'd said the words, Marta assumed it was Jack who had come to join them. His expression looked a little hurt but he seemed to get over Gigi's disinterest pretty quickly when he saw Marta looking at him.

"Hi, I'm Jack Forge. We've had a few Auckland boys staying with us too. Marta, isn't it? You're Mrs Ingles' daughter, aren't you? Bert told us all about your kiss with Peter on the field yesterday. You're very pretty, but Pete's a bit old for you, don't ya think?" Jack cinched his eyes at Gigi. "It appears I've picked up the scraps this time, so if you ever want to go out sometime, I'm free."

Gigi stormed off and Suzy followed, leaving Marta standing there with Jack.

"Would you care to dance?" He asked. Marta was delighted that at least someone had asked her and was about to accept when Peter arrived by her side, giving Jack the quick word. "Sorry mate, she's taken." He handed Jack the drinks he'd brought and spun Marta out to the dance floor before she knew what was happening.

Marta couldn't remember a time she'd felt happier than she did right then. She smiled. She laughed. She jived. She spun and she twisted - all to the beat of the band. Peter was such a good dancer and knew just how to hold her. She could trust him with her whole body and she knew he'd never drop her or tread on her toes. Marta realised then just how badly she had fallen for him. She loved him. She couldn't bear the thought of him leaving on Monday. But rather than dwell on it, Marta decided to replay the words he'd said to her yesterday. 'I can't stay here in Masterton, Marta. I really like you a lot and I hope we can at least enjoy our last few days together.' Marta was determined to do just that - enjoy herself as much as possible. She was in love with Peter and she could only hope to convince him of it before he left. Praying and hoping that he might love her back too.

Marta's cheeks cramped every time she smiled, which was almost constantly. She'd never felt this happy before in her whole life. Peter 'liked' her and paid her so much attention. No one, not even her mother or father, had paid her so much attention before or made her feel so special the way Peter did.

Peter grabbed her hand and led her to get a drink. With their refreshments in hand, he said, "Let's go outside and get some fresh air." Marta was hot and flushed and some fresh air was exactly what she needed.

Outside the night had finally come and its stars twinkled in off-beat waves. Moths flipped around the hall lights making shadows dance on the pavement. The night's dew was already in the air and it wasn't long before Marta felt a shiver run over her bare arms. Peter removed his jacket and placed it around her shoulders. It was warm and smelled of his citrusy cologne. Marta drew the fabric around her more, trying to yield an unmanned hug from it.

"Come on," Peter said, "Let's get out of this light so we can see the stars better. I don't get to see them much in Auckland, it's usually always so cloudy."

Peter directed them to the end row of parked cars, furthest from the town lights. He jumped up on the hood of a car and offered Marta his hand to pull her up. Leaning back against the windscreen they looked up at the black expanse dotted with stars above. Peter's hand searched for hers between them, and finding it he wrapped his fingers around hers. His warm touch surged up her arm and then caused her skin to goosebump as she cooled again. With his other hand he tried pointing out some of the constellations, and eventually stopped at one, singling it out. He made sure she knew which one he meant. "See that one, the one next to those two really close ones? That's your one, Marta. It's just for you. I will always look at your star and think, 'That's my girl's. What a beauty she is.'"

Transfixed by her twinkling star, it was unexpected when Peter's face stole her view and hovered above her own. He kissed her, full, hard, and eager. Sucking her lips, and delving his tongue inside her mouth, dancing his with hers. She wasn't sure if she'd done it right, but his passion and urgency made her lose all care. This kiss was much stronger than either of the two they'd shared before. She was sure now. Peter was the one. He loved her and she wanted him just as much as he wanted her. There was no question about it. So she kissed him back with a ferocity that made him moan. "Marta." His kisses intensified and she felt his hands search her body for anything it could get a hold of. His hands were addictive and strong. She couldn't breathe without them touching her. He slid them both off the front of the car and tried the back seat door handle to see if it was unlocked. It opened and Peter ushered her inside.

In frenzied excitement, and kissing without stopping for air, Peter pulled down her dress' zipper and explored what lay beneath. Marta let him have free reign, and he made short work of her bra and knickers.

It was all over before she knew it, and it hurt a little more than she expected. But she didn't care. Peter was hers and she was his. In that moment, that was all that mattered.

Without giving her time to process what had just happened, Peter helped her out of the car to get themselves reassembled. He caressed her face and helped smooth her hair which was now a little bent out of shape. He zipped up the back of her dress for her and kissed her neck. Then, like nothing had happened, he led her back to the dance floor and they continued their evening like they'd never left the hall. The only thing that had changed was their starry-eyed gazes at each other, and subtle grins that belied the truth of their rendezvous. A secret code that only the two of them knew, and Marta loved it.

It wasn't until the next morning that she had her first doubt. She'd thought Peter might have snuck into her room once Mum and Dad had gone to bed, but it was probably best he hadn't. She wouldn't have known what to say if someone discovered him there.

Breakfast was eaten as usual and then it was time for church. Marta wasn't feeling too great but she'd gone anyway so as not to encourage her father's judgment. Dad didn't like how friendly she and Peter had become, but Mum didn't seem to mind. As Marta sat there in the pew, pleading forgiveness for her sins, she couldn't help but let the guilt of last night's weakness take over. She knew she was a wretched girl who should be punished for allowing herself to succumb to - as Dad would say - 'the temptations of the devil'.

She wanted to smile but she couldn't. When Peter asked if she was okay after the service, she only shrugged and would neither confirm nor deny there was anything wrong. She loved Peter, but the more she thought about what had happened, the more she realised how very foolish she'd been. Peter had given her no promise, no proposal, no ring of engagement. This was not how she was raised. She couldn't equate her love for Peter to the misery she now felt inside.

Peter tried again to offer her some comfort on Sunday night. The sorrow in his eyes when he couldn't console her made Marta feel even worse. She came to the point where she just wished he would leave her alone.

"You don't really want me anyway," she said before they parted for bed. "You're going home tomorrow and you'll forget all about me." Tears streamed down her face and she knew her words were true when Peter made no attempt of denial.

Marta stayed in bed on Monday morning and wouldn't come out of her room. She said she felt sick. It wasn't true in the physical sense, but she was definitely sick with something. She just couldn't figure out what it was. Guilt perhaps.

Peter stood at her door when the others had left. "Marta? Please open the door, Marta. Can't I at least kiss you goodbye?" There was silence and she wondered if Peter had left. "I will never forget your star, Marta. And I'll think of you always when I look at the night sky. I love you."

There. He'd said it. Did he really mean it? Or was it merely spoken out of sympathy. No more words were spoken and all Marta could do was dwell on every one of them that had passed from his lips through her closed door. By the time she eventually opened it. Peter was nowhere to be seen. Mum's car pulled out of the driveway.

That's it. I'll never see him again, and I'll never love anyone else - ever. Goodbye Peter.

CHAPTER EIGHT

Monday 1st August 1960

Peter

PETER WONDERED IF he was losing his mind. Something wasn't right. He'd felt it on the bus this morning on his way to work in the city. It was a route he'd taken countless times, but today it felt odd again, different somehow and he couldn't quite give any valid reason why.

He'd been working as an intern at Wheeler, Baxter & Frye Law firm for nearly six months and had been selected as one of four candidates up for a promotion. He was confident the position would be his and even bought himself a new suit. But now he wasn't so confident at all.

Was he losing his mind?

Ever since Mary agreed to his proposal three weeks ago he'd felt a little different, not in a bad way. But, for some reason he couldn't shake the feeling that something bad was about to happen. Mary tried convincing him it was just nerves. Once they were married any doubts or reservations would simply evaporate. Mary was right. She always was. They'd met at their graduation ceremony in May. It was a whirlwind romance and Peter had every incentive to make her happy. At the time, he didn't realise Mary was the daughter of one of the partner's at the firm. He knew their liaisons were dangerous, but the thrill of keeping their relationship hidden from Mary's father, Mr Frye, had added a whole new level of duplicity to their encounters - much to Mary's delight. With boundaries crossed and risky rendezvous at the office, the only thing preventing them from getting caught was Peter's own ambition. It was Walter Wheeler who had him under his wing and if Peter kept his head on straight long enough to please all the partners then his confidence of getting the promotion was well founded.

Now he wasn't so sure.

Peter raked a hand through his hair and analysed every person who got on the bus. None of the faces were hers though.

He'd seen a face he recognised at Victoria Markets on Saturday while he and Mary were shopping. He couldn't shake the feeling that he knew the girl more intimately. But he couldn't remember where or even when he'd met her, the latter bothering him most.

It wasn't just her face that haunted him - the girl was pregnant.

A strange knot twisted in the pit of his stomach and no matter how much water or coffee he drank the sickening feeling just wouldn't leave.

She'd seen him. He was certain. But she'd not approached him or aligned her path with his so they would meet. Maybe he was mistaken. He hoped he was. But thoughts of the girl tormented his dreams. Not only was he losing sleep, but also his sanity. It seemed like everywhere he went, there she was!

His head pounded, reverberating like footsteps down an empty stairwell. The headaches were getting worse, and painkillers no longer had any effect. He was relieved to be meeting Tom for lunch today. Maybe he might set his mind at peace.

Entering the office, Kelly handed him his cases for the day along with a seemingly never-ending list of amendments and clauses to check or rewrite. He was glad of it though. If he could busy his mind with work then there'd be no space left for him to think about the girl.

What was her name? He ran through his fingers the names of some of the girls he'd slept with in the last nine months. There hadn't been as many as he thought, not since he got back from their away games for cricket. And none since he and Mary had crossed that line three months ago.

Marta. It was Marta - he was sure of it. Her face was almost the same, but her hair was very different. Normally she had it styled and set, but not this girl at the markets. Her hair was dark brown and it was tied into a plait. A wig maybe? She was obviously trying to disguise herself. But she had seen him. Why hadn't she tried to speak to him? She must have seen him with Mary and decided not to risk an awkward introduction. That made sense.

But if Marta was pregnant, was he the father? He hadn't known her very well. He was enamoured by her kitten-like eyes and the way she bit her lip when he talked to her. Her body was phenomenal - supple curves perfectly rounded in all the right spots. She had a terrible crush on him and he hadn't the heart to make her feel foolish for it. The night of the dance came rushing back in a series of flashes. He'd had a few drinks but not enough to impair his better judgment. The feelings were mutual, he'd never forced himself on a girl.

Had she come to track him down? What would he do if Mary found out? His career would be over - all hopes of the promotion gone. Six months wasted. He'd have to start again.

Maybe that's why Marta had come. To find out if he wanted her, if he knew the child was his.

Peter slammed his fist on the desk annoyed that his thoughts were consumed by the girl even more so now than they were before.

He felt sick. Sick to his stomach. His heart raced and his palms tightened. He couldn't breathe. Peter loosened his tie as sweat beaded on his temples. Was he having a heart attack? It sure felt like it.

Drawing in deep breaths he reined in his wild thoughts. A mild panic attack, that's all it was. He made his way to the men's bathroom and splashed a little water on his face.

Breathe. In and out. In and out. There. Everything is fine. Everything will be okay.

Peter wiped his face with the back of his sleeve and walked back to his desk with a little more calm to his semblance.

"You okay? You don't look so good." Kelly asked.

A lie was less hassle and often best practice in workplace environments.

"Yeah, I'm fine. I think my milk might be off." Suffering from food poisoning was far more preferable than suffering from a panic attack. At least at the office it was.

"I might go for a walk. Get some fresh air."

"Not much chance of that out there," Kelly grimaced.

"I won't be long."

"Okay. But if Mr Frye asks where you are, I'm not covering for you." Kelly called after him.

He walked away, waving a dismissive hand behind him.

At quarter to twelve, when Peter returned, Walter was waiting in his office. "Where have you been?"

"Sorry. I've had a bit of tummy trouble this morning. Think my milk's soured."

"Oh. Well, I wanted to tell you that the partners and I have agreed. You've got it, Peter. They've decided you have the drive and ambition we're looking for here at the firm. You're to be our newest, and, I might add, our youngest solicitor we've ever had. Congratulations, son. You deserve it."

Walter's accolade was the start of what Peter hoped would be a long and profitable career at the firm. One day he even hoped he might make partner.

Peter clasped his mentor's hand firmly, shaking it with as much enthusiasm as Walter did.

With a grin pinned to his ears he couldn't wait to share the good news with Tom. And, as soon as Walter left, Peter grabbed his coat and headed for the exit once more. He'd stay late if he needed to catch up on any deadlines.

"Oi? Where are you off to? You only just got back." Kelly crunched her brows and her mouth.

"The newest associate of Wheeler, Baxter, & Frye has a lunch. Back in an hour!" He waved again.

Kelly muttered her displeasure much louder than he expected, but he didn't care to stay and listen.

His feet seemed to glide over the linoleum corridor without a hitch or a stumble. This was how life was meant to be: easy and ordered, with not a care at all.

Peter considered taking a longer route through Albert Park, past the very buildings he'd studied at during his time at University. But as neither time nor weather was on his side, he hastened his step and took a direct route straight to O'Grady's on High Street. Spits of rain plinked the pavement, each drip holding more water than the last.

Despite the rain, Peter walked on a cloud of elation, barely noticing the other pedestrians about him. His arrogant bubble pushed everyone out of his way, making his journey most enjoyable. He was almost at O'Grady's when he felt something brush past him. A familiar waft of rose drifted in the air, along with the head of brown plaited hair. Ducking through the crowd ahead of him, she moved quickly and was in the far distance by the time he registered who it was. There was no doubt in his mind now.

Tom slapped him on the back breaking his gaze from the crowded street.

"Tom! It's so good to see you." Peter held out his hand in greeting. Tom shook it formally as was customary now that they had graduated. High fives and chest bumps were no longer considered suitable for men in their profession. But the two of them still managed a good old back slapping now and then, and the occasional elbow jeer.

Peter often had a hankering for the good old days, when a Sunday afternoon cricket game came with a Monday morning hangover, and life seemed far less difficult than the corporate world they now lived in.

Over their meal Peter shared the good news of his new promotion.

'That's fantastic, Pete. Looks like your proposal worked then." Tom smiled with a cheeky glint in his eye.

Peter had kept him appraised of his courageous courtship with Mary and although Tom didn't approve of their secrecy, he was pleased Peter had finally found someone he wanted to settle down with. "She's a great girl, Pete. I don't know what she sees in you though. Don't go giving her an excuse to call off your engagement. You won't find another girl like her. I can promise you."

Tom's warning was a stark reminder of the trouble he could be in. If it was Marta stalking him, and she was pregnant with his child, he knew that his toughest road may yet still lie ahead. But how would he ever find out if it was really her or not?

"Tom. I've got to tell you something. You're not gonna like it, but I have to tell someone, or I'll go mad."

"Sure, what is it?" Tom took a last sip of beer and clamped his lips tight.

"I think Marta might be here in Auckland. I saw this girl at the market last Saturday. It looked a lot like her - but she had dark hair and it was tied in a plait."

"Who?"

"Marta. Remember? Maggie's daughter, in Masterton?"

"Oh, Marta. Yeah, okay, so what?"

"She's pregnant, Tom." Fear faulted his usually confident mask. "I know I didn't tell you at the time, but that night at the dance. Marta and I... well we kind of took things a bit too far in one of the cars out in the lot."

"Oh, for God's sake, Pete! You didn't."

"I didn't mean to, but we were looking at the stars and she was so beautiful. God, she was beautiful. You know it. The whole team thought she was a stunner. She wanted it, Tom. I didn't force her."

"You're an absolute idiot, Pete. That girl had such a huge crush on you, but I never thought you'd take it that far. She was only sixteen! You're a damn fool!"

"I know. I'm an idiot. And I know I don't deserve Mary. But if I lose her, I'll lose my promotion and maybe even my job. What should I do?"

Tom paused to think a little before he answered. "Well are you sure it's Marta? Has she spoken to you?"

"Well no. But I'm ninety-nine percent sure it's her. She was just here, before you arrived. I didn't talk to her but she brushed past me. I'm sure it was her. She smelled like roses. You'd know it was her if you saw her."

"Well if she doesn't make contact with you, Pete, there's not a whole lot you can do."

"I know. But what if she does and Mary's with me?"

"Well I don't think she'd do that, Pete. The last thing a girl wants to do is meet the new girlfriend, I mean, fiancée, of a guy who got her pregnant."

"I guess you're right."

"I know I am. Marta will only talk to you if you're alone. If you really must know if it's her, then give her an opportunity to meet you alone. Sit in a park for a while. And don't talk to anyone. That's my advice."

"You're right. I will. Thanks. I'll let you know if I see her."

"I'm not so sure I wanna know. But if you need any help. I'm here for you. I know Iris doesn't like you much, but it's only because she thinks you're a little sleazy. I'm beginning to wonder if she might be right. But, no matter what, we'll always be friends."

"Thanks. I really appreciate you saying so. I've got a lot of mistakes to make up for, and when I marry Mary, I hope to start by making a good life for us together."

Tom dipped his head. "Just see that you do, Pete. See that you do."

Peter shook Tom's hand and they gave each other a hug. Peter left and made his way back to the office.

For the rest of the afternoon he buried his head in his work and when five o'clock came, he picked up his things and headed straight for Albert Park. It was always the place he went when he needed to clear his head or think things over. It seemed the perfect place to be alone.

Once he arrived he wasn't sure what to do next. He'd not thought to bring a newspaper to read, so he did as Tom suggested and just sat. The central park bench out in the open seemed best.

Since the rain had eased after lunch, the bench was mostly dry. Grey clouds still blanketed the sky and scattered winds churned the nearby trees. Shifting his back to the draught, he snapped his collar around his neck and tucked his chin to his chest.

Beneath an anxious brow he scanned the pathways and grassy clearings. His mind wandered, easily gravitating to the night of the dance. Conjuring the foggy memory to mind he attempted to place himself back at the scene. The night was a bit of a blur. They'd won their game - he recalled that much - but his memories beyond that were a mix of booze, music, and euphoria. Marta was obviously a virgin, but he didn't care. She wanted it.

He leaned forward, elbows on knees, his palms clutching his face. His chest burned and a tightness constricted his throat. What had he done?

He hadn't stopped to think how Marta might have felt about their quickie in the car. He'd enjoyed himself and that was usually all that mattered when they were away playing cricket. They'd won by eighteen runs. A good win, considering their start and the fact it was a blistering hot day. Marta wasn't quite herself the following day. Her provocative looks and subtle suggestions gone. She was just being a typical girl, emotional and manipulative. That's how all girls behaved. His sister was a master, and so was their mother. It's how she got him to choose law over cricket. The face she made when he told her he wanted to play cricket professionally had etched in his brain. Bitter disappointment laced with horror and fear. She'd blubbered something about wasting a perfectly good brain on a silly old game.

The death of his dream left him devastated too.

A gust of wind nudged him sideways, snapping him out of his thoughts. He looked up. Marta's face moved towards him. He dipped his eyes, too scared to look but curiosity changed his mind.

There she was. Kitten-eyed, freckled, button nose and all. Her body flaunted a spectacular bump wrapped in a red mini skirt.

Red. He liked her in red.

"Hello Peter." She fiddled with her sleeve, then put a nail between her lips. "I've been waiting for the right time to talk to you." She looked at her stomach, a smile held in reserve. "I'm pregnant." Her lashes sprang wide and her eyes bore into his, "It's yours." Her statement seemed so final, so definitive. Irreversible.

Peter didn't want to ask, but couldn't stop himself. "Are you sure?" Marta looked hurt.

"Yes. It could only be yours." She looked out to the buildings in the distance and spoke with a pain in her voice he hadn't heard before, "Dad kicked me out. He was so mad at Mum for allowing me to go to the dance with you. Dad said that the only way I can come back is if I give the baby up for adoption. I'm not welcome home if I decide to keep it. Mum sent me up here so no one back home will know. She said it's best if I give the baby away to a family. Someone who can take care of it better than me."

Tears rolled down her cheeks, taking the stain of mascara with them.

"It took me a while to find you, but Mum said that if I did, I should ask you what I should do." She paused and bit her bottom lip. It reminded him of the first kiss he'd placed on them. He couldn't help but stare. They were just as intoxicating as before, round and rosy like a cherubs. His crotch responded and he shuffled in place, shunning his instincts before they took over.

Marta sat beside him. "If you want, we could get married. If you still love me that is. We could be a family, you, me, and the baby. I know we could raise it together and be happy. You have a good job, don't you?"

Peter thought a moment as he stared out beyond the patches of grass and concrete paths that wove through Albert Park. How was he going to let her down? He felt wretched about it, but he had to. He was engaged and his whole future was now in jeopardy. He'd have to be brutal. He didn't want Marta thinking there was still a chance for them.

"I don't love you, Marta." It stung his own heart to say it as much as it clearly stung hers. Marta's tears sprang fresh from their wells and she tried her best to flick them away. "It's...it's just not as simple as you might think," He reasoned. "I've been promoted at work. Truthfully, I think I only got it because I'm engaged to Mary, my boss's daughter." Peter paused, waiting for Marta to register what he'd said.

"Oh, I see." A new stream of tears made their journey over her freckled cheeks once more. He handed her his handkerchief and she took it gratefully.

"I don't know what else to say. You knew we could never be together. We're from two different worlds you and I. I'm going to marry Mary, she is my future. I think it would be best if you gave the baby up for adoption. I don't mind helping with any expenses. I'll buy your ticket home. But that's all I can do. Mary mustn't ever know about this. You can't tell a soul. I don't think Mary's father would be so forgiving if he knew. Please, Marta. Give me your word you'll never tell anyone I'm the father."

Marta nodded.

He prayed she meant it. He was about to put his arm around her but stopped short of making contact with her. He didn't want to encourage her feelings for him. An ache moved from his hand up his arm. She was still so beautiful and his heart swelled with compassion. "I'm so sorry, Marta. I really am." He caved, letting his arm rest on her shoulder. In a heartbeat she wrapped her arms around him and held on so tightly that he almost couldn't breathe. Bubbles of panic popped in his chest and he fought the urge to push her away. Instead, he wrapped her in his arms and let her head rest on his chest. When her sobs had subsided she lifted her head and sat upright, smoothing her shirt and then skirt.

"I'll be okay. I'm due on the twenty-sixth, just four more weeks. I'm a little scared of how much it's gonna hurt though. Sharon - a girl at the home - she had hers two weeks ago and she said it hurt like hell. She had a boy, but he still hasn't been adopted yet. I really hope they find him a good home soon." Marta rubbed her belly. "Here. You want to feel?" She held out a hand. His throat hitched and no words came out. She grabbed his free hand and flattened it on her stomach. "There. You feel that?"

The roll of movement beneath his palm caused a flutter in his chest. He wrenched his hand away, and Marta giggled. "This little one needs a good home too. I can't bear the thought she might end up in foster care."

"She? You think it's a girl?"

"I think so. At least I hope she is. Girls have a much better chance of being selected."

He hated the way Marta talked about the baby. Like it were some sort of prize to be auctioned to the highest bidder. Even though he couldn't be a father to the child, he wanted to provide for it, no matter how much it cost.

A thought popped into his head. "Marta? What if I could find the child some parents? Ones that I knew would take really good care of her. Would you like that?"

Marta's smile was small but he sensed she was pleased at his suggestion.

"I guess that might help. But they would have to be really good, Peter. I don't want her going to just any old couple. Especially if they have children of their own already. They may not love her the same way otherwise."

He nodded slowly. "Leave it with me, and I promise I'll do my very best to find her the parents she deserves."

Marta's lips spread wide and a weight in his heart lifted. Finally he had said something right. Now all he had to do was keep his promise.

Tuesday 2nd August 1960

Marta

When Peter called her the day after they'd spoken in the park, she was surprised to hear that he'd already found a couple that were willing to adopt the baby.

"It's Tom, Marta. He said he and Iris would love to take her."

Marta wasn't convinced. She was dubious about Tom. He wasn't at all what she had pictured a father should be for her baby. But he had been very kind to her when he and Peter stayed with them.

And what about Iris? She'd only ever heard Tom talk about her at the farm. It seemed like he loved her a lot. He phoned her every night and made sure he paid Mum and Dad the toll fees for the calls too, which would have been expensive.

"Tom's got a great job. He and Iris are getting married this Saturday and then they're taking their honeymoon up in Paihia for a week. He said it wouldn't be difficult to talk Iris into adopting the baby as she is desperate to start a family straight away."

"I don't know, Peter. Will she even know how to look after a baby?"

"Iris is the eldest of six children in her family. I think she'll do just fine."

Peter sounded pretty convincing. He had good intentions and she knew that no matter who Peter found, she would always believe no one would be good enough. She had dreamed she and Peter would raise their child together and be a happy family of their own. It's what she prayed for every day since finding out she was pregnant. If being the mother of Peter's child and carrying it all this time did not persuade him to love her, then there really wasn't anything else she could do. Peter had made his choice and she would do whatever he thought best. If he thought Tom and Iris would make good parents for their baby, then she would just have to trust him.

"I'll agree to Tom and Iris on one condition," she said.

"What's that?"

"I want to meet her, Iris that is. I want to see what she looks like. I don't have to talk to her. I just want to know what she looks like and to hear the voice that our baby will know as her mother's."

"I don't know, Marta. Iris doesn't know that I'm the father. If she did, I'm not so sure she would agree to adopt her."

"Why not!?!" Marta's voice dipped before it peaked.

"Well she doesn't like me much. We just don't see eye to eye."

"And this is the woman you want to raise our baby?"

"Yes. I do. She's a very loving and kind person, Marta. The fact that she doesn't like me much should only prove that she is wise and can spot a bad apple a mile away."

"You're not that bad!" She still loved him, even if he didn't love her back.

"You're sweet, Marta. But Iris is right. I've not been very thoughtful of others and I've been selfish when it comes to love and relationships."

'Well then, I definitely want to meet her."

"But I don't see how."

"What about at the wedding? There'll be plenty of guests around and she'll have no idea who I am. Just say I'm a distant cousin of Tom's if she asks. You won't even know I'm there."

"I doubt that. You're pretty cunning, I'll give you that." Peter paused as if mulling it over. "All right. I'll tell Tom you're coming. But please don't cause a scene. Iris, and Mary for that matter, must never know that I am the father and that you are the mother of the child they'll adopt, okay? And for goodness sakes, do something with your hair. It is a wedding and we don't want you sticking out like a star in the night sky.

You need to at least try to blend in with the other guests - so no red. Okay?"

Marta smiled at his hint of the star he'd chosen just for her, the night their baby was conceived.

"I'll do my best. But as far as the sticking out part, there's not a whole lot I can do about that." Marta giggled. "I can't wait till this thing is out of me."

Saturday 13th August 1960

Marta's heart vibrated when she saw Peter again. He looked so smart in a suit and tie and it reminded her of the last time she'd seen him dressed that way. He held her in his arms so closely at the dance that she'd bathed her own neck in his cologne as he kissed her.

Looking at him now, standing near the church alter with Tom grinning beside him, she felt as helpless as she did that night. Her racing heartbeat and longing to be desired clouded her better judgment. It never occurred to her to question how virtuous Peter's sudden and urgent attention was. Confused and overwhelmed by her own instinctual behaviour, she'd followed his direction and surrendered herself completely. He did say he loved her before he left, but she never saw the look in his eyes when he said it. She questioned how true it was from the moment he spoke the words through her bedroom door. For the rest of her life she'd never forget the inside of that car, parked outside the town hall. The music, the punch, the cheering, the awards. All the men were sportingly pleased with themselves, their joy infectious. She hadn't a heartbeat of hope of keeping herself chaste, evidenced now by her ever-expanding belly.

Marta stroked and held the protrusion between her hands like a ball. 'One more month and it will all be over,' Matron had said. Until then she just had to, 'Be good, eat well, and try not to get into any more trouble'. Marta had laughed at Matron's last suggestion. How much more trouble could she get herself in? Pregnant at sixteen was about as unforgivable for a country girl as it was for a city girl not to have a new dress and a date for the high school social.

Marta was ever hopeful that when Peter saw her all dressed up, he might regret his decision to marry Mary, and fall madly in love with her instead. She knew it was a fantasy, but there was no denying they still had a spark between them, she'd felt it at the park. At least he still cared for her. Just not as much as she would have liked.

The church's organ volume increased and a flurry of notes heralded the beginning of the wedding march. Marta watched as a beautiful smiling bride made her way down the aisle towards Tom and Peter. She wondered if she would ever get to be a bride. She felt as though she had skipped ahead in the time-line of her life. She couldn't envisage how she was ever going to get back. Maybe it would be easier once the baby was born and her body shape returned to normal. Would she ever really be able to forget about her baby though? Surely no one would want to marry her now that she'd disgraced herself. Her only consolation was at least nobody knew about the baby back home. Well no one except Mum, Dad, and Dr Fredrickson.

Not even her best friend Cherie knew the truth about where she really went or why. Mum used a made up excuse of a widowed aunt in Auckland who wanted Marta to accompany her to Europe for the summer. Her 'make-believe' Aunt Rosemary was apparently very wealthy and was paying for the whole thing. The rouse did seem a little far-fetched, but Marta went along with whatever Mum said, nodding and trying to seem excited about the grand adventure.

Inside she felt terrible about all the lies they'd told. Dad didn't liked it at all, but he would rather beg forgiveness for a few lies than have the whole town know of Marta's disgrace. He was so ashamed of her. She had never seen him so angry.

As the minister's monotone voice led the ceremony at the front of the church, her father's voice echoed in her head. 'You little Minx! How could you have been so stupid. Do you not listen to the sermons on Sunday? You're just as bad as... never mind. I can forgive, but it's much harder to forget. You will not be so fortunate. You will give this baby up for adoption. If you won't, you must leave this house and never return. The choice is yours and I'll have nothing more to do with it. Maggie, she's your daughter you sort it out.'

So many things went wrong after that. Dad got grumpier, and he couldn't even look at her without screwing his face in disgust. She was devastated. She didn't even want to go back home. But, since Peter didn't want her either, what choice did she have? She would return to Masterton and continue her life as if nothing had happened.

Lying was becoming a bit of a pattern. Sweeping feelings from her heart and locking them away in the back of her mind like a carpet concealing debris. It wasn't wise, and it messed with her head, but hide her secrets she must.

The minister's pitch changed, and seconds later he announced Tom and Iris to be husband and wife. She watched the two people who would raise her daughter, kiss briefly and grin at each other with pride as they walked down the aisle hand in hand.

Outside, the church guests threw rice and confetti in the air, hailing the couple with a chorus of best wishes and congratulations. Flashes popped and film wound on ready for the next photo. Marta watched the happy couple kiss and hug, opening their arms to friends and family. A tall woman with gold blonde hair, like the colour she had just dyed her own back to yesterday, draped herself on Peter's shoulder and whispered into his ear - giggling afterward. Marta's jaw clamped tight. It must be Mary, his fiancée. She'd seen her with him before. Though Mary's slender eyes twinkled, and her cheeks were round and delicate, her wired limbs and pointy chin lacked the same tender form. She wasn't curvy like Marta.

Marta rolled her palms over her belly until they disappeared beneath it. She promptly drew them back, crossing them over her swollen breasts and resting her forearms on her tummy.

Perhaps it's my weight Peter doesn't like?

Peter smiled and kissed the woman and then they walked out of sight. She never saw him again that day, which was lucky.

Marta made her way to the bathroom inside the church. Her feet were sore and starting to swell in the only decent heels she had. Safely hidden in one of the cubicles, she could hear the other ladies as they came and went.

Finishing, she opened her door and proceeded to wash her hands at the sink, leaning in to check her eye makeup in the mirror. Mary walked in and Marta tucked her head to her chest in an attempt to hide.

"Wow, you look like you're ready to burst. When are you due?"

"Um," She didn't want to talk to Mary. Not ever. This was the woman who had ruined her chance with Peter. Marta bit her bottom lip. "Um… in another six weeks or so." She lied, her voice slightly quivering.

"Gosh! Are you scared? I'd be scared." Mary looked herself over in the mirror and primped her hair. It was fine and limp, and a little dull close up. "It looks like it would be quite difficult to have a baby. You look very young. How old are you?"

Mary's questions were beginning to grate, and she didn't know what to say. She frowned then feigned a looked of shock at the rather personal question. "I'm eighteen, not that's it's any of your business. I'm Tom's 2nd cousin. My husband works in the forest up north so I'm staying in Auckland till the baby arrives. There's no midwife where we live."

Lying had become second nature by now and all kinds of stories slipped past her lips without hesitation. She'd told so many that she could almost believe them herself. The more she lied the better she got. The only problem was, it was difficult to keep track of what she had said to who. That was the trick if you didn't want to get caught.

Mary looked apologetic and tried to paw her shoulder. "How exciting. Well"- her smile brightened - "Good luck. I hope it all works out for you." She turned to leave.

"Thanks. I'm sure it will." Marta poked a tongue at the mirror.

Back outside, Iris looked perfect. Marta could tell she would make an excellent mother simply by the way she paid extra attention to the children in attendance. As long as Tom kept his promise and never told Iris who the baby's parents were, Marta was confident the baby would be accepted as their own. Content with all she had seen, Marta slipped away unnoticed and would wait for news from Peter when the newlyweds were back, hopefully with confirmation that Iris was happy to proceed with the adoption. Until then, she could only pray that the baby would not arrive before they returned.

And for once her prayers were answered.

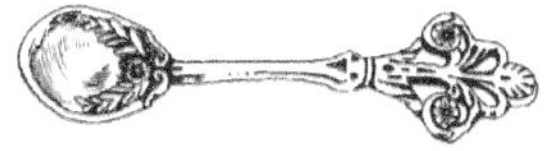

CHAPTER NINE

Sunday 28th August 1960

MARTA AWOKE WITH a dull ache in her pelvis. It felt familiar but was one she hadn't experienced for a while. It was still dark outside and she thought if she could just fall back to sleep it might go away.

When the pain came in waves she considered if there might be more to it. She tightened her eyes and breathed deeply. Normally she would rise and make herself a hot water bottle for any pain she experienced.

A sharp pain tugged her insides and took her breath away. She couldn't help but cry out a little.

It was Marlene who turned on the light and asked if she was okay.

"I'm not sure. It's probably nothing." Marta said, denying what she suspected were the first signs of labour. She wanted to believe her own words more than anything, but another surge made her clench her teeth and she whimpered as she clutched the bed sheets in her now sweating hands.

"You're in labour, aren't you?" asked Marlene. "I'll go tell Matron."

Marta gritted her teeth until the pain subsided. "No wait. I'm okay. I don't want to go anywhere. Leave it a few more hours. You know labour can takes ages. I don't want to bother her. It'll only make her grumpy."

"You're right about that," said Marlene.

When Sharon Naples woke matron in the middle of the night five weeks ago, Matron had been very cross with her. Sharon's labour lasted twelve hours and by the time she finally had her baby, Matron was terribly grumpy in the afternoon. Her eyes were blood shot and she had an infectious case of the yawns. Matron informed the girls that the early stages of labour could go on for hours. In future, they were to hold off any urgent call outs until the morning if it was at all possible. "Just grin and bear it. It won't get any easier. So try and get some rest if you can until the morning."

After that, they had all feared a night birth as some of the girls who'd already had their babies looked to be in terrible pain. Now Marta knew exactly how they felt. She would rather wait until a little light had dawned than risk Matron's disapproval though.

Less than twenty minutes later she found herself praying so hard for the sun to rise, and promised God if he granted her wish she would commit to becoming a Nun.

God obviously had no need for more nuns and the sun rose as usual at 7:27 am, precisely the time she was wheeled into the delivery suite at the opposite end of the home for unwed mothers.

Two hours later, and with a final excruciating push, a baby girl cried her first shouts of life. Marta lay back and rested, finally relieved from her duty of bearing a child and relinquishing her role as it's mother.

Tears streamed down her checks as a cocktail of emotions flooded her heart and mind - a toxic swamp of love, despair and grief. None of the feelings could be processed, enjoyed or considered for any length of time or they would surely overcome her and lock her inside her head.

She wanted to see her baby, to hold her, to know that she was all right. But she would never have the chance to bond with her baby, to see and touch her own flesh and blood. All that was left to hold onto were the bed sheets.

"It's for the best," they said. "It doesn't help you or the baby to have contact, and then be torn apart. Better the bond be severed at the umbilical cord than later from your arms." Keeping a mother's maternal instincts from taking root was considered, best practice, but she wondered if it ever really worked the way the doctor said it did.

The stories from girls who'd had their babies, offered testament that 'best practice' was a joke. Most of them felt sad and empty and were not at all unaffected by the whole experience. Marta wondered how she would fare, now her time had come. The only thing she could liken it to was feeling like a limb was missing, a sensation of feeling it was there, but no evidence to back it up. It was as though she'd left a big chunk of herself in that delivery room. Not just in the actual physical sense. Yes a living human being had been removed from her body. But along with it went a small piece of herself. What part, she couldn't quite put her finger on. But it was definitely gone and her body's response was a constant reminder that it was a part she would probably never ever get back.

In the next few hours she had expressed off a few mils of milk and then been washed and bound snuggly about her waist. It felt like the nurses were trying to convince her she was back to her old self, long before it would actually be true (if, in fact, she ever did return to the way she once was).

Peter sent her flowers and they were a sweet reminder that he still did care about her. Matron had put them in a glass vase and relayed that Marta could return home in about three weeks, when her body was more fully recovered.

More presently concerning were the size of her well expanded breasts. The swollen masses resembled two giant trough floats as she sat in the bath tub, bobbing about her chest without a hint of their former glory. Fitting them into her brassiere was like trying to fit a size sixteen body into a size ten swimsuit. It was of little concern to the nurses who continued to bind them flat, no matter how painful it was. She did hope that all the bandages wouldn't flatten her shapely curves too much. They had been one of her best features. Her freckles on the other hand, if being pregnant could have removed those, then the whole thing might actually have been worth it. Still they remained, although they did seem to have faded a little.

In order to avoid any chance of the baby being offered up for adoption to another couple, Peter had contacted the Social Welfare department and had the adoption papers drawn up himself. He had added legal clauses which would seal the adoption records shut for the remainder of the baby's life. As far as Peter was concerned, the baby would only be known as the child of Thomas and Iris Johnson. He had submitted a request for a birth certificate to be issued without any record of the birth-parents' names. Marta suspected he did so more for his own benefit than for hers, or the child's for that matter.

Two days after their little girl was born, the papers had arrived and were shuffled in front of her by Matron with a pen to sign. Dutifully she had done what was asked, but all the while with the greatest reluctance, knowing she would never get to see the baby again.

The day Tom and Iris came to pick up their new baby girl, Peter collected Marta from the ward and took her for a walk in the hospital garden, likely to distract her. She wasn't much in the mood for talking so she left it to Peter instead.

"She's so beautiful, Marta. She has your nose and lips and my eyes. I know this is hard, but it's for the best. You'll come to agree once you return home and settle back in. Our little girl has the best parents a child could hope for. She'll do well with Tom and Iris. You've got a bright future ahead of you too. You'll be able to do whatever you like with your life now. You're pretty good with your hair, why don't you become a hairdresser? Your mother would probably like that. Those girls in Masterton could learn a thing or two from you." Peter looked as though he wanted to touch her hair but he tucked his hands in his pockets instead.

Marta liked his suggestion and thought it was at least worth considering. She hadn't given much thought about what she would do when she returned home. Mum had instructed her to learn French while she was in Auckland, but she hadn't the patience for it and given up only two pages in to the book. Sharla had taught her the few phrases that she knew of, but she hadn't a clue what they meant.

Peter reached inside his jacket and pulled out a white envelope. He handed it to Marta and she accepted it without checking what might be inside.

"It's just a bit to get you home safely and with a few new things. Your friends might not believe you spent the summer in France if you don't return with at least a few new dresses."

Marta said nothing and just looked at him. She wasn't sure if she should be grateful or annoyed by his gift. It felt more like payment for services rendered than generosity.

Peter kicked at the ground and she couldn't tell what thought might be consuming him. Finally he broke the silence once more. "Let's head back shall we? No point in dragging things out. I'm due for dinner at my parents soon."

It was the first time Peter had ever mentioned his parents. Marta wondered who they were and if they knew that Peter had a child. A child that was no longer theirs anymore, and a grandchild his parents might never know existed.

"What's your mother's name, Peter?" Marta's words sounded sharp. They obviously cut Peter because he jumped a little in fright. "The cat hasn't got your tongue then?" He joked. Marta tried not to smile. Her desire to reward Peter's jokes with such a gesture had vanished. Strangely all she wanted to do was hit him. Hard. Right in the face. Everything about him seemed so smug and arrogant. She wouldn't of course - hit him. She couldn't. She still loved him, even though she hated him right now.

"My mother's name is Valerie. She doesn't know about the baby, and she never will. She would be very cross with me if she did."

"Well that would make two of us then," she scowled and shoved him in the chest. He stumbled backwards, keeping his hands firmly in his pockets. He bowed his head, and she strode off without looking back.

She never looked back and she never saw Peter again.

As Marta neared the entrance of the hospital she spotted Tom and Iris leaving, Iris cradling their new baby in her arms.

Marta concealed herself and started a film rolling in her mind, recording every detail from the baby's bonnet on her head to the stockings on her legs and the wide smiles on both Tom and Iris' faces. Every muscle in her body wanted to run up to them and grab her baby back. But instead she stood very still and silent. Her mind screamed so loud she could hear no other sound than that of her baby's cry. Tom and Iris tucked themselves into their car and drove away.

It was over. Really over, and there was nothing for Marta to do but go home.

Monday 19th September 1960

Marta's face turned red in front of the class.

"I'm sorry, Sister Fletcher. I don't know what you mean. I didn't hear those words very often while I was away. My Aunt liked to stay in places where they spoke more English. I hardly got to practice my French because everyone wanted to practice speaking their English with me."

Marta wished her mother hadn't made up such a lie. It made it virtually impossible to slip back into her old life. Half the town expected stories about all her travels, and the other half just wanted her to say something in French. Her useless attempts at some basic phrases were so bad that Sister Fletcher suggested she would have been better off staying in school. Sister Fletcher was the hardest of anyone in town to fool as she had travelled extensively through Europe before moving to New Zealand. Marta made a point of finding any excuse to be elsewhere if Sister Fletcher was around. Not the easiest task when she saw her practically every day.

Although Marta had become better at lying she still found it difficult when put on the spot. Her poker face was hardly well practiced. Spinning a yarn was one thing, but biting her bottom lip and blushing were two tells she'd not yet conquered. Not that she cared much. She didn't care much about anything anymore. Secretly she wished that everyone knew the truth so she wouldn't have to pretend she was fine. The look on

Mum's face when she suggested she just tell everyone was one of severe panic.

"No one must ever know, Marta. Do you understand me?" Mum clenched her fingers around her arm and glared at her with eyes like hot pokers. "No one. Got it!?"

Why would it bother her mother so much if someone found out? There would be talk of course, but Mum was used to being the topic of gossip. There had been all sorts of rumours about her mother over the years. Mum weathered them all, and generally, most of the other women in town respected her, at least in public.

"If people knew that you'd had a baby out of wedlock you'd be known as 'easy' and believe me that's not a reputation easily denied or overcome. I was given that label once by someone I trusted. She told everyone that I was like the town bike, anyone could have a ride. She made me sound like I was a whore, and that if other girls didn't watch out, I'd be after their fellow too. It wasn't true. But it didn't matter. Once a rumour gets started it's nigh on impossible to correct. I don't want you to have to suffer as I did. It was one mistake. You shouldn't have to live under it for the rest of your life. It's best if people don't know. So please, be a good girl and keep your mouth shut, for all our sakes."

Mum wasn't just concerned about Marta's reputation, but also her own. Mum was certainly well talked about in town. She was brazen and outspoken, not to mention so stunningly beautiful that others found it hard not to notice her, or what she was up to. It was the sole reason Marta thought it would be all right if people knew the real story. Mum would explain and everyone would go about their business as usual. Mum's stern warning, however, made her rethink the situation. She would have to keep the baby a secret. If not for Mum's sake, then for Dad's.

He was neither happy nor relieved to see her home again. The fact that she had done as he requested and given the baby up for adoption didn't seem to soften his disapproval of her immorality. His annoyance at her frequent teary outbursts at home only exacerbated the situation. All she could do was keep her head down, attend church, and attempt to keep her tears in check.

Sunday 9th October 1960

Everything seemed to be returning to normal once the initial transition was over. People stopped saying "Bonjour" when she met them in the street, and Sister Fletcher stopped eying her with suspicion every time she asked Marta to answer a question in class. Mum and Dad continued in their jobs, and the boys were doing all right too.

Everything was fine until today. It had been four weeks since she'd returned from Auckland and Sundays were usually a day of reprieve. Everyone made an extra effort to be kind to each other - even Dad. So the luncheon to be held at church after the service was no cause for concern. That was until Mrs Fitzherbert loosened her lips in the circle of women she was sitting in, Marta and Maggie included.

"I'm not one to gossip, but my sister rang me last night and asked if it was possible for us to host a young girl for a few months. Seems she's got herself in a bit of trouble" - she frowned and muttered - "Of the mothering variety. Of course I said I would consider it. I am after all a willing servant of the Lord. It's a Christian's duty not to lay judgment on those too stupid to know better. Poor girl. She's only seventeen. I do hope the townsfolk won't scorn her too badly."

Marta's hairs on the back of her neck stood up and she looked at her mother. Mum met her panicked stare only for a moment but gave no reassuring nod.

Mrs Dawson replied, "It's not for us to judge. The Lord alone will judge her on the day of reckoning."

The topic was hence forth discussed at length among the other church ladies.

"I don't know what's happened, but today's young people are so reckless."

"I agree. They give no consideration to the consequences of their actions."

Marta lowered her head and plucked a fingernail. She was so caught up in eavesdropping on the various conversations around her that when Mrs Dawson asked her a question, she froze. "You left town for quite a while, Marta. You didn't have a baby while you were in Paris, did you?"

Marta's face turned pink and she bit her bottom lip. To be asked so blatantly about her baby had caught her off guard and she had no words to say. Worried she might stutter in denial of the question, she did the only thing she could think of. She ran out the door of the church and as far away from Mrs Dawson as she could get. Which, as it turned out, was worse than if she had tried to reply.

According to her mother, all the women stopped their conversations and awaited her response. She attempted a dismissal stating what Mrs Dawson had suggested was outrageous. But the only thing that the ladies could really judge the situation by was Marta's prompt disappearance.

From that day, rumours about where Marta really was for six months began circulating, gathering momentum at every street corner.

"It certainly wasn't Europe," said Mrs Heslop, who had been known to gather information from Sister Fletcher about the girls at school. (Under the guise that she might better be able to pray for them of course). "She doesn't know a lick of French after six months abroad and when she was asked about the Louvre, she hadn't a clue what it even was. I tell you, that girl did not spend even one month in Europe. I doubt she even has an aunt."

From then on Mrs Heslop made sure that every woman in town knew about Marta Ingles and where she suspected Marta really went.

Mum kept up her denial at every meeting she attended and rebuked any woman who tried to tarnish Marta's name. There was no evidence to their rumours after all.

That was until Jimmy, her youngest brother who was only eight, admitted to his friend Frankie that he didn't think he even had an Aunt Rosemary, and that he only knew his sister had gone to Auckland. That set the cat amongst the pigeons, the sparrows, and the ducks in the park pond too.

Now, wherever she or her mother went, they were whispered about in every corner of the room and every shop doorway. Marta was distraught with shame, but Mum handled it better. That was until they were accosted by Mr Young, a well known sheep-shearer, outside the hardware store one Friday afternoon.

"I see the apple doesn't fall far from the tree there, Maggie. You up for it? I'm all alone now since Jackie died. No one need know. The girl can come too if you like."

"You dirty bastard. Go stick your filthy undies up your own arse, Barry Young! And don't you dare speak to me or my daughter that way ever again. You do, and you'll find out just how far a little rumour can travel." Mum gave him an eye, pouted her lips and waved a single pinkie finger at him. Marta didn't understand what the gesture meant but Mr Young did.

He promptly shook his head and crossed his arms across his chest, "Uh… Sorry Maggie. I…ah…only meant it as a joke."

"Well no one's laughing, Barry. And the only joke around here is you, you mangy moron!" Mum's hot head all but exploded with another string of unsavoury descriptors, some even made Mr Young blush. As shocked as Marta was, she listened carefully, enjoying Mr Young's recoiling response. It was the first time she had heard Mum batter another man verbally. Dad copped it occasionally, but Mum always apologised and never let it escalate into something worse. Mum would certainly have to pay penance for what she'd said to Mr Young. Although the situation was awkward, Marta loved how her mother stood up for herself. She hoped she too would one day have the confidence and courage her mother possessed. No wonder people envied her. Mum had the nerve of a bull, and it was one that most others lacked. If Marta had any hopes of becoming like her, she needed practice, and lots of it. Her dreadful performance in front of the ladies at the church luncheon was nothing short of an embarrassment. Why hadn't she held her ground? They had no real proof.

After their run in with Mr Young, Marta was more determined than ever to grow a thicker skin. Her reputation was at stake and if anyone thought they could tarnish her name with their silly opinions, she'd make sure they got a dose of their own medicine.

Each night before bed, rather than say her prayers, she'd practice her insults and comebacks at home in front of the mirror. Sometimes she'd go for a long walk on the farm and hurl abuse at the wind, or a cow, or even a stray fence post. Not even the rabbits were safe. Even though her ability and confidence had grown, her courage to test them out within earshot of Dad hadn't. His punishments were far more terrifying than those dished out at school. The Sisters were quick to admonish her answering back, and great effort went into shaming her when she stepped out of line. But she would rather write lines and wash chalk boards than be slapped by her father.

Early on she'd forgotten where she was, and muttered something about how he and the boys hadn't a clue about cooking and wouldn't survive a day without her or Mum looking after them. Dad came down on her like a felled Macrocarpa, and left the sting of his hand on her cheek.

"You little brat! You may not be my own flesh and blood but I am still your father! Don't you ever speak to me like that again, or I'll toss you out on your ear so fast, the only thing you'll remember is the slam of the door in your face."

His words were more painful than the slap to her face.

Not his flesh and blood? What did that mean?

Confused and hurt, Marta withdrew inside herself hoping his words might be forgotten. The only way to express her pain became the very thing she had wanted to master. Sass.

That was until Sister Fletcher decided Marta's verbal outbursts had become intolerable and required a more fitting deterrent. A firsthand experience of having her mouth washed out with soap and water remedied the situation for a while. At least until Marta figured out how to use sarcasm and innuendo in place of blatant profanities.

Things became strained at home, and Mum and Dad argued more too. She could barely remember the last time they actually smiled at each other.

Then one night, without warning, Dad announced that he had sold the farm and they were moving to Scotland before the end of the year.

Mum was crying and so was Harry. They both had a lot invested in their lives and friendships in Masterton. The only one who didn't seem to mind was Jimmy, and he had a string of questions a mile long.

Dad answered them all calmly and when Jimmy seemed satisfied, Dad continued.

"I'm tired of all the talk and this nonsense. Mr Kendall, next door, has made a generous offer for the farm and I've accepted. Mum and I agree that it's best if we leave Masterton. We can make a fresh start somewhere completely new. Somewhere where no one can tie our name to anything unsavoury. We should have left years ago."

Mum's next flood of tears suggested she wasn't in as much agreement with Dad as he implied.

"Pull it together, Maggie. You'll come to like it in Scotland. It's pretty much like it is here and we can still farm a bit of land - me and the boys. You'll see. You'll make new friends, and Marta...well, she won't be able to cause us any more trouble. I'll see to that."

Marta wondered what Dad meant by his last comment, but she dare not ask, fearing the truth more than her own speculation.

PART THREE

2017

London –

United Kingdom

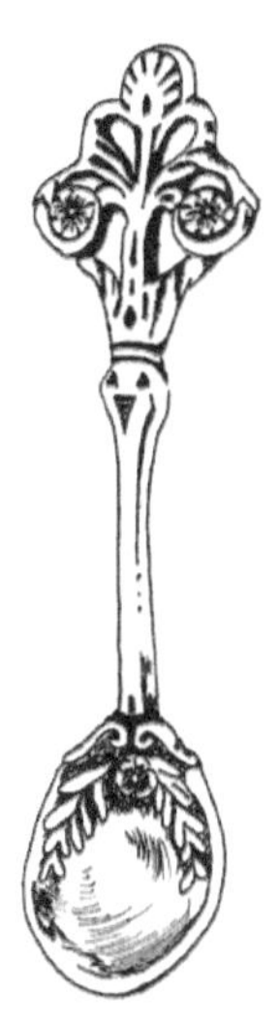

CHAPTER TEN

Tuesday 22nd August 2017

CHLOE BLINKED HER eyes when the main cabin lights turned on and the captain's announcement of their descent came crackling through the aircraft's PA system. Hostesses bustled down the aisles handing out hot moist facecloths in a last ditch effort to wake those passengers who had actually managed to get some sleep during the flight. Chloe cricked her neck and ran fingers up each side of her vertebrae, attempting to free up the muscles. A pair of tongs offered a steaming rolled towel. She unravelled it quickly and placed it over her face. The towel, performing its magic, wielded her brain back from the dead, and her eyes took a slap of cold air soon after. She was definitely awake now.

Reality dawned and her dread of arriving in London returned. She'd watched the TV shows about Heathrow, Britain's busiest airport, and felt at least a little prepared to run the gauntlet of arrival procedures. But as passengers around her confidently prepared themselves, readying passports, bags and every other attachment they'd brought along, Chloe couldn't bring herself to do anything.

What would happen if she just refused to disembark? Would they leave her on board and send her wherever the plane was headed next? Unlikely. And who knows where she might end up if they did. The thought of staying on board the aircraft vanished when the fatigue of her almost three day journey made a comeback in her memory log. Twenty-one hours she'd been travelling since leaving Auckland. And that didn't include the seven hour lay-over in Sydney to meet Peter.

She'd been very lucky to meet him, and his reception of her couldn't have gone better. But now the novelty had disappeared and all she could think of was the daunting task of finding the right train to get her to where she needed to go next.

Chloe stood and went to the bathroom to see if she bore some resemblance to the human who had boarded the flight in Sydney. Her hair hinted something wasn't right. She took a comb to it and after a few strokes it came to order. She leaned into the mirror. Her sunken eyes wore heavy shadows from the cubicle's overhead light. It made her look sick. No doubt airport health officials would pull her aside and ask if she had been in contact with anyone with the flu. Or, more to the point, was she in fact feeling ill herself.

Chloe washed her face again with marginal improvement over the steamy towel. Taking out her nude tinted compact powder she brushed it over her face in sweeping circles. Squeezing the brush flat she took a bit more dust and angled it onto her cheek bones and down her neck. There. At least now she had some colour. Picking a deeper shade of bronze shadow she brushed it lightly on the bone of her brow - giving her eyes some warmth. Lastly, she smeared her 'Flatout Fabulous' lipstick across her lips and puckered them at the mirror. Her mask now complete and no longer looking like a corpse, she felt a little more prepared to fake her way through customs as an actual human being. Settling herself back in her seat she fastened her seatbelt and felt ready to make contact with the planet once more.

Rubber bounced along the tarmac and Chloe's tummy rolled in response. She hoped she wouldn't throw up. Remembering the food trays that were being collected when she awoke, she was probably just hungry. Breakfast sounded pretty good right about now. Or perhaps it was lunchtime? But finding food was the least of her concerns. The mysteries that lay ahead in the queues of arriving passengers took precedence over stomach grumblings.

When the final approval of her two year work visa landed with a thump of ink in her passport, Chloe felt almost euphoric, like she'd graduated teachers college all over again. Walking as if floating on a cloud, the other passengers streamed past, overtaking her like she were a vintage caravan on holiday. Strolling her hand luggage towards the baggage claim she caught sight of the family of five that had been on her flight. They were now entangled in a heated debate over whether they should get luggage carts for their bags or not. Chloe beamed a smile at the probably three year old who was stamping her feet and about to have a tantrum the size of Hurricane Harvey (which incidentally had stalled over the Yucatán Peninsula but could develop into a category 4 at any moment). Chloe giggled when the child spotted her staring. The little girl didn't seem to know whether she should continue with her performance, or smile back at Chloe. She opted for both, giving Chloe a cheeky grin and proceeding to escalate her tantrum in both volume and velocity.

Chloe couldn't help but laugh out loud.

Distracted by the escalating drama, she didn't see the male passenger with his cup of coffee about to cross her path. Two more seconds and she would have missed him altogether. Alas she didn't.

Hot liquid seeped through her shirt and they both leapt backwards from their accidental encounter.

She inhaled sharply and tugged the shirt away from her chest. Only then did she looked up to see the damage she'd caused. The guy wasn't as badly soaked, but his hand was wet and he shook it before patting it dry on his shirt tail. She was mortified.

"Oh No! I'm so sorry, it was my fault. I wasn't looking where I was going." Chloe clenched her teeth in a 'finger's crossed' kind of smile. She kept her top angled from her chest and searched in her bag. "Ah here. Let me help clean this up." Chloe pulled a rogue but unused tissue from her bag and began pressing it against the splosh of coffee on the guy's pale blue designer sports shirt.

Her simple gesture caught him off guard. But once the initial shock wore off, he put one hand in his shorts pocket and proceeded to watch her hand on his chest with interest. His grin went from third to first gear in a matter of seconds. She ceased her dabbing and her cheeks flushed pink.

"Don't worry about it, luv. It'll wash out. It's just coffee." His eyebrow cocked and a smile creased his cheeks like speech marks at the corners of his mouth.

Wow! This guy could melt the ice at Scott's base. Chloe dipped her eyes fearing he would see how strong the magnetic pull was for her to look at him.

Don't look, don't look. Do something else, anything else.

Chloe pulled at her sodden top again and assessed her own damage. She looked around for a sign to the nearest restroom.

The guy gulped what little liquid remained in his cup and then crushed it in one hand. "Look, I'm the one who should be sorry. They ran out of lids and I should have been more careful. Are you all right. Can I help? You're not from around here are you?"

"No. No I'm all right. I can manage." Chloe's face warmed but her voice still wavered.

His forehead wrinkled and his razor blue eyes searched her with concern. "Nah, Com'on. Come with me and we'll get you cleaned up. We can't 'ave you arriving in the great city of London looking like a drowned rat when it isn't even rain'n. The bathroom's just over there." He pointed with the crushed cup.

Her sheepish grin seemed to be all the permission he needed to usher her towards the restrooms. The touch of his palm on the middle of her back radiated heat and she felt like a ship being nudged to a safe harbour. She smiled in gratitude before entering the ladies restroom. He'd likely be gone by the time she was finished.

She entered a stall and grabbed the spare top from her hand luggage, thankful Danielle had suggested she pack one in her carry on. How was her sister always right about these things?

Chloe exited the stall and checked herself over in the mirror. She reapplied her lipstick and fluffed her hair. The guy was probably long gone, but secretly she hoped he wasn't. He was the first genuinely kind person she had met and her terrible first impression needed rectifying.

There he was, glued to the same spot she'd left him. Her heart fluttered. Anxious yet excited to speak with him again, she caught his eye and waved. He was talking to some girls, but he looked pleased to see her. He urgently waved her over. She hoped he wasn't just some creep playing a politeness card, only to see if she was an easy target. He hadn't come across as that sort of guy though, and seemed like he actually cared. It didn't hurt that he was hotter than the coffee she'd just ruined. Even though his eyes were alluring, she couldn't help but put her sensors on high alert. She felt like an antelope leaping about the plains of the

African Serengeti hoping to survive her next encounter with a cheetah or lion. 'Adult-ing' was much harder than expected and her next task: navigating the extensive rail network of London, seemed insurmountable right now. It's a wonder she hadn't already sat on the floor of the airport and had her own meltdown. She needed a friend, even if they were just a temporary one.

Chloe wove herself through the bustling crowds, taking more than a few seconds to reach him.

"Hey, there you are, sweetheart," he extended his arm for Chloe to stand beside him. She hadn't a clue why, but let him rest an arm over her shoulder. He nodded at the teenage girls he'd been chatting with. "Well, it was nice meeting you." His polite dismissal was a welcome relief. The girls walked away happily giggling and looking back over their shoulders at them. His term of endearment hadn't gone unnoticed and Chloe wondered what kind of game he was playing at. He turned from waving at the girls.

"Sorry. Thanks for saving me. You...you look"- his eyes swum in hers for a prolonged moment before dropping to her chest - "much..." - He splayed a wavering palm at her pale green t-shirt - "dryer." Chloe sensed he was more nervous than before.

He turned his palm and offered it to her.

"Hi. My name's Matt."

Smooth move.

She shook it, and squizzed him with bemusement.

"What I meant to say was, you look - *very* nice." The movement of Matt's mouth as he emphasised the v, along with the glint in his eye, halted her thoughts, and her heart thumped a little harder. "Can I offer you a lift? I have a ride waiting. I can take you wherever you wanna go."

Matt. Chloe liked the name. Matthew or Matty never sounded as nice as just plain Matt. He looked like one too, homely and warm with a hint of mischief. His face wasn't as chiselled as Jeremy's, and nor did he have the dimple in his chin that she'd grown to think of as sexy. A clean-shaven man was Chloe's preference and Jeremy happily obliged. He said he thought it unprofessional of men who didn't anyway.

So, her attraction to Matt's neatly trimmed facial hair was unusual and yet oddly intriguing. Maybe she liked it because her father had a moustache. She'd never known him without one, and a memory of stroking her fingertips over it when she was very young came to mind. Her heart warmed. The hairs in Matt's moustache were much shorter than Dad's, but it still framed his thin upper lip in a similar way. The exception being Matt's draped further down the corners of his mouth too, much like a garland over a fireplace mantel. Matt also had a small, but wide, tuft beneath his thick lower lip - which looked more like a shadow than actual hair. A small amount framed his whole jawline, jutting in slightly at his cheekbones and on his chin too. What would it feel like to kiss him? The thought caught as a lump in her throat and she sent her attentions further north as distraction. The only problem was there was more glorious hair up there too. Longish tresses of sun-kissed brown hair, tousled up and to one side with short side burns combed forward. If Chloe hadn't seen the great city of London from above, she could have sworn she'd just landed on a stormy Caribbean island.

She moistened her lips with her tongue and realised she was staring - completely deaf to every word he'd spoken.

"Where are you headed? A hostel or hotel? Honestly, I don't mind. In fact you'd be doing me a favour. I hate making small talk with the driver. They always ask how my holiday was, and this time it was rubbish. I really don't want to talk about it or pretend I had a great time."

Chloe watched his lips move but not a sound from his mouth was making any sense. She knew she'd have to say something soon as Matt was beginning to look a little disappointed.

"Uh, I'm staying with a friend in Holloway."

"Well that's not far out of the way at all. I'd be happy to give you a ride."

Chloe heard him this time. He didn't seem keen for their meeting to end, but why?

Maybe he liked her too. Was she silly to hope that he might? He wasn't creepy, but he was dangerously attractive. Chloe flipped her hair through her fingers and hunted through her list of dos and don'ts that Danielle had recited to her over and over before she left. Nothing came to mind with resounding alarm bells, apart from 'don't accept rides from strangers'. She'd have to remedy that and fast.

Chloe held out her hand. "I'm Chloe, by the way. I'll accept your offer for a ride. So long as you promise not to abduct me and sell me as a sex slave."

Sex Slave!?! Good grief. Had it really only taken her three minutes to say something she regretted instantly? Her giggle afterward carried more nerves than she wanted, but that's because she was genuinely nervous.

Matt looked straight into her pupils. They were probably dilating given their close proximity. Heat rose to her cheeks once more and she glanced sideways, biting the edge of her bottom lip. She prayed he wouldn't respond to her sarcasm with a sarcastic joke of his own. She didn't think she could trust herself to read his real meaning if he did.

"I would never do a thing like that. People who do that are just sick and demented. But with a face like yours, Chloe, you're wise to keep your wits about you." Matt lifted his brow as if complimenting her scepticism.

Chloe had to look away, his gaze kept making her temperature rise and she feared she might overheat or worse, pass out. Then where would her wits be?

During her ride in the back seat with Matt, Chloe learned he was a professional football player, and he was returning to train for their upcoming season. She tried to listen to his friendly chatter but with her eyes preoccupied by the sights out the window it had been difficult to pay really close attention. She hadn't meant to be aloof, but he thanked her anyway for not asking him any questions about his terrible holiday. The truth was she didn't really care. She was finally here. She recalled the times she had watched Prince William on T.V waving from the balcony of Buckingham Palace. Back then she had promised herself that if she couldn't marry a prince then she would at least visit the palace one day. It was a silly school girl fantasy but, nevertheless, it had brought her around the globe to this very day and given her enough confidence to actually come and see London for herself - in person (not just via Google's satellite maps).

Strangely she was relieved Jeremy wasn't there. His pessimism had endeavoured to ruin many of their trips and it was only because she was able to laugh off his pithy comments that either of them could smile and enjoy themselves at all. He definitely needed her more than she needed him, it was so blatantly obvious now.

With him now out of the picture, so was his personal raincloud, unable to drench her good mood. Now she could enjoy it all. The red brick and white stone buildings, pointy church spires, double-decker bus-sized billboards, and every unique shade of human one could possibly imagine. Every opportunity would be experienced through her rose mirrored sunglasses and not one drop of rain would ruin it for her, no matter what weather was forecast. Although Jeremy's company gave her the reassurance and confidence she often lacked, being free of his disposition focused her effort to become more self-reliant in that area of her life. She had done well so far, basing her verdict on the fact that she was still able to function relatively normally and hadn't fallen to pieces on the flight over.

Matt was very kind to offer her a ride and she would definitely make sure he knew how grateful she was, but as she gazed out towards the city's skyscrapers she knew she would have found her own way there if she'd been left to her own devices. Danielle would be waiting for her call once she reached Joy's place and achieving that first milestone preoccupied her thoughts. Well that, and the amazing smell of Matt's cologne.

Matt's driver didn't seem to be in a hurry to reach her destination, but Chloe felt sure they would get there eventually. So when Matt mentioned a quick detour her heart skipped a few beats and her worry bugs found their way back into her conscience.

"I promise it won't take a minute. I just thought you might want to see it, that's all."

'See what?"

Matt's top lip curled spreading the whiskers above wider. "You'll see."

As they rounded a corner on what seemed to be just another ordinary street Chloe wondered what on earth he so desperately wanted to show her. Edging their way down a long street with a convoy of other London commuters, a distinct golden statue and set of buildings came into view as they neared the end.

"Is that..." she tugged her seat belt loose and shuffled towards the middle. She leaned in, hovering her head over Matt's lap for a better view out his window. "...Buckingham Palace?"

Matt sunk backwards and nodded. "Ah-huh."

"But how did you know I wanted to see it?"

"Pretty much every tourist does. I figured I'd save you the trouble and give you a quick drive by." He cleared his throat and looked down at her with an impish grin. "Is it what you expected?"

Too enamoured by the stones of the Palace walls, she hadn't registered her awkward position. She sat up. "It's lovely. But it's not quite a castle is it. I really want to see some castles while I'm here. And…I'm not a tourist. I have a job. I'll be teaching at Millfields Community School." She swung a glance at him and caught him staring. Meeting his eyes momentarily a tight wave of heat surged up her neck. She shuffled herself back toward her seat and fixed her attention to the car in front. "I start in two weeks. I came a bit early so I could see some of the sights and find my way around the city." She looked to her left and then cranked her neck hard to look out the rear window for one last peek at the shrinking Palace. "I…" She was about to say that her boyfriend was meant to come too, but as Jeremy was no longer part of her life, she changed the subject "…I'm glad we came this way. Thanks for showing me, Matt."

"Well I'd love to show you around some more if you'll let me. I train most days until around three, but after that I'm free. Except for Thursdays. I coach a kids football team on Thursdays." Matt's grin widened.

Chloe liked that Matt seemed grounded for someone clearly used to being in the limelight. Just before they got in the car at the airport, a boy and his sister, along with their father, asked for his autograph. Matt offered to have his picture taken with them too. It was then that she cottoned on that Matt was a little more than just a random guy she ran into at the airport.

Curiosity burrowed a tunnel in her thoughts. *Just how famous is Matt Knightly?*

She held no great prejudice against famous people. Matt seemed genuinely nice about it, not full of himself or glamorous like celebrities on magazine covers in hair salons. Rugby boys back home were nice enough, but she'd never met any of them in person. The only thing she could remember about the New Zealand soccer team right now was that they were called the All Whites. Which was a nice change from Black, but seemed a bit silly really. The fact that the names of New Zealand's top sports teams seemed to always include a reference to the colour black was not lost on her. The All Blacks, the Black Caps, the Black Sticks, Not to mention the most controversial of them all - the Black Cocks! (She'd learned about that one at a pub quiz night in Wellington.) Almost every American she had met thought it might be offensive to label a team by the colour of the people's skin who played it. Chloe had laughed and attempted to point out that not all the players were darker skinned. But she did accept that they might have some merit to their argument since a majority were.

Soccer (or football as the British and most other nations preferred to call it) was not a sport she followed with any great interest. Rugby didn't rank much higher either. Only really big games offered a night out at the bar with friends who were hard core followers. Granddad's cricket career ended before she was born and it seemed New Zealand Cricket's golden era had come and gone with him. She could appreciate all the effort and training that went into the national sports, but she was no great contributor to it.

Pulling away from what felt like the centre of London, the car now headed alongside a river which she easily surmised to be the river Thames.

"We have a place called Thames back home, but it's nothing like this. Well the city part anyway." She continued chatting about all the various places in New Zealand she could think of with place names derived from

British places, Palmerston North included. Matt smiled and nodded, captivated by her every word. It seemed as if he never took his eyes off her. Just as he was about to start up a new conversation the car pulled to a stop.

The driver turned his head. "Thirty-seven, Elstone. Here we are, Miss."

Chloe looked out at the row of skinny houses, each with its own unique door. A few had decorative windows, some gold knockers, while others had numbers, or simply a few potted plants. Some of them even had two doors, one for the upstairs portion, and one for the lower. A reference to sardines sprang to mind and she sucked in a breath in preparation for the confined living quarters. The idling car perched awkwardly to one side of the street as there wasn't a car park free anywhere.

"We can't stay long, sir, I'm double parked, sir." The driver winked in the rear-view mirror.

"Yes, Paul. We won't be a minute." Matt frowned. He was already out and around to open her door before Chloe had collected her bag and things from the floor of the car.

"Here you are, safe and sound, as promised. I hope you see now that not all Londoners are bad, and some of us can be trusted." Matt indicated the accolade went to himself in that department, standing tall beside the car. "Case in point," he said, offering his hand as she exited the vehicle.

Chloe smiled at his attempt to look gentlemanly, or was it irresistible? She couldn't decide.

'Thank you. I really am grateful for the lift. I hope your shirt doesn't stain too badly."

"Don't worry about it, luv. It wasn't even my shirt. I borrowed it off a mate. He won't notice if I don't tell 'em." Matt winked and laughed at himself a little. Chloe couldn't tell if he meant it as a joke to ease her mind, or if he was actually telling the truth.

"Well I guess this is me." Chloe said, trying to part ways politely.

He lifted her suitcases from the rear of the car and set the larger of the two on the pavement. "Ah, Chloe? Would you like to have dinner with me on Saturday?" A car tooted as it veered around them adding a sense of urgency to respond.

'That'd be nice. I don't have a UK sim-card for my phone yet, and I can't remember Joy's number here, sorry."

"That's fine. I'll come pick you up from here at seven, that okay?" His eyes sought her favour.

"I look forward to it." Chloe smiled. She wasn't sure if she should hold out her hand for him to shake, or offer him a hug. Both seemed out of place. She felt a little sad to see her new and only friend about to leave. She reached to take her suitcase and he handed it to her. With both her hands now full, she resigned herself to a simple farewell. He gave a chuffed grin, ducked inside the car, and lowered the window. "Bye, Chloe. See you Saturday."

She set the suitcase on the ground and waved as he drove away. If everyone was as nice as Matt, perhaps London wouldn't be so scary after all.

Tilting her bags to wheel them up the steps, one twisted on a wheel and threatened to escape. Her arm wrenched and she lurched it back in line. As she was about to ring the doorbell, the door swung open.

A short, curvaceous, rosy cheeked woman with bleach blonde cropped hair appeared with a smile that beheld a fence of white teeth.

"Chloe?"

"Yes, it's me. Sorry I know I was supposed to call you when I arrived but I ran into this guy and he offered me a ride. So I figured it might save you the trouble of coming to pick me up from the station like we'd planned."

"Never mind that. Was that Matt Knightly I just saw talking to you? Is that who gave you the ride?!" Joy squinted down the street as if trying to spot the car in the distance.

Chloe nodded. "Yes. He was very nice. I didn't think he'd give me any trouble since it seems he's not a stranger to anyone else around here."

"You've got to be the luckiest girl alive, Chloe Spencer. I can't believe that of all the people in the world to meet at Heathrow, you got to meet Matt Knightly, and he gave you a ride, no less."

Joy's enthusiasm was a little over the top, but Chloe had heard that British people were big fans of their beloved football teams, and their players too. Joy pulled her inside the entrance and motioned Chloe to follow her into a sitting room.

"He's gorgeous isn't he! God, if I'd had him all to myself in the back seat of a car, there's no telling what I might have done to him."

Chloe couldn't help but giggle at her host. Joy sure thought a lot of Matt and probably a lot more lustfully than Chloe had during their ride together. Chloe glanced around the tiny room and seated herself on the grey modern sofa. Joy's taste in furnishings were not at all what Chloe expected. Unlike her host's comfy appearance, her sofa was rock hard. Chloe's body ached from the long flight and all she wanted to do was sink into a soft bed.

"He's not bad-looking I suppose." Chloe tried to sound nonchalant but only to drive Joy mad.

"You're kidding right? Well maybe where you come from that's normal. But here in the UK, Matt's a frigging fifteen. None of this nine or ten rubbish. He tops the charts and then some. Oh, you've got to see him play, Chloe. He's so determined to win and he can kick that ball like a school boy's arse. Did you give him your number? Or mine?" Joy's face held an air of hope for her own sake, rather than Chloe's.

"No, sorry. I haven't memorised your number yet. And I haven't got a UK sim-card either. I need to get one a-sap."

"Hell yeah. Otherwise how else is Matt gonna track you down again? You've got to think of all the odds, Chloe. If you want Britain's sexiest man alive to call you, then you've got to give him your number, silly."

"Well he is taking me out to dinner on Saturday."

"Really? Huh. I thought he had a..." Joy paused, then shrugged. "Well, never mind. Things change all the time. Who knows - maybe it's over. So where's he taking you?

"I don't know."

"You didn't ask?"

"No. It's just dinner. It's not like he asked me to marry him."

"I can't believe you didn't ask?! If you weren't Danielle's little sister, I'd give you an earful of what's what and who's who. But, seeing as you are" - Joy jabbed her in the arm playfully - "I'll forgive you this once. But" - she held up a finger with a stern glare - "You've got to promise to tell me all about it Sunday. Deal?" She held out her hand to Chloe. Joy was funny. Chloe liked her hobbit-like fireball host and knew she'd get along with her very well.

"All right. I promise." Chloe shook her hand. "But you've got to promise to show me around and also how to navigate the underground. Buses I can manage, but the trains - not so much. Wellington only has four main lines and they all end up in the city. But I'm guessing it's a little more complicated than that here."

"Deal." Joy dumped a heavy nod and then beamed a bright white smile. It was then that Chloe remembered her host was a dental assistant.

Chloe chuckled. "Now. Speaking of my sister. I promised I'd give her a call once I'd arrived. Can I use your Wi-Fi?"

"Sure, but first, let's get you settled in and then I'll make us a cup of tea. You look exhausted."

"You're not wrong there. I feel like a zombie. My adrenalin's spent and I couldn't stomach the thought of food until I landed. I'm sure I'd still be studying the transportation options if Matt hadn't given me a ride. Don't get me wrong, I would've figured it out eventually, but I really could use something to eat, and a shower. I didn't actually tell you how I met Matt did I?"

Chloe talked as she hoisted her two suitcases up Joy's narrow staircase and continued to relay the whole story whilst Joy pointed to where everything was. So enthralled by Chloe's tale, she wouldn't dare interrupt, except to ask for further details.

By the time Chloe retold the story to Danielle on Skype, she'd begun skipping some of the details. In particular, Matt's full name. Chloe figured Danielle would be far more interested in hearing about how her meeting with Peter went. She couldn't have been more wrong. When she finally spilled about accepting a ride from Matt Knightly, Danielle all but choked on her own saliva.

"Hold up, hold up. Say that bit again," she palmed the screen.

"Which bit?" Chloe nibbled a fingernail.

"The bit about Matt Knightly."

"Oh, that. Why? You know him?"

"Ah, ye-ah. He's only Arsenal's hottest player?"

"Well. I didn't know that."

"Oh no! And you spilled coffee on him!" A look of horror scraped her face.

"Well I didn't do it on purpose, and it wasn't even mine. The cup had no lid. I mean who carries an open cup of coffee around the world's busiest airport anyway?"

"Oh my god, Chloe. Good thing you had that spare top then." As soon as the words left Danielle's mouth Chloe knew she was out of the woods for accepting a ride from a stranger.

Chloe sighed, "Uh-huh."

"So. What did you guys talk about, in the car? He's pretty hot, don't you think? Does he still have that goatee?"

"I suppose so. Yeah, but I'm not sure I like it." Chloe loved seeing reactions to her indifference, and she'd never tire of it, no matter what supporting evidence Joy or her sister had.

"Well. He's at least a step up from Jeremy, surely?!"

"Maybe."

"No. Not maybe, Chloe. He is!"

What was it about this guy that had every girl crushing on him so badly? Had she just not truly registered how incredibly appealing he was? He looked good - yes. He smelt good - definitely. He was nice and very gentlemanly - that was confirmed. Yes on first impressions he seemed like a great guy. But Chloe wanted more than just surface attraction and good etiquette. Jeremy turned out to be not so great a guy and he had all the same things going for him as Matt, except for the facial hair of course.

"Well he did ask me out Saturday. So I guess I'll see if I agree with you after that."

"Seriously? No way! You have a date with Matt Knightly? Someone pinch me. How on earth did you get so lucky?"

"It wasn't luck, Danielle. It was an accident."

"Well don't tell him that. No one wants to be considered an accident."

"No of course not. I just meant that it's not something I planned. Seriously though. I'm not looking for a new relationship right now. I've got a job to do, and a new grandmother to find. I don't care how famous he is."

"I know. But no one would blame you for wanting to move on with your life, from Jeremy I mean. You don't need him. This just proves there are other guys out there. Don't throw away a chance at love, just because you're too 'busy' to give it another try. Think of all the things that have fallen into place so you can be exactly where you are now. I just think you're in a good space and place to move forward. At least give it a try."

Later, her sister's words chorused in her head like one of Mum and Dad's old 80's love ballads. Chloe pictured Matt's face as the steam in the shower rose to the ceiling and she let the water beat it's rhythm on her neck and chest. She was definitely attracted to him, but only in the physical sense. Maybe once she got to know him a little better his personality would have merit too. But that's not the reason she had come half way around the world. Chloe had things to do, things to see, and things to accomplish - not only for herself, but for her mother too. A man could wait. If it were truly meant to be, any man would wait until she was ready for another try at love.

CHAPTER ELEVEN

Saturday 26th August 2017

COME SATURDAY, CHLOE was more than a little anxious about her date with Matt. Every day since she'd arrived it seemed she learned some new fact about him, or had seen his image in product advertisements on billboards around the city and at train stations.

Joy had kept her promise and shown her every which-way to get about the city. Chloe seemed to pick it up all right and only came unstuck when she tried to get from Victoria to Wimbledon on the district line. She had unwittingly hopped on a train and gone completely the wrong direction. Several embarrassing conversations later with various locals and one station master, she found her way back, arriving much later than expected. Joy hadn't teased her like Danielle would have.

She'd encouraged her to just keep going, she would get to know it all very well eventually. Chloe felt a little homesick the first few days and wasn't sure if she would last a whole year. Joy's plan to take her out most nights had kept her busy to the point where she didn't get too much time to dwell on life back home.

Chloe's thrill at getting a new SIM for her phone was short-lived when she found herself being spammed by a barrage of questions from her sister about what she was doing. She didn't really mind though. Danielle's constant texts often included updates on how Mum was doing and how she and Granddad were going to see what further information they could find out about Marta. She was even going to take Granddad to Masterton for a day trip to see if he could locate where he and Peter had stayed with the Ingles family.

Chloe had spent a good hour Skyping Danielle, relaying all that Peter had told her about how he met Marta and how she had moved with her family to Scotland around 1961. Chloe was thrilled when Peter mentioned Scotland as it was possible she would be perfectly placed to continue searching for her mother's birth-mother.

Now that Saturday was here, Chloe's stomach sickened at the thought of meeting Matt again. He wasn't just a fine-looking, fit footballer, he was famous. And she was - well - just a newly graduated school teacher from New Zealand with barely an inclination to watch sport on TV, let alone actually play sport herself. What on earth would they ever find in common? She felt more intimidated than Eliza Doolittle, and, to make matters even worse, she was completely stumped about what she should even wear. She had changed three times in the course of half an hour and still wasn't sure what she had on would be suitable. For Chloe, there was always 'comfort vs. curve appeal' to consider. Striking the right combination of both was every girls' goal when it came to dressing for a date with a guy you actually liked. She had no idea where he was taking her and whether she should wear heels or flats?

Of course, Joy had voted for the calf-tightening kitten-bow pumps that Chloe had brought with her. She couldn't fault that her legs did look decidedly more sexy in them. But if he had any plan to whisk her off to a private tour of his football stadium then wearing heels would surely be a death trap. Chloe flumped herself backwards on the bed and stared at the ceiling.

"Come on. You don't have time to day dream, Chloe. He's gonna be here in ten minutes. Man, if I had a date with Matt Knightly, I'd have been ready hours ago!"

Joy was right. Chloe plucked herself up from the bed covers and smoothed down her dress. Given her dilemma, she'd opted for the black knit wrap dress on the basis of its merits, apparently it was magic. It tied just beneath her bust, offering just a hint of cleavage without looking like a hooker. The slinky knit draped nicely about her waist and floated off her hips like chocolate off a fountain. Hailed as the female traveller's highest rated companion, the 'anywhere' dress could be paired with a cardigan and flats for casual daytime wear. Or, if teamed with heels, a lace shoulder wrap, and diamante necklace, it could also suit an intimate dinner for two. Not only that, it didn't need ironing and it could be washed and dried overnight. Basically it was a one piece wardrobe, and every girl must own one, or so the lady at Danielle's party plan evening said. The whole sales pitch had her believing she would step out in style, looking like a movie star. Chloe was impressed by its versatility and been convinced by Danielle that she should purchase one, so they could get the 'buy one get the second half price' deal. Chloe had agreed and she was now grateful she had.

"So you're sticking with that then?" Joy's question raised Chloe's doubts once again.

"I dunno. What do you think?"

"Good lord, woman. You look fantastic! We can't have you leaving the house half-naked so I think you should stick with what you've got on. I'm sure Matt won't mind whatever you wear, so long as *you* are wearing it."

Joy's confidence boost was exactly what she needed to get herself on her feet, and buckle her ankles into her pumps.

"Take your flats with you if you want. Or just go barefoot. I hear Matt has a thing for girls' toes." Joy giggled.

"Are you kidding? I can't tell. Oh Joy, that's not funny."

Joy was chuckling so hard that they almost missed the doorbell.

'Shhh! Now best behaviour, Joy. Please don't embarrass me any more than I already feel."

Joy sobered up and found her serious face, only to then burst into a new fit of giggles.

"You're impossible, Joy!" Chloe marched downstairs and opened the front door, pulling a considerable amount of air inside along with it. It was cool but not uncomfortable and Matt's cologne was a memory she'd inhale any day.

Matt's eyes twinkled as the lights reflected off his ocean blue eyes. She'd not really noticed them before. Was it cliché for her to think she would probably drown in them by the end of the evening? They were certainly captivating and a lump caught in her throat. It seemed Matt was equally speechless as well.

"Wow. You look smashing." Matt finally gushed and took her hands in his own.

Chloe felt the heat rush to her neck, then finally found her tongue. "Thank you. I wasn't sure where we were going. Should I bring these?" Chloe held up her white canvas shoes.

"No I think we'll manage just fine. I've booked us a table at Lumière at the Parkway. The assistant chef, Lucas Flavigny, is a good friend of mine. I think you'll like it."

"Sounds lovely," she said, looking back up the stairs for Joy's confirmation.

"God yeah." Joy said arriving at the bottom of the stairs. "It's fancy all right. Hi I'm Joy, friend of Chloe. It's very nice to meet you, Matt." Matt shook the hand that was offered, giving a polite smile in return. Chloe worried Joy might grab him for a quick hug or a selfie but she maintained her self-control. Chloe breathed deeply and relaxed her shoulders a little.

Matt gestured to his car. "Shall we go?"

"No driver tonight." Chloe said it as a statement rather than a question. Matt looked at her a little puzzled.

"No. Just the two of us this evening. I usually only have Paul pick me up from the airport so I can be available to the fans and not have to worry about my bags." Matt's explanation, although odd, seemed logical. What must it be like to be famous and deal with other people's demands on you all the time? Maybe he would enlighten her tonight.

Joy shooed them off her front steps. "Well, have a great time tonight, you two." She waved as they got into the car and drove off.

Chloe smiled at Matt feeling a little embarrassed by Joy's fond farewell. But he didn't seem to notice or care much about that. Every chance he got he looked at her sitting next to him in the front seat and Chloe feared she would become too distracting to his driving than was safe. In order to keep his eyes on the road she asked him about all the streets and buildings they passed. Some of them she knew a lot about already and would mention random tourist book facts that she'd read on her flight over. She was smart like that. She could remember the oddest things she read from books, and people loved to ask her questions just to see what strange thing she might know about it. It's what made her so loved by the students she taught during her practicum at Naenae Primary School. Well, that and she stuck out like white chalk on a blackboard and spent a lot more time in the playground than most of the other teachers did. Kids just seemed to gravitate to Chloe. One little girl told her that she liked her because she had the prettiest long hair, just like Rapunzel. And when she grew up she wanted to be just like Chloe. Although the child was of Maori decent, Chloe wouldn't make mention of how unlikely she was to ever look that way. Instead, she told the little girl that she could look however she wanted, as long as she brushed it fifty strokes every day. She then proceeded to help the little girl with her counting. Her hair was in much nicer condition by the end of term, and the girl had learned to count right up to 100.

Chloe smiled at the memory and wondered how the little girl was getting on now. She had wanted to apply for the position at the school but was advised to get some experience teaching overseas first. It was what had sparked her idea about travelling around Europe and the UK with Jeremy.

Jeremy. Why did every thought seem to end on him? Her devastation over their breakup was warranted. She was certain he was close to proposing and had even dreamed he might do it while they were in Paris, or Venice perhaps. Now that the dream was over, she realised just how deluded she'd been. With no one to please except herself, Chloe now enjoyed the thrill of freedom and was wary of giving that up again, whether that might be to Matt, or any man for that matter. Not only did Matt have a mountain to climb, but a fiord, a desert and an ocean to cross as well if he stood any chance of winning Chloe's heart. She wouldn't try to make it difficult on purpose, but if Matt thought she was another easy conquest or a notch to his belt, then he was sadly mistaken. The unfortunate thing for Chloe was that he was fascinatingly different than any guy she'd ever dated before. Perhaps Matt felt the same way about her. Given how little she knew about him, before running him over at the airport, he had no need to present her with an altered persona of himself.

Matt's sudden interruption of her thoughts made her happy to be relieved of them, and she was determined not to spend another minute thinking about Jeremy ever again.

"Here we are." Matt pulled up to the front of a giant building which looked more like a roman palace than a restaurant. Two giant columns stood guard at the entrance alongside two formal trench-coated doormen, Chloe's mouth fell open in awe at the structure while Matt got out and went to open her door. She liked that he did that. Jere… No. No one had done that for her before. She took his offered hand and climbed out of the car all the while feasting her eyes on the stunningly grand entrance before her. Next thing she knew Matt was beside her with his arm firmly wrapped around her waist and from out of nowhere a camera flashed. Matt paid no heed to it, so Chloe followed suit. Matt led her up the wide set of stairs and the car was taken care of by one of the parking attendants.

"I think you're going to like it here." Matt's eyes flickered.

"It's… it's magical. I thought places like this only existed in France, or Italy but this is magnificent." Chloe's voice slightly echoed in the entrance hall and she wondered how often the place would be dusted. Frequently she concluded as there wasn't a spec of it in sight. Matt led her off to the right towards a set of open glass doors which welcomed visitors to the hotel's fine dining restaurant, Lumière.

Chloe was relieved she'd dressed a little more formally and wished she'd never brought up her silly shoes. Following the maître d', Chloe felt the warmth of Matt's hand on the small of her back as he guided her to their table. The heat of his touch remained until well after they were seated, and Chloe pressed her back into the chair to revel in it as long as she could. The setting was opulently faultless. From the decorated walls to the highly polished tableware, everything looked as if it were made for royalty, and she felt like a princess at a grand dinner party. Seated in a prime position at a table raised above the main central floor, the table was dimly lit and allowed patrons to take in the view over the whole restaurant and up to the glass atrium roof overhead.

I could get used to this.

Joy's jealousy was not at all misplaced. How Chloe had managed to bump into Matt Knightly and be invited to dine with him at such an extravagant restaurant was surely a fairy-tale. Or at least that's what it felt like. She pinched her arm under the table just to be sure she wasn't dreaming.

Sitting opposite, Matt watched her every move, seeming to enjoy her wonderment of their surroundings.

"Good evening, Mr Knightly. Can I get you anything to drink?" asked the grey attired waiter in an aristocratic accent. His dark brown hair was slicked back solidly and his face was so cleanly shaven that Chloe couldn't tell if he might actually be able to grow facial hair at all. He almost seemed as if he might have been wearing makeup, but maybe it was just the lighting. A lot of city men these days had regular facials and some even had their faces waxed in a bid to keep their 'look' neat and modern. The waiter's fresh face was in stark contrast to Matt's sculpted stubble and she looked at them both equally as Matt ordered the recommended bottle of wine. Matt was definitely more appealing when viewing the two options side by side. She wondered if her opinion would change if he attempted to kiss her. Her eyes glued to his lips as he whispered something to the waiter. She hoped he wasn't ordering them escargot or a string quartet, or something else equally as embarrassing. He was clearly trying to impress her and it was unquestionably working.

The waiter nodded. "I'll see what I can manage, Sir."

Manage what?

Matt's school-boyish grin made her wary.

"I've asked him if Chef Flavigny would mind giving us his recommendation for our meal in person." Matt looked as if he was about to say something else but stopped himself. He obviously liked to keep a bit of mystery going. It was a nice change from predictable Jere…boys. She shrugged as if it was neither here nor there to her and Matt chuckled.

"You're a hard one to read, Chloe. I've just realised I don't even know your surname. Forgive me for not asking you sooner. I mean, you've known my surname this whole time. It's a little embarrassing."

"Not as embarrassing as Spencer. Yup, I'm Chloe Spencer. You know, like the long sleeve undergarment. Or like Frank Spencer off 'Some mother's do have 'em'." Chloe cringed at her pitiful references. It's what her mother used to say when asked the same question. Chloe asked her mother once who Frank was and she showed her a clip on YouTube. Chloe thought Frank was funny, in an old-fashioned sort of way. She told her mother that a girl at school talked a little like Frank. Her mother laughed so hard. Chloe missed that sound, a soft tinkling chuckle, sometimes accompanied with the huskiness of Muttley if she were bordering on tears. Chloe looked off into the distance, praying Mum's health was improving. Her face must have finally betrayed her thoughts because Matt looked at her concerned.

"Are you okay, Chloe?"

"Yeah, I just miss my… home." She said, deflecting her real sentiment. She couldn't say she missed her Mum. That might sound a bit childish, even if it was the truth.

"I miss me Mum too," Matt admitted.

How did he know?

Chloe dipped her eyes sideways, embarrassed.

Matt smiled like he'd read her thoughts. "I miss her even when I'm just out of town for a game. I know, it's silly. I'm nearly 24. Even though Mum's a ball-buster, she's the reason I am where I am today. She's sacrificed a lot to give me the opportunities I've had. When I made the first grade squad, I was still in high school. The training was intense and it was really hard. I had to study at night and train during the day. She tutored me so I wouldn't fall behind. I only passed my GCSE's because of her. I don't know how she did it, working full-time, cooking, cleaning, and taking me everywhere. She's my hero. I'd be lost without her. All that work paid off, mind you. Mum doesn't have to work anymore if she doesn't want to. I told her I'd support her. But you know what mums are like. She won't let me no matter what I try. I thought she'd be thrilled to retire, but she really likes what she does. I respect her for that."

Chloe digested Matt's story and decided to pry further.

"So, what does she do?"

"She's an accountant. She used to work for a big company, just down the block from here. But when I went pro and needed tutoring she gave up all the benefits at her old firm and became a private consultant for a few smaller businesses. It suited her well and she was able to work from the road when were away for games. The lads love her and think of her as part of the team now." Matt joked.

"She sounds like a formidable woman," Chloe took a sip of water from the crystal cut glass before her.

"She is." Matt grinned.

"And do you have any brothers or sisters?" Chloe continued her inquisition.

"Yeah, I had an older brother. But he died in a car accident when I was just a toddler. I was buckled in a car seat but he wasn't. He used to take it off without Mum realising. He was killed instantly they said.

Another car struck the side of ours right where Sam was sitting. It's a blessing in a way, or so Mum says. Had he lived, he would have been badly brain damaged and wouldn't have had much of a life. Still it would be nice to have an older brother around now." Matt gazed past her as if trying to shove the memory back in his vault. "What about you, Chloe, any siblings?"

"Yes I have an older sister, Danielle. She's engaged to this guy, Mark. He's a second year junior house surgeon doctor or something like that. I dunno. He's a bit of a wise guy. I don't like him much, can you tell? Anyway they're getting married in April next year. I'm a bridesmaid, so I'll be heading back for a few weeks during term break. I just hope she doesn't choose too ghastly a dress for us. Danielle and I didn't really get along too well until just a few weeks ago actually. We've had a few more heart-to-hearts since, and also a common cause which has helped. I do wish her the best and everything with Mark. I just think she could do better."

"What's better than a doctor?"

"No. I don't mean it like that. Mark isn't around much, and I can tell she gets lonely sometimes. Anyway, she's been too busy lately, what with wedding preparations and looking after Mum." Chloe hadn't intended to mention Mum. It just sort of came out with the rest of her babbling. She grabbed for her glass of wine and sipped a large gulp, filling her mouth quickly and making it tricky for Matt to question her further. It didn't work though. He seemed very interested in anything she had to say. Since he'd shared so much about his family, he was obviously hoping for the same in return.

"Why does your Mum need taking care of, is she unwell?" He was intuitive she'd give him that. But just how he'd garnered such a talent for it was what really fascinated her.

"Uh, well... My Mum has cancer. She was diagnosed with it two years ago and she was doing really well. But a couple of weeks before I was due to fly out she collapsed, at her own vow renewal ceremony no less. It was my parents' thirtieth anniversary. Everyone was there. Poor Mum. Gave Dad an awful fright. One minute she was walking up the aisle grinning like a newlywed with that ridiculous wig Danielle got her. And the next, she was on the floor right in the middle of the church. I'm pretty sure I screamed. Dad ran so fast, I thought he might trip and fall too. But that's Dad. He never thinks about himself, just Mum."

"Oh, Chloe, how heartbreaking for you. I'm surprised you're even here."

His words stung her more than he knew. She already berated herself daily for leaving when her mother was so obviously unwell.

"I didn't want to come." Chloe bit back. "But Mum made me promise to keep on 'playing my game' she said. She wanted me to see if I could find her birth-mother for her you see, and ever since that day in the hospital I've been working on finding out what really happened the day my mother was born. She's adopted you see."

Chloe looked up from staring at the empty space where she hoped a dinner plate might soon occupy. She looked at Matt and stopped herself from chattering any further. She was getting too entangled in telling her story that she'd almost forgotten she was on a date. Matt Knightly didn't want to know about her dying mother back in New Zealand. That wasn't the sort of thing you discussed at a romantic dinner for two, was it?

"I...I don't want to bother you with all that though. This place is incredible. Let's talk about something else, shall we?" Chloe took another swig of her wine. She had better pace herself, or Matt would be scraping her up off the floor if she kept up her current rate of consumption. Chloe's eyes darted around the room, anywhere she could rest them without making direct contact with Matt's again was most preferable.

But they were drawn in an instant to his Atlantic blue eyes when she felt his hands touch hers. He cupped them between his palms.

"I'm so sorry to hear about your mother, Chloe. Truly I am. You must be finding it very difficult to be so far away from her at a time like this. I hope she'll recover for Danielle's wedding. I bet she's trying really hard to get better for it. If she's anything like my mum, she'd probably climb through hell if that's what it took." Matt's eyes were awash with such kindness that Chloe had to divert her eyes again to keep herself from crying.

Good grief. I'm a mess. Why on earth would Matt Knightly want to date me when I have so much turmoil in my life? If I were him, I'd probably be looking for the nearest exit.

'Needy' was the last thing any guy wanted in a girl they were seeing. Heck, it's probably why Jeremy had cut his losses and bailed too come to think of it. She wouldn't blame Matt if this one meal was all he ever asked her out for.

"Sorry," she ducked her head to blot her eyes on the napkin. "I might just use the ladies room."

"Sure. It's over there and to the right." He pointed. "Do you want me to come with you?"

His offer, although odd, was sweet.

"No. I'll be fine. I just need a minute."

Upon her return she was relieved he didn't push her further on the subject of her mother or life back home. Instead he seemed very keen to keep her mood as upbeat and excited as possible.

"Aw, you just missed him. Lucas was here and he recommended we try the fresh Truffle salad followed by the Venison Wellington. I went with his suggestions and ordered. I hope you don't mind. He's also got a new chocolate dessert he's been trialling. It isn't even on the menu yet. He's asked if we would mind being his guinea pigs this evening."

"Well that's just fine by me." Chloe leaned back in her seat. "I'm so hungry I could probably eat a whole deer right now." Matt burst out laughing and promptly called the waiter over to bring them some rolls to tide them over. Chloe was impressed. He obviously didn't want to risk having a mentally unstable hungry woman at a Michelin star rated restaurant. That wouldn't bode well for any potential future they might have. Chloe chomped on a roll as soon as they arrived and then lashed what remained of it with butter. She didn't care what Matt might think of her stuffing her face full of what essentially was deemed 'pauper's food'. Fancy or not, bread and butter was just the kind of comfort food she needed right now. Especially since she had drained her glass of wine and was starting to feel a little light headed.

The meal was divine. Each new flavour had been well savoured in Chloe's opinion, thanks in part to Matt, who took eating with purpose to a whole new level. She'd never seen a guy relish each subtle ingredient in his food before, or even discuss it with her afterward. Her taste buds were well tickled and she couldn't bear the thought of spoiling it with dessert. In fact, it was the first time she felt no desire to eat something chocolaty after a meal in a long time. Normally dessert was the first thing she'd look at on the menu. But since 'Chef Flavour' or whatever his name was, had offered them a treat that no one else could have, it did seem a shame to turn him down. Chloe was relieved then, when the plate that landed in front of her held a portion so minuscule that she doubted there were more than three or four bites to it.

Matt picked up his spoon to scoop up a mouthful but stopped to watch Chloe take her first bite. She hoped he wasn't one of those guys who got off on watching a girl eat dessert. She wasn't sure if denying herself the decadent pleasure would have any effect on Matt's gratification though. He seemed to be enjoying every moment of their evening together regardless of what subject or situation came up.

Stuff it. Who cares. Chloe placed the spoon in her mouth.

It melted and floated on her tongue like the tiny bubbles in a wave as the last of its waters reached the shore. Then came the dense satisfaction of rich chocolate and tart raspberries rolling between the layers of mouse and mascarpone. If Cadbury ever made a chocolate bar version of this dessert Chloe would buy the entire first batch she concluded before she'd even swallowed.

Matt grinned at her - but not in a creepy way - so it was safe to take another bite without intense scrutiny of her enjoyment of it.

"Looks like Lucas has hit the jackpot with this one," said Matt as he swiped another mouthful off his spoon.

Four glorious mouthfuls later and it was all over. Chloe felt a little cheated. Normally she'd expect to feel gluggy and about to burst if she ate dessert with a meal out. But this time, she felt fine. Content even. Happy. Yes, she felt very, very happy.

"That was de-licious. I want the recipe." Chloe demanded.

Matt laughed. "I doubt you'd be able to get it, but I'll ask him if you like."

"Oh, that's sweet of you, but if I actually tried to make something like that, it would probably turn out very differently. I am no chef."

"Well maybe I could ask Lucas if he'd give us a private cooking lesson. Would you like that?"

"Really he'd do that? I wouldn't think he'd have the time working here in this fancy place."

Chloe's words had started to slur a little. She could tell she was mildly intoxicated. She'd had two glasses of wine which was more than usual for her, but it didn't usually make her feel like this. Had the dessert been laced with some liqueur perhaps? She doubted she'd ever find out. Matt wiped his face with his napkin and as he did his face became a little blurry.

Matt observed Chloe's change in demeanour and sounded concerned, "What on earth did he put in that?"

Within fifteen minutes of them finishing dessert, Lucas stood beside them at their table. A worried look on his face.

"Uh, my humblest apologies, Matt. But it seems that I may have given you the wrong desserts. Those two had a secret ingredient that wasn't supposed to have been given to anyone. I used my own specially infused coconut oil in it, which may have some side effects…uh…how are you feeling?"

"I feel a little happier than normal but I put that down to your wonderful food, Lucas. Chloe on the other hand does seem a little more affected than me." Matt frowned. "What did you infuse it with, Lucas?" Matt's tone was strained, like he was trying hard to stay calm.

"Um, well…it has a small amount of…" Lucas whispered something too close to Matt's ear for her to hear properly, and judging by Matt's response it wasn't good.

"I wouldn't recommend driving tonight, Matt. I am so very sorry. I hope I haven't ruined your night. Please let me make it up to you. I will talk to the concierge and see if he can offer you a room for the night. No charge. I'm truly very sorry."

Chloe giggled. Was this a joke? Now she was inebriated and was going to spend the night with Matt Knightly in one of London's fanciest hotels? She began to wonder. Had Matt planned this from the start? How devious of him, she grinned to herself, much too happy to care what his true intentions were. Joy was going to tear her eyes out with envy when Chloe told her about this later.

Matt stood and seemed a little less intoxicated than she was. Chloe's alarm bells began ringing in her head when Matt came to her chair and helped her upright. Clutching her tightly about her waist the room began to move and she thought it must have been an earthquake, only nobody was screaming. She didn't mind. It felt wonderful. "Chloe, let me take you upstairs so you can rest. I promise you'll be fine. You'll feel better after you get some sleep.

Although she knew it wasn't wise on a first date to let a guy take her anywhere other than home, she did feel quite sleepy and was more than willing to lie down. She'd do it right now if Matt weren't holding her upright. She only hoped that he would be there in the morning and that she'd remember what happened.

Fortunately, he was, and she did.

She couldn't quite tell if it was morning or not given that the curtains in the room were still drawn and blocked out the most light of any curtain she'd ever encountered. It took her a moment before she remembered where she was. Fumbling in the dark she tried to work out how to turn on the bedside lamp. Once found, she flicked the switch and glanced over at the other side of the bed. It was untouched. No one had slept next to her. She felt relieved but also slightly disappointed. Not that she would have slept with Matt on a first date, or any guy for that matter. She did have some moral code. But where was he? A quick scan of the luxurious suite revealed Matt's jacket lying over the edge of a couch. It was then that the door to the room cracked open allowing a smattering more light to enter.

"You are awake." Matt's eyes sparkled and his arms glowed with a sheen of sweat. "I was wondering how long you would sleep. I didn't want to wake you. You looked so peaceful."

Chloe felt slightly embarrassed. How long had he watched her sleep? She didn't really mind though. She'd done it to Jeremy herself on occasion. To her it was a kind of endearment.

"I've just been down in the gym for a quick workout. Would you like to as well? I mean, I don't know if that's a part of your daily routine or not. I usually run 10K or so on the weekends. Just so I'm keeping my fitness up." Matt discussed his life like it was something she ought to know if she was going to be dating him.

How could she not want to date him!

Although his grey singlet was wet with sweat, it was the muscles and skin left visible that had her attention. He wiped the sweat from his brow with the gym towel draped around his neck and waited for her reply.

Chloe was a little flustered. She sensed Matt was aware it was his current state of undress that was the cause. She was almost certain he'd timed it that way. This guy sure could elicit whatever reaction he wanted from a girl. He'd obviously had a lot of practice too.

He chuckled to himself as if he had heard her inner dialogue.

Chloe, determined not to let him frazzle her, changed track and gave him her best excuse to avoid sweating profusely in front of him.

"Uh...no I don't think I need a run today. I feel like I've walked so many miles since I've arrived in London. I know there's really no need to walk everywhere, but I much prefer it to the bus or a train. I'm sure I probably won't always feel this way, once I've lived here a bit longer that is."

Matt nodded. "Well. Hyde Park is just across the road. We could take a walk if you like."

"That sounds great." Chloe smiled, and then frowned. "Oh wait. I didn't bring my flats. Blast." Why hadn't she brought them along? She could have left them in his car.

Matt walked across the room to the untouched side of the bed. Leaping over it like a country runner would a gate, he landed butt first close beside her. She was still wearing her black dress, which although bragged it never needed ironing, looked decidedly like it did right now. Matt offered his hand to help her up. He didn't seem to notice nor care how sweaty he was.

She recoiled from him, teasing, "Eww, Gross. You need a shower before I'll go anywhere with you."

He laughed and wrapped his sticky arms around her in a side hug.

Chloe squealed and tried to wriggle free. Eventually he released her a little.

"There, now that makes two of us in need in of a shower. Or…I know. How about we take a swim? The hotel has a really nice lap pool. We could just go for a walk in that if you like."

Chloe ceased resisting and twisted her eyes at him, "You're very persistent aren't you."

"Well I kind of feel like I let you down last night and I didn't get to take you where I had planned to after dinner…"

"Really." Chloe butted in. "Where were you gonna take me?"

Matt nodded and smiled. "…Well, as I was saying, I was hoping that you'd let me make it up to you today. That is…if you haven't anything else planned." The look in his eyes hinted she should put him out of his misery quickly if her answer wasn't favourable.

"Well, the only thing I had planned for today was laundry and a complete download of how our date went with Joy. I'll be glad to delay both if possible. So yes, I'm free. A swim does sound really nice. I expect the pool will be heated so that's not an issue, but like my shoes - I don't just happen to have a swimsuit on me."

"You could wear your underwear, couldn't you?"

"Matt. I don't think they'd allow me to wear what I've got on underneath this dress." Her coy eyes and soft blush had him right where she wanted him. She saw his eyes widen and wander over her body as if wishing he had some kind of X-ray vision. Chloe giggled ashamed that she had teased him so shamelessly.

"I'm only kidding, Matt. I'll wear my bra and knickers, but only if you wear yours." Chloe hadn't a clue what Matt might be wearing beneath the shorts he had on. She expected some sort of expensive silk boxer's or something like it.

He stripped down to his underpants immediately for her to inspect whether she thought them appropriate enough or not. She felt her insides flutter into a knot and tried to conceal her arousal with a hand over her eyes. "Matt!" She breathed.

"All right. I'm down to me jocks. It's your turn."

Chloe felt incredibly uncomfortable but what else could she do, renege on her own deal?

Tugging on the strings of her wrap dress. She unfolded herself from the fabric layers and stood with her arms across her waist nervously awaiting his response.

"See, it's not so bad. I knew you were hot!" Matt said assuredly. He moved towards her, but Chloe pulled away. Her body language speaking well enough for Matt to know not to come any closer.

"Well let's go, shall we. I'll go grab us some towels from the bathroom."

As Matt turned, Chloe nearly choked on her giggles, covering her mouth in a bid to try and stop herself from laughing out loud. It was no use, they all escaped along with a few tears as well.

Matt's butt cheeks rubbed together and his black thong disappeared between his flexing glutes.

Chloe didn't feel so bad now. At least her black lingerie looked somewhat like a black bikini. She wondered how long Matt would be able to swim in his Brazilian-like speedos before security showed up and kicked him out.

She'd certainly enjoy finding out, that's for sure.

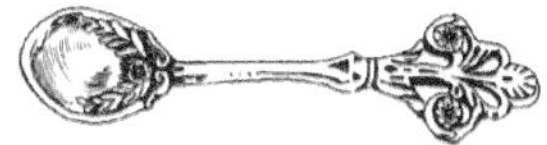

CHAPTER TWELVE

Sunday 27th August 2017

THEIR FIRST DATE had certainly been memorable, and for that she was grateful. Although she hoped Matt would want to see her again, she still hadn't decided if she should accept. Her break up was still so recent, and she didn't think it was really fair to either of them to jump straight into a new relationship. Even if her head said she was fine, her heart was trying to assert some sensibility. For now she really had to focus on what she was here for in the first place. To teach and try new experiences (and also to find her grandmother).

Matt pulled his car up outside Joy's flat. Chloe looked up at the building to see if it gave any clue of Joy's whereabouts. Not a single curtain fluttered. Chloe turned to face Matt.

"Thank you so much for…everything, Matt. It's been…surreal."

His lips curled at the edges.

"You're welcome. I've enjoyed your company a lot." His eyes and cheeks crinkled and she liked that she was the cause.

Her resolve started to melt. She had to get out of the car before all that was left of her was a giant puddle on the seat.

Matt took her hand. "So, I promised I'd spend some time with my Mum tomorrow, and then I have training to get back into. But how about I take you out Wednesday? Say around four? And somewhere not quite so fancy this time."

"So soon? Don't most guys adhere to some weird unwritten code of conduct post-date? Like, don't you have to wait three days before calling or something?"

"Well I guess that might be considered normal practice. But you're not normal, Chloe Spencer. And there's no way I'm going to let some other creep weasel their way into your life without having my own chance with you first."

Chloe's stomach flipped. Matt wanted a chance with her?

Danielle's voice echoed in her mind.

Play it cool. Don't be a beaver.

"Well, what if I have some sort of girl-code? Maybe I should make **you** wait a bit." Chloe kept a look of all seriousness in her eyes. It was a risky move, but this was how you played the game, wasn't it?

Matt looked a little stunned and she regretted playing him that way. *Who invented these silly rules anyway?*

She added quickly, "I *do* want to see you again, Matt. Just as much as you seem to want me. I mean - to *see* me." Heat rose up her neck and threatened to take her cheeks too. Chloe dropped her eyes to her knees.

Matt let go of her hand and lifted her chin with one soft finger. His steely blue eyes were alight, a precursor of his instinctual intent. He bent towards her. Her cheeks were now fully flushed and there wasn't a chance she could hide it. She had to regain her ground. So, rather than bend to meet him halfway, her hand reached towards his cheek and gave it a light pat.

"You'll keep," she chuckled, mentally crossing her fingers he wouldn't take offense. She wanted so badly to kiss him, but some invisible force held her back.

Matt's expression turned to confusion. She couldn't help but laugh out loud.

He groaned and tapped at the steering wheel. She knew she wouldn't be able to resist him the next time he attempted to kiss her, but for now she'd kept him at bay.

'Treat 'em mean - keep 'em keen' was Danielle's motto. She swore it had worked like magic on Mark. And it had certainly won Chloe Jeremy's affection. Though, considering neither of those two men were really worth winning over, she wondered if it really was the wisest advice. Chloe hated the thought that perhaps she was playing games with Matt. But Matt was, well, different somehow. She wanted their first kiss to be somewhere memorable, not inside his parked car. A first kiss was very important. If it wasn't great with Matt, it could spell the end before any kind of relationship could ever begin. It was then that she finally understood how she really felt about him. She liked him, a lot, and she wanted it to work out, if it could. For now, avoidance was in both of their best interests.

"Well, Miss Chloe." Matt's brows furrowed like a butler's. "I do hope you'll agree to see me Wednesday. I know I won't be able to concentrate on training without knowing I'll get to see you afterward."

Chloe's car door swung open by its own volition, and she jumped with a gasp. Half expecting to be held at gunpoint for her purse, Chloe clutched it tightly in her lap.

"Thank heavens you're back," Joy said, leaning her blonde tipped head into Chloe's space. "Danielle is on Skype and she wouldn't wait once she knew you were parked outside. Sorry, Chloe. She insisted I come get you. It's late over there and she wants to go to bed."

Chloe rolled her eyes. Even from half way around the world her sister still had the ability to interrupt her.

"I'll be in shortly, Joy. I was just about to give Matt my answer about another date." Chloe smiled and then frowned.

Joy's cheeks glowed with a mixture of embarrassment and excitement.

"She'd love to go on another date with you, Matt." Joy thrust a piece of paper into Matt's face. "Here's my number. Call me anytime. Day or night, I don't mind. I'm available, even if Chloe's not." Joy laughed. "Or maybe you have a friend at the football club you could introduce me to. I love a good double date."

Chloe felt the pit of her stomach sink lower into the seat. She hoped Matt wouldn't take Joy's forwardness too seriously.

"I know just the fella, Joy. I'll see if he's free."

Joy's delight was barely contained and her urgency to get Chloe inside had disappeared.

"Fantastic. Saturday good for you? We could meet at O'Leary's, you know it?"

"Let me talk to Gary first, and I'll get back to you."

"Gary Macknavern?!" Joy all but squealed, and exited the car before Matt could say anything more. Judging by the look on his face he wished he could take back his last words. Chloe laughed and patted his thigh. "You walked right into that one didn't you."

Matt smiled sheepishly and seemed to be struggling to keep his eyes on hers. "Well. I'd do anything if it meant I'd get to hang out with you again. I'll swing by around four thirty if that suits. I promise. This time there'll be no laced desserts on the menu."

"I look forward to it." Chloe leaned towards him quickly and placed a light peck on his cheek. It prickled more than she expected, but it was worth it to see his face light up in response.

Joy tugged her outside the car and Chloe gave a feeble wave goodbye.

Danielle was busy working on her nails when Chloe finally got herself seated in front of the computer.

"Hey, how's it going?" Chloe asked.

"Well, hello to you too. What took you so long? I thought Joy had forgotten I was still here? Never mind. How was your date last night? Where have you been? You didn't stay at his place did you?"

"No. I didn't stay at his place. There were just circumstances that prevented me from coming home last night."

"What? What circumstances? How big was this circumstance? Must have been pretty big if you couldn't get home last night." Danielle teased.

"Danielle, can you get your mind out of the gutter. It's wasn't like that."

"Yeah? Well what was it like then?"

"Never you mind."

"You know I'm just going to ask Joy if you don't tell me yourself. She said you'd promised to tell her every juicy detail about your date. So why not tell me too?"

"Ah...maybe later. What's up, why are you calling? Did you and Granddad find something?"

"Ugh, you're killing me. Come on Chloe. At least give me a hint. Will you see Matt again?"

"If you must know, yes. He's asked me out Wednesday, and on Saturday we might do a double with Joy and one of Matt's mates. It's not serious or anything. We're just friends. He seems nice. I just need to get to know him better."

"I'm surprised you don't already if you spent the night together."

"He's nice Danielle. I want to take things slow. I'm kind of liking not being attached at the moment. I have time to figure things out on my own, without the influence of a guy. I don't want to give that up if I'm just a fleeting fancy to him. Besides, I start my new job next Monday and that's going to take a lot of my time. Plus there's Jeremy to consider."

"Jeremy?! Why on earth would you be considering him? He certainly didn't consider you when he bailed on your trip." Danielle's words contained the bite of a protective dog. "I'm pleased you're adapting to being single again. But it's Matt Knightly, Chloe. Don't pass up the opportunity if you actually like him. You'd be hard pressed to do much better."

"Well thanks, Danielle."

"I didn't mean it like that. You're a great catch. Any man would be so lucky. I just meant, don't close yourself off to possibilities. You're there to try new things. Just think of Matt as one of those *things* you're there to experience." Danielle's cheeks bloomed.

Chloe sighed. "Can we move on please? You're tired, remember, it's late." Chloe tapped on her watch.

"I guess it is. What time is it over there?"

"You know what time it is, Danielle. Why are you stalling? Is Mum okay?"

"Yes, she's fine. They said she'll be able to come home in a few days. But that's not why I'm calling."

"It isn't? Well that's a relief. How was Masterton?"

"Well Granddad had a wonderful time reminiscing their cricket trip and we even visited Rathkeale College, where his team was hosted. There wasn't a whole lot else they could tell us though. They confirmed that Maggie Ingles did leave her employment at the college for Scotland. But beyond that they had no further information about them. Granddad took me up to where he remembered dropping Marta off at St. Brides School, but he said that the old school is gone now. We asked at the Library and they told us it was amalgamated with St Joseph's College and the girls all moved there in the seventies. There's a new primary school where the original St. Brides was. I thought the whole trip was going to be a bust until we ran into a few older locals at a cafe downtown. Suzy, one of the women, said she attended St. Brides in the sixties and I asked her if she knew of Marta Ingles."

"And, did she?"

"Suzy's smile confirmed she did before she'd even said a word. Her stories were wonderful, Chloe. I was thinking I might try to take Mum to visit her as she seemed to know an awful lot about Marta Ingles and her family. Marta had two younger brothers: Harry and Jimmy. She said it was a very sad time for the whole family when Marta's father announced they were leaving. According to Suzy, Marta's mother, Maggie, was on a few different boards in the community and the loss of her presence was felt enormously. Suzy remembered the big cricket match and the dance they had afterward too. She didn't say as much, because of Granddad I think, but I reckon she might have even seen Marta the night she and Peter - you know."

"Really!? Wow."

"Yeah. Suzy said she regretted the part her family played in the whole thing. She said that it was Marta's brother, Jimmy who spilled the beans about Marta not going to Paris. He said she went to Auckland for a while. But it was Suzy's own mother who was really to blame for fanning the gossip about Marta. Apparently she didn't like Maggie much. Suzy said that none of the mothers did. It sounded like Maggie was a bit of a flirt from what I could gather. Nevertheless, it was nice to have some more information about the Ingles' and confirm what we suspect happened."

"That's great Danielle. I've done an initial search for Marta Ingles but it's led nowhere. She's probably married and goes by another name. It might be easier to locate her brothers. What were their names again?"

"Harry, and Jimmy."

"Great. I'll also pop to the Library tomorrow and see if anyone there can point me in the direction of where to start. I hope you relayed all this news to Mum. She may not want to know her Grandmother was a woman of questionable repute, but maybe Marta was different. We're not all like our mothers, are we?"

"No. But I sure wish I was as brave as Mum, Chloe. I do try, but it's so hard keeping up appearances sometimes."

"Well then don't. Mum's not as tough as she may appear, Danielle. You don't have to wear a brave face for her. She knows it's been really hard for us. Just show her you're not as brave as she thinks you are. You'll see. She'd love to know you still need her, and her support. You are allowed to breakdown once in a while. Don't wait till she's gone. Talk to her."

"I will. Thanks. You're wising up fast little sis. Travelling suits you. I wish I was there. I really miss you."

"I miss you too. I'm so glad that you're there for Mum though. I never would have come here if it weren't for you. So, thank you."

"Nawww. Think I'm gonna cry. But enough of that..." Chloe once again marvelled at how much restraint Danielle had when it came to her emotions. "Now, there was one other thing I was calling about and I'm not sure you're gonna like it. In fact I'm not sure I should even be telling you because it's about Jeremy."

"Danielle! What? You can't say that. Now I've got to know."

"All right, since you forced me. I was visiting Mark at work two nights ago and I saw Jeremy in the ER. He was fine but he was with a girl. Apparently she'd passed out at a party and he was taking care of her, or so he said. She was okay. Mark put her on fluids and they left after a few hours observation. Jeremy said he'd take her home."

"Oh. Well. Good. Who was the girl? What was her name?" Chloe stuttered.

"Uh, Amy? Emily? I don't know, something ending in y. Anyway, that's not all. I may or may not have mentioned that you were doing great in London and that you were dating a famous football player."

"What! Why'd you say that?"

"I don't know. It just kinda came out. I wanted him to know that you were doing great without him. In fact - better than great. Awesome. Call it a sisterly reaction. Sorry Chloe. Besides, what does it matter? It seems he's moved on, and I think you should too, with Matt."

"You don't know that! I swear Danielle. If I could kick you right now I would." Chloe forced her foot into the air in front of the screen till it consumed the whole picture.

"I'm sorry. But look at it this way. He sure was shocked when I told him. He looked so worried, like he really regretted what he did to you. He deserves to feel bad for that at the very least. I'm just looking out for my baby sister."

"Ughhh." Chloe growled. "I really don't know what else to say. I think I should go before I say something I might regret."

"No wait, Chloe. Please don't be mad at me. Please. I'm really sorry. I'll never do something like that again, I promise."

"Pinkie swear?" Chloe held up her crooked finger.

"I swear." Danielle mimicked.

They both giggled.

"All right," said Chloe. Danielle's brows relaxed and she wasted no time reverting back to the big date.

"Now. Matt. Tell me everything."

Chloe relaxed back in her seat. "Joy!" She yelled.

"Yeah?" a voice echoed back.

"Come chat with us. I'm gonna spill about what went down on my date with Matt."

A faint squeal and a thud from the kitchen was followed by rapid footsteps and the door swinging open to the living room.

"I have popcorn!" She announced sliding into the couch beside Chloe.

Chloe gave a full run down on what happened at the restaurant, followed by her inebriation, or at least what she could remember of it. Both girls were horrified and so relieved how Matt handled the whole situation.

Joy shook her head. "Jeepers. You're so lucky Matt was a gentleman. Not many guys these days would be able to resist an opportunity like that."

"Heck yeah. I mean that's practically how most rape stories go," said Danielle. "Matt sounds like a pretty decent guy. Please tell me you'll at least consider dating him."

"I will. I am! I think I might like him." Chloe blushed.

"That's great. I'm sure dating Matt will make you forget all about Jeremy."

"Maybe. But I still do miss Jeremy. We were together for three years. I think forgetting him might take a little longer than a few weeks."

"Well. Maybe. But don't let that stop you from making new friends, and dating whoever you want, as long as Joy and I approve of them first of course. No tinder meet-ups unless Joy is in the vicinity. You got it?"

"Yes, Dad." Chloe saluted her sister.

CHAPTER THIRTEEN

Monday 4th September 2017

CHLOE'S FIRST DAY at her new school left her in no doubt. She really was born to teach. She loved everything about it. The children, their smiles, the challenge of getting her message across and the joy when it was received. She even loved the not so cooperative children.

The day would have been a complete success if it weren't for one slight hiccup. During lunch, Carol, one of the year six teachers, pointed to the staffroom table where a *Heat* magazine sat.

"Is that you?" she asked.

Chloe turned the glossy magazine the right way up to see what she was talking about.

Air hitched in her throat and for a second she couldn't breathe. The headline read, 'Mystery date Knight'. Heat flooded her cheeks. She wanted to deny it, but there was little point. There on the front cover was her own face, smiling next to Matt outside the Parkway Hotel.

"But how did they get this? I mean, it was only last week."

The teacher just smiled and said. "Better get used to it, Chloe. The paparazzi are crazy around here. So this thing with Matt Knightly, is it true?"

"Is what true?" Chloe asked naïvely.

"You and him stayed the night?"

"What?!" Chloe's voice carried a shrill of panic. She flipped through the pages to find the article.

"Don't worry about it. It'll be old news before you know it. Maybe just keep that out of the boss's sight for now though." Carol nodded at the magazine.

Chloe hugged the glossy pages close to her body, looking around for anyone else whose curiosity may have been peaked. Most of the other teachers were busy reading or talking amongst themselves. Carol patted her shoulder and left.

Chloe stood paralyzed for a moment and took a deep breath. The far corner of the room was empty and she made her way over to the window. From there she could see the playground with clusters of children enjoying their games together. She loved how simple life was at that age. How making friends and sharing whispers held none of the hang-ups of adulthood. Chloe glanced around the room once more before unfolding her arms and fingering through the magazine pages. It didn't take long to find the full spread article. With the pages resting against the window ledge, Chloe cupped a hand across her mouth. Her heart sank as several other photos were displayed alongside the article. The picture from the cover was used as a two page background showing a wider view of the hotel. Other smaller pictures dotted the page giving glimpses of the rest of the evening. One at the restaurant table with them holding hands. One of her cloaked in Matt's jacket, her head resting on his shoulder at the reception. The last picture near the bottom made her take an almost audible breath. A slightly blurred picture featured both of them in the pool, their heads bobbing together at an angle that made them look like they were about to kiss. Chloe read every word, each one painting a story that made them both sound like a callous couple.

Her heart drummed against her chest as other internal organs clashed around like cymbals. She hugged the magazine again, attempting to crush its very existence against her sickened stomach. She darted her eyes around the room. Who else had seen this? The pictures were pretty damning in and of themselves, but the story they had come up with for Matt's date was completely wrong. Apparently she wasn't just Matt's 'Mystery Date', she was his 'Rebound Romance'.

Not once on their date did Matt mention a recent breakup. She felt stupid now for telling him about Jeremy during their swim in the pool. His compassion had surprised her, but now with reality in print, Matt's sensitive response only came from shared experience. Chloe couldn't help but feel a little duped. Why didn't he say anything?

Chloe's heart sank. Was she about to lose her reputation for a one night stand that never happened? What would happen if her fellow teachers or pupils found out? Would she lose her job? How had she landed herself in such a mess so quickly? She'd barely been in the country two weeks!

Her heart ached for the comfort and anonymity of home, and she listened for a moment for her father's calm voice to kick in.

"For now, I think your best course of action is to cut all ties to Matt Knightly. I know it's not fair, but until you've built up some rapport with your new school and it's families, you're at risk of losing your reputation

as a good teacher. Don't throw it all away on a man. You've worked too hard for this. You're better than that, Chloe Spencer."

Damn right I am.

The bell blared. Chloe turned and watched the other staff members file out. She lifted her chin and pulled her phone from her pocket. She had to call Matt and cancel their date again. Stringing him along like this wasn't fair to either of them, and she had to do it now while she still had the nerve to do so.

"Hi Matt. Sorry. I know it's going to sound like I'm repeating myself, but something's come up and I have to cancel our date tonight. I know I promised to make it up to you, but I just can't right now. My job is more important. I hope you can understand. Bye, Matt."

Chloe hit the end call button and felt certain that it really was the end. Not only had she cancelled their date last Wednesday (due to a dinner invitation from her new boss, the school principal, Mr Lyles and his wife), but she had also put off Matt's attempt to reschedule for Saturday. Her excuse that she needed to prepare for the following week wasn't entirely untrue. Although the whole term's lessons had been planned well before she'd left home, a few minor changes were still necessary. In truth her stomach was in knots about starting her new job and she hadn't been able to think about anything else. Sadly her excuses did little to dissuade him. He wouldn't take no for an answer when he'd offered to take her out for a first day on the job celebratory drink tonight. When she finally relented (promising one drink only), she thought she might feel differently about seeing him again.

The tiny window of hope she had dared to look through, a view of herself together with Matt, was now gone and closed forever. For good measure, she'd glue it shut, nail it, and paint it black. If Matt tried to talk his way around it this time, she'd show him the magazine and question his integrity. Surely cancelling a third time would seal their fate.

Near the end of the school day Mr Lyles came to her classroom. Chloe's heart pounded beneath her pale blue print shirt dress. The questioning look on his face had her mentally scrambling for her best excuse and apology about the article. But, much to her relief, Mr Lyles simply commended her quietly on a great first day and gave her a quick smile before asking if he could make an announcement to her class.

Chloe nodded, relieved she wouldn't have to start building a case for herself on the spot.

"Good afternoon, room eight," Mr Lyles scanned the children sitting at their desks around the room.

"Good afternoon, Mr Lyles," they replied in unison.

"Given that Miss Spencer has done a wonderful job today, I've agreed to let her share a special surprise she has planned for you all. So if you could pack up your things and make your way out to the playground, she has someone there she would like you all to meet."

Chloe scrunched her brows. "What? Who is it?"

The class laughed.

A sudden sense of fear crept up her arms and gripped her shoulders. *Please don't let it be him.*

One of the boys asked in a loud voice, "You mean you don't even know who you invited to meet us, Miss Spencer?"

Then Melody, a little girl who seemed to like asking more difficult questions added. "Well if you don't know who it is, then how did you plan the surprise?"

Chloe tucked her head towards the principal and whispered discreetly, "I really don't know who is here, Mr Lyles, I haven't planned any visit. Are you sure it's safe for the children to meet whomever it is?"

"Who is it, Mr Lyles?!" One of the bigger boys in a dark grey t-shirt yelled. Chloe couldn't remember the boy's name presently as her mind was now fixated on just one person.

Mr Lyles frowned and raised both hands above his head. He pushed them down slowly to engage the children in lowering their voices. "Shhh. Quiet please everyone, you too, William." The whole class became silent. "Even if Miss Spencer knows nothing about this visitor, I'm sure you will give him a warm welcome."

Chloe looked at him blankly, desperately hoping it wasn't the one person who could ruin her reputation and new position at the school.

As the children bumped and skipped out the door of the classroom, Chloe's feelings about the surprise visitor were far different from those of her students. Dread sat on her shoulders like a guilty student being sent to the Principal's office. Dragging her heels at this point was futile, not to mention childish. All she could do was nod politely and hope to dodge whatever bullets came at her.

There, standing in the middle of the playground was Matt, grinning wide, with a huge bundle of footballs.

"Miss Spencer!" He waved. "Thanks, Mr Lyles."

"No. Thank you, Mr Knightly." Mr Lyles waved back. Matt tossed him a freshly autographed ball, which he landed on his knee and then caught.

Chloe wandered over to where Matt waited.

"Hello, Miss Spencer. I got your message, but I had to come and hear it in person. Besides, I think that your class deserved to get out early on their first day back. What do you reckon kids?"

All the kids cheered and swarmed around Matt and Chloe.

"I want a ball," said one.

"Great surprise, Miss Spencer," said another.

"Can you sign one for me? I'm Molly."

"Sure. Here you go, Molly." Matt smiled at the little girl.

"Is he your boyfriend, Miss Spencer?" Melody asked.

Chloe quickly responded, "He's just a friend."

"Oh. That's good." Melody replied. "It must be nice having a famous footballer as your friend, Miss Spencer. Mum's always drooling over Mr Knightly when she sees him on the telly. She said that if she wasn't married to Dad, she'd go out with you." Melody looked up at Matt and cocked her head to one side. "Would you like to meet my Mum? I know she'll want to meet you. You could come for dinner." Melody's offer was genuinely cute, and Chloe wondered what excuse Matt might give her.

Chloe restrained a chuckle.

Matt looked at her with a grin and winked. Then he looked back at Melody. "Well, I don't know, luv. I wouldn't want to upset your dad, or anything."

"True." Melody replied, "He does get mad sometimes, especially if Mum's been drinking too much. She acts a bit silly when she has the red juice. I'm not allowed the red juice because Mum says it's only for adults."

Matt laughed.

Chloe clapped a hand over her mouth. Concealing her laugh wasn't going to cut it, she needed to regroup. She raised her hands and clapped loudly three times. "Right everyone, gather around. Mr Knightly has put a lot of work into planning a special challenge for you all, so listen up and do exactly as he says."

Chloe licked her smile. Matt froze for a second looking deep in thought. If he had the nerve to waltz into her place of work, sign some autographs, and play with the kids, then he had better be prepared to work for any favour he hoped to gain. Did he not understand the position he had put her in? She could lose everything. Her job. Her reputation. Her dignity. Her self-respect too for that matter.

I'm in charge here - not him.

"What are we to do with all these balls, Mr Knightly. Are they all for us?" Chloe asked in a loud voice.

"They sure are, Miss Spencer. I thought your class might like some new sports equipment."

"Well that's very nice of you. Isn't it kids? What do we say to Mr Knightly?"

All the children chorused back at different times, "Thank you, Matt." Or, "Thank you, Mr Knightly."

Chloe smiled at her class and then stepped back. "Over to you, Mr Knightly."

Matt quickly grouped the children into two teams and set them each to a task. One group was to run a tagged relay kicking the ball along the ground around five cones and then back. The other group was to knee kick the ball in the air five times while moving up to a single cone and then back again. Matt gave them each a few minutes practice at the skill and then lined them up for the race.

Chloe was impressed at how organised he was, and also that he managed quite successfully to keep everyone's attention, including hers. But it still didn't change how she felt about seeing him.

Final cheers rang out as the teams raced to the finish. Matt picked up a little girl and dribbled the football around the cones for her, making it appear like she was doing it herself.

"Hey, that's cheating!" One of the boys yelled. His team still won so there was no animosity at the end.

Chloe laughed. "All right children." She clapped. "You can all go and play until your parent arrives to collect you."

All the children dispersed about the playground with their new balls and happily played. Chloe was about to have a word with Matt but he jogged off to join the kids. Kicking the football into the air on one foot and keeping it off the ground for several more kicks with his knees and feet, Matt encouraged the kids to give it a go. Some weren't too bad.

After a while the final bell rang and the children brought the balls back to where Chloe stood. She dismissed them into the care of their waiting parents, watching them jump and laugh as they wandered away. Matt kicked a ball towards her, forcing her to decide whether to stop it or not. Thankfully she did so successfully. She was mad at him, yes, but staying mad at him was no easy task. Matt looked pleased when she landed her foot on top of the ball. Her stomach flipped with nerves as he jogged towards her.

His gaze only diverted when an excited woman, holding Melody's hand, hollered, "Yoo-hoo, Matt!"

Matt stopped in his tracks.

"Matt Knightly?! Oh my gawd, oh my gawd, oh my gawd! Pinch me now," the woman all but squealed.

He grinned at her and she melted into another fit of gushing.

"I love you so much, Matt. You're the best player, *Arsenal,* has ever had." Melody's mother fished for something in her handbag and pulled out a pen. "Would you mind signing my top?"

Melody's mum had on a really nice sleeveless shirt, not the kind of garment you'd normally expect to have autographed. Matt didn't seem to mind, but he pulled out his own sharpie and permanently marked his name across it. Melody's mum giggled as the pen stroked across her chest. Matt just smiled his for-the-fans grin that Chloe was now used to seeing every time someone approached him. It was nice that he enjoyed making another person's day, but she'd seen more than enough for now. Chloe began collecting the balls and dropped them into the over-sized mesh sack.

When most of the parents and children had left, Matt finally caught up to her.

"Well I guess we better get these balls put away." He said with a sly grin, nudging the last few balls with his toe off the ground, into the air, and then into the giant bag.

"Show off," Chloe huffed, moving the edge of the bag, so the last ball missed its entry.

Chloe stifled a smile when he leapt to prevent it rolling away further. His freshly showered scent wafted past her, making her eyes roll down the length of him. Her interest reignited. She wished it hadn't. She hated noticing his toned physique like every other female within a 500 metre radius appeared to. She didn't like making him feel like he'd done something wrong, but her desire to keep her job took precedence.

"Can you bring those?" She gestured to the sack and moved towards the sports shed before giving him a chance to reply.

Matt followed with the bag over his shoulder, awkwardly swaying under the weight.

"You Okay, Chloe? Did I do something wrong?" His innocent tone made her stop and spin around to face him.

"I don't think you really get it." Her annoyance weighed heavier on herself than at him. He looked confused and dropped the bag. He took a step towards her.

"Just forget it, Matt. You wouldn't understand." She turned and kept walking.

Now at the shed, she unlocked it, and heaved the door open. When Matt caught up she pointed to a spot inside. "There." She avoided contact with his eyes.

Matt hauled the giant bag inside and dropped it.

He turned to face her, waiting until her eyes would meet his. "Why don't you try me? I'm tougher than I look." He came within arm's reach and she watched his chest rise and fall from the exertion of carrying the bag.

"You sure?" Chloe aimed a feeble punch into his bicep and then regretted doing so when he went to grab her hand. She pulled away and headed for the door.

Matt jumped to block her exit. "What did I do? Tell me. I can't make it right if I don't know what I did wrong." He reached to take hold of her hand again but Chloe folded her arms high across her chest.

"Have you seen today's *Heat* Magazine?"

Matt looked puzzled. "No. I forgot to pick up my copy this morning." His subtle sarcasm sounded almost legit. "Why? Is there a picture of me in it?" He grinned, placing his hands on his hips. The stance caused his shirt to tighten across his chest, and Chloe struggled to stay focused. Matt's body seemed to have some kind of gravitational pull and the only way to break free was to confront him with a stare. "You're on the front cover," she paused. "And so am I!"

Realisation dawned across Matt's brow but his smile remained.

"Oh, I see. Can I see it?"

Chloe huffed and side stepped him through the doorway. Matt spun around to follow.

Taking the key from the lock, she looked at him. "It's in my bag. Wait here and I'll get my things."

Matt took a step to follow her.

"For God's sake, Matt. Just stay here. You've already done enough damage for one day. I can't afford to have any more rumours circulating about us, and certainly not at my school!"

Matt stepped back and let her leave. She felt her heart wrench a little. She wasn't trying to hurt him, just as he hadn't purposefully tried to hurt her. Chloe hoped he understood how serious she felt about the situation. Maybe his celebrity status was just too much for a Kiwi girl from Palmerston North.

When she returned, Matt was engaged in conversation with Mr Lyles. She rendered herself with a false smile and gingerly approached them, hoping against all odds that her new boss remained as clueless about the magazine article, as he was about their date. The fact that the men were laughing by the time she arrived only heightened her anxiety further. She dropped her shoulders and forced what little dignity she had left into her smile.

"Hello, Chloe. I must say we are very lucky to have you here at Millfields." Mr Lyles patted her shoulder, just like her father did when he was done giving one of his students a congratulatory farewell at the end of a school year. "Matt, you'll look out for her for us, won't you? The children already like her I can tell, and don't worry about the article, Chloe. If I hear any complaints from the parents, I'll set them straight about the virtue of your character. It's just a gossip mag. Your references were exemplary, and Matt here has told me exactly what happened. You'll not have to explain it any further to me. Right. Well, I've a bit more paper work to catch up on. But you two have a great night." Mr Lyles held out his hand to Matt and he shook it like the two of them had just struck some kind of deal. Mr Lyles walked back inside leaving Chloe alone with Matt once more.

Chloe narrowed her eyes at him, simmering her thoughts into words she might actually be able to say out loud.

How dare he! Did he have no sense of how humiliating that was?

Refusing to give him a chance to explain, she turned to walk away.

"Hey wait. Hang on. Where are you going now?" Matt's confusion resembled that of someone who'd just had the wind knocked out of their sails.

"I'm going home. I'm tired and I don't want to fight with you."

"Well, what's there to fight about? It's all fine with Nathan." Matt jerked his head back in her boss's direction. Then, spotting the magazine in her hand he reached towards her. "Can I see that?"

Chloe stopped and handed the magazine to him. He fingered through it. "It's just nonsense, Chloe. It'll be old news by tomorrow. I'm sorry. I should have protected you better. I didn't know they were going to be there. Someone must have tipped them off. It'll be different next time. We'll be more careful."

"See that's just it. You're not getting it, Matt. There's not going to be a next time." Chloe moved away.

"Wait. What?" Matt stopped following her. "You mean that's it. You don't want to hang out with me anymore? But why?"

"It's not that I don't want to, Matt. It's just…I can't do this right now. I've got higher priorities than becoming Matt Knightly's newest fling. You do know I recently broke up with Jeremy. You don't want to be the rebound guy, and I don't want to be yours." Her accusation brought a flicker of shock to his eyes. "I deserve better than that, Matt, and I can't do this right now. Other than finding Mum's birth-mother, and focusing on my new job, that's really all I have time for. Do you understand?"

"Okay. I get it. I really do. But can we at least still be friends?"

Chloe let a tear slip. "So I really was just a one night thing? You have no interest in me at all - like that," she said, the words devoid of all hope.

"What? Of course I'm interested in you. What fool wouldn't be? Why would I be here otherwise? You cancelled our date, a date I was very much looking forward to by the way. You're not just a fling to me. I really like you and I hoped we could get to know each other better. Don't you want that?" Matt reached to cup her cheek but she turned and wouldn't let him.

"I don't know," she stammered. She didn't know what she wanted. Part of her really liked Matt and part of her was terrified of being hurt again. "I...I like your company, but I'm just a nobody from the bottom of the world. Besides, I'm still not over Jeremy and I really don't know how long that will take. You don't want to get involved with me. I can't make promises I'm not sure I can keep."

Matt opened his arms to her, but she was reluctant to enter them. He moved towards her slowly, encompassing her whole upper body in his arms. "I won't pressure you" - He kissed the top of her head - "But I'd rather have you as a friend than lose you altogether." He let her go, moving his hands to her shoulders. "Maybe I could help you with your search. Strictly platonic, I promise, I won't hit on you." Matt eyed her whole body. "Just as long as you promise not to look like that. Seriously. You need to do something about your clothes."

Chloe wiped her face. "What? What's wrong with my clothes?" She glanced down at her dress.

"For starters, you're showing too many curves. Rein it in will you. A man's gotta think around here and you're not making it easy on me."

Chloe giggled, confused. "But I'm not wearing anything clingy. This dress is about as loose as any of my clothes get."

"Yeah. But I know what you have on underneath it, and that's an image that's burned in my mind." He grinned.

He was teasing her on purpose. But why would he risk making such a remark? Perhaps it was his way of trying to get her to think of him as just a friend.

Chloe's lips twitched indignantly. Gratifying him with a response would only encourage his behaviour. So instead, she marched out the school gate without so much as a glance behind her.

Matt laughed. Then ran to catch up with her again.

"I know you like me, Chloe Spencer. So, remind me again. Why can't you come out with me tonight?" Matt blinked innocently.

"This, Matt, is the very definition of you hitting on me. Didn't you just promise you wouldn't?" Chloe scowled and he took it like an arrow to his chest.

"Ouch!" He placed his hand on his heart without losing his smile. "Yeah but you haven't changed your dress yet so my promise is not valid. Maybe if you were in track pants and a sweatshirt - maybe then I'd be able to resist...I bet you'd look cute in that too..." Matt trailed off when Chloe's phone blinged. She stopped to grab it from her bag, and Matt bumped into her unprepared for her sudden halt.

A tiny envelope sat in the top corner of her phone. She smiled and tapped it. It was from Jenny at the local Library. They'd only met yesterday, but Chloe felt certain her new friend had found more information about the Ingles family.

Chloe read the message.

'Success! I've found an article from 1966 about Jimmy.

Call me as soon as you can.'

CHAPTER FOURTEEN

C HLOE FELT A surge of urgency. Although her mother wasn't yet at death's door, she was painfully aware that her condition could change in an instant. There was little time to waste waiting for answers to come to her. Jenny understood and had sent multiple inquiries with names and dates to various departments. She had even contacted a friend in the police who might be able to assist with the search.

Chloe felt the heat from Matt's body behind her.

"Who's that?" He asked, his words warm against her cheek.

She pulled away, tucking her phone out of sight quickly. Should she tell him or not?

Her voice wavered, "Uh. It's nothing. I'll call them back later."

"It's all right, Chloe. You can tell me, we're friends." His eyes sought hers to confirm their new status. The moment she smiled, she wished she hadn't. He winked back with a grin, implying they were anything but simply friends. His gaze lifted from her lips. "Is it something to do with your search? Can I help?"

"Yes. And, No." Chloe glanced around the street, then turned about face and headed in the direction of the library.

"Well. Hold up. Where are you going now?"

Her actions must have looked like she was in some kind of video game. Taking a walk in Pac-man's maze and being hemmed in by ghosts. "Uhh…I'm going to the library." Her answer was intentionally vague. Without giving Matt specifics she hoped he'd give up, and go home. Unfortunately it had the opposite effect she was after.

"Well, which one? Winchester, Glenfield, Holloway, Ilswich? I could give you a ride if you like." Matt stood, waiting to hear whether he'd won her approval or not.

Firstly, she was amazed Matt even knew the names of the libraries nearby, and secondly, a ride might get her there faster than waiting for the bus. Was it wrong to take advantage of Matt's offer when she had no intention of rewarding his efforts? She pitied him a little. The poor guy had spent the better half of an afternoon trying to impress her and all she'd done was push him away. Keeping her face as straight as she could, she looked him in the eye. "All right. But this is not a date. It's just you giving me a ride to the library. Got it?"

Matt looked pleased having finally been able to offer her something she wanted. Even if it was just a lift down the road. The car he'd come in was not the smart sports car he'd driven her to the hotel in. This car was an ordinarily white SUV and although it was still smart, it was far more practical for carting sports gear and people. Chloe climbed aboard and within seconds the air-con blasted an icy breeze. Chloe pushed the vents away. She had no wish to arrive half frozen at the library. Even with what little sun was out, it was barely enough to keep the chill off her arms. She couldn't wait to get home and put her fluffy jumper and slippers on. She would miss New Zealand's long summer break over Christmas and wasn't sure what to expect in London. Danielle had rabbited on about how cold winter was in the UK, but as it was still the tail end of summer, Chloe only had a vague idea of what was yet to come.

Matt pulled into a side street and parked the car. He was out and around to her door before she'd even unbuckled herself. Clearly he wasn't about to let her escape his company that easily. Without a word he walked her inside the library and to the front desk. Perhaps he thought keeping his mouth shut would aid in prolonging their time together.

Jenny looked up from the help desk.

"Chloe, Hi. I wasn't expecting you to drop by so soon. How was your first day at school?" Jenny, looked at her and then at Matt, making the assumption that they had come together. She extended her hand for him to shake. "Hello. I'm Jenny. And you are?"

Matt looked at Chloe. "See, not everyone recognises me. Hi Jenny. I'm Matt. Just so we're clear - this is not a date." Matt's face creased with lines of seriousness and Jenny laughed.

"Okay. If you say so, Mr Knightly." Jenny smiled at Chloe with a knowing grin.

Matt looked displeased.

Chloe rolled her eyes at Jenny and giggled.

Jenny tapped the *Heat* magazine on her desk. "You two have been keeping the tabloids busy haven't you?"

Matt was not amused, and this time, neither was Chloe.

"So what have you found?" Chloe asked, trying to forget Matt was even there.

"Well, I was trawling through a number of old phone books and came across a few of the Ingles here in London. I figured it was worth a shot to call and see if any of them had a link back to Marta. Anyway, the long and short of it is, I've found a woman called Annette Ingles. She says she was married to a David Ingles. And get this - David's father's name is Harry Ingles. If it's him, Marta's brother, then maybe he'll know where Marta is. Annette said her husband, David, died three years ago. Apparently he was Harry's only son. She still pops in to visit her father-in-law occasionally."

"That's wonderful, Jenny. Well not the bit about her husband of course, but surely Harry must know where Marta is. Did you ask her if she would be willing to meet me? Maybe she could introduce me to Harry."

"I did ask, and she agreed." Jenny handed her a piece of paper with Annette's number scribbled on it. "Annette sounded nice on the phone, but she said Harry lives in Thornton-Heath. That's not the sort of area you want to go visiting on your own, if you catch my meaning."

Matt touched Chloe's arm resting on the counter and shook his head. "There's no way I'm letting you go there alone. I'm coming with you."

Chloe frowned. "Who says I want you to come? Maybe Jenny wants to come with me. She's the one who's done all the hard work after all. What do you say Jenny? Want to come with me?" Chloe leaned further over the counter, hoping to hide the plea within her eyes from Matt.

"Well I'd love to, but I'm swamped here at the moment. Plus I have a number of evening events I'm running this week. If I can, I will. But perhaps Matt would make better company anyway." Jenny smirked in his direction, and a non-verbal agreement exchanged between the two of them.

Matt let go of Chloe's arm and placed his palm on the desk. "I'd be more than happy to look after Chloe, Jenny."

"I thought as much." Jenny smiled.

Chloe pursed her lips. "All right, you two. But do I get a say in any of this?"

"No." Matt said. "I'm coming with you and that's that. I won't have you going alone, Chloe. I'd never forgive myself if anything happened to you."

Although she had mixed feelings about Matt, she was glad that at least someone in London, other than Joy, would care enough to notice if she went missing.

"Now what's this article you found about Jimmy?" Matt asked.

"Hey!" Chloe dropped a scowl in his direction. "You did read my text."

"Sorry. I just really wanted to help. Pleeease?"

"Don't you have somewhere else to be right now?"

"No. We had a date planned and you cancelled - remember?"

"Oh, right. I forgot. Sorry."

"You two are adorable," cooed Jenny.

Chloe lowered her already low brow even further. "No we're not. You're not helping, Jenny."

"Right. Well…follow me." Jenny stood and took them to a small back room where a microfiche machine was set up. Jenny grabbed a film and threaded it into the machine. Clicking through each page she found the one and offered Chloe her seat. "Read that. It's not great news I'm afraid. But at least it confirms your story of Marta's family moving to Scotland. It's tragic really."

Chloe absorbed all of Jenny's words and began reading the article aloud. "Ambulance crews were dispatched to the accident near the River Donn in the area of Strathdon, on February 2nd 1966. Three young boys from the Aberdeenshire area are all thought to have been killed instantly at the time of the accident…"

Jimmy, Marta's youngest brother, was one of those boys. No direct mention was made of Marta in the article. Other than to say that, "All three of the boys' families are being supported by the community in this harrowing time of grief."

With this news, Chloe couldn't help but feel discouraged. Now there was one less person to ask about Marta's whereabouts. Unless Harry offered her solid information, Chloe would be no closer to finding out what happened to her grandmother than when she first started.

"Have you heard anything back about Marta from your other contacts?"

Jenny turned the machine off. "No, not yet. You'll be the first to know as soon as I do though."

"Thanks, Jenny. I really do appreciate your help. I'll let you know how it goes with Annette."

Chloe stood to leave and Matt, who had been silently participating in the afternoon's research, now felt it necessary to raise the awareness of his presence once more. "Why don't you give Annette a call now? I could take you to meet her tonight if she's free. We could grab dinner on the way."

Jenny smiled at both of them. "Are you sure this isn't a date? Sounds like one to me."

Chloe opened her mouth to speak but Matt's voice jumped in. "Of course it's not. I'm just helping out a friend. But, let's be honest, we've all got to eat sooner or later, don't we?"

Although Matt's question was clearly rhetorical, it was obvious he expected her to give him an answer. And, preferably one that would have him escorting her to the nearest food vendor.

"I guess I am a little hungry." Chloe said, a slight pang jabbing her stomach. Her eyes widened, adding in haste, "How about you, Jenny, you want to join us?"

Eating alone with Matt worried her. Every time he spoke, his words endeared her to him, further weakening her resolve. Not to mention that eating food with Matt was an experience all of its own. The way he savoured each mouthful sent a pang through her body, making her saliva ducts weep. She realised then that secretly she hoped Jenny wouldn't be able to join them after all.

"Dinner sounds great, but I think you two should eat without me. I'm a picky eater and there's not much around here that I like." Jenny eyed her with a glare encouraging her to accept Matt's offer.

"All right. Let me call Annette first and see what she says. If it's on, I'll let you take me to dinner. If not, then I'm afraid you'll be taking me home."

Chloe dialled the number and wandered away from Matt and Jenny towards the library's main entrance. Matt appeared beside her when he finally realised she was not intending to return back inside.

"Well, are we eating or not?"

"Fine. But nothing fancy. Fish 'n chips is about all I can manage right now."

"Sure. I can do fish 'n chips." Matt opened her door and she climbed inside. She couldn't help but smile at the attention he was giving her, even if all he got was a measly meal of deep fried potatoes and who knew what sort of fish.

When Chloe informed Matt they were to meet Annette at The Princes Arms, he asked her to search and input the address into the app on his phone. She couldn't help but feel nervous when he handed it to her. Did he trust her that much? She couldn't deny her curiosity of what photos it contained. Would his ex-girlfriend be on there? She presumed as much and her interest died just as quickly as it had arisen.

"In 200 metres, take the next right onto A104." A voice spouted through the car's speakers, making Chloe jump in her seat.

Matt laughed. "It's all right, Chloe. Gigi doesn't bite."

"Gigi?"

"Google Maps."

Chloe nodded. "Right. Do you always name your tech? Don't you find it weird?"

"Nah. I figure sooner or later we'll all be talking to robots. Asking them to find this or that, update us on what they think is relevant to us, and let's not forget, they'll probably even help select what toilet paper we should wipe our own arses with. Heck, maybe they'll even do it for us." Matt's straight face made it impossible to keep up with his jokes sometimes. He glanced at the phone in her hands. "Looks like that Pub serves food. Why don't we just eat there? I'm sure Annette won't mind."

"Okay."

"So. If this Harry guy turns out to be the person you think he is, what will you ask him? What if he won't tell you where Marta is? He might not want you prying into his family's business."

"Well, Marta is my family's business. I'll just have to make him see that."

"I'm just saying, he might not be as receptive as you hope. Imagine how you'd react if a stranger you just met wanted to know where your mother or sister was? Would you just tell them?"

"Well no probably not. But I think I would know better than you how to get someone to talk. I am a school teacher, remember. We have our ways."

"Sure, but I'm just saying, not everyone wants to dish the dirt on their family - especially if there's some nasty skeletons in the closet."

"What skeletons? There are no skeletons here. Harry is Marta's brother, so was Jimmy. What could they possibly have to hide?"

"I don't know. But if you expect them to just welcome you like a long lost relative, you might be disappointed."

Chloe huffed. Why did Matt feel the need to rain on her excitement? She finally had a genuine lead to finding Marta and he seemed intent on making her feel like the big bad wolf come to blow the Ingles family house down. Of course she could see his point. She'd be lying if she said she wasn't worried. Harry might not want to meet her as readily as Annette did. But what choice did she have. The promise she made to herself and her mother was simply one she had to fulfil. Even if it meant losing her personal pride in the process. She'd do anything to reunite her mother with her birth-mother. Giving her the chance to talk to her in person was the ultimate dream.

Once again Matt's presence caused a stir when they entered the bar. The busty waitress who tended their table seemed intent on ignoring Chloe's existence, disregarding any attempt she made to place an order.

Matt looked at Chloe and seemed to nod from the corner of his eyes. He curled his lips with his irritating for-the-fans grin, and searched the waitress's top. "Ah, thank you..?"

"Macy," she beamed back under a flutter of lashes. "But you can call me Mace if you like." She placed her hand on Matt's bicep and gently squeezed.

"Thank you Macy. But, if you wouldn't mind, could you take my girlfriend's order, please. She's very hungry and I'd like for that to change as soon as possible." Matt's pearly-whites glistened from the dim light towards the flirting waitress.

Matt returned his attention to Chloe and his brow jumped.

Girlfriend?

"Sure thing, Matt." Macy smirked. She twirled a pen between her fingers. Then, placing it between her lips, she sucked at its end before yanking it out. "What'll it be?" she asked Chloe curtly. Chloe startled at the noise and her appetite recoiled. She wasn't sure who to be more annoyed at, Macy or Matt?

"Um. I'll have the chicken burger, no tomato, and a Sprite, please."

Macy scribbled on her pad and Chloe wondered if any of her order was actually written down. Macy looked like the kind of waitress who was used to getting acquainted with those she took orders from. But, she would also more than likely tag her customers with some hideous name to remember who was who. Chloe presumed her name would be *Hungry Bitch*, and Matt's would be, *Bae* with heart emojis.

When Macy finally left the table Chloe only had one word for Matt. "Girlfriend?"

Matt shrugged his shoulders and brows in unison. "I think that's appropriate. Don't you? How else was I meant to get her to treat you with a little respect?"

"Friend would have sufficed."

Matt smirked, seemingly pleased he had made her feel uncomfortable once again. She hated to admit it but she kind of liked how he made her feel around him. Annoyed, flattered, angry, noticed, respected. It was a mixed bag of emotions. Even she thought herself irrational at times. Although she wouldn't allow things to go any further than light-hearted flirting, she still liked that he bothered to try.

Their meals came and were consumed in relative silence. Chloe was anxious about what to say to Annette. Keeping a steady eye on the entrance of the pub, and a continuous sip on her straw, Chloe hadn't seen anyone enter who fit the description. Two drinks later and another on the way, she was desperate for the loo.

Just as she excused herself from the table, a woman entered the bar fitting Annette's self-description perfectly. Mid-thirties, short, with straight dark hair to the shoulders, a pasty complexion, and a narrow nose. In contrast, her full round cheeks were anything but pasty, looking like they'd just taken a brisker walk than usual. Most notable were the woman's blood red lips which looked like a painted Russian dolls. More striking than her lips though was her well defined nose, chiselled like an Egyptian statue with a severely pointed tip.

Chloe changed route.

"Hello, are you by chance, Annette?" She asked holding out her hand timidly.

"Yes. And you must be, Chloe." The woman took her hand and shook it lightly, her dark brown coat dwarfing the pale hand it offered. Chloe beamed.

"Wonderful. I was just about to use the rest room, but my friend is at our table over there." Chloe pointed towards Matt and he waved back at them. Annette turned back to Chloe. A hint of concern laced her questioning eyes.

"Yes. It is Matt Knightly. He's a friend of mine and offered to come with me tonight. I hope that's Okay? He's nice. I promise."

Annette smoothed a hand over her hair and Chloe couldn't tell if she was nervous or frightened.

"Sure," she said, nodding with little enthusiasm.

Chloe ducked to the restroom as quickly as she could. The thought of leaving Annette alone with Matt for too long made her worry. Her fears were allayed when she spotted a smile on Annette's face when she returned. Matt always seemed to be able to put anyone at ease. It was a refreshing change from Jeremy. Trying to coax a conversation out of him at times was like clawing at a soft toy in a gaming machine.

"Ah, nice of you to join us, Chloe. I thought Macy must have drowned you in there." Matt teased.

Chloe shook her head unamused. "Sorry Annette. I drank a little too much before you got here. Not alcoholic drinks, I can assure you. Not that I'm not old enough to drink, because I am. But, I only had lemonade…but I had two, which is more than usual for me. Oh no I'm babbling, aren't I?" Chloe looked at Matt for assistance. He patted her hand.

"It's all right, Chloe. Annette understands. She was just telling me that she hasn't sat alone at a table with a man my age since she dated her husband. Then I told her I was twenty-four and she turned that lovely shade of Manchester red. I think you two just need to breathe." Matt looked towards the bar. I'm going to go find out what happened to your drink, Chloe. Can I get you anything, Annette?"

"A Gin and tonic thanks. No ice."

Matt raised his brow. "All right then. I'll be right back."

Once Matt was out of ear-shot Chloe made her confession. "I'm sorry, Annette. Matt insisted he come along. I'm not familiar with the area and it can be a bit confusing at night. I was so anxious to meet you that I thought having him here might help."

"Oh, for sure. It doesn't hurt that he's not half bad to look at either." Annette rested her elbows on the table and leaned to catch a glimpse of him at the bar. Chloe followed her gaze and was not surprised to see Matt engaged in conversation with Macy. It bugged her more that it bugged her seeing him chatting away with the waitress in the first place. Why did she care? They weren't really boyfriend and girlfriend. But Macy didn't know that. The audacity of the pierced black and white waitress was what really bothered Chloe, not Matt's friendliness towards her. Chloe shook her head and tried to focus on what she'd come for.

"I believe Jenny told you who I'm looking for and why. Do you think there's any chance Harry would agree to meet me?"

Annette pulled her attention from Matt back to Chloe without any indication she had good news.

"Well. Maybe he would. I'm not really sure. He's a pretty recluse kind of man, and he has a bit of a temper. The only good thing David used to say about his father was that he genuinely loved his grandkids. David has two sisters. One's out west and the other, Vicky, lives in New York. We don't see Vicky much. She left when she was quite young. My son's at high school and my daughter is just seven. Ben, my son, offered to babysit so I could come tonight."

"That was good of him. Where did you tell them you were going?"

"Oh they know. I told them about Jenny's call. It's strange. We really don't know much about David's side of the family. Harry's wife left them soon after David and the girls finished high school. David didn't speak much about his mother. And Harry...well he's about as open as an ice-cream shop on a rainy day."

"I figured that might be the case. Do you think your father-in-law really is Marta's brother?"

"I believe so. He has mentioned on occasion that he lived in New Zealand when he was a child. That's how I knew Jenny probably had the right person."

"I hope you're right, Annette. That's why I need your help. Would you consider taking me to meet Harry? Please? He's more likely to open up if there's a friendly face in the room. Don't you think?" Chloe looked for Matt at the bar and was surprised to see him staring at her when she did. She darted her gaze away from him and grabbed hold of her empty glass on the table. Sucking up a tiny bit of melted water from the ice cubes in the bottom, she almost choked when she saw Matt heading towards them.

Annette looked up as Matt arrived with two glasses in hand. "Thank you," She said taking her drink from him before he could set it on the table. She sucked the tiny straw. "He might, Chloe. I'll give him a call tomorrow and see if I can set something up for you."

Matt glanced between them. "Set up what? What'd I miss?"

"Uh nothing." Chloe took her drink and gulped down several sips before realising how much the fizz would burn her nasal passages. She placed her palm between her eyes and blinked. She'd best get it over with and tell Matt what they were planning before he charmingly inserted himself into the scheme anyhow.

"Annette has agreed to set up a meeting with Harry. I'm fairly certain he's our man." Chloe looked to Annette. "Perhaps don't tell him we're looking for Marta just yet though. I don't want him thinking we're digging into his family without good reason. I think it might help if he learns it directly from me as to why I'm looking for her."

"Well, what should I say to him?" Annette asked before taking another sip.

"Tell him…" Matt said, thinking fast. "Tell him you've found a distant relative from New Zealand and they would really like to meet him. Would that peak his interest enough?"

"Yes. I think that'll work. I should think he'd definitely want to know who it could be."

Matt caught Chloe staring at him. He grinned. "Great. Well that's settled then. Let me know when and where and I'll be there." Matt said it like he'd been part of the whole conversation, and Chloe knew it would be difficult to refuse his offer.

Annette looked at Matt with concern again. "I'm not sure you coming is such a good idea, Matt."

"Oh. Why's that? If you don't mind my asking."

"It's just, Harry can get a bit tetchy around people he doesn't know. One of you is probably enough."

"Oh. Okay. But if you think about it, Annette. There aren't too many people in London who don't know who *I* am."

Annette gave him a sympathetic shrug. "Harry's not a big fan of football. He follows the cricket and rugby mainly. Sorry."

"Well, if I can't meet Harry himself, perhaps I can just drive you there, Chloe. I can wait outside. I promised Jenny I'd accompany you, and no offense, Annette, but I'm not in the habit of breaking my promises - to anyone."

Annette seemed to concede via a shrug.

Chloe played with the straw in her drink. Drawing the last of the liquid into her mouth, she swallowed slowly. "I'll be fine, Matt. Annette will be there. And besides, I can get an Uber ride home if necessary." Chloe looked back to Annette. "You'll stay with me till then, won't you?"

"Y-yes sure." Annette stammered.

Matt reached and touched Chloe's hand making her insides flip. "Are you sure. I really don't mind. I'm not happy letting you go on your own."

Chloe skirted her eyes from his, wishing he would stop trying to pin her with them. Finally she gave up and bore a stare directly into him.

"Nothing bad is going to happen. If Harry doesn't want to talk to me, I'll just leave. I promise I'll let you know how it all goes." Chloe widened her eyes to Matt's look of disbelief. "I promise."

Matt squeezed his hand over hers and then removed it, his warm touch suddenly gone.

"I'll only agree as long as you keep that promise." He held out his hand. "Deal?"

"Deal."

CHAPTER FIFTEEN

Saturday 9th September 2017

CHLOE MET ANNETTE at the Thornton-Heath rail station so they could walk the three blocks to Harry's flat together. Annette knocked on a white door with 56b on it. Paint flaked from its grooves and the stench of rubbish hovered nearby. Not a single sign of a garden graced any of the street's edges, just, concrete, metal gates, and rows of wheelie rubbish bins. Chloe crinkled her nose, shortening her breaths to avoid inhaling it. Soft footsteps shuffled towards them from inside, accompanied by a fit of coughing, each rasp growing louder as it reached the front door. A latch turned and the door pulled slightly ajar, tensioning against a chain.

"What do you want?" a man grumbled.

"It's me, Harry, Annette. Remember, I said I was bringing someone from New Zealand to meet you."

"Right." The door closed and the chain was released. The door swung open revealing a man in black sweatpants and a half-open terry cloth dressing gown over a grey shirted swollen belly. The stench of alcohol drifted on the current escaping the confines of the narrow hall in which he stood. White whiskers stuck out like tiny cactus thorns all over his jaw. He drew his hand over his chin and scratched.

"Come in, come in." His tone gave no impression he was pleased by their visit, but Chloe held out hope his tune might change once he'd heard her story.

"Who's this?" Harry asked.

"This is Chloe Spencer. She's the one from New Zealand I told you about. I think you'll be interested in what she has to say." The old man barely acknowledged her before heading off down the hall. He disappeared through a doorway to the left.

"Can I get you anything, Annie? Tea? I don't have milk. But if you don't mind drinking it black, I can make one." Harry's voice echoed from the other room.

"Thanks, Harry. We'd love a cuppa." Annette called back immediately.

Chloe knew it was best to go along with whatever Annette said regardless of whether she could drink a cup of black tea or not. Her stomach skittered. It had taken all her nerve to make it this far tonight. The whole ten minutes it took to reach their destination she wished she hadn't been so stubborn and accepted Matt's offer of a ride. Her silly pride and determination to prove she could manage on her own lacked any ounce of common sense and she dare not dwell on the journey she must take to get back home.

Earlier that day, Danielle called to go over the facts as they knew them. Chloe was anxious to tell Harry what she knew about Marta and his family during their time in New Zealand. What concerned her most now though were Danielle's parting words, which still echoed in her ears.

"Don't scare him off, Chloe. He might not want to tell you where Marta lives. You might need to convince him we're not after anything, except to honour Mum's wishes."

Annette guided her to a sitting room at the front of the house, motioning her to take a seat on the sofa. The room wasn't cluttered but it certainly hadn't been cleaned in some time. Dust caked the coffee table and various bits of dirt and debris littered the floor. A single recliner with a rip in the vinyl looked as if its stuffing might escape. Chloe took a seat on the wooden armed settee, its cushions at least were not about to pull apart at the seams. Sinking into the sofa, much further than expected, sent her clutching for the armrest to prevent her slipping completely to the floor.

Annette giggled. "Woops! Looks like the springs are gone again." Chloe pulled herself up and Annette lifted the cushion on her side to re-hitch the springs where she could. She threw the cushion back in place and moved to repeat the process on the side where Chloe had tried to sit. There was nothing. Not even a spring to rehome. Harry shuffled up the hallway and Annette settled the cushion back over the hole with a look of worry on her face. The growing weight in Chloe's chest sank to her abdomen. She knew the task ahead had potential to go south if she said the wrong thing. She could only hope that her dignity didn't end up on the floor along with her backside.

"Here you go, Annie." Harry deposited a mug into her waiting hand. He looked at Chloe, nodded, and passed her a cup of the dark stained water. She took it with as happy a grin as she could muster and perched herself on the edge of the sofa like a bird balancing on a swing.

"Thank you, Mr Ingles," her voice barely a whisper. She cleared her throat, dislodging the growing tension within her vocal chords.

Annette took a sip of the tea and placed it on the coffee table. Harry was quick to grab a coaster and place it on the dusty surface. He hunted for another briefly, but gave up and put a newspaper down for Chloe.

"Mr Ingles, I'm so happy you've agreed to see me. I wasn't sure if you would, given that you're probably wondering why a twenty-two year old woman from Palmerston North would have any sort of connection to your family. I want you to know that no matter what you learn tonight, I only ask that you understand that it is at my mother's request that I have come, and it is she who would like to know the truth about her past."

Harry, now fully reclined in his chair, took a slurp from a mug and screwed up his face. He grunted with a nod, indicating Chloe should continue her story.

"My Mother's name is Elizabeth Spencer. She is currently quite ill with cancer and we're not sure how much longer she has with us. You see, Mr Ingles, my mother was adopted at birth and I believe that your sister, Marta Ingles, was her birth-mother."

Harry eyed her over his next sip, spluttering it down his chin and chest when her words set in.

"What the hell, Annie. Who is this you've brought here. Why on earth would she make such an accusation? My family has been through enough without this. What do you want? Money? I have none. Gloria took it all, and my Aston Martin. I don't even have anything to leave my own grandchildren. I don't need this nonsense. You're not welcome here, Missy. New Zealand was my home once, but not anymore. I never want to see you again." Harry then squinted his eyes at Annie, gritting his teeth. "You understand, Annie. Not a word. I'm going to bed. You deal with this. Get rid of her."

Harry was already on his feet, as was Chloe. She could scarcely believe how quickly things had turned for the worse. Why had he been so quick to dismiss her?

"Harry. I'm sorry if I've upset you." She caught hold of the old man's sleeve. He whipped around, his breath heavy with a wheeze. "You've no right coming here."

"No. But I just need to know where Marta lives. I promise I won't bother you any more. I know Jimmy's death must have been such a blow to your family and I know he knew the truth about Marta having a baby. Surely you wouldn't want to deprive a child from meeting their mother, would you?"

Harry hissed. "Get out! Get out of my house now, before I throw you out!" He barked with the ferocity of a Bull Terrier.

"I will find her, Mr Ingles, with or without your help." Chloe said before running from the room.

Standing on the front doorstep with the door still open slightly, she could hear Annette trying to console her father-in-law. She felt bad she had put Annette in the position of having to mediate the situation. Chloe looked up and down the street. It was cold and getting darker now. The beat of her heart thickened in her ears, and she lowered her head, drawing her coat around her.

Annette arrived at the doorstep looking sympathetically grim. "I'm so sorry, Chloe. I didn't realise he'd react like this. I don't think he's been taking his meds. I should have visited him sooner. He's normally a little more polite than this. Maybe it's best if you go. I need to stay and try and settle him. Will you be all right getting home? You can call for an Uber and wait inside if you like. Harry will understand."

"Thanks, Annette, but I think I'll walk to the station. It's not that far."

"You sure?" Annette clutched Chloe's arm.

"Yeah. I'll be fine." Chloe didn't want to stay in Harry's house any longer than she had to. He clearly didn't want her there and she felt a brisk walk might help her head. Where had she gone wrong? Maybe she shouldn't have mentioned Jimmy. Maybe Harry had forgotten or didn't want her bringing his sister's reputation into question. They were both valid possibilities, but the one that hurt the most was his accusation she was after his money. Chloe wondered if perhaps he had been quite wealthy in the past given his mention of the car and his wife taking it all when she left.

Annette let her go. "Let me talk to him. I'll try and make him understand. He's had it pretty tough lately, with David's death and all. We all have. It's just bad timing."

Chloe nodded. "I understand. But please do try and see if he'll tell you where Marta is. For the sake of my mother, I won't let it go. I have to find her, with or without Harry's help."

"I'll do my best, Chloe." Annette closed the door behind her.

Tears trailed her cheeks as she walked in the direction of the station. It wasn't any later than eight o'clock but as the sky dimmed, it was late enough to keep her ears alert for any sound of trouble. As she neared the end of the first block a group of three teenage boys loitered outside a convenience store. Although it was darker on the opposite side of the street she crossed over to avoid having to walk past them. She tucked her head low and wrapped her coat tight around her middle. It wasn't until she had passed the store that she realised she was headed straight into the path of a hobbling older man coming towards her. Should she cross again? That might make her seem fearful, which she was. Denying her fear a foothold, she stayed her course, keeping her head low. When she was within a few metres of him, she nodded at him, sidestepping to let him pass. She continued on, picking up her walk - almost to a trot. The closer she got to the station the better she felt. Lights were ablaze at the platforms entrance and she knew if she could just make it there, she would soon be on the train and heading home. The problem was she hadn't anticipated this outcome and hadn't the first clue which train she should catch to get herself home. Maybe she should call an Uber to come get her from the station. At least she'd get where she needed to go and not end up somewhere even further from home.

She pulled out her phone as she reached the final crossroads before the station. Swiping the screen and tapping on the Uber app, she heard the sound of a few footsteps closing in behind her. She gave a momentary glance over her shoulder and sure enough it was the boys from the corner. Were they following her, or simply heading to the station to catch the train like she was? One set of footsteps quickly grew louder and before she knew it one of them had snatched the phone from her hand.

"Hey. Give that back. That's mine." Chloe regretted her words the moment she uttered them. The other two, still behind her, quickened their pace and tripped her up. In the process they attempted to snatch her handbag. She clutched it to her stomach and fell to the ground, waiting for the blow that would inevitably make her let it go. She knew it was a mistake but her fingers gripped hold of the strap so tight that every time they attempted to wrench it free, the strap cut a little deeper into her skin.

All reason had left her, and her only instinct was to lash out and defend herself. She stretched an arm, trying to claw at one of the boys' faces. She let out a scream pitched so high that it pierced her own ears. Both boys jumped away and took off at a sprint towards the station.

Now what? Where could she go now? The station wasn't an option anymore, not if they'd be waiting for her there. Her phone was gone, but at least she still had her bag and wallet.

Crouching on the path a beam of light flooded the street from a doorway a few houses ahead.

"Come. In here." A faint voice whispered.

Could she really trust a stranger and enter their house? Maybe she should just walk back to Harry's place. Annette would help her. Before she could turn in the opposite direction a woman with dark skin and glowing white teeth stepped from the door. "In here. You'll be safe."

Chloe stood and took a step towards her. Her left shin throbbed and she limped the rest of the way.

"Oh my days. They dun yu good, did'n they." The woman's Jamaican accent was comforting as was her arm around her as she helped Chloe inside the house.

Chloe looked around the hallway and a breath shuddered from her chest.

"It's irie, luv. You're in shock. Here. Sit down. Is there anyone I can call for ya?"

Chloe fished inside her handbag and took out a card with Matt's number on it. The woman took it and fetched a phone from the next room. Chloe sat on the stairway and looked at her leg. It was dampened with a stain of blood through her jeans. The woman dialled the number and handed Chloe the phone.

Chloe waited while it rang praying Matt would pick up.

"Hello?"

"Matt. It's me. Can you come get me...I've been attacked."

"What? Oh God, Chloe. Where are you?"

"I'm..." Chloe winced at her stabbing leg before letting out her breath, "...I'm not sure."

The woman gestured she pass her the phone. Chloe felt a little dizzy so she let the woman take it.

Chloe wasn't sure how much time passed, but enough that she was now comfortably seated on the old woman's couch. Her wounded leg had been cleaned and bandaged and the woman had brought her a proper cup of tea. Chloe drew in the scent of spiced leaves like it were medicine for her pain.

A knock on the door made her jump and the woman left the room.

Matt's face appeared around the sitting room doorway and her pent up emotions could no longer be contained. Tears slipped down her cheeks like prisoners making a run for it. He rushed to her side.

"Oh, Chloe. I never should have let you talk me into letting you come alone."

"But I wasn't alone." Chloe blubbered. "At least not to begin with."

"Well something must have gone wrong. Why didn't you call me straight away?"

"I had to get out of there. Harry was so mad! Annette didn't know what to do. She did offer to let me stay till an Uber arrived, but I figured it wasn't that far to the station." Fresh tears travelled south once more and Matt pulled her into his arms.

"It's all right. It's over now."

There was another knock on the door. The woman looked confused and then worried.

"It's okay. I called the Police." Matt said.

She nodded but seemed not entirely happy by his news.

After the police had taken Chloe's statement, Matt thanked the woman and lifted Chloe from the couch. Supporting her hobbling effort to the front door of the house, he paused once they were outside and scooped her clean off the ground. Chloe wrapped her arms around Matt's neck and rested her head against his shoulder. Matt carried her to his SUV and tucked her safely inside.

Red lights spiralled the street as the Police car pulled away.

Chloe leant her head against the cold glass window and closed her eyes. She was finally safe.

When the car pulled to a stop outside Joy's, Chloe couldn't remember the journey there at all. She felt sleepy and exhausted. Matt opened her door and as she fumbled for the seat belt's latch, she couldn't seem to make her fingers work. Matt reached across and pushed the button, pulling the strap free. Chloe tried to lift herself out but her whole body felt so heavy.

"Easy. I got you." Matt wrapped his arm around her waist and took the majority of her weight till she was vertical.

"I forgot to thank Dara." Chloe mumbled.

"I took care of that. You were lucky she heard you scream."

"I know. I'm so sorry, Matt. I should have listened to you."

"Never mind. Let's get you inside and into bed."

Chloe slid a smile across her lips. "Are you trying to seduce me, Mr Knightly?"

"Me? No, never. But I'm not leaving you, Chloe. I'll sleep on the couch. I'm sure Joy won't mind."

"No. Not a bit. But maybe you should ask her to refrain from informing the press of your location."

Matt eyed her a little confused before he twigged about what she was implying.

"Got it. I'll have a word."

Sunday 10th September 2017

Chloe awoke the next morning to find Matt's arm wrapped around her middle. The bed covers lay between them but her memory of how he came to be there was a little foggy.

Flashes of the attack and how she had cowered on the ground conjured memories of Matt coming to her rescue. It was she who had asked him to stay beside her so she could sleep.

He stirred at her attempt to slip beneath his arm and out from the covers.

"Chloe?" He hitched up on one arm and rubbed his eyes with his fingers. He blinked a few times and then ran a palm through his hair.

"What time is it?" He yawned.

"It's morning. Thanks for staying, Matt. It really meant a lot."

Matt pulled himself to sit on the edge of the bed next to her before standing. "Sure. I wouldn't want to be anywhere else. Breakfast? I could take you out if you want." Chloe watched him stretch, His t-shirt raised and she spied his stomach muscles straining against the tension. He caught her staring, so she dipped her eyes to her pyjama sleeves, tugging the ends over her hands. She looked back up at him.

"No I just want to stay home today. Can you stay?"

"Of course. I'll just make a few calls. I'm sure I can work something out. I'm going to have to order us some breakfast though. I'm hungry and we can't stay in without provisions." He smiled and bent to kiss her head.

Chloe caught hold of his hand and wouldn't let go. He helped ease her up off the bed and encircled her in his arms. The tension building between them became too intense. Afraid of what she might say or do, Chloe tucked her chin to Matt's chest and rested her cheek there a moment. His heart thumped in her ear and she knew she had stirred him. She drew herself away without meeting his eyes and shuffled towards the bathroom.

When she returned, Matt was nowhere to be found. She threw on her dressing gown and went in search of him downstairs. The voices from the kitchen confirmed Joy was up and no doubt ready to fire her with questions about last night.

"Thanks." She heard Matt say. "I'll go help Chloe get down the…"

Chloe entered the kitchen and headed for the cupboard containing the mugs.

"Morning. Did you sleep well?" Joy's tone and smirk left little to guess what she meant by it.

"Fine thanks. You?" Chloe replied, without biting. Matt looked between the two of them.

"Would you mind if I took a quick shower, Joy? It'd be nice to freshen up a bit." Matt thumbed a gesture upstairs.

"Sure. There are towels in the hallway closet. Help yourself. Do you want a clean shirt? I'm sure I can find something for you if you like."

"I'll be fine. Thanks." Matt strode from the room like he'd just lit a fuse and his safest position was as far away from the kitchen as possible.

No matter how many questions Joy asked, Chloe couldn't pry her mind from the man in their bathroom.

"Matt Knightly is taking a shower in my house!" Joy's words - not hers. It was nigh on impossible not to imagine Matt standing under the streams of water. She'd already seen more of his body than most when they swam in the hotel pool together. But to have him so close made her tingle all over.

Chloe rinsed her cup in the sink and headed towards the stairs.

"Where are you going so fast?" Joy asked with a wink.

"I'm going to get dressed if you must know."

"Sure." Joy giggled. Chloe half expected Joy might offer to help her up the stairs. But only to make sure Chloe did what she said she was going to do.

Joy's keys rattled as she snatched them from the table and headed for the front door. Chloe knew then that Joy was more than a little miffed at her, and had no intention of hanging around for what might become an awkward situation.

"I'll be back in an hour. That long enough?" Joy didn't wait for Chloe's answer and the door slammed behind her. Chloe shrugged and hopped herself back up the stairs. She was a little out of breath when she neared the top, and was glad Matt exited the bathroom to help her the rest of the way.

"You want to go next?" Matt asked.

Chloe nodded. "Joy's gone out for a bit. She'll be back later."

Matt nodded. "Well I can't say that doesn't make me feel a bit better. I thought she was going to bite my head off before you got down there. She's been grilling me hard about why I wasn't with you last night in the first place. I tried to explain, but Joy wouldn't hear it. She'll make a great mother one day." Matt laughed. Chloe did too.

"Can I help you to the shower?"

"Hmm. You'd like that wouldn't you?" Chloe crooked him a smile, and his eyes glistened back.

"I won't deny that the prospect is enticing."

"I'll be fine." Chloe turned and shuffled towards the bathroom. But before she could get too far, he grabbed hold of her elbow and turned her back to face him again.

"Chloe?"

"Yes?"

"Please, don't be mad, but..." Matt raised both his hands to each side of her face and stroked his fingers into her hair. He lowered his mouth towards hers, pausing only a moment before pressing his lips gently against hers. She raised her chin, willing him to offer more. She clutched his wrists softly, yielding to his touch.

He withdrew a moment, resting his forehead on hers, seeking the permission he desired to continue. The intoxicating linger of his breath, and his hand slipping around her waist, sent a shiver though her body. She could take it no longer and leaned in towards his mouth for another kiss. Pulling herself tighter to his torso, she clasped her arms around his neck and let his tongue caress hers.

Her legs weakened and he slipped his other hand around her waist, lifting her from the floor entirely. The toes of her right foot wrinkled before stretching to the floor. He didn't seem to want to release her, but he eventually let her back down. Chloe pulled her eyes open and ran her teeth across her lower lip, sliding it into a grin. Matt's cheeks dimpled. She'd not seen that smile before. His eyes lingered on her lips a moment more before he pulled his gaze to her eyes.

His hands remained around her waist and he kept his face as close to hers for as long as he could. Chloe cleared her throat and his trance came to an end when the sound of the doorbell chimed throughout the house.

"That must be the food." Matt stroked her cheek. "I'll go deal with that while you go take a shower."

Chloe nodded rubbing a hand up the back of her neck.

The doorbell rang again in three quick successions.

"All right, I'm coming." Matt called.

Chloe hopped towards the bathroom with a silent squeal swirling in her head.

Wow! Just, wow! Matt sure knew how to leave a girl wanting more.

She turned on the shower and quickly got in. The warm water felt nice, even though it stung around the gash on her leg. It got worse when she tried to add soap.

Patting herself dry she thought she could still hear two voices downstairs. The delivery guy was either still chatting with Matt, which wouldn't be surprising. Or, perhaps Joy was back sooner than expected.

Chloe limped back to her room and quickly dressed into some sweat pants and t-shirt. She tugged on her slippers and headed for the door. It was only then that she thought she recognised the other voice.

Jeremy?

CHAPTER SIXTEEN

CHLOE HOPPED AS quickly as she could to the base of the stairs. The sound of keys rattling at the front door warned of Joy's return. So it definitely wasn't her Matt was talking to. Chloe waited till the door opened and Joy stepped inside.

Chloe warned her to keep quiet with a raised finger. "Shhh."

Joy looked confused.

"Matt's talking with someone," Chloe whispered.

"Okay. But why are we whispering?" Joy replied huskily.

The voices in the sitting room ceased and the door swung open.

There, standing before her, was Chloe's worst fear. Jeremy in the flesh.

His eyes looked drawn and his chin was unshaven. In fact he looked quite terrible if she were entirely honest.

"Jeremy. What are you doing here?" A sudden flush of his after shave hit her, its jarring woody scent conjuring memories she didn't want to relive right now.

"Babe. I missed you so much," he said, pulling her into his arms and resting his chin on her shoulder.

Chloe's tongue froze. She hadn't the slightest clue what to say in return, but words just seemed to fall from her mouth on some kind of autopilot. "I missed you to." She looked towards Matt with a glint of an apology in her eyes.

Jeremey pulled away releasing her just a little from his grasp. "Now that I'm here. We can start all over. What do you say, Babe? I should never have let you come on your own. I was stupid and foolish to suggest we take a break. I just thought you'd benefit from some time to grow up on your own. These past few weeks without you have taught me one thing. I can't live without you, Chloe. You're the one for me." Jeremy got down on one knee and pulled a small box from his pocket. He opened it and held it up to her. "Will you do me the honour of becoming my wife, Chloe Spencer?"

Tears stripped her cheeks. What should she do? How could she make him stop? Her heart ached in a mixture of emotions. Just minutes ago she felt like she was starting to move forward. Towards a life of her own making and choosing. Now she'd been tossed back in time to a moment she thought she always wanted - Jeremy on one knee.

She touched his arm. "I...I can't give you an answer, Jeremy. I do love you, but..." Matt eyed her as if hanging his hopes on every word she spoke. "I'm just not sure that I'm still *in* love with you anymore."

Jeremy's eyes dropped and he snapped the box shut. "What do you mean, Babe? We're meant for each other. We make a great team, you and I. Plus, your Mum really likes me."

Jeremy hit raw a nerve, and he knew it. Betting the one chip he had left, Jeremy knew she couldn't argue with him over it. Perhaps he considered it his only real means of winning her back. Chloe didn't know what to say. She had to stall him for an answer before she agreed to something she'd likely regret.

"I know. But, I just need more time. It's a big decision and I'm not ready to make it yet. I appreciate you've come all this way, but… Hang on. Why have you come all this way? Why now? Why are you really here, Jeremy, did Danielle say something?"

"No. But she did say that you were moving on. I didn't like the thought of you with anyone else. So I told my boss that I had to take a few weeks off and win back the heart of the girl I love."

Chloe didn't doubt his words, just their timing. So it was only his fear of losing her for good that motivated him to act. How romantic - not.

Just then the doorbell rang again. Who else was about to join their band of merry men? Matt pointed to himself. "Ah…that'll be the food." He left the room and Chloe worried he might not return. When the front door closed and Matt's return wasn't forth coming. Chloe knew she had to do something.

'Wait here, Jeremy. I'll be back in a minute."

Chloe left him with a grinning Joy who appeared to be enraptured by the real live drama unfolding in her living room.

"Matt?" Chloe called.

She opened the front door to find him sitting with a plastic bag filled with baked goods and two cups of coffee in a cardboard holder. She lowered herself to the step beside him.

"I'm so sorry, Matt. I had no idea he would just turn up like this. I…I don't want him here. Truly. I came here on my own to prove to myself that I didn't need a man to look after me. But here I am, completely in that position. I mean, look what happened last night. If I'd just listened to you and accepted your offer I could have avoided being attacked on the street. Maybe I'm not as strong and independent as I hoped."

"Nonsense, Chloe. You are not the weak thing you make yourself out to be. You are strong and brave to come all this way on your own. You have a job you love, and friends who care about you. That's not weakness. I don't care what Jeremy says or thinks. You belong with whoever makes you happy. Not just someone who needs you. Do you really want to live your life dreaming about what your life could have been? I don't expect anything from you. I'll understand no matter what choice you make. But, I have to say this. If you go back to Jeremy, will anything be any different than what it was before you left? You split for a reason. Just don't forget that. You deserve the best. And, in my wholly biased opinion, Jeremy ain't it. He was right when he said he was a fool. I already know I'd be a fool to give you up without a fight. I know you felt something upstairs. But if you want me to go, I'll go, and I won't bother you again."

"I...I don't know. It's a little hard to think right now. I...I did feel something for you. I still do. I'm just scared I'll make the wrong choice and ruin everything." Chloe's bottom lip trembled. Matt wrapped his arm around her shoulders and reached a finger to lift her chin. Chloe searched his eyes for an answer and she found one in his gaze. He liked her. Maybe he even loved her. But was he the one who would be the right fit for the future? He came from a completely different world to hers, and she couldn't see a safe way over the fence between them. Despite her floundering thoughts, his lips pressed into hers with such tenderness that she forgot for a moment and let the intensity of their chemistry ignite once more. Her insides swirled, as did her thoughts. She never felt that way with Jeremy anymore. In fact she couldn't remember the last time she had any kind of lovely flutters from his touch. They certainly weren't there when he'd dropped to his knee. Shouldn't she have at least felt something for him?

Matt left her lips and Chloe's eyes remained closed. She didn't want the moment to end, to have to face reality. Why couldn't Jeremy just leave well enough alone? Danielle would have to answer for this. She just knew she had something more to do with Jeremy's presence here. How could she do this to her own sister? And why? Didn't she like Matt? She'd encouraged her to date him and said Chloe couldn't do any better. So why send in the cavalry when there was no war to fight.

Ah, but now she guessed there could be. Was this Danielle's way of making Chloe see where her true heart lay? The only problem with that was, she didn't know. How could she? She'd even told Matt that she was still not over Jeremy. But she had at least admitted to Jeremy that perhaps she was no longer *in* love with him. Was it really that big of a difference? Even married couples said they weren't always *in* love with their spouses. It didn't mean they didn't still love each other.

All she knew was that she wasn't ready to choose.

"I'll leave you to it." Matt said as he stood. "I've a few errands to run, but I'll give you a call later."

"Promise?"

"I promise."

"Good. I'll hold you to it, Mr Knightly. I know you're not in the habit of breaking your promises and I'd hate to be the one who breaks your record."

He smiled. "Not a chance, Miss Spencer. Only a fool would break a promise to you." He bowed formally, handed her a coffee and pastry, and turned to leave.

"You sure know the way to a teacher's heart." She smiled and waved until he drove away.

Back inside only turmoil awaited. If only she could stay out here on the sunny doorstep and enjoy her breakfast, alone. Any hopes of a peaceful brunch were scrapped as soon as the front door swung open. Joy stood with a weird kind of grin on her face. "Please take care of your visitor. He's come all this way to see you. Don't you think you should at least talk to him, rather than hiding out here? He deserves a decent explanation at the very least."

Chloe skulled her coffee, which was only just warm, and tugged a mouthful of pastry from the bag. She stuffed it in her mouth and then promptly repeated the process until her whole mouth was full. At least the time it took to chew and swallow it all would give her a few minutes to consider what she might say. She had a mind to make Jeremy run a gauntlet of questions. Questions she'd long hoped he'd answer ever since their breakup.

What made him think he deserved another chance? Why did he really break up with her in the first place? Who had he been with at the hospital when Danielle spoke to him? How did he ever hope to regain her trust? Why should she agree to marry him? What was it that he truly loved about her? All these and more burned in her mind for answers. Yes she would make him work for her trust. And, no. She would not make it easy for him. If she could send him home on the next flight, she would. But given that he'd come all this way, she couldn't bring herself to dismiss him without first hearing him out. Maybe once they'd had it out, her mind would be at ease. She had far more pressing worries than whether or not to accept a proposal of marriage. It was that thought that bugged her the most. She had dreamed of the day Jeremy would propose. Wished for it so desperately that she thought she must have jinxed it for herself. But now, with his declaration made, she didn't feel the joy she once imagined she would. No. She felt something entirely different than what she expected and it scared her.

I don't love him, and I don't think I ever really did. I like the idea of us, but the reality is not what I've longed for all these years.

The thought of committing herself back into their co-dependent relationship wasn't as enticing as it once was. No longer could she envision herself as Mrs Jeremy Riggs. In fact the thought almost repulsed her. Yes her mother liked him. But Dad didn't. Not to mention her grandfather's words. They still rang as true as the day he'd spoken them. "He's a bastard, Chloe, and he doesn't deserve you. You're too good for him." Thomas' curt words brought a smile to her lips, promptly followed by a tear. She missed him. She missed all of them. Her family meant everything to her. How could she stay here another day when she felt so miserable away from them. Jeremy at least lived in New Zealand. Matt had a big career here. It wasn't as if he'd promised to up-sticks and move country to be with her.

For now she had to remain here. Men aside, she had a promise of her own to fulfil, and no man, not one who'd proposed marriage, nor one who was famous and made her heart melt, would distract her from what she set out to achieve. Finding Marta was all that mattered and if Jeremy or Matt couldn't respect that, then neither of them deserved to be a part of her life, full stop.

"Jeremy. I think you should leave."

"You can't be serious, Chloe. I've only just got here."

"I know. But I never asked you to come, and there's no room for you to stay here. I suggest you go home if you've nowhere else to go. I'm not giving you an answer to your proposal right now. I have other priorities. If you really want me back, then you're going to have to prove it. Give me time. I'll be home for Danielle's wedding in April. I'll give you my answer then. If you can't wait that long, then we would never have lasted anyway."

"Babe. Surely you don't mean that. I love you. You're my cupcake and I'm your teddy bear. We belong together. Is it because of that footballer? He'll never love you like I do, Chloe. His first love will always be the game. You're just someone new to play with. He'll never be able to give you what I can."

"And what's that, Jeremy - a long list of reasons why he needs me? Matt doesn't need me. He likes me for who I am. He encourages me and makes me feel like I can do anything on my own, if I really want to. I feel free with him. We weren't like that. You rely on me to pick you up when you're feeling low. And I expected you to put me back together when I fell apart. But is that really good for either of us? I want to grow, to learn more about who I am and where I come from. You seem to want nothing to change. I can't be with you if that's the life you envisage for us."

"Chloe. You know that's not true. We have changed. Look at us. You're so much stronger than you give yourself credit for. I'm just sorry it took me so long to realise it."

"Please just go, Jeremy. I need to be alone."

"I'm not leaving until you give me a straight answer, Chloe. Yes or no?"

"If you can't respect me needing time to think about it, then I'm afraid my answer's no. I think you should go now."

Jeremy looked at Chloe. "I have to believe you don't mean it, Chloe. You'll see. In time I think you'll change your mind." Jeremy pushed the small box with the ring in it into his pocket. "I'll see *you* at the wedding."

With that, Jeremy withdrew from the sitting room and a few seconds later she heard the front door click shut.

Chloe sunk onto the couch, butted her head into a cushion, and screamed.

It was getting close to 6:00 pm when Chloe's vow of silence was interrupted. Joy poked her head around the door of her bedroom.

"Chloe. There's a delivery for you. It just arrived. Do you want to open it?"

Joy's tone had lightened and it was evident she felt some sympathy for her.

Chloe pulled her head from beneath the pillow, and, in a groggy daze of moist eyes and a red nose, she mumbled. "Who's it from?" Chloe's heart skipped at the thought of a package from back home. A week or so after she'd arrived, Dad had sent her a small packet containing a hand written letter and a block of Whittaker's Jelly Tip chocolate. He knew her so well, and to hold a piece of paper with his handwriting on it made him feel all the more closer.

Joy handed over a white box about the size of an old large Bible, and sat next to Chloe on the bed.

"I don't know. There's no return address."

Chloe knew as soon as she saw it that it couldn't have come from New Zealand. It was too clean and clinical to have travelled all those miles. Joy handed her a pair of scissors so she could cut the tape along its edge.

Reaching inside, Chloe pulled out another small box. It was a new cell phone. A simple post-it note stuck to its front gave the only clue as to who had sent it.

"So I can keep my promise," Joy read over Chloe's shoulder. "Well that's cryptic."

"Not to me." Chloe smiled. "It's from Matt. He knew mine was stolen and he promised he'd call me later. That's so sweet."

Chloe unwrapped the phone from the rest of its packaging and noticed it had already been opened once before. She hit the power button and the screen lit up. Matt had already charged it and entered some of the numbers she might need.

His. The school's. Her boss. Joy's, Jenny's, and Annette's. He'd even added some emergency number's and put them on her home screen. The best part was, he'd already selected a photo for her background. It was a close-up picture of them outside the Parkway Hotel. There were others in the Gallery too, ones Matt had snapped of them in the hotel room after their swim. She looked so happy. Nothing like how she'd been feeling for the past several hours.

It was strange to see herself looking so put together, relaxed, and confident. It was like looking at an image of a completely different person.

"Hey. You want to order some Chinese and watch Netflix with me?" asked Joy.

BEEP-BOOP-BEEP-BOP-BO-BO-BEEP.

The phone's buzzing vibrations freaked Chloe out and it jumped from her hand onto the bed. The two of them laughed so hard it made Chloe's inside ache.

"Wait, it's Matt. I should answer it." Chloe said in a sighing voice trying to regain her composure.

"I'll leave you to it." Joy smiled.

Chloe grabbed her hand so she wouldn't leave. "Wait." She swiped to answer and then put it on speaker.

"Hey Matt. Joy's here with me."

"Hello, Joy. So you got my package then. Your new number is on the back of the sticky note."

"Thank you so much. I have to say, you're the first person I've met who'd go to such extreme measures to keep their promise. I'm impressed."

"Finally! Do you know how hard it is to impress this girl, Joy?"

"Oh I have my suspicions." Joy giggled.

"Anyway. I have news, and it's not the kind I want to share over the phone. Is it okay if I pop over? It's important, Chloe. You'll want to hear this."

"Uhh, I guess so. Joy and I were going to get Chinese and watch Netflix. Will it take long?"

Joy smiled and seemed pleased she had at least been considered in her decision.

"I don't know. That depends on you. I'll see you soon." Matt hung up before Chloe could ask him anything more.

Two minutes later the doorbell rang. Chloe's heart sunk. She hoped it wasn't Jeremy - back again for another round. Chloe cast her eyes to the ground.

Joy patted her hand. "I'll get it. If it's Jeremy, I'll tell him you're out."

"Thank you. I just can't face him again. Not yet anyway."

Joy padded downstairs. Chloe pulled herself out of bed and wriggled her feet into her slippers. She was surprised to hear Matt's voice enter the house. Had he been parked outside their flat the whole time? How else could he have arrived so quickly?

When she made it to the kitchen the aroma of soy sauce and lemongrass made her tummy grumble. Now that she was up she realised she hadn't eaten anything since the pastry and coffee Matt brought earlier.

Her eyes widened at the cartons of noodles, chicken stir-fry, and rice spread across the table.

"Looks like your boyfriend's a mind reader, Chloe. Worth keeping around if I were you." Joy set three plates on the table and then went back to the drawer for cutlery and two remaining glasses of water on the bench.

"Wait, did you order already?" Chloe picked up one of the carton's and sniffed it. It was warm in her hand. It couldn't have come from the fridge.

Matt grinned. "I figured you girls might be hungry. So I took the liberty of picking up food before I called. Lucky guess I suppose." Matt winked at Joy and Chloe couldn't tell if the whole thing had been planned or if it really was just a lucky guess. Her stomach gurgled regardless and she promptly sat in a chair and started scraping out contents from each carton onto her plate. The others took their seats.

Chloe looked at them and stuffed noodles in her mouth, sucking them in quickly so she didn't look entirely like a pig.

She nodded as she chewed and held a hand over her mouth.

"This is so good. Thanks, guys."

Joy smiled and ate also. Matt held off starting his meal until Chloe had already swallowed two mouthfuls.

"So. What was it you wanted to tell us?" Chloe asked between bites.

Again Joy smiled. "Yes. We're glad for the food of course, but what's so important it couldn't wait? "

Chloe liked that Joy felt included. She had been a wonderful support, but it can't have been easy watching Chloe be fawned over by not just one man, but two! (One a famous footballer no less.) It's probably what a lot of girls dream of. But Chloe knew the reality of her dilemma was certainly not the fairy-tale Joy thought it was.

Matt eyed Chloe over his next mouthful and promptly shovelled in another two after it.

She leaned back in her seat as if resigned not to eat another bite until he offered his explanation.

Finally he spoke. "Please don't be mad. I..."

Chloe's mind instantly hitched to the kiss they'd shared this morning. He'd uttered those same words, but no sentiment of an apology followed. He wasn't sorry at all, not one bit, and neither was she.

"...I couldn't let last night go. So, after I left here this morning I went and saw Jenny. I told her what happened and she gave me Annette's number - so I could tell her what happened to you. Annette was terribly upset and blamed herself for the attack. She knew it wasn't safe for you out there, but she couldn't leave Harry in the state he was in. I asked her if she thought Harry might be willing to speak to me. She was reluctant to give me any hope he would. But when I told her I could get their family season pass tickets, she gave me Harry's address."

Chloe almost choked on her own saliva.

Matt paused. "I know what you're probably thinking, but I didn't do anything really stupid. Well, kinda."

"What did you do, Matt?" Chloe's eyes widened.

"Well I sort of made up a story that he'd won season tickets for his whole family. I went there around lunchtime, dressed in my full football garb and told him that someone had entered him in the draw for the prize. He was blown away. He knew who I was, but he didn't ask for an autograph or anything - said he preferred rugby. I think maybe he was trying to say in not so many words that he didn't really want the tickets for himself. He then asked me if it would be all right if he just sold them. I knew then that it might be my only shot to see what other family he might have who might like the tickets. He mentioned he had a grandson who might like one and then he also mentioned his niece had a son who was a big Arsenal fan. When he started talking about the boys, I knew then he'd probably accept a ticket for himself too. So I asked for the boys names. His grandson, Annette's son, is Ben Ingles, and the other boy's name was Brody Warren. But he said something about how he thought Brody and his mother, Vera, had moved back to Scotland."

Hints of smiles spread across Joy's and Chloe's faces.

"Well that's something." Joy gushed. "Scotland! Maybe this other boy's mother is one of Marta's children." Joy suggested.

"That's what I was thinking too," said Matt.

Chloe blinked at Matt wondering if that was the end of his story, or was there something more he was keeping to himself until he'd garnered her reaction to his first bombshell.

"Chloe. I know I should have asked you first, but I wanted to do this for you. After what happened last night I just thought you deserved to get some answers. Any answer. Just something to continue your search."

Chloe twirled a fork in her noodles once more. "And is that all? Or is there more to your little ruse you're not telling me?"

"Well. I wasn't going to say anything, but I did take the opportunity to ask Harry about how I might find an address for his niece. I think he suspected then that something wasn't quite right and he asked me why he couldn't just pass the ticket along to Brody himself. I gave him some excuse that I just had to confirm that the winners could actually attend the games. He sort of bought it - I think. Anyway, the last he knew of Vera's whereabouts was that she worked at the Whittington Hospital. I thanked him and gave him six season passes. He seemed pretty pleased. I'm sure he'll just scalp them, but at least we've got a lead." Matt grinned at her like he'd just provided her with enough intel to take down a crime ring.

"We?" Chloe said with speculative caution.

"Well. You. Of course I meant you have a lead. But surely you're ready to accept my help now. Won't you?" Matt's eyes were full of hope and Chloe knew she had better not jeopardize losing the second best asset she had in her hunt for Marta.

"You're right. I do need your help. Would you take me to the hospital and help me find out more about this Vera?"

Matt started closing up the empty boxes of Chinese and stood to clear the table. "Umm. I guess so."

Chloe caught hold of his arm before he could take two steps towards the rubbish bin. "There's more isn't there?"

"Well I might have stopped in there after my visit with Harry. What can I say. I was on a roll and I was already in my gear. You know how it goes. It wasn't hard finding the nurses manager, but getting her to talk was near impossible. She's a tough one. Eventually she confirmed Vera had worked there. But as far as any forwarding address she just wouldn't budge. I tried to explain your situation. But she kept citing the hospital's protocol about personal information. I told her I understood. But I've not given up hope yet. I've let Jenny know the new family names to search for and she's scouring the Internet for Vera Warren."

"Well. You have been a busy boy, haven't you?" Joy smiled.

Chloe cleared her throat. "Yes. It seems you've got this whole search under control. I'd still like to talk to that nurse myself though. If it's not too much trouble for you to take me."

"Of course it's no trouble. I don't know what else you think you'll be able to learn though. I tried all my tricks, but it seems the manager is a stickler for the rules."

"Well, that may be. But I've a few of my own tricks that no amount of cologne, flirting, or grins could gather."

Matt jumped his brow. "I bet you have. I can't wait to see them. Shall we head over there now?"

"It's getting late and Joy and I have some shows to catch up on. How about you pick me up after school tomorrow and we'll see if the nurses are a bit more chatty when the manager's not around. Okay?"

Matt nodded. "Right-o. I guess I'll leave you to it then." Matt finished washing his hands and went to wipe them on the dish towel. Joy shook her head and handed him the hand towel.

"Thanks for the food, Matt. And I'm still keen as mustard if you ever do get around to fixing up that evening with your friend for us." Joy giggled.

Matt grabbed his jacket from the back of the dining chair and shrugged it on. "Ah. Yeah. Sorry I haven't organised that sooner. He's been quite busy with work. He's a trader and his hours can be a bit irregular. Let me check back with him and I'll let you know." Matt walked towards the front door with Joy and Chloe in tow.

"Sure." Joy nodded like she was trying to believe him. "You do that."

"I will. I promise."

"Matt?" Chloe asked. He spun around like he couldn't wait to know what she wanted.

"Yes?"

"Thank you. You've gone above and beyond today and I'm not sure how I'll ever repay you."

"Well I've an idea." Joy laughed. She ducked out of the way and behind the sitting room door.

Chloe blushed and then boldly clutched the fronts of Matt's jacket in her fists. She pulled him towards her body slowly and lifted up on her toes. He leant to meet her lips and placed his hands on her hips. Her body pulsed with a sweep of euphoria. His mouth opened to hers, and his body tensed, yearning to take things further. He wrapped one arm around her waist, and with the other, wandered his fingers through her hair. Keeping a firm pressure on the small of her back, he pulled her to him as if fusing them together as one entity.

Dizzy and breathless, he released her a little. She dropped to her heels and their lips parted.

He traipsed a finger down her face. His gaze, thick with desire, mirrored her own feelings. She regretted having to say goodnight so soon.

He smiled, laid one last kiss on her, and then turned the door handle and slipped outside.

Chloe crushed her fists together over her chest, trying to calm her thumping heart. It was only when the sound of his car had disappeared that she could move herself again.

CHAPTER SEVENTEEN

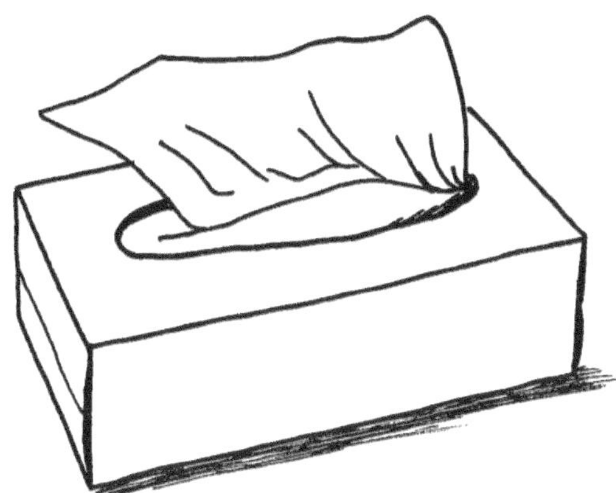

Monday 11th September 2017

WHEN THE FINAL bell rang, Chloe's heart skipped a few beats. She had eaten through four fingernails and read the clock more times in one day than she could count on her own hands.

Relieved Matt was already waiting for her outside, she promptly got in the car and pulled out a spiral-bound notebook. Fingering through the pages she read several notes about her search and the facts as she knew them. If Vera Warren had any link to Marta then Chloe simply had to find out where she'd gone.

Chloe's pulse quickened upon entering the hospital. The familiar scent of chloroform and washed linens permeated the air and pulled her stomach into a knot. Instantly her eyes wandered the corridors as thoughts of her mother's illness returned to the forefront of her mind.

"It's this way." Matt said, and took her hand.

Tears began pooling in her eyes as memories of her mother lying in a hospital bed overwhelmed her. Matt kept them moving at a steady pace until he stopped in a small waiting area in front of a nurses' station.

Chloe burst into a flood of tears and Matt wasn't sure what to do. He eased her into one of the chairs and wrapped an arm around her.

"It's okay, Chloe. We don't have to stay here. You don't have to do this. We'll come back some other time. Or maybe we could get Jenny to ask her police friend to look into it for us."

Chloe wiped her eyes and reached into her bag for a tissue. With no luck finding one she glanced around the waiting room. "No. I'll be all right."

Spotting a box on the nurses counter she stood and went to fetch a few. Behind the desk sat a single nurse whose badge indicated her name was Wendy. The young woman looked at Chloe and concern flooded her eyes.

"You all right. Miss?"

"Yes. I will be. I was wondering if you could tell me if anyone here used to work with a nurse called Vera Warren? I was told she moved, but I haven't been able to locate her. Vera tended my mother you see, before she passed, and I just wanted to thank her in person." Heat flooded Chloe's cheeks and she tucked her chin to hunt for something in her bag. The only thing she found was her father's letter, still inside its blank envelope. It remained in her bag so she could read his words anytime she felt homesick. Chloe longed to read it now. She pulled it out and held it in front of the nurse. "My mother also left something for Vera in her will."

Matt's eyebrows flew up his forehead then quickly dropped to play along.

The nurse, although sympathetic to her plight, seemed reluctant to divulge any information.

"Oh, I see."

Chloe tucked her hair behind her ear and stood the envelope upright on the counter. "I understand it's not really allowed. But our lawyer has met a dead end. He thought maybe one of Vera's past friends would better know how to find her. I'm not exactly sure what it is" - Chloe waved the envelope towards the nurse momentarily - "but I promised I'd hand it to Vera in person myself. It may be money, I'm not sure. It wouldn't surprise me if it were though. My mother was a very generous woman, and she liked Vera very much. She often spoke with her about her son, Brody."

The nurse's eyes brightened. "Oh yes, Brody was such a hoot to have around. Vera brought him to work with her a couple of times when she had no one else to look after him. All the nurses kept him busy and the matron never said anything."

Chloe lay the envelope flat on the counter, flattening her hands neatly over top. She gave a shutter speed look towards Matt. Even she was surprised that she might actually get the answer she was looking for.

"So, do you know where she went?" asked Chloe. "I heard she may have gone to Scotland."

"Oh, yes. You're correct she did move to Scotland with her kids. That was a little over a year ago now. Your lawyers must be really desperate to settle the estate if they've sent you looking for her."

"Well they didn't exactly send me. This is more of a personal request my mother made of me before she died. Mum's lawyer was a little less than sympathetic to my cause so I've been left to try and fulfil her final wishes myself." Chloe rubbed the edges of the envelope between her fingers. At least most of what she had told the nurse was true. Her mother did ask her to find Marta, and finding Vera was just a small step along that journey.

"Oh, I see." The nurse looked back to her computer.

Chloe sensed Wendy was about to clam up again. Leaning over the counter, she locked the nurse with a watery stare. "Please. If you know anything that might help me find her. I'd be eternally grateful. I can't move on until I know I've done all that I can to find Vera."

Wendy leaned towards her. "I understand. I do. But I'm just not allowed to hand out staff details. Even those who no longer work here. I really am sorry, Miss. The nurse glanced down the hallway to her right and then down the one behind her. Then she whispered, "My friend invited me to her birthday party. I think I'm going to go. I've never been to her house. It's over on Freegrove Road. Do you know where that is?"

Chloe turned to Matt. He nodded and cleared his throat.

Chloe backed away from the desk hoping distance would sever suspicion of any unusual discourse. She blew her nose. "Well, I hope you have a great time." Chloe replied. 'Thank you,' she mouthed at Wendy.

Matt took her hand and started for the exit. Chloe planted her feet, tensioning the pull until Matt noticed she wasn't going to leave. He looked back at her, confused.

She couldn't be bothered explaining, and spun back to Wendy.

"Ah...Nurse? Can you tell me which room they're in perhaps?"

Wendy glanced around before looking at a folder on the desk. "I believe it's room 63 you're after."

Chloe smiled like she'd just beaten her sister at a game of Uno. "Thank you."

Matt nodded in disbelief. And together they hurried along the corridors towards the exit.

Once they made it back inside the car Matt shook his head. "Man! And I thought I had sway. You, Chloe. You've got a whole pied piper thing going on. I don't know how you pulled that off, but you did. Sixty-three Freegrove Road here we come."

Chloe bobbed her head in the same disbelief. Heat crept up her neck and threatened to suffocate her words. "I...I don't usually lie like that. I hope you don't think I do it often. I could tell Wendy wanted to help. I just needed to find a way so that she could."

"Well I bought it. You almost had me choking up. If this teaching gig doesn't pan out, you'd make a damn good actress."

Chloe rubbed her hands over her face as if rubbing away an invisible mask. If it was that easy to deceive Matt, then maybe continuing to lie about her mother would help their search further. But was lying really the way she wanted to get answers? It didn't sit well with her. She was always on at her students about the pitfalls of telling lies. But was stretching the truth in this instance okay? Time and a moral compass were not her friends presently, and desperation seemed to strangle her conscience.

Standing at the red door of the terraced house, Chloe rapped on its painted timber as if checking for a stud in a wall. Matt reached across her and buzzed a camouflaged doorbell. Chloe looked at him as if he'd provide an answer as to why she hadn't spotted it herself.

A few seconds later the door swung open and a little girl about the age of four stood looking up at them with a finger up her nose. "Mum! It's for you." She screamed as she raced back down the passage and out of sight. Within seconds a woman could be heard speaking in a firm but kind voice. "Vicky. How many times have I told you that you're not allowed to open the front door? You must come and tell me if there's someone at the door first."

"You were busy." The girl reported more matter-of-factly than in defence of her actions.

Chloe smiled at Matt briefly before the mother appeared at the door wiping her hands on a dish towel.

"Hello. Can I help you?" The little girl stood boldly beside her mother looking up at them again with the same screwed up face she had previously. The mother lay a hand on her hair and the girl attempted to squirm free.

"Uh, I hope so. My name is Chloe Spencer and I'm looking for a woman who used to live here. Her name is Vera Warren. You don't happen to have a forwarding address do you?"

"Oh. No sorry, I don't. I recall the name, but the only mail that's come here is advertising. I used to return it, but now I just toss it."

"Oh. I see." Chloe replied.

"Maybe ask the Jackson's next door"- She gestured left - "They knew her. They might know where she lives now."

"Thank you," Chloe replied, and dipped her head towards the little girl. "And thank you." She gave her a big grin.

Matt and Chloe slipped themselves around the fence line and up to the Jackson's black front door.

"I hope we aren't just chasing our tails here. It'll be getting dark soon." Chloe sought the sky in hopes of a few extra twilight minutes. Contrary to her hopes, the days were actually getting shorter (not longer as they would be back home). There, spring lambs would be dotting the paddocks and in between farms, flowers would pop up as if from nowhere. The daffodils were her favourites and a good deal of them had already surfaced before she left.

The door before them creaked open just a little and an elderly man's face peered out from the darkness. "We're not interested. Sorry." He went to close the door but didn't quite succeed before Matt propped a foot against it.

"Excuse me sir. We don't want to bother you. We're not selling anything..."

The man pulled the door open a bit further and the whites of his eyes broadened. "Hey, don't I know you?"

"Maybe."

"Yeah. You're that football player. You play for Arsenal." The man wasn't asking for confirmation, merely stating what he believed.

"Yes that's right. Matt Knightly" - he proffered his hand towards the gentleman - "And you, Sir. Are you Mr Jackson?"

"I am. But why do you want to know?" he squinted. Chloe liked the old man's aloofness. It reminded her of her grandfather.

Chloe held out her hand for the man to shake also. "Mr Jackson. My name is Chloe, and I'm looking for a woman who nursed my mother in hospital. Vera Warren. Do you know how I might get in touch with her?"

"Oh yes, Vera. I know her. She took care of my Bessie too. She was a good nurse. A good neighbour too. Not like this other racket we've got next door now. I sure do miss 'em."

"Well I bet they miss you too." Appealing to Mr Jackson's sentimental side might be the only way to gain his trust. Bessie, she assumed was his wife, and perhaps the common chord of family sickness might draw them closer. Chloe took a deep breath and prayed she had the right end of the stick.

"Is Bessie doing all right now? Is she home?"

"Yes, she's home. I buried her in the back yard. There's wasn't anything more we could do for her."

Matt plugged the void left by Chloe's stunned silence. "Well that's nice. I had a Springer Spaniel once. He died when I was only seven. The vet said he had some rare genetic disorder and we had to put him down."

Chloe absorbed the new information about Matt, eying him sympathetically, and simultaneously realising that Bessie was not Mr Jackson's wife at all.

A guttural voice echoed from inside the house. "Who is it, Geoff. Is it those Mormons again?"

"It's a football player and his wife. They're looking for Vera." His voice croaked back.

Chloe looked at Matt in a panic. "Oh no, we're not…"

"We're not Mormons." Matt finished. He smiled with a twinkle in his eye. Chloe knew any further protest would only make their quest for information worse.

"No. We're not Mormons." Chloe said with the warmth of an ice-pack.

"For heaven's sake, Geoff. Invite them in and close the door. It's as draughty as St. Alberts in here already without you fanning the breeze." The voice from inside moved towards them and was accompanied by the softest round face Chloe had ever seen. The woman's brown beaded eyes smiled from sunken dimples on her well powdered face and her cheeks bloomed in a soft baby pink. She held out her cushioned hand, offering more warmth than a fireplace.

"Come in. I'm Mary. Geoff, Take their coats. Come. Will you have some tea?"

"That would be lovely, thanks." Matt replied and took Chloe by the hand.

For a moment she considered he only did so to confirm their lie of being married, but it wasn't the first time he'd placed his hand in hers. In fact, she was getting so accustomed to him doing so that it almost felt strange if he didn't. This simple gesture made her feel safer than if she had been accompanied by a whole squad of body guards.

He squeezed her hand and shook it a couple times. From that moment she knew he was on board with whatever tale she had brewing in the pot.

Excitement bubbled, fostering a sense of confidence she hadn't felt since leaving home.

"So you're looking for Vera?" Mary asked as she filled a kettle and flipped the switch. "Well she's been gone for a while now."

Chloe pressed a short smile between her lips. "Yes. I know. We tried looking for her at the hospital. I had no idea it would be this difficult to track her down. My mother left her a little something." She fished for the envelope again. "She asked me to personally deliver it into her hand. She loved Vera and I think she just wanted to show how much she appreciated her, now that she's gone."

"You're not from around here are you, deary?"

"No. I'm from New Zealand." Mary raised her eyebrows and Chloe could finally make out the whites of her eyes.

"Well. What do you make of that, Geoff? New Zealand. That's a million miles away. How on earth did you come to be all the way over here, then? Tea, Coffee?"

Chloe nodded. "Tea thanks. I got a teachers position at Millfields Community School."

"Mr Knightly?"

Matt nodded to the tea.

Mrs Jackson dumped four tea bags into a pot and followed it with the boiled water. "Well, I bet they're glad to have you. How was it your mother came to be in Vera's care then?"

Chloe dipped her eyes to the table, while Mrs Jackson poured tea into the cups before them. If only an answer were as easy to brew as a cup of tea. "Well, we've lived here for a while now. When Mum was diagnosed with cancer, Vera was the one who stopped by to check on her the most."

"Ah, yes. Vera is very good at what she does. She never said she worked in the oncology department though. She must have taken a liking to your mother if she visited her often. Oncology is clear across the other side of the hospital from the ER.”

Chloe knew then that her efforts to deceive Mary were on very thin ice if not completely sunk already.

“Uh, yes. Well, Mum knew Vera from quite a young age.” Chloe knew as soon as the words slipped from her tongue that she had only just deepened the hole by another foot or so.

“Oh, I see. Well, your mother must be very well travelled then. Scotland, New Zealand, London. Vera only returned home because she couldn’t secure the house on her own. Grant said she could stay in the house, but when the divorce settlement came through, she just couldn’t manage it. We were both terribly sad to see them go. Jess took it pretty hard. That girl was born for the stage.” Mrs Jackson’s cheeks blossomed with fondness.

“Sorry, who is Jess?” Matt asked. Chloe was glad that he did. If he hadn’t, she might have slipped up in her lie even further.

“Vera’s daughter. Jess.” Mary replied. “Vera said she was finally settling in now that her drama teacher had seen what she could do.”

Chloe’s heart lifted. This meant that Vera had been in touch with Mary after they left London. And fingers crossed it meant she had a means of contacting her?

“Mrs Jackson. Would you be able to give me a phone number or an address where I might find Vera? I’d like to deliver Mum’s letter to her before I return to New Zealand in April.”

“You’re not leaving the team are you, Mr Knightly?” asked Geoff.

Matt swallowed his tea and set the cup down. “No. Of course not. Chloe’s just going to visit some family.”

Geoff nodded. “Well. I know Brody would be over the moon to meet you.”

"Oooh, yes. He really would. He's a big fan of yours, Mr Knightly. He's a pretty good player too I think." Mary's cheeks puffed once more and her eyes almost disappeared entirely.

"Well, I'd love to meet him, Mrs Jackson. Perhaps I could get him some tickets to a couple of games too."

"Oooo. He'd like that, wouldn't he, Mary. Where's that letter they sent?" Mr Jackson looked around the room.

"Mary rose from the kitchen table and left the room. A few minutes later she returned with an envelope in hand. She placed it on the table in front of Chloe.

"Here you go. She moved back home to live with her brother, Max. But she said she was looking for her own place in the village."

Chloe read the tiny address in the envelope's top corner.

'C/- M. Lockheart

287 Tullynessle Lane,

Alford, Scotland'

Chloe took out her phone and quickly took a photo of the handwritten address.

Mary picked up the letter and took out the single page from inside, and handed it to Chloe.

"We haven't heard from her in a while. I think things have settled down now. I think I'll write her tomorrow and see how she's getting on."

Heat gathered at Chloe's collar. What if Mary divulged all she had told them to Vera? It then dawned on her that aside from her slip about her mother knowing Vera at a young age, she hadn't really said anything to cause suspicion that her story wasn't true. That was, unless she went into detail about visiting her in the oncology department. That might catch them out.

There was little she could do now other than to continue with the lie.

Chloe skimmed the letter quickly. Most of it was to do with how Mary and Geoff were getting along with the new neighbours. Vera mentioned that Jess and Brody were settling into their school well and that Jess would be starring as one of the leads in the school's production of A Midsummer Night's Dream. She also mentioned that Brody was missing his chats over the fence with Mr Jackson and that he had joined a soccer team. They were doing very well in their games, apparently. Vera said she would write again once she had found a new home for themselves. Since this was the only letter Mary had shown them, she presumed they hadn't found one yet.

Mary picked up the empty tea-cups and put them in the sink. Matt took that as their cue to leave and stood.

"Well. Thank you, Mr Jackson" - he shook the man's hand again - "and Mrs Jackson." Matt held out his hand but the elderly woman engulfed him in her arms. Matt smiled sheepishly upon being released.

Mary hugged Chloe also. "It's been lovely meeting you both. You do make a smashing couple, don't they, Geoff? Oh yes. You'll have beautiful children, most certainly."

Chloe blushed. "Not yet, though."

Matt grinned. "Oh, I don't know. I quite like the idea of starting our own football team sooner rather than later." Matt's grin wiped Chloe's from her mouth. She bit her lower lip momentarily before giving a tentative laugh.

"Thank you for the tea, Mary. And thank you for all your help."

Mary winked at her. "Goodnight, Mrs Knightly. I hope you find what it is you're looking for."

PART FOUR

2017

Alford –

Scotland

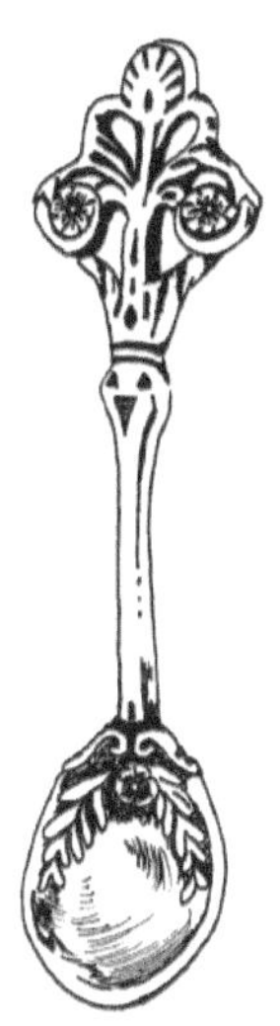

CHAPTER EIGHTEEN

Saturday 16th September 2017

Chloe

JESS WARREN WAS as she expected: a teenage girl, whose Facebook photos, although short on number, accurately represented the girl Chloe was poised to meet within seconds.

Once Jess confirmed her as a Facebook friend three days ago, Chloe had studied Vera's daughter's online photos in great detail. In some, she looked far more than her fifteen years and by anyone's reckoning could have easily passed as someone in their early twenties. But other photos gave her lack of maturity away. Snap-chat filters with animated features and younger looking friends placed her squarely in the high school age bracket.

The Alford Academy car park was scarcely populated when they arrived. A fact Chloe thought Matt might have preferred given he wasn't supposed to leave the city after his first game of the season. They only planned to stay one night and would be back in time for school on Monday.

Jess had asked them to meet her and her cousin, Ella, at the school rather than at the address on Mary's letter. Mutual territory was probably best all round, but Chloe wondered if perhaps there was more to it than that.

Matt followed two steps behind, a fact she appreciated given the trip was really about her journey and not his.

Jess cocked her head to one side as they approached straining her eyes against the low sun.

"Chloe Spencer?"

"Yes. That's me. And this is -"

"Matt Knightly!" Jess fizzed. "I don't believe it! Ella look, it's Matt Knightly."

A demure girl with brown curly hair and large eyes looked over Matt as though he were a new dress she was trying to decide if she liked or not. It was clear Ella hadn't a clue who Matt was, and it amused Chloe. Finally! There were still people on this continent who had no idea who Matt was. She only had to travel nearly 900 kilometres to find one of them. She was certain that if Matt ever came to New Zealand he'd practically be anonymous.

Nevertheless, it seemed Jess knew exactly who Matt was.

"Brody's gonna be pure static when he sees you. You won't remember, but he asked for your autograph nearly a month ago when we flew in to see Dad." Jess looked back to Chloe. "So how do you two know each other? You said you're from New Zealand, didn't you?"

Jess' question wasn't unwarranted and if Chloe weren't so impatient to stay on course, she'd have made more of an effort with her response.

"Matt's just a friend. That's all."

Jess looked at Ella. "Is he now? Well. I bet friends like Matt don't fall in your lap every day. How'd you meet?"

Chloe sighed. "We met at the airport. Now if you don't mind I really would like to know if we can meet Marta. She is the reason we've come all this way. I don't mean to sound rude or pushy, but I really must speak with her."

"Hey, I know you. You're the lady who took our photo with Matt at the Airport! Remember? I told you, Ella?"

Ella looked confused and then as if in pain she spoke. "Oh yeah. We understand you're eager to see our Grandma, but she isn't always up to seeing visitors. We popped down to see her during the game this morning and I'm afraid she doesn't seem to be very co-operative today. Maybe we could try tomorrow?"

"Oh"- Chloe frowned - "I see. Well…" she spun round hoping Matt might add more weight to her request.

He shrugged a shoulder and looked around as if there was little else to say.

"Well…" Chloe hadn't a clue what might change the girls' minds and resigned herself to the fact that meeting her new grandmother would have to wait until tomorrow. "Well, I guess we'll go tomorrow then. We're staying at an Airbnb nearby. So, what time shall we meet tomorrow?"

"Grandma is usually best in the mornings," said Ella. "Say ten-thirty, by the war memorial in the Village. Will that be all right?"

"Sounds good to me," Matt said, stretching his arms skyward with a yawn.

Chloe saw both girls take a momentary peek at his displayed abs.

"Where's a good place to eat around here?" Matt said following his yawn with a pat on his belly.

"The Forbes Arms is pretty good, isn't it, Jess?" said Ella.

"Yeah. I suppose. I like the Bistro better. It depends what you like."

"Whatever is closest," said Chloe. If she knew anything about Matt it was that food was important, and if the quality was poor she'd learn so soon enough.

Chloe was about to say goodbye when a minivan pulled in nearby and tooted.

Jess looked back over her shoulder. "That's our ride. We'll see you tomorrow. And remember, Chloe, Mum and Uncle Max mustn't know who you are. Not until we've talked to Grandma about it."

Chloe nodded she understood. She was not about to jeopardise her chances of finally meeting Marta. Not even if it meant going behind Vera and Ella's father, Max's, backs.

Matt stood behind her enclosing her in his arms about her waist. He propped his head on her shoulder and whispered, "It'll be fine, Chloe. We'll meet Marta tomorrow and if all goes to plan, she'll get to meet her newest granddaughter."

Chloe circled into his embrace and looked up into his eyes.

"I hope you're right."

Jess

Jess would have bet a field of cows they'd succeeded in concealing what she and Ella were up to. Were it not for Uncle Max's questions at dinner, her confidence would have remained unshaken. Great care to avoid entangling themselves in a web of lies was no mean feat and it was a wonder they hadn't given themselves away before dessert.

"Who were you two talking to at school this evening?" asked Uncle Max.

Ella, never one to lie with ease, let Jess take the lead. "That was Matt Knightly from the Arsenal football team. He wouldn't say why he was up here. Maybe he's looking to change teams."

"Doubt it." Brody scoffed. "Matt loves Arsenal. He'd never move."

Jess flashed him a scowl. "Well maybe he's scouting for someone to mentor - a player with great promise."

Brody and Steve both looked at each other, each competing with a proud grin.

"I wonder if he saw us play this morning?" said Steve.

"I bet he did. And I scored our only goal too." said Brody, his cheeks puffing at the seams. "Did he say how long he was staying, Jess? Maybe I could get him to sign my shirt."

Jess shook her head. "I don't know, but I wouldn't hold your breath. If he was here to see anyone, it's probably the senior team, not you runts."

Ella's eyes rang alarm bells at her from across the table. *Woops - bit far.*

Uncle Max frowned at her. "Steady on, Jess. Who was the girl with him?"

"Dunno. Probably his girlfriend." Ella interjected.

Jess nodded her brow at Ella.

"Pa? We'd like to visit Grandma again tomorrow. She wasn't quite herself today and I want to check in on her, make sure she's all right."

"Maybe. I should pop in and see her too," said Uncle Max.

"Och, Pa. She knows you're busy here. We'll just check in and say hello. I'm sure she's fine."

Uncle Max eyed them with what Jess considered a glimmer of suspicion.

Jess raised an open palm towards her uncle, "If you really want to see her, go ahead. Don't let us stop you. She'd be pleased to see you I'm sure. She said you'd been in yesterday, which probably isn't true. But you know how she is - she forgets."

Jess prayed her suggestion wouldn't jeopardize their own visit, but she had to say something to throw him off their scent.

"I'll pop in and say hi when I pick you up then. If Matt Knightly is coming to see the senior boys play tomorrow, then I want to be there."

Ella bugged her eyes at Jess.

What had she done? Maybe if she told Matt and Chloe tomorrow about what she'd said, he might take pity and offer to stick around for the game. She sure hoped so. Otherwise the town may become suspicious of why Matt was there at all. If not, she was certain Chloe's big reunion with Marta would be headline news at school come Monday.

For now, Uncle Max seemed none the wiser about what they were up to. And, if there was anything more Jess had to do to keep it that way, she would.

Her mother, on the other hand, had been easy to fool. She seemed so caught up in her own worries lately, that keeping Chloe's visit a secret had been easy. She hadn't the slightest clue what was bothering her mother, but nor did she want to pry. Having Chloe turn up to meet Grandma was difficult enough without adding the complexity of her ties to their family. If Grandma confirmed her mother had an older sibling, it might be more than Mum could cope with at present.

A letter arrived in the mail yesterday and once Mum read it she went as white as a winter fog. Jess wondered if it were from Dad requesting she and Brody return to London to live with him. They had talked about the possibility with Dad during their last visit. But even doing that seemed a betrayal of sorts. Jess missed London and her friends, but could she really leave her mother, alone, up here?

Jess figured her mother might like some alone time and organized herself and Brody to stay the night at Ella's. Uncle Max was fine with it, and Mum seemed relieved. A night off would do her good.

Now all they had to do was get Grandma to remember.

Max

"Something's not right. The girls are acting weird." Max pushed his new cell phone hard to his ear. Having the damn thing that close to his brain kept his eyes leaping to the clock. Normally he'd put it on speaker, but at the risk of one of the girls overhearing his conversation with Vera, he'd resigned himself to paying the price.

"Weird how?" Vera sounded distracted, like she was attempting to do housework at the same time as talking.

"They don't want me to visit Ma tomorrow."

"Why? Were you going to?"

"No. But now I think I should. I'll pop in when I go to pick them up. Want to come?" His offhand question was worth a shot, even if he did already know the answer.

"No. If the girls are up to something, then we're better off letting them think we're clueless. They'll come clean eventually. And if they don't, they'll learn the consequences the hard way."

Vera's words were like listening to their mother's and he thought it uncanny how similar they sounded. If only Vera would talk to her. Then maybe she'd see just how much they actually had in common. In truth, visiting Ma or not wasn't really what concerned him.

"They were talking to someone outside the school this afternoon. A guy. And he was far from looking like a pig's ass. Jess said he was Matt Knightly - the Arsenal player. You know him?"

"No!" she snapped. "I mean, Brody has his poster on his wall. But I've never met him." His sister's voice then changed pitch, stiffening through teeth as if escaping a bitter tongue. "Did he happen to have a girl with him?"

Would the truth be the worst he could utter at this point?

"Aye, a blonde lass. There was something strange about the two of them. I'm just not sure what it is. I suppose it could be that she and Jess looked a bit similar - with their long hair and all."

"Where'd they go?"

"I dunno. The boys' game finished and I called the girls over to leave about two-thirty I guess. I suppose Matt and his girl left too. Jess said the Arsenal player had come to watch the senior boys play tomorrow. Does that sound right to you? I would have thought the school would make a big deal if they knew someone like him was coming to watch."

"They would. On second thoughts, Max, I think I will visit Ma tomorrow. What time are you going?"

"About midday I suppose."

"Good. I guess I'll see you then." Vera paused. "Max?"

"Aye?"

"If you run into the footballer and the girl. Don't believe a word they say."

CLICK - the line went silent.

What did she mean by that?

Something was definitely going on, and based on the girls' mysterious behaviour, they knew more than he did, maybe Vera did too. He just had to find out what it was before all hell broke loose for the Lockhearts once more.

304

CHAPTER NINETEEN

Sunday 17th September 2017

Chloe

A GREY BLANKET shrouded all hope of the sun making an appearance, and a desperate wind shunted the few who ventured out along the footpaths. Were it not for the dark granite buildings and narrow streets, Chloe would have picked it as any number of the far south towns back home.

"I hope they get here soon or my fingers are gonna go numb." Chloe puffed a breath into her cupped hands and pulled the ends of her sleeves over her knuckles.

Matt wrapped an arm around her, his heat radiating through every layer of clothing she had on including her down jacket. How could he be so calm, so warm, so self-assured? Her whole body felt like an ungreased engine - seized with worry, yet desperate to move.

Hands on her wristwatch mocked every glimpse, and she wished she had the courage to wind them forward out of spite.

Why she insisted they leave the comfort of their room at the castle so early now seemed unforgivable. The room Matt booked at Castle Ferlie was far more decadent than she ever would have splurged on, but the few short hours they had spent there far exceeded anything she could have conjured in a dream. Never did she think, on such a monumental trip as this, that she would ever get to walk the hallways of a centuries old castle. Now her memories of Scotland would be like every other traveller who journeyed there. Not that she minded. She had always dreamed of coming here, to walk a highland trail, visit a castle or two, and explore the historical sites of the cities. But for all her grand ideas of travelling, never did she once contemplate the severity of how the weather would impact her experiences of it.

Chloe tugged the hood of her jacket up over her slapping hair and jiggled on the spot to keep circulation in her legs.

"Why don't we go wait in that shop over there?" Matt pointed towards an old building with a green painted door. "We should be able to see when they arrive. Beats waiting out here."

The sign above the store indicated it was an old mercantile, now selling an odd mix of electrical appliances and craft supplies.

Chloe nodded and they strode towards it, accompanied by a flurry of leaves.

Tucking themselves inside, an elderly gentleman looked up from behind the counter.

"Good Morning. Can I help you?" came his thick Scottish accent beneath his thick greying moustache.

Chloe acknowledged him with a smile. "Oh no thank you. We just needed to get out of the wind. It's pretty cold out there," she puffed another breath into her hand, the heat lingering much longer than it had on the street.

"Not from around here then. Where're you from?"

"London." Chloe replied keeping her eyes firmly fixed on the monument across the street.

"Are you now? Sounds like you've come a bit farther than London. I've not heard the likes of yer tongue in these parts in a while. From the land of kangaroos, aye?"

Chloe brought her gaze inside, giving the man a curt smile with a pinched eye. "No. I'm from New Zealand. I'm a Kiwi, not an Aussie. Not that it really matters round here."

The man shook his head and scrunched his brow low. "Oh Aye, It matters. If you'd 'ave thought me Glaswegian, I'd be more miffed than a bat with no wings. So what brings you round these parts then?"

Chloe wasn't about to tell her life story to a storekeeper, but she also didn't want to cause any offense and get kicked out of the warm shelter. "Just visiting - the castles - you know. That sort of thing."

"Oh aye. Grand. Have you seen Craigievar or Dunnottar?"

Out the corner of her eye Chloe spotted Jess and Ella arriving at the monument. She touched Matt's shoulder and addressed the man, hopefully for the last time. "No. Sorry. Maybe next time. Thank you."

Matt followed her outside, back into the gusty wind.

Jess spotted them first and crossed the road to meet them. She pointed down the road and together, Chloe and Matt fell in step behind the two girls. Jess looked over her shoulder before scanning the rest of the surroundings. "It's about five minutes away."

Jess and Ella kept their heads low and no one spoke until Jess turned in towards a gate at the edge of a larger sized house.

"Wait here. We'll go and check if she's able to see us." Jess and Ella disappeared inside.

Matt placed an arm on Chloe's shoulder. She exhaled and let them drop a little. Her hands trembled inside her pockets and she turned to look at him. If there was any confidence to be gained from his presence, she'd already taken it. Matt's eyes held hers like they were the only two people who existed. "You got this, Chloe. Your Mum is going to be so proud when you tell her you've found her."

Chloe placed a hand on his chest. The steady beat of his heart calmed her own.

He lent to kiss her, just as Jess emerged from the front door.

"She's up."

Chloe turned before Matt could land his lips on hers and he kissed her cheek instead. She looked back towards him, her face awash with hope. He nodded with a smile.

Together they climbed the stairs and followed Jess down a hallway to a room near the back of the house. Once they reached the doorway, Chloe knew there was no turning back. Everything she'd been through to reach this point all seemed to pale by comparison to taking this final step. From Palmerston North to Alford, she was finally here.

Inside, Ella sat on a sofa next to an elderly woman with platinum blonde hair coiled on top of her head. A grey shawl swaddled the woman's narrow shoulders and seemed to make her look older than she really was. The large room was nicely decorated with a single bed, the sofa, and a couple of mismatched dining chairs, which appeared to have been brought in just for their visit. A large tapestry of a castle with bright flowers all around it graced the opposing wall of the sofa. It was the castle they had just stayed at, and Chloe was lost in it for a moment. The intricacy of the work was incredible and must have taken a number of years to complete.

Chloe pulled herself back to reality and glanced over her shoulder at the elderly woman. As soon as their eyes met, the woman lowered her gaze to her hands.

Ella gestured towards Chloe, "Grandma. This is Chloe Spencer. She's come all the way from New Zealand to meet you." Ella's tone was sweet, but a little condescending.

Chloe conceded her new relatives probably knew best how to talk to Marta, given the unique situation. According to Jess, Marta had bouts of forgetfulness and they weren't sure if she'd be able to tell them anything about the past. Despite the obvious hurdle, Chloe still had to try.

Marta stood and moved towards her bed, keeping her back turned on Chloe, and her head bowed low at Ella. "I don't really feel like visitors today, Ella. I'd like to take a nap."

Jess moved to intervene, "But, Grandma, she's come all this way, just to meet you. Wasn't that nice?"

The woman looked back at Chloe again and appeared to be making a summary of her looks. "Aye it is. Where abouts in New Zealand are you from?" she asked, her eyes wincing with worry.

"Palmerston North." Chloe's voice cracked. "But I'm working over here in London for a while."

Chloe turned at the sound of short footsteps coming down the hall. A woman about her own height, with shoulder length sandy-brown hair, shuffled past Matt, who was waiting at the door, and entered the room.

"What's going on?" the woman asked the girls. "Are you two out of your mind?" - she glanced at Chloe - "And what are they doing here? They've no right to see Ma."

The elderly woman pulled her shawl tighter about her shoulders and sunk back into the pillows propped against the bed head.

"Ma, are you all right?" the woman asked.

"I'm fine, Vera. Don't burst your boiler, the girls just wanted to check on me. I'm much better today, thank you. It's lovely to see you, and it's nice that you've come, but why are you here?"

"I was worried about you, about this…this…about them?" Vera moved towards Chloe until her face was within inches of her own. She lowered her voice, grating her words over the edge of her tongue. "What are you doing here? You've no right. A word, if you will." Vera gripped Chloe's elbow and motioned her towards the door.

Of course Vera deserved an explanation, but so did Marta. Why leave the room?

Once out the door, Vera let her go but remained constant in her haste to move her away from Marta's room. Chloe stopped at the top of the stairs thinking that was far enough, but Vera motioned she should continue down. Knowing Matt remained upstairs gave her hope she would return once her story had been explained.

Chloe lifted her chin, glancing back up the stairs once she reached the bottom. Why hadn't Matt followed her? He'd been there every other step of the way. Was it out of respect, or did he fear he was becoming far more involved than he ever wanted.

Vera pointed to a small dining room that was currently unoccupied. She entered and closed the door behind her.

"Well?" she asked, before turning to pace the room.

"Well. Hello. It's nice to meet you" - Chloe held out her hand - "I'm Chloe Spencer."

Vera stopped momentarily to look at her and crossed her arms tightly across her chest. Chloe wrung her palms together feeling foolish for having extended the civil gesture. "I've been looking forward to meeting you ever since I learned of your existence. You're not so easy to find you know."

Vera swiped a rogue tear from her cheek and continued treading the linoleum floor as if her legs couldn't stop.

She shook her head and wiped another tear from existence. "No. No. No. Why are you here? What do you want? I don't want you here. Ma won't be able to handle it. It's not fair to her and it's not fair to me. Why after all these years have you come here?"

Chloe was confused. She would have thought Vera might be pleased to learn she had a new niece, not to mention an older sister. She hadn't expected her to be so callous about it.

"I couldn't wait any longer. Mum is very unwell and it is her dying wish to meet her birth-mother before she passes. Please. If you've any compassion, please let me meet your mother. She is my grandmother too, and she deserves to know what happened to her daughter."

Vera's creased brow eased into a glare. "Like bloody hell she does. She does not need you or anyone else unsettling her. She's been through enough already."

"But wouldn't a mother want to meet her child? A child she dearly loved but had to give up."

"What?" Vera stopped dead, her face contorted in a mix of worry and confusion. Chloe wondered which part she hadn't understood.

"Your mother, Marta. She had a baby in New Zealand - my mother - and she had to give her up for adoption. My grandfather said she had to because her father wouldn't let her go home if she didn't."

Vera sat down at a table and placed a palm on her forehead. Her face had drained of colour but eventually she started nodding.

"You mean, Ma had another child? But how? When?"

"Marta met a man named Peter in Masterton, in 1959. They, you know, and Marta got pregnant. Peter was a bit older than her, but he wouldn't marry her - he was already engaged. So Marta had to give the baby up. My Grandparents, Thomas and Iris, adopted the baby. They called her Elizabeth. She is my mother. Please. She has cancer and she's..." Chloe's eyes swelled with tears, "...she's dying. I only wanted her to have the chance to meet her mother. It's what she's always wanted. She asked me to find her for her." Chloe chugged the last word out like it was the only one that mattered. "Please."

Vera's expression went from utter confusion to one of relief and then pure joy.

"So I have a sister in New Zealand. Wow! Oh my god. Wow!" Vera jumped to embrace her.

"Chloe. I'm so sorry. When Mary said you were looking for me I thought...well, never mind. I had it all wrong. Wow. So I have an older sister!"

It was then that the gravity of all the information Chloe delivered hit.

"But is she really dying? Oh Lord. How long does she have? I don't believe it. I have a sister."

"We're not sure. The doctor said it could be as much as six months, but it's really an unknown."

"Well. Let's see what Ma has to say about all this. I have no idea how she'll take it. But knowing her and secrets she may just want to deny it. I'll do my best to help her come clean - if I can."

"Thank you" - Chloe eyed her new relative cautiously - "Aunty Vera. Is that all right? Can I call you that?"

Vera looked her up and down, nodding her head with a smile.

"Yes, of course!"

Chloe followed Vera back upstairs and was relieved to be reunited with Matt. He was the one constant in all the turmoil of the situation.

Seeing how severely the news had affected Vera, Chloe was more than happy to let her new aunt take the lead with Marta. How would she react once she learned who Chloe really was? The moment Chloe had hoped for was also the one she feared most. Would Marta confess all? Would she even remember?

Of all those gathered in the room, Chloe's hopes of reuniting her mother with Marta now lay in Vera's hands.

Chloe drew a sharp breath and pressed her fingers tightly over the smooth photograph in her pocket. She almost couldn't bear to watch.

Vera knelt on the floor next to Marta's bed and cupped the old woman's hands in her own. "Ma? I know the truth, and it's all right, you can tell us. What do you remember about the baby you had in New Zealand? Chloe has told me what happened, but do you remember anything?"

Vera's imploring gaze held such compassion that Chloe's eyes swelled with tears. Was this what her mother had missed out on all these years, knowing her mother as only a daughter could? She knew it wasn't true. Mum had a mother. Iris. She loved her. They loved each other. Mum never lacked a mother. But somehow, deep down, it must not have felt the same once she learned she was adopted.

Marta looked at Vera with a weighted brow, one that had carried the burden all these years.

"Of course I remember, Vera."

Tears dripped from Marta's swelling eyes like buckets filled to the brim. "How could I ever forget? My little girl was the most beautiful baby in the world. But I couldn't keep her. I was so young."

Vera pulled a handful of tissues from the box on the side table. Marta took them gratefully and clutched the wad to her face. Fresh tears came once more. Eventually the old woman twisted the tissues around her nose making a short toot sound before absorbing the last of her emotional discourse. "I have a picture in my box over there." Marta pointed with a shaking hand. The jewellery box was much like the one Chloe's mother kept their baby bracelets in. Vera looked at Jess and asked her without saying a word to bring it to her.

"Under the tray." Marta nodded and raised a finger in her own familiar motion.

Jess handed the open box to her mother and Vera lifted a base tray from the box. She took a small photograph from the bottom of the box, looked it over for a brief moment, and then handed it to Marta.

Marta looked at it and smiled as new drips trailed her cheeks. "I named her Claire. Isn't she a beauty?"

Vera smiled. "Oh yes, Ma. She's beautiful. Did Pa know about her?"

"Yes. I told him eventually. I almost lost everything, but he forgave me. Your Pa loved you kids too much to break up our family over my transgressions. Claire was taken care of and I knew she would have a good life."

"Still. That must have been really hard letting her go like that," said Ella.

Vera broke down into big sobs and Marta stroked her daughter's head as she lay it on the bed next to her.

Jess and Ella seemed stunned to silence and kept a keen eye on Vera.

With all the swirling emotions in the room, Chloe let her tears slip too. Marta must have been a good mother and grandmother to have her family care so much for her now.

Chloe's heart ached for her own family, her mother, father, sister, and grandparents back home. The heavy weight of sadness finally made her turn into Matt's embrace. He held her tight and let her soak his shoulder with her pain. She pulled away when the tears eased and he swept the dampened hair from her cheek.

Jess looked at Chloe and then back at her mother. "Well, is someone going to explain what's going on?"

Chloe walked over to Marta and looked at the photo in her hand.

"That's my Mum." Chloe fetched a similar photo from her pocket and handed it to Marta.

Marta's watery gaze looked momentarily at the photos and then searched Chloe's face for...for what? What was it the elderly woman wanted to say to her?

"Claire? Is that you?"

"No, Ma. This is Chloe. Remember. You just met her. Chloe is your little girl's daughter. Chloe is your granddaughter. Do you understand?"

"Oh yes, but you look like her, like Claire, don't you?" Marta cocked her head to one side and traced Chloe's face with her eyes.

"What makes you say that, Grandma?" asked Ella.

"Because. She looks just like me when I was her age."

"Well I guess I look a little like Mum. But she doesn't have hair like me. Mum's is a bit darker. Marta, would you like to meet my Mum?"

Vera drew her attention away from Marta and looked wearily at Chloe. "But how can Ma meet her? She's sick and in New Zealand. That's what you said, didn't you? How can Ma meet her daughter if she's so unwell. Can she travel?"

"Well, No, but I thought maybe..."

Marta sat up on the edge of her bed and jutted her chin forward. "What do you mean I'm unwell, Vera? I'm perfectly fine thank you very much." She took both photographs of the baby and clutched them to her chest. "I must see her. I must! I need to see my little girl."

"But, Ma. You can't. You can't travel to New Zealand. Do you know how long the flight is? Hours and hours. You won't cope with it."

"Well Claire can come here then." Marta looked at Chloe. "Tell her to come. Would you, please?"

"I'm afraid it's not possible, Marta. You see Mum's quite unwell and I don't think her doctors would agree to let her go."

"What's wrong with her?"

"She has cancer I'm afraid and she may not have much longer with us."

"Oh no, Vera. I must go. Claire needs me." Marta grabbed hold of Vera's arm the way Vera had grabbed hold of Chloe previously. Desperation tensioned every muscle in the wrinkling jaw of the old woman. "You can't stop me, Vera. I'll go by ship if I have to, but I must go. Please." Marta held Vera's gaze until her daughter dropped her head in concession.

"I don't know how. But I'll try, Ma. I'll talk to Max and see if we can work something out. But I can't guarantee anything, all right? If the doctor says you can't travel, then that's final. You'll just have to talk to her on the phone."

"Or we can Skype call her." Chloe interjected. "But Mum would be over the moon to meet her real mother in real life." Chloe met Marta's hopeful gaze with a smile, and nodded.

"I'll be fine. You'll see, Vera. I'm not so senile yet that I can't return to my homeland. Claire needs me."

Chloe wanted to add as much weight as she could to Marta's plan to travel to New Zealand.

"She sure does, Grandma." Chloe paused to gauge Marta's reaction, and the older woman beamed.

"But maybe it's best if you call her by her name now. It's Elizabeth. But everyone just calls her Lizzy."

Warmth radiated from Marta's smile. "Lizzy. I like it. Yes. Lizzy needs me."

CHAPTER TWENTY

Friday 1st December 2017

Chloe

IF EVER THERE was a good reason to panic now was the time to do so. Chloe closed the lid of her laptop and burst into tears. How could this be happening? Never had she been so desperate for a bridge to span the distance between New Zealand and London until right now. Mum was back in hospital and the doctor said she may only have weeks left. Danielle's unscheduled call not only contained news she never wanted to hear, but also an urgent plea for Chloe to return home as soon as was humanly possible. Her sister's normal diplomacy over the matter had not only gone out the window, but appeared to have landed in the loony bin.

Her calm controlled facade was now replaced by blubbering tears. If Chloe had not witnessed her sister's disposition for herself, she might never have believed how serious their mother's condition was.

Danielle was going to bring the wedding forward so that Mum could attend, and Chloe agreed it was a good idea. Reeling from her new reality, the consequences of that decision would only suffice to unscrew her hinges even further.

Wiping away tears she opened her laptop once more to view the coming week's schedule. She never intended to return home for the Christmas break. Seventy-two hours on home soil seemed hardly worth all the days of travel to get there. But now, there was no question. She must return - the sooner the better. With barely enough time to think let alone pack, her body flicked to autopilot and she emptied her drawers onto the bed. Several thoughts still managed to emerge, knocking her to the bed in great sobs each time.

First there was the matter of the school's Christmas play. Not only was she directing it, half of her class had main parts, and without her there to guide them, how would the show happen at all?

Then there was the not so small matter of Matt's football club's Christmas party. It took him three whole dates, and one master-chefs dessert class, to talk her into attending the important function with him. He'd spent the better half of last month bringing her into the fold of the footballer's life, not to mention the lives of their better halves as well. What Chloe had accomplished in the few short months since she'd arrived was as much of a surprise to herself as it was to everyone else. She had a job she loved, friends and co-workers she liked and trusted, and Matt - the icing she never expected, nor knew she even wanted. Not only had he spread himself so thickly on her cake, but she doubted life could ever taste as sweet again without him. It was he who would be most disappointed. Her boss and friends would understand, but Matt? He may not be as agreeable as she hoped.

Since their trip to Scotland, their relationship had gone from 'strictly platonic' to 'I want to see you every day'. The results of which were as mixed as a bag of M&M's. There were parts of him that she really liked. His care for his mother, his generosity, the way he challenged her to try new things, and how he always listened to her opinions, even though he may disagree. But there were also things that she didn't like. Like his sense of entitlement above others, or when he laughed at people's clumsiness, even if they were injured. And although she'd become used to it, she still didn't like his affection towards his female fans.

How would he react to the combination of her sudden departure and excessive distance? Would it prove too difficult for either of them to overcome? Although there was attraction, and friendship in spades, was it enough for a life changing commitment? Why had she not remained pragmatic and avoided the new relationship? She knew her mother would eventually need her back home, and now it felt reckless to have become involved with Matt at all. Her worst fears were about to play out, just as she predicted, and she only had herself to blame. Matt would be hurt. She would be hurt. There was no winning in this situation, only heartache and sadness.

And then there was Marta. She would be devastated to learn of Mum's decline in health. Although her mother did get to see and talk to Marta before Chloe and Matt left Scotland, the blubbering words over the terrible connection could barely be counted as a reunion. Further efforts at the school library, for a better connection weren't much better. As fulfilling as the whole experience was, it had given Mum that glimmer of hope that one day soon she would get to meet her mother in person.

Marta was as determined to meet her daughter as Chloe was for her to come visit. Just yesterday Vera called with news they planned to travel to New Zealand in early January. But now Chloe feared even that may be too late.

She swiped her phone to call Matt. It went straight to voice-mail. A sobbing message to call her back wasn't advisable, given their past experiences, so she hung up. It would be better to tell him in person anyway. Then she'd be able to see how he took the news and not simply listen to words without real meaning. Her fingers and toes were well and truly crossed in hopes he'd be supportive of her situation.

Next on the list was her boss. She was fairly certain he would appreciate how urgently she needed to return home, but she was also aware how difficult it would be to find a substitute over the Christmas holiday period.

Mr Lyles took the news better than she expected, offering his deepest sympathies for her mother and family. Chloe tried to insist she would return to her position at the school just as soon as she could. She couldn't give him any assurance of how long that might be, but Mr Lyles was quick to put her mind at ease.

"We'll be fine, Chloe. Life happens to us all. I will put my recommendation to the board that we hold your position open for your return for up to six months. They should be satisfied with that. You have proven your worth around here and I know I speak for all the staff when I say that we dearly hope you'll be able to return to us just as soon as you are able. But..." There it was. Chloe held her breath. "Should you decide not to return, I only ask that you inform us as soon as possible so we can start to look for new applicants once more." His last words were drawn and weary. Chloe understood how he must feel. A Principal's job was never straight forward and was as much of a human resources role as it was an educational one. Her father had taught her that.

With promises made to Mr Lyles, Chloe biffed her phone across the bed as if she hated to make the last call the most. Marta. If there were any way she could smuggle Marta back home to New Zealand in her suitcase she would. Chloe needed all the help she could get so she fired off a message to Jess via Facebook.

'I need your help! Mum is back in hospital. She may only have a few weeks left. If Marta really wants to meet her, then she needs to come to New Zealand ASAP! I'm on the next flight home tomorrow. Please - I beg you. If there is anything you can do to convince Vera to make the trip now, please do.'

Chloe hit the send button and dropped her phone on the bed again. There was little else she could do now other than pack. It would be getting warmer back home, but not so warm that she wouldn't require her jeans and a few sweaters. The dry summer days in the Wairarapa wouldn't come into full swing until late January. At least Danielle's wedding might benefit from the last of the spring flowers. *Mum would love that.*

Chloe grabbed her suitcases down from the top of the wardrobe and began folding her things into neat rolls, just as her mother had taught her to do before going off to school camps.

Entranced in her own thoughts a beep from her phone jumped her back to reality and she grabbed it. It was a reply from Jess. Chloe loved how quickly her new cousin responded to messages. It was like being back in high school, and their tennis match messages were always laced with comic relief.

'We are on it. Headed to Grandma's now. Uncle Max said we can stay at the farm while Mum's in NZ with Grandma. I'm sure we can fit in their suitcases. Gonna give it a shot anyway.'

Chloe smiled. Then it hit her - she still hadn't booked a ticket home. Maybe she had been waiting until she could speak to Matt. But regardless of how he'd take the news, it was sensible to at least look at what flights were available. It wouldn't be cheap given the peak season in the southern hemisphere, not to mention how close it was getting to Christmas. Chloe flipped open her laptop and searched for the earliest flight. Preferably one that would prevent having to donate a vital organ. Her phone beeped again. This time it was a message from Dad.

'I've booked you a flight home tomorrow on Air New Zealand. Mark will pick you up from Wellington Airport and bring you up when you arrive. I've emailed you the ticket. See you soon. Love Dad'.

She opened her email and sure enough there it was with her ticket files attached. For a split second disappointment sunk her lower into the bed. The ticket was just for one. Not that she expected any different, nor was she ungrateful. She should be, and was, relieved. Soon she'd be reunited with Mum and able to offer her comfort and reassurance in person. But that didn't ease her concern about whether Marta would make it to New Zealand in time. Or give Matt the opportunity to... to what? Come with her? She'd be lying if she said she didn't want him to come. But now he wouldn't have the choice. She was going and that was that. If he couldn't, or worse, didn't want to, where did that leave them?

Chloe pushed her tears aside and continued packing. Maybe Matt would at least give her a ride to the airport. Without realising, Chloe had begun packing even the non-essential things in her room.

Was she subconsciously planning to not return after all?

She looked around searching desperately for something to leave behind. Her collection of sentimental items were few and small, and her only belongings that wouldn't fit were two rather chunky winter coats that she had recently purchased. Neither would be needed back home, and neither were expensive enough to be considered a realistic reason to return for.

The hardest thing to pack was the dress she had just bought for the Christmas party. Now, instead of wearing it to the red carpet event she would likely wear it to Danielle's rehearsal dinner, if in fact there was even going to be one.

Given the limited time they might have left with Mum, Chloe doubted any of the usual customs would be adhered to. Danielle had been planning her big day for months already so it wasn't unreasonable to imagine she would succeed in bringing everything forward. But summer weddings weren't cheap and were notoriously difficult to achieve given how few venues would be available now. Aside from the obvious hurdles, Chloe didn't doubt her sister's ability to pull it off. Danielle had worked harder miracles than that for their parents' anniversary. Chloe was quietly confident she would do it again.

Her greatest wish at this point was that Marta and Vera would be able to make the trip too. With them in mind Chloe picked up her phone once more and called Vera directly. It took a few rings, and 'Please hold's', but eventually Chloe had Vera's full attention.

"Chloe, I know your Mum's not well. I'm just not sure if I can make the trip right now. I've made an urgent request for leave from work and fingers crossed they'll grant me the time off, but I have no guarantee. I'm so sorry."

"I understand. I'm just grateful you've tried. Danielle has brought the wedding forward and I know she'd be glad to have you both there for it as well. I know it's a big ask. But please, if there's any way you can make it happen, Mum will be overjoyed to meet Marta."

"You know it's not just Ma who wants to come. I want to meet Lizzy too. I can't help but wonder what life would have been like if I'd known I had a big sister." A soft sniff made its way through the receiver. "I'll hopefully know more by tomorrow."

"Okay. Well, I fly out tomorrow morning. After that I'll be out of service for a good twelve hours or so - until I reach L.A. My stopover there is brief and then I'm on another flight for another eleven hours. It's a long haul, I know. But you could still take a day or two in L.A. or go through Singapore and break up your travel. It's up to you. Dad's paid for my ticket home, so perhaps I can give you some money towards your flights if that helps?"

"Oh, that's sweet of you, Chloe. I'll speak with Max. We'll work something out. I'll let you know as soon as I have things organised. Ma's been in my ear for weeks now. I thought she'd forgotten how to use a telephone, but it seems she's more capable than we realised, given the right kind of motivation." Vera chuckled. "Ma is determined she's going, 'come heaven or high water', as she would say."

If only Vera knew how lucky she was to have a mother so close by. Chloe could use a hug from her mother right now. Soon. It wouldn't be long till that wish could come true, if only it wasn't under such devastating circumstances.

Chloe ended her call with Vera and paused - hovering a finger over the button to call Matt again. He would be here in a few hours anyway. It was their Netflix night, and the new series, The Crown, had already won her vote for their evening's watch.

She'd only seen Matt briefly yesterday - after school. Arsenal had a game that evening with Huddersfield and he'd only had a few minutes to spare before heading to the stadium. She wanted to go watch him play, but a mountain of marking and a ton of props needed to be ordered for the play. He understood and didn't seem too upset she wouldn't be there.

Her finger landed hard on the call button, and she clutched it to her ear. This time the phone rang only twice before Matt answered.

"Hello gorgeous. What's up? I've just come in for a quick break. You called?"

"Yeah, Sorry. It can wait. I don't want to distract you."

"But I like your distractions. You're worth any reprimand coach might give."

"Something's come up, but I'll tell you about it later. Just come straight here after practice if you can. It's important."

"Sounds like it. Just give me half an hour and I'll be there as soon as I can."

"No, Matt -" Too late, he'd already hung up.

His practice usually went until four on Fridays but today they'd be at it until six. Arsenal's next match was against Manchester United on Sunday and the whole city was buzzing with anticipation. Chloe promised she'd take Joy, who was very excited about watching the game from the club's viewing box. It was a big deal and on Arsenals home turf too. Chloe hoped Matt wouldn't get into trouble for leaving training early. The roads would be even more congested with the influx of both teams' fans. That meant the airport would be equally congested too. Chloe swiped her phone and set an alarm for the morning, hopefully with an hour to spare for the traffic.

6:30 am, she winced at her phone. It would still be dark, and freezing. She'd been praying for snow for her first Christmas abroad, but all hope of that was now gone. At least for her anyway. In less than eighteen hours she'd be high above the city and on her way home.

Chloe lay on her bed and let her mind wander at will. Would Danielle's wedding take place before or after Christmas? Would Vera be able to get the time off to bring Marta to New Zealand?

Chloe's thoughts sent her on a wave of mixed emotions and she eventually drifted off to sleep, hugging a jacket Matt had loaned her, and tears soaking into her pillow.

A loud bang on the door downstairs followed by multiple 'ding-dongs' from the doorbell startled her awake.

It had become dark and Chloe leapt up brushing her hand over the wall by the door to find the light switch. She rubbed her eyes to gain some semblance of vision before thumping down the steps to answer the door.

Matt. It must be him. Chloe looked at her wrist. How long had she slept? 5:10 pm. Thirty minutes, but it felt like three hours, at least that's how her head felt. She brushed a hand quickly through her hair and again over her eyes before opening the front door.

"Oh thank God, you are here. I thought something terrible had happened. There was no answer when I rang the bell."

"Sorry. I fell asleep." Chloe let her body fall into his arms, resting a good portion of her weight on his shoulders. "You stink." She scrunched her nose.

"Gee, thanks. Is that all I get for rushing over."

Chloe blushed. "No." She pulled the front of his sweaty shirt towards her and kissed him softly. Matt lingered, awaiting more.

She gently pressed him away, biting at her lower lip. "I meant…would you like to take a shower?"

"You know I would." He sunk his eyes into the gap of her shirt collar as if ready to undress her right there in the entryway.

Chloe dropped her eyes and fiddled with her fingers, tugging at a nail that wasn't in any way rough enough to be removed.

Matt took a step back. "What's so important? You sounded upset on the phone. Is everything okay?"

Danielle's call rushed back into her mind, and tears swelled, dripping down her cheeks as she looked up. All strength in her legs departed and her knees dipped without thought to a landing.

Matt caught her, his eyes widening. "Are you all right, Chloe? You don't look so well."

"It's Mum."

"Oh God, is she all right? Is she…she's not…?"

Chloe knew exactly what he was trying to say. She didn't want to say it either, but the fact was, her mother really was dying and no amount of avoiding the word would change it.

"No. She's not dead. But she doesn't have long. Dad's booked me a flight back home." Chloe paused and lifted her chin. "I leave tomorrow. I'm so sorry, Matt, but I won't be able to attend the Christmas party with you - or any party here for that matter. Danielle has moved the wedding forward. She hopes Mum will be able to attend. I…I…" Chloe searched for the right words to carry on but the air caught in her throat and a fresh set of tears overtook anything she might have tried to say.

Matt pulled her into his arms and guided her to the sitting room. He settled them on the sofa and cradled her head on his shoulder. "It's okay to cry, Chloe. I can't imagine how you must be feeling right now. Well that's not entirely true. I can imagine. Mum got really sick with the flu last year, and she ended up in hospital. I was playing in Switzerland when they called. I felt terrible, and so helpless."

Chloe looked at him through a watery haze and in that moment they shared a deeper connection than she had ever felt with anyone else. Matt had her heart, wholly and completely. But did she have his? She guessed maybe she was about to find out.

Handing her some tissues from a box beside the sofa, she recovered her wits so they could talk.

"Matt?"

"Yes?" He placed his warm hand over her tissue clutching fist.

"I'm not sure what the future holds for me - for us. But I want you to know, before I go. That I think maybe, I'm in love with you, Matt."

Matt jerked his head up to meet her stare. For once it appeared he was at a loss for words. He pulled her towards him and hugged her tightly.

"I thought maybe you were going to break up with me." His voice mumbled amongst her hair.

Chloe couldn't deny the thought had crossed her mind. Maybe if they parted ways now they'd save themselves the long and painful break up.

"Is that what you want, Matt?"

"I...I don't know. Will you be coming back?"

"I don't know. It's okay. I wouldn't expect you to wait for me or anything. Your whole life is here, your career, your Mum, your friends. You don't have to say anything, Matt. I get it."

Matt withdrew his hand and rubbed it across his forehead. Chloe felt sorry for him. He probably hadn't been expecting to be put on the spot like this, and nor did she like making him feel like he was cornered. She could never ask him to give up his life here - not when her own future was so uncertain. Maybe she'd be back - maybe she wouldn't. Nothing was certain. Tomorrow is never promised - only hoped for.

"Will you take me to the airport?"

"Of course I will," Matt shot back. "Oh wait. I can't. Coach has us coming in tomorrow first thing. He wasn't pleased with our fitness today, so the lads are having an early session at the gym."

Matt searched her, hoping to give a better answer. "I won't go. I'll call coach and tell him I have an emergency."

Chloe shook her head. "No. You go. I'll get someone else to take me."

"What about my driver, Paul?" He clutched her hands between his as if to pray. "I'll get him to drive you in my car. He'll make sure you get there on time."

"Thank you. I need to leave here at 6:30 am."

Matt didn't say anything else. He just grabbed her for another hug and wouldn't let go.

"I'll miss you." He dropped his head to her shoulder. If he had tears she couldn't tell. Was he even like that?

When he finally let her go, the wet salty marks had laid their evidence.

Chloe kissed the tops of his cheeks. "I'll miss you too."

PART FIVE

2017

Palmerston North – New Zealand

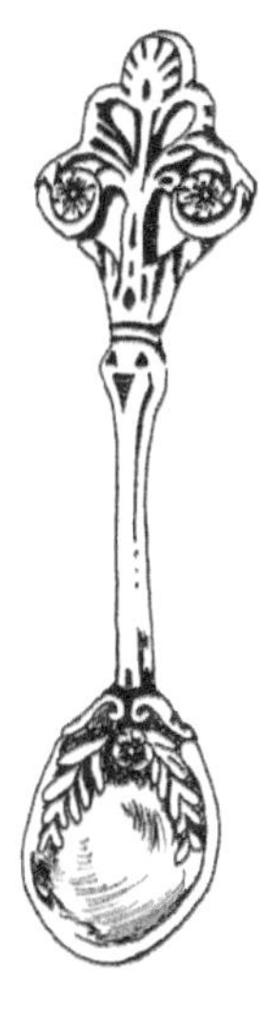

CHAPTER TWENTY-ONE

Monday 4th December 2017

Chloe

CHLOE PULLED MATT'S jacket up close around her neck. She'd made him wear it the last night they were together and his fresh cologne still permeated the fabric. When she asked if she could keep it, Matt not only complained that she'd be depriving him of his favourite piece of clothing, but his favourite person as well. Chloe's heart tingled at his compliment, but she still had doubts about his sincerity. Secretly, she was hoping that if Matt missed her as much as he said he would, then maybe he might find his way back to her. Having a piece of Matt's clothing hardly compared to having his arms around her, but she took comfort from its empty sleeves nevertheless.

Chloe's arms, drained of all strength, slumped in her lap beneath the jacket. In less than ten minutes they'd be landing in Wellington, and, although she was excited to be back on home ground, the two hour drive with Mark felt like it could be the final shove over the edge of a very tall cliff. She hoped she could retain some sort of decorum, and stay awake long enough to locate him.

She closed her eyes and took a deep breath. A sharp blast of cool air streamed into her nostrils and her eyes flew open. The guy sitting next to her had turned his air vent in her direction. Even though the blast was unwelcome, it did at least blow a little fog away from her brain. Similarly, the same could be said for the airport. A low mist threatened their early morning flight into the capital, and Chloe found herself praying for a diversion directly into Palmerston North. But as kiwi luck would have it, a keen westerly kept the fog at sea long enough to land the wavering aircraft on the strip of land bridging the gap between the harbour and the Cook Straight seas.

Touch down. Chloe expelled all tension in a single breath as the plane turned at the end of the runway. It felt like she'd been holding it since they left Los Angeles - and that was fifteen hours ago. It was a miracle anyone in Europe ever ventured this far south of the equator at all. But, despite how long it took to get here, it was home, and nothing felt so good as stepping off the gangway into Wellington Airport. It seemed an eternity since farewelling Danielle there three months ago, and for a split second she wondered if she would ever be able to face going back to London.

It was 8:30 am on a Monday morning and though she had skipped a whole day ahead of her students back in London, she couldn't help but wonder how they had taken the news of her sudden departure. She didn't even get the chance to say goodbye or explain anything to them. She hated that more than anything. Most of them would take it in their stride, but, for a few it would break their hearts. One little boy in particular was making excellent progress and his confidence was growing daily. She hoped her disappearance would not affect him adversely, nor any of the students for that matter.

Waiting by the carousel for her luggage she thought she caught sight of Jeremy. But when the man turned she realised she was mistaken. Where was Mark anyway, and why was he picking her up and not Danielle? She guessed her sister had enough on her plate with rescheduling the wedding and couldn't spare the time to pop down to Wellington. Mark was more likely to be transiting between the two cities anyway. It made sense he would offer to bring her home. Unfortunately, the thought of two more hours travelling in a car with Mark did nothing but make her feel more miserable. She was surprised to admit it, but she actually missed London. How could her allegiance have turned so quickly? Not only did she wish she was in her class teaching, but she also missed the close-knit streets and terrace houses.

Scanning the sea of heads, she caught sight of Mark waving a hand in the distance. He dodged his way over to her, offering a quick, emotionally devoid hug on arriving. With both her bags secured, he turned and led the way towards the car.

Seated in the car, Mark turned to face her. "We've missed you, Chloe. Danielle made me promise not to dally, but would you mind if we made one stop before we head north?" He pulled his belt across his chest. Chloe reached over her shoulder and did the same. She hadn't worn a seat belt in weeks and it felt strange to have the restraint across her chest.

"Umm, I guess not. Will you be long?"

"No. I just have a patient I promised to look in on before leaving town. This wedding move has totally messed with my schedule. But hey, what can I do. It's important to Danielle that her mother attend the wedding, and I'd do anything to make your sister happy."

"I'm glad to hear it." Chloe's heart softened a little towards Mark. He wasn't so bad. He did love Danielle, and if he could make changes to suit her, then maybe he did deserve her after all.

If only she could be so lucky. She couldn't imagine Matt giving up his football career for her, but neither would she want him to. It was such a big part of his life. To have achieved such success at something you love so young was rare, and she would hate to be the one to blame for him giving that up. There was little doubt she would ever have to make a choice like that. Now that she was home though, it was becoming clearer about where her heart belonged. New Zealand was home no matter what. Even if she could make herself return to London to finish out her contract, she could never live there long term. Everything about home seemed open and less crowded, even in town, parked amongst the masses outside the hospital.

"I'll wait here." Chloe yawned, covering her mouth with the back of her hand, while simultaneously attempting to wave Mark off.

"Won't be long."

Mark closed the door and jogged off towards the entrance.

Chloe watched a few birds in the sky as they made their way towards the main city harbour. The sheltered waters were well littered with fish scraps and human rubbish and would no doubt leave their tummies full and ready to take flight over the Cook Straight once more.

Chloe pulled out her phone to check for messages. One from Jess caused her tummy to flutter.

'Success! Mum and Grandma are on their way. Fingers crossed they make it. Love Jess & Ella.'

There was also an email from Vera. Chloe tapped it open and waited for it to load. Vera informed her they had in fact caught a flight to New Zealand and would arrive in Palmerston North on the 7th of December.

Chloe's heart swirled with joy. Now she could rest knowing she had done everything she could to fulfil her mother's wishes. Only time and misfortune would be to blame if anything should go awry.

Chloe searched the hospital entrance for any sign of Mark's return. Knowing him, she presumed he'd take much longer than the few minutes he had suggested. She didn't mind. The warmth of the car made her drowsy and her eyes rolled in her head trying to fight off sleep. Saving her nap for the drive may not be an option for much longer. Ten minutes passed and she was just at the cusp of drifting off when the driver's door swung open.

"Right. Let's hit the road," Mark said.

Chloe righted herself in the seat and tried to hold her heavy lids open.

"That was quicker than expected," her voice slurred.

"I said I wouldn't be long. Now. Let's get you home." Mark turned the key and the car grumbled back to life.

Chloe half smiled back as her eyelids drooped. Prying them open she tried to focus her vision. "Thanks, Mark."

He smiled in amusement. "You get some rest, Chloe. I'll wake you when we're close."

Chloe curled herself sideways and balled Matt's jacket up against the window. In no time at all she succumbed to sleep, dreaming of her own reunion with her mother.

Chloe felt a shove against her shoulder and she pulled herself back into reality.

"Nearly there, Chloe. Now I should warn you that your mother is on some pretty strong drugs. She may not recognise you at first, but give her half an hour or so and I'm sure she'll figure it out. Danielle has kept her apprised of your return, but I want you to be prepared, she really doesn't have much time left. We're doing everything we can to keep her comfortable, and when I saw her two days ago it seemed likely she'd be well enough to attend the wedding. But…I encourage you to savour every moment - there may be fewer than you think."

Before any moisture could accumulate, Chloe rubbed her eyes, and then her forehead. She pressed her hands down the length of her thighs and shuffled in her seat. "Oh yes, of course. Thanks, Mark. I really appreciate all you're doing for us - for my family. When is the wedding by the way?"

"Friday."

"But that's…" Chloe paused trying to recall what day it was again.

"Four days from now. I know. It's soon. I've still got to get my suit sorted. In fact, I'm off for my fitting just as soon as I've dropped you off."

Chloe stared at him like two and two made three.

"We had to take it. It was the only venue with an opening. It's much smaller than we planned, and I know it's not what Danielle dreamed of, but she would rather have a small wedding with her mother there than a large one without her. She is happy, Chloe, and I've promised I'll make it up to her."

"I'm sure you will, Mark. And I'll be here to make sure you do." She smirked.

"So you're staying? I thought maybe you'd head back to the U.K."

"I'm not sure. There's a lot to consider. I guess it depends on how… how long Mum needs me." She couldn't bear to say anything else. The word, death, wielded so much pain that to utter it prematurely was almost akin to welcoming it.

"Well I'm sure you'll figure out what to do. And if I know anything about your sister, she'll have a whole plan mapped out to help you decide." He winked.

Mark pulled the car right to the front entrance of the hospital then sat with it idling. I'll drop your bags to your parents' house later if that's okay."

Chloe nodded.

"She's in room 232 - same floor."

Chloe nodded again.

"Give Danielle a kiss for me, and tell her I'm on track for a perfectly fitted suit. I'll catch up with you all a bit later."

Chloe opened the passenger door and took only her handbag with her. She watched Mark drive out to the curb before turning to go inside. Her feet seemed to weigh a ton and each step grew more difficult the further she made it inside. Grateful for the wall of the lift, she leaned her shoulder against it, hoping against all odds that the stringent smell of the hospital would keep her awake long enough to make it to her mother's room.

Pushing on the door, Chloe entered, drawing in a sharp breath when she saw her mother lying motionless on the bed. Danielle was seated in a chair nearest the window and looked up from the magazine she was flicking through. She motioned her to come in quietly.

Chloe nodded. She was beginning to wonder if she had lost her ability to talk at all. Every new piece of information seemed so overwhelming. She wouldn't know what to say anyway.

"She's just fallen asleep," Danielle whispered as she rose from the chair and opened her arms for a hug. "I'm so glad you're here, Chloe." She wrapped her arms around Chloe so tightly that she wondered if she were in the right room.

"Who are you, and what have you done with my sister?" Chloe smiled. "I'm here now. Everything will be okay."

"But it won't be." Danielle sniffed. "I'm not even sure if Mum's going to make it to the end of the week."

"Sure she will, Danielle. She has to. Marta's on her way. They arrive Thursday. If Mum can hold on till then, I'm sure she can make it to your big day. Now, tell me all about the wedding plans. And where's Dad?"

"Oh, he just popped home for a rest. He's been taking the night shifts, so Mum's never alone. It was almost impossible to get him to go home. He's exhausted, Chloe. He's wearing a brave face but I can see he's struggling.

"Of course he is. He's losing the love of his life. Wouldn't you be?"

"Yes. I don't know what I'd do without Mark. He's been so good. I know you might think otherwise, but he does love me, and I know he's the right one for me." Danielle clutched her arm, and Chloe wrapped her hand over her sister's. "I know. He's totally on board with the wedding changes. I'm completely blown away. You picked good, Danielle, and I know Mum approves."

"Chloe is that you?" came a croaky voice.

"Mum!" Chloe sprang to her mother's bedside. "It's me, Mum. I'm home."

"I thought I was dreaming, but it is you." Mum's dry lips spread wide across her face puffing out her cheeks a little.

"I'm home Mum. And I have news. Marta is coming. She'll be here in just a few more days. You have to hold on for her...for us, and for the wedding. Marta's desperate to meet you and she's coming all this way. You'll like her Mum. She's feisty and stubborn just like you." Chloe smiled, letting the tears slip endlessly from her eyes. She wrapped her arms around her mother as much as she could as she lay in the bed.

Mum pointed to the glass of water on the bed table, and Chloe brought it to her. Once she had rehydrated, her mother insisted they sit her up.

"I want to hear all your news, Chloe. Tell me everything. How is London? Danielle tells me you've been seeing someone. Is it serious?"

Chloe shrugged. Mum frowned.

"Well. How did he take your leaving?"

"As well as to be expected I suppose." She dare not give her mother any sort of false hopes for her romantic future. Heck, she dare not hope at all, for the sake of her own heart.

"All right. Hint taken. But I won't be here forever you know." Mum pointed a finger at her, but then waved her hand to change the subject before Chloe could say anything. "I talked to Peter on the phone. He sounds real nice, but what's he like - in person I mean? I've not seen him at all besides Dad's old cricket photos."

Chloe's heart swelled with joy. Her mother's spirits appeared to be lifting, and it was comforting to know she had some part in it. What she hadn't expected was her mother's surge of inquiry about her love life these past three months. But then again, that hadn't really changed. Mum was always interested in chatting with her about life, and she hadn't realised just how much she missed their talks until now.

"I'll tell you everything, Mum. But first you have to promise to tell me if you're getting tired. Marta is coming, and I don't want to talk your ear off completely. Because, in a few days, you two will have a lifetime to catch up on."

Her mother nodded with a narrow smile. "Agreed."

After a steady stream of chit-chat, relaying every detail of her time teaching at the school to her encounter with Marta's brother, and the attack thereafter, Danielle eyed her with a stare hinting their mother was growing weary.

Chloe nodded and looked at her watch. "Mum it's been so great to catch up with you, and Danielle too, but I'm so tired. If I don't get some sleep soon I think I'm going to have to stay right here and take a nap."

"Oh goodness, yes. Sorry Chloe. I'd forgotten you have just come from the airport. You must be exhausted. Dad will be here soon. Why don't you two go home and get some rest. Truth be told I'm a bit tired myself."

Chloe cocked her head sideways and dropped her jaw. "I told you that you had to tell me if you were getting tired."

"I thought I just did," Mum said, twisting her smile.

With little warning other than the few heavy footsteps as they reached the door, Jeremy pranced in. He cast a desperate eye over Chloe, and then finally addressed her mother.

"My apologies, Lizzy, Danielle. But I must speak with Chloe. It's urgent."

Mum and Danielle looked just as stunned as she felt.

Chloe stood between the bed and Jeremy with a hard frown. "What are you doing here. How did you know I was back?"

"I didn't. And I'm guessing I never would have if I hadn't run into Mark. I had no idea you were back in hospital, Lizzy." He looked over Chloe's shoulder at her mother. "If I had known, I would have come sooner. Why didn't you tell me, Chloe?" he pulled his gaze back to her.

Chloe didn't like the familiarity he shared with her mother. Yes, her mother had told him to call her Lizzy, just two days after they began dating, and yes, they connected on some weird level reserved only for boyfriends who exceeded a mother's expectations. It was a fact Chloe once admired. Now, however, it seemed inappropriate given they were no longer in a relationship. Just his mere presence in the room felt like an affront to Chloe's absence. Every muscle tightened throughout her body and she folded her arms firmly across her chest.

"What does it matter to you if my mother's unwell?"

"Chloe!" her mother breathed. "Don't be like that. It was very nice of you to come, Jeremy. I'm a little tired though. Perhaps you could visit another time."

"Sorry, Lizzy. But if I'm honest, I really came to see Chloe. Did she tell you?"

"Tell me what?"

Chloe shook her head at Jeremy with a 'don't you dare' glare.

"That I asked her to marry me."

Chloe turned to face her mother, knowing she was about to receive an earful. Hurt furrowed her mother's brow. Chloe's omission was practically as good as a lie.

"Sorry Mum. I didn't think it mattered. I told him no in London. I can't marry a man I don't love."

Jeremy grabbed her elbow from behind and turned her back to face him.

"You don't mean that, Chloe. You can't. You're the only one for me. I know this now. I know I didn't always show you how much you mean to me, but can't you see, I've changed. I have. If you'd just give me a chance, I know you would come to love me again." Jeremy caressed a hand down her cheek and she swatted it away like a fly.

"No, Jeremy. It's over, and nothing you can do or say will change my mind. Now would you please go away? I'm tired and I don't want to talk about this anymore." She turned her back to him and buried her head in her hand.

"But, Chloe...I love you."

Mum held a hand to her mouth, and reached a hand towards Chloe for her to take hold of. "Oh, Jeremy. You do?"

"Yes. I love your daughter. I always will. For the rest of my life, I want to love her and support her, and make her every wish come true. I want her to become my wife."

Chloe turned to face him once more, hoping like crazy it would be the last time. "No you don't, Jeremy. You only think you do. You and I will never work. We're not good together. I've changed and I'm not the same person you fell in love with. Just go. Please!" Chloe's words held the bite and slight whimper of a cornered dog and she hated the fact that she had raised her voice. A nurse had come running to their room to see what all the fuss was about.

Jeremy lowered his shoulders in defeat. "I'm sorry. I'll go. But my offer still stands, Chloe. When you've come to your senses, or perhaps when you're not so tired. You'll see. I only want what's best for you."

Jeremy slipped out the door, and Mum, who was now sitting even more upright, slumped back into the pillows on her bed.

"What's going on, Chloe. Why didn't you tell me he proposed?"

"I wanted to, but his arrival was so sudden and I needed time - time he wasn't prepared to give me. So I said no."

"You mean to tell me he flew all the way to London just to ask for your hand, and you refused. But why? It's what you always wanted, isn't it? You and Jeremy were supposed to get engaged in Europe on your trip anyway. Why the change of heart? Is it because of this new guy? What's his name" - she looked at Danielle - "Matt?"

Chloe sighed at her sister. "Not now, Mum. You need to rest and so do I. Danielle, can you take me home?"

"Of course." She avoided looking Chloe in the eye, and grabbed her handbag.

"Thank you." Chloe replied. "I'll see you tomorrow, Mum. We'll talk more about it then, I promise."

CHAPTER TWENTY-TWO

CHLOE REGRETTED LEAVING Matt's jacket in Mark's car. If she could just wrap herself inside it everything would be all right. How long would it be before Mark brought her bags to her parents' house? Chloe closed her eyes and let her head fall against the car's headrest.

Danielle eased to a stop at the lights and indicated left.

Watching the busy intersection, Chloe felt the cut of the seatbelt in her neck and tugged it away from her chest. The traffic blurred and Chloe let her thoughts float away, hoping that some might disappear completely. "I'm sorry if I upset Mum. She doesn't need any of this right now and nor do you. If we could just leave it till I've had some sleep, I'd be grateful."

Danielle nodded, easing her foot off the brake and cruising towards the next set of lights. "Consider it forgotten. Mum will get over it. She only wants to see you happy. Maybe she thinks Jeremy can do that - make you happy. I see that might not be the case now." Danielle stopped at the lights again and turned to face her. "You've changed. I can see it." Danielle smiled with a fixed gaze.

"He's the one, isn't he?" She grinned. Chloe had no answer and therefore gave neither confirmation nor denial. But as her sister would say, silence speaks volumes, and she was right.

They pulled into the driveway of their childhood home and Chloe sighed, letting a tear slip down her cheek. "Home. It's so good to be home."

Mark's car was already parked in the driveway and Chloe went straight to it's window to peer inside for signs of the jacket.

Nothing. He must have already taken her bags inside.

Chloe followed Danielle through the back door and into the kitchen.

"Dad, we're home." Danielle called, ditching her keys on the counter.

"In here."

Chloe almost burst into tears at how close his voice sounded. Holding them back she marched towards the sitting room and promptly into her father's arms. She wound her arms around him, noticing instantly how much thinner he felt.

"Dad!" - she pinched around his ribs - "What have you been eating? There's hardly anything left of you."

Her father let her go and shook his head. "I haven't had the appetite lately and hospital food is hardly nutritious. I hadn't really noticed. I guess my pants are feeling a little looser."

"Well we need to sort that out and soon." She drilled her eyes into him. "I don't need two parents wasting away on me."

Dad pursed his lips in a brief smile and scratched at his whiskered chin.

Danielle moved in to hug Dad, then motioned Chloe with a nod towards the door. "You head off to bed, Chloe. I'll take care of him. You need to sleep. We have a lot to get through in the next couple of days and I need you well and rested."

Chloe was happy to oblige and headed straight to the bathroom. She hadn't changed clothes since leaving London and wouldn't be surprised if they up and walked off to the laundry of their own accord.

Chloe could have stayed beneath the streaming water for another hour were it not for the raised voices. Turning off the shower she couldn't make out who the voices belonged to, but they were definitely arguing.

She scurried to her room, threw on some clothes, and ventured towards the lounge. Patting her hair dry with the towel as she entered she found Granddad mid-sentence standing over Grandma Iris.

"…it's just how it is and you're going to have to get used to it."

No one else was in the room and Chloe presumed Dad had gone to the hospital, and Danielle and Mark must be elsewhere. What she couldn't figure out was how her grandparents had come to be in her parents' home at all.

"You can't do this to me, Thomas. It's not fair. Lizzy doesn't know what she wants and upsetting her like this won't help anyone."

"You mean upsetting you won't help anyone." He bounced his hand at her.

"It's not about me!" Grandma said with fumes of exhaust.

"For once Iris, I agree. It isn't about you and that's the end of it. Lizzy wants to do this and we're not going to stop her." Granddad huffed.

"Stop what?" Chloe asked, making both her grandparents jump.

"Oh, good. Now you can back me up," said Granddad.

"Back you up how?"

Grandma pointed a finger at Granddad. "He wants Peter to attend the wedding and I don't think it's necessary."

"Well I think that's a wonderful idea," said Chloe.

"See!" Granddad beamed his pleasure in his wife's face. Grandma slapped him lightly on the cheek. "Oh, Thomas. Why can't you see?"

"It's not me who's blind, Iris, it's you." Granddad looked to Chloe. "Now. You tell her the rest of the news. I haven't the heart to say anything more."

Chloe held her Grandmother's hand and led her to the couch. "Grandma. I'm not sure how much Granddad has told you, but do you remember that photo I showed you months ago - the one that looked like me?"

"Yes. What's that got to do with anything?"

"Well, you see. I had reason to believe that it might be mum's birth-mother."

Iris looked at her in horror. "You don't mean to tell me that trollop was at our wedding, do you?" Grandma looked at Granddad, "Thomas?" she growled. "Did you know about this? Did you know she was there?"

Granddad cowered towards the door as if trying to escape the room.

"You come back here this instant and tell me what's going on, or so help me... I'll not share another night in the same bed with you ever again!"

Chloe wanted to laugh but bit her tongue. Granddad sure was in hot water, but Chloe knew it was long overdue. She'd promised to take some of the heat, back when they first began the search, but Granddad had made his own bed and now he had to lie in it, even if it meant doing so alone for the rest of his days apparently.

"Iris, sweetheart." He said, lacing his words in sugar. "You must understand. Peter was in a tough spot, He was engaged and the poor girl was to be disowned by her own family if he did nothing. He saved her, really."

"No, Thomas, *we* saved her, and him by the sounds of it." Iris gritted. "I only wish I'd known sooner. Maybe then I would have understood why Lizzy was so reckless as a child."

"Iris," Granddad twirled her name in candy floss, "Lizzy was a good child, we raised her well, and she loves us. She loves you. Nothing will change that."

"I know. But I just can't help thinking that her last days with us, won't be spent…well…with us."

"Can you blame her? You know how much meeting her birth-parents has meant to her. Why can't you let her enjoy them? We've had her our whole lives. Peter and Marta deserve the chance to get to know the girl - the woman they missed out on, don't you think?"

Granddad was now close enough to pull Grandma into his arms. She resisted at first, but was helpless to refuse the comfort he was offering.

"She's my daughter, Thomas. I only want what's best for her. Can you guarantee this Marta woman can say the same?"

"I know I can." Chloe interrupted. "I've met her, Grandma, and she's really nice. She had a pretty rough time of it by the sounds of things, and when I met Peter, he said it was really he who was to blame."

"Oh, I see. So you've met them both already have you? Well that's just great. Once again I see I'm the last to know anything."

"Don't blame Granddad, Grandma. He was only trying to protect you. He knew you'd be upset if we went snooping in the past. But I did it for Mum. I did it because she asked me to. I never would have done it without her blessing. She wants to meet them, and I think we should let her. She may not have long left with us, but if she wants to spend time with them then we have to respect that. We'll see her tomorrow and the next day. But when Marta arrives on Thursday, I think we should give them their space. Mum needs to heal, and so does Marta. Honestly, that's the best gift you could ever give Mum right now, and I think you know it."

Grandma bowed her head as if considering Chloe's words.

"Well aren't you all grown up?" She smiled. "I worried for you, Chloe. I thought you'd lost your way when that fella left you. But look at you now. So confident and strong."

Granddad laughed. "Looks like you've found some of your Grandma's gumption, my dear. Use it wisely. And for the sake of your future husband, whoever he might be, don't chuck it at him all at once - It can hurt."

Grandma patted his hand on her lap. "Don't think you're completely off the hook yet, you've got some introductions to make and I'm going to enjoy watching you squirm when you do." Grandma chuckled.

Granddad stood up quickly, pulled Grandma to her feet, and into his arms as if he were going to waltz her. "Frankly my dear, as long as I have you in my...bed" - he winked - "I don't give a damn." He dipped her slightly, and Grandma let her head roll back laughing.

Chloe marvelled at them. Yes this is what she wanted, a love like no other. One where even fighting contained its beauty. Chloe remembered her fight with Matt in the sports shed, when she thought his celebrity status would threaten her job. She laughed.

Fights with Jeremy were never like that. She always felt like she was to blame, that she hadn't compromised or understood what he needed from her. It made her heart twist sharply.

Sleep could no longer wait, but nor could Matt. She had to talk to him. Now.

She picked up her phone to dial. It was mid-afternoon. It would almost be 2:00 am in London. She wondered whether his team won their game against Manchester United.

She searched the news. 3—1 to Manchester.

Matt would be so disappointed. If it weren't such a terrible hour maybe she could cheer him up. She dialled anyway. It went straight to voice-mail. She held the phone to her ear with both hands, listening to every word of his message. She'd give anything to talk to him right now.

"Hi Matt. I just wanted to say, I miss you. Call me when you can." Chloe ended the call, curled into bed and was asleep before any other thought or memory could detain her.

Thursday 7th December 2017

Marta

Marta tucked her handbag under her arm and attempted to lift her bag onto the trolley.

"Oh, Ma, for heaven's sake. Here let me do that." Vera yanked the bag onto the trolley with little grace. She eyed her with a stern glare. "If you injure yourself you'll have a terrible time travelling back home again. Remember what the doctor said, 'no heavy lifting'."

Marta nodded, mimicking Vera as she regurgitated the same phrase for the twentieth time since leaving Scotland. She fanned herself with a Skyways magazine, and watched Vera and everyone else as they plucked their bags from the circling snake of luggage.

"What have you got there?" asked Vera. "You weren't supposed to take that. That stays on board the aeroplane for the next passengers." Vera snatched the magazine from her and looked around for anyone she could return it to. Finding no one, she handed it back to her and proceeded to search the carousel once more. She eventually spied another bag and went to haul it off the carousel. Wheeling it over she heaved it on top of the two others and patted them to check their stability.

"Is that all of them?" Marta asked.

"Aye, it is." Now all we have to do is find the domestic terminal."

Both scanned the cavernous glass walled Auckland Airport for any signs that might point the way. It was then that Marta spotted him. At first she didn't believe he was real, but once he was standing two feet in front of her she figured it was safe to pat Vera's shoulder and inform her of their added companion.

"Max!" Vera squealed, her cheeks puffing in delight. "What are you doing here. Who's with the kids?" Her eyes flashed.

"Joe offered to come down and take care of things. He wouldn't take no for an answer, so I hopped on the first flight out. I got here an hour ago."

"You're joking! You mean to tell me I've been travelling this whole time and you still managed to beat us here?"

"Aye, and I've been waiting for you to get here so we can check in for the connecting flight together. The domestic terminal is this way. Seems they keep the international and domestic travellers separate here." Max took over their luggage trolley and led the way.

When the pilot announced they'd be landing in Palmerston North in five minutes, Marta stuck her nose on the small aeroplane's window. "Heavens, it's so big! I wasn't expecting it to be this big. When I was here last the city never went beyond the railway line. Look at it now." She pointed out the window. Max, who had taken over Vera's parental supervision duties, simply nodded and smiled. "Aye, it's not small at all. It looks even bigger than Paris. How many people do you think live here, Ma?"

"I read online that only 86,000 people live in the city."

Max looked surprised. "Did ye now? And where might you have read that - online?"

"Wikipedia." She nodded back. "Ella showed me on her phone. I do like that I can call her more often now, you and Vera too."

Max huffed, "Aye, but you don't want to be spending hours on the daft thing. There's no telling what it might do to yer brain."

"It can't do much worse than old age, son."

Max chuckled. "Aye, true enough."

On the ground Max was a much greater help than Vera. He had all their bags piled high on another trolley in no time at all. Marta looked around the scarcely populated little terminal for any sign of Chloe. Then she spotted her familiar long hair, swept up to a high ponytail. It reminded her of younger days when she too wore such a style. Marta shot a hand in the air to wave. As Chloe neared them, she was just as surprised to see Max, as she and Vera were in Auckland.

"Hello. I wasn't expecting to see you too, Uncle Max. But welcome." She opened her arms to each of them for a hug. "Come. I'm parked just outside. Mum's at home under strict orders to rest. She's so excited to meet you all. And I know she'll be even more excited once she sees you here too, Uncle Max."

Chloe and Max crammed their luggage into the car and when they were finally underway, Marta's stomach started to swirl with sickly anticipation.

Chloe started the car. "I'll take you to your hotel first, so we can drop off your luggage. Have you eaten?"

It was nearly noon but the thought of eating a meal was the last thing on her mind.

Max cleared his throat. "Aye. I had a bite before we left Auckland."

Vera leaned forward to speak. "Ma and I haven't. I'm starving. Is there anywhere you would recommend, Chloe?"

"Well, what do you feel like? If you don't mind fast food, I'm sure we can find something for you."

"I'm not hungry. I just want to meet Lizzy. The sooner the better." Marta's words were blunt, but sharp enough to sever any plans to detour for food.

Chloe smiled into the rear-view mirror. Marta knew she would find a solution to Vera's hunger that wouldn't impede a timely arrival.

"I'll get Danielle to bring you something, Aunty Vera. She won't mind. Grandma Iris will be popping in later with Granddad and she always brings food. I'm sure there'll be something you can eat." Chloe eyed Vera in the mirror and she nodded.

"Good. Now how much further?" Marta asked.

Chloe and Max laughed.

"Not far. About four minutes if we don't hit rush hour." Her granddaughter's eyes wrinkled at their corners, as did her smile. Palmerston North may be large in size, but certainly not in population. All the roads were dotted with cars but none ever stopped for long.

Chloe ushered them all inside her family home. "Would anyone like a drink?"

Marta wrung her hands in knots and she worried Chloe might think she were cold. If her stomach wasn't so queasy she might have been able to sit down, but since it wouldn't settle she had convinced the others that she needed to stretch her legs. Vera agreed.

It's just nerves. I'll have some tea and all will be well.

"I'd love a cup of tea, thank you, Chloe," she said turning at the corner of the room. Vera and Max agreed to tea also and Chloe decided to make a pot. Finally when the tea was served and she'd taken her first sip, a man entered the room. She could only presume him to be Chloe's father, judging by his silvering hair.

"Everyone." Chloe said in a slightly higher pitch than usual. "I'd like you to meet my Dad, Jack Spencer. Dad this is Max, Vera, and this is Marta." Chloe gestured him towards her.

"Max. So great you could make it. It's so lovely to meet you all. Lizzy is understandably nervous. As I'm sure you all are too. I'll take you to see her when you've finished your tea."

Marta stood and moved closer to him. She held out her hand and he took it in both his hands. "Thank you, Jack. You've no idea how happy I am. I've waited nearly sixty years for this day, and I'm not about to let a simple cup of tea stop me now."

Jack touched her shoulder and flattened his smile. "I understand. Very well, follow me."

Marta wanted to chide herself for her impatience, but there was no time now. Her stomach swirled like a bowl of soapy water and continued to swish with every step behind Jack. The others followed, but she dare not look back to see who.

Entering the softly lit bedroom, Marta stepped inside dipping her head slightly as she did so. She wanted to look up and straight into her daughters eyes but she was scared. What if she was still mad at her for giving her away?

Jack spoke softly. "Lizzy, this is Marta. Marta, this is your daughter, Lizzy. And you're in luck, Lizzy, even your brother has made the journey."

Marta looked up and to her left where she felt Max's presence beside her. She eyed him anxiously and he smiled, gesturing her it was okay to go to her daughter. Marta turned and saw Lizzy for the first time. Her beautiful baby was so grown and old. It was hard to imagine she was ever her child, this stranger in a bed sick with an illness that would soon take her life. Marta's swirling stomach ached so hard, and in an instant the pain surged to her chest. She rushed forward, into the awaiting arms of her full-grown baby, hugging her tight. In her mind Marta pictured the little baby she had seen flail it's arms soon after she'd given birth to her. Back then she had wanted to hold her. To brush her finger across her baby's nose and cheeks, and stare into her eyes. She was so innocent, and ignorant of the fact that she would never get to look into her mother's eyes. The only thing left to do was cry, and eventually the waters came, thick and salty with all the pains and memories that she had tried so hard to lock away. Not only did she cry for her own loss, but for Lizzy's too. The woman in her arms shuddered with a pain Marta could only imagine. What must she think of a mother who gave her away? Marta pulled away for a moment to memorise her child's face as it was now. She caressed Lizzy's cheek and wiped away her tears. "It's all right. I'm here now. I'm here, and I'm not going anywhere." Marta smiled.

Lizzy wiped her eyes and seemed to be searching her face for a similar familiarity. "I can't believe it...it's you. You're real. You're here."

They embraced once more and then Marta motioned for Vera and Max to come closer.

"These are my two children. Max. He's my eldest...well I guess not anymore." She laughed. "And this..." she took Vera's hand, "...this is my Vera. She's a nurse." Vera's eyes were watering already and she leaned forward to give Lizzy a hug. "Hello, Sister. You know, I always wanted a sister. Max was okay as far as brothers go, but a sister! I can't believe my wish came true." Vera wiped her nose with the back of her hand. "I only wish I'd met you sooner."

"I know. Me too," said Lizzy. "And I am truly blessed to call you my sister, and a Scottish one no less."

Everyone laughed.

Marta's heart was full - right to the brim. Like an old darned sock, the hole in her heart began to mend, closing the gap her child had left. Never again would she have to wonder how her daughter was, or where she was, or who she was with. Lizzy would forever remain in her heart no matter how much time she had left on this earth. The thought of losing her so soon pained her already. Would it have been easier to have not come at all, staying ignorant of all she had missed? In spite of everything she was desperate to know it all, no matter how much harder it made their parting. The dam holding her questions broke, flooding her mind in a great rush.

What was Lizzy like as a toddler? Did she like school? What was she really good at? Who was her first kiss? When did she marry? Did she always know she was adopted? What hurt had she experienced? *Did she think about me?*

All Marta could do was begin at the start, and pray like crazy they'd make it to the end. Lizzy would have questions of her own, and if Marta's patience could bear it, she would wait as long as she could for answers to her own questions. At the very least they now had a start, and that was more than either of them ever thought they would get.

CHAPTER TWENTY-THREE

Friday 8th December 2017

"CHLOE. SOMEONE'S HERE to see you," her mother's voice echoed down the hallway.

Chloe looked at her sister, delicately dressed in fine lace and chiffon, with a veil pinned at the base of her wispy balled hair. In half an hour they'd be at the church and down the aisle.

Danielle looked at her - her eyes sparkling, "I'll be fine. You go."

"Just a minute," Chloe called back, wafting the veil into even ruffles down her sister's back. She hadn't the slightest clue who it might be, an old school friend perhaps. Mum said she had a surprise for her today, but she hadn't hinted it might be a person. Chloe presumed the surprise would be a piece of Mum's jewellery she wanted her to wear, or a keepsake for the momentous occasion. As Chloe had little desire for anything other than her mother's presence at her sister's wedding, she hadn't put any more thought into the surprise at all. All of Mum's other wishes had been fulfilled. Marta was here, her sister and brother too, and, thanks to Granddad, Mum had met Peter yesterday as well. All of them were attending the wedding, so what more could her mother possibly want?

Chloe patted her lips with a little gloss, looked herself over in the full length mirror, then slipped out the door of her sister's room. The voices gathered in the living room sounded familiar, and although she hadn't the slightest idea who had come to see her, her stomach flipped into a knot beneath her blue shift dress (the one she was supposed to wear to Matt's Christmas party).

Chloe entered the room and scanned the bodies.

Jeremy?

Surely he wasn't her mother's surprise.

Mum, beautifully dressed in her new summer dress and hat, sat poised in a wheel chair and motioned Chloe to come to her. She held both of her hands, and eyed her solemnly. "Hello, sweetheart. Jeremy's just popped in to see you. Don't be too long. We need to leave in a few minutes." Her mother's voice held no celebratory tone, and yet her faint smile led Chloe to think her mother may have put him up to it.

Dad wheeled Mum out of the room, and was followed by Grandma Iris. Eventually Granddad left too, but not without shaking his head first. The cars were already parked in the driveway and Danielle would be making her exit soon.

Jeremy watched the others leave and then turned to face her.

"Chloe. I know you said you don't want to marry me. But I know in my heart that you still love me..." He clutched her hand and lifted it to his chest, cupping it against his shirt. "And, I'll wait for you until you're ready."

His heart was beating fast and his eyes were glazed with moisture. "Don't break my heart, Chloe," his puppy eyes yelped. "We belong together and I think your Mum thinks so too."

"Why? Did she say something?" Chloe raised one brow.

"Well not in so many words. But I can tell she just wants you to be happy. I can make you happy, Chloe. I promise. I'll never leave you again the way I did before. You have my word."

Chloe searched his eyes for the truth, and seeing he was sincere, she dropped her shoulders and bit her bottom lip.

"I'm just not sure if I can trust you again, Jeremy. You broke my heart and I've spent the last three months trying to fix it. I was finally starting to get over you, and now...well, now you're back again."

"I know, and I'm sorry. Can you forgive me?"

"I do. I have. But I'm not sure if I can go through that again."

"You won't have to. Just promise me that you'll give us another chance." Jeremy dropped down on his knee and offered her his ring again. Chloe looked at it and tears swelled in her eyes. Jeremy took it as his cue to put the ring on her finger, and she didn't resist.

She looked at it and felt the band around her finger with her thumb. It felt strange, yet exciting all at the same time. The pea-sized diamond glistened in the light. Jeremy had spared no expense and the ring was far bigger than she ever expected.

Jeremy stood and took a chance on a kiss. Chloe's lips pressed softly against his and his dimpled chin brushed smoothly across hers. It was strange, yet warmly familiar. Somehow it felt like nothing had changed - like they'd always been together and not a day had passed since August.

Chloe pulled away. His breath was heavy and satisfied.

His unfettered grin left no doubt of his conviction. But Chloe's mind was still cloudy and not ready to invest herself completely.

"You can't tell anyone." Chloe pressed her hands against his chest and looked up into his eyes. "Promise me. This is Danielle and Mark's day and I won't spoil it for them by announcing anything. We'll tell them all tomorrow."

"But Chloe...don't you want to share the news - at least with your Mum. I'm sure she'll be thrilled to know that both her daughters will be happily married."

"I'm sure she will, but we'll tell them tomorrow. Until then, keep your mouth shut." She drew her lips tight. Telling Jeremy to keep his mouth shut was like telling a six year old to put the cap back on a coloured marker. The intention was there and maybe even a feeble attempt. But inevitably it was never clicked on securely enough to prevent it from falling off.

Danielle entered the living room and Chloe sprang back from Jeremy.

"Are you ready?" Danielle asked, passing her eyes across the two of them curiously.

"Yes. I'm ready." Chloe blew a burst of air up the right side of her face. It was a little too warm for her liking.

"Let's go then." Danielle hitched up her dress to make walking a little easier.

Chloe gave Jeremy another stern glare ensuring he knew exactly how to behave if he wanted to stay in her good graces.

Chloe spun the ring on her finger inwards and grabbed her and Danielle's bouquets from the dining table. The size of her bouquet alone hid both her hands formidably well, and Chloe wondered if much of her dress would be noticed at all beneath the monstrosity. At least she wouldn't have to hold them all day, as opposed to wearing the dress Danielle had originally picked for her to wear. Perhaps the flowers were her sister's attempt at some form of control. Now, Chloe was nothing but glad for their size.

Danielle questioned her almost the entire way to the church. By the time they arrived Chloe had almost run out of wits.

"It's nothing...*really*. Let's just focus on your wedding. This is your day - not mine." Chloe exited the car and helped Danielle lay her small train out behind her. Together they made their way up the stairs of the church and into the entrance alcove. Dad had been summoned and would be there soon to accompany Danielle down the aisle.

"All right then," Danielle looked at her sideways. "But you would tell me if it were anything important, wouldn't you?"

Chloe couldn't imagine a bride looking more displeased right before entering the church on her wedding day. She huffed and handed Danielle the flowers from her left hand.

"Chloe!" Danielle grabbed her hand and flipped it over.

"Shhhh!" Chloe frowned. "It's nothing. You saw nothing. Okay?"

"But, but, but you, you. Oh no. What have you done?!"

"Nothing. I've done nothing."

"That's not what it looks like. That looks like a giant piece of something right there."

Chloe pulled her hand away and buried it beneath the foliage.

"I might have agreed to marry Jeremy. I'm not sure."

"Well that rock says otherwise."

"No it doesn't. We're just going to try again. He asked for a second chance, and for Mum's sake, I'm going to try."

"Oh, Chloe." Her sister's face drained of any remaining happiness it might have still had. "You're an idiot!"

"Well thanks, Danielle. I'm glad you still think so. I was beginning to wonder how long our new peace agreement would last."

Danielle buried her forehead in her palm. "I'm sorry, Chloe. I guess, if it's what you really want. Then…I'll support you. But just so you know, Jeremy was not Mum's surprise for you today."

Dad arrived just as the stringed music in the church sounded. He wrapped Danielle's arm around his and smiled. "You ready?"

"I am." Danielle drew up a fresh smile.

Chloe marched down the aisle first, pacing her steps in time with the music. Danielle's orchestra friends had formed a quartet and were positioned up on stage off to one side.

Chloe smiled at the small gathering of friends and guests that could make it to the weekday wedding. Nearing the front of the church Chloe spotted Marta, Vera, and Max sitting next to Mum. Peter and his wife, June, were seated in behind them. They all beamed in joyful chorus. At the end, Chloe turned and watched as her father and sister started their progression towards her.

Her sister looked beautiful and her smile was now genuinely gleeful. Chloe looked at Mark. She had barely noticed him during her walk up the aisle. His smile was full of teeth and his hair was more slicked than usual. Beside him was his older brother, clutching his hands across his front like he was about to get kicked in the crotch. Chloe sniggered through her nose. She swam her eyes over the heads of the gathering and thought she spotted a familiar head of hair. The face was obscured by someone else and by then Danielle had arrived at the front of the church. Chloe turned to face the minister and let her mind go numb in the moment.

Within minutes a flood of terrifying thoughts consumed her. Danielle was right. What had she done? She didn't love Jeremy any more, but was it really possible to love him again? Maybe she could if she just tried. But what would that mean for her future? Should she go back to London? There was something else that bugged her. If Matt truly cared for her, why had he let her go so easily? Had he really done anything different than Jeremy?

Jeremy said he wanted to let her grow up and become her own person. And now she had. So why then did she now feel like her future had been decided for her? Had she not learned anything? Why had she allowed Jeremy to convince her to marry him? Granted, he'd not pressured her with a set time frame. But still, it felt as though it really wasn't a choice she had made independently. Had she really only accepted him to please her mother. What would that mean then when she was gone? Who would she be pleasing when she was gone?

"Chloe," she heard Danielle whisper. Chloe looked at her in stunned silence. Her sister held out her bouquet for her to hold while she and Mark said their vows. Chloe watched Mark across her sister's shoulder. He loved her sister and would do anything for her. Would Jeremy do the same? He'd promised to make her happy. But what if she would be happier without him? Did she really matter to him?

Danielle spoke her vows and within seconds of Mark accepting his ring, the two of them were kissing their union into wedded bliss.

Chloe looked down the aisle momentarily. At the back of the church sat Jeremy, smiling at her with a subtle grin that made her insides lurch. He'd caught her. She was his, and he knew it. Her heart thumped hard and her breathing shallowed. She had to escape. But the service wasn't over. Danielle tugged her flowers back out of Chloe's hand and nodded her head sideways. Chloe followed her sister to the table set up with the registry and took her seat to sign the official documents. When she looked up she could now see who the person was that was obscured earlier.

Matt.

Her breathing stopped and all she could see was his face. Everything around him blurred and the next thing she saw was the carpet on the floor. When she blinked her eyes open, a fanned breeze was attempting to provide needed air as well as dry the hairs on her arms. Mark's brother lifted her upright and someone else passed her a glass of water. She took it and skulled the lot. If only it had contained something stronger, vodka perhaps. Had she really seen him, was he really there? Chloe looked around in a daze and then up to see Danielle bent over her with worry lining her forehead.

The string quartet started playing again and the minister made some jovial remark which made the wedding guests chuckle, likely at her expense. Chloe stood and eventually the minister had them all back in position. The minister nodded at her to affirm she was okay to continue. Chloe smiled feebly and it was then that she realised her flowers were still on the registry table. She looked down at her hand momentarily. She had to get it off. Grabbing at the ring on either side of her finger she tugged at the metal band and giant rock, trying to pry it off her finger. Gone was her desire to reconcile with Jeremy, and gone was any sense of dignity at all. She tucked her head to one side and licked her finger, hoping to slicken it free. Heat rose throughout her body as her struggle became harder to hide. Danielle micro-frowned at her to stop jiggling.

Chloe eyed her back, nodding desperately in the direction of her bouquet. Danielle didn't seem to comprehend. Chloe tightened her fist into a ball, jamming the rock into her hand as a form of self-flagellation. How could she have been so stupid? Why did she accept Jeremy's offer so readily? Did Matt really mean that little to her? He would certainly think so if he saw she had Jeremy's ring on.

When the minister finally announced to everyone, "I give you, Mr and Mrs Hughes," Danielle smiled and seemed to have a moment of clarity. Perhaps she too saw Matt. She handed Chloe her bouquet, took Mark's hand and together they sauntered off down the aisle flower-less, waving their arms in the air. While the crowd was distracted Chloe grabbed her lost bouquet and quickly followed the happy couple out to the church steps. Once outside she handed Danielle her bouquet, and was about to quietly step aside to find a bathroom when someone grabbed her arm.

"It's our turn next." Jeremy winked.

Chloe looked around for anyone who may have overheard. Seeing no one she pulled Jeremy aside with her and into the women's bathroom.

"Chloe. I can't... well, I suppose I could..." his mouth parted and he licked his bottom lip.

"Ew. Not a chance, Jeremy."

"Well I just thought because you..."

"Just shut up. I can't marry you, Jeremy. I'm sorry. It's a terrible mistake. I can't marry you just because my mum likes you. I don't love you anymore, and I don't want to try either." Chloe had her hand under the cold tap and was frantically pumping soap into her other hand. She smothered her hand with it and twisted the ring free from her finger. She rinsed it briefly then handed it back to him.

"Good-bye, Jeremy." Chloe marched out with her chin high and a huge weight off her shoulders. Finally she could breath. She stepped into the sunlight on the church steps and stood beside Danielle.

Her sister tucked her head to her neck and whispered, "Is it over. Is he gone?"

"I don't know if he's gone, but it sure is over. Thank God."

"Well I don't know if God had anything to do with it, but I know Mum did." Danielle pointed towards where Mum was sitting talking with a man. Chloe walked up from behind unwilling to fully accept what she had dared to hope for without seeing it first with her own eyes.

"Chloe! Are you all right?" Mum reached for her. Chloe entered her mother's arms and stayed there for a good twenty seconds. She was hesitant to let go and turn around, but eventually her mother gave her no choice.

"Sweetheart. Look who's here." Her mother gestured.

She turned to the smart waistcoated man. "Matt," she said nervously meeting his gaze. He smiled and dipped his head. Her gut whooshed like petrol on a flame. She wrapped her arms about his neck and kissed his cheek. "It's you!" She let go and stepped back. "Are you really here?" She grabbed his arms and biceps to be sure he was real. Every last bit of muscle beneath the sharp rolled shirt sleeve was his, and she leapt back into his embrace with a squeal.

"I missed you too, Chloe." He kissed into her hair. "I couldn't stay in London a minute longer. I had to come. I hope you don't mind."

"Mind? Why would I mind - you goose! You're everything and more to me."

Chloe pulled away again. She realised she might have just made a fool of herself. Matt hadn't professed anything for her other than he missed her. A cat can miss it's kittens - it doesn't mean it loves them. Chloe ran her fingers down the back of her hair and folded her arms across her waist.

"Why are you here, Matt?"

"To see you, silly."

"Okay. Well. Here I am." Chloe turned sideways as if not to look while he gleaned her body.

"What's up with you all of a sudden?"

"Well. Are you here just to see me? Or are you here for some other reason? Perhaps to make sure I come back."

"Well I'm hoping you'll come back with me of course. But I really came because I wanted to meet your mother. I mean, if we were to ever get married one day, I'd like to say I at least had the opportunity to see where you got your good looks from." Matt looked at her father who had now joined Mum's side. "No offense, Mr Spencer."

"None taken." Dad quipped.

"Well in that case, and if I'm not being too presumptuous..." Matt turned and lowered himself on his knee before her. He took from his waist coat pocket a diamond ring and held it up to her. "Chloe, would you do me the honour of becoming my wife? You face your challenges head on, and I admire you for that. I'm not sure what the future may hold, but whatever comes, I want to face it with you - together. I love you, Chloe Spencer. What do you say...will you marry me?"

Chloe held a hand to her heart and looked over her shoulder at her mother. She had tears trickling down her face, not tears of disappointment or sorrow, but tears of pure joy.

Chloe turned back to Matt.

"Yes, yes, yes! Of course I'll marry you."

He stood and took her into his arms, lifting her off the ground and hugging her so tight she thought she might pass out again.

He placed her down, took her left hand, and placed the ring on her. Chloe hoped it wasn't red or bruised from removing Jeremy's ring. She looked down and saw no evidence of her recent mistake. Only the beautiful hexagonal set vintage ring stole her attention and her breath. Chloe looked around the crowd hoping she hadn't caused too much of a scene. Danielle was making her way over.

Chloe hugged her. "I'm sorry, Danielle, I didn't mean to ruin your wedding."

"What do you mean? You haven't ruined it! Look how happy you are. I would never begrudge your happiness, little Sis. You deserve it every bit as much as I do. I just wanted to be the first to congratulate you." Danielle smiled and wrapped her bare arms around her. "I think you just put the icing on Mum's cake."

Now it was Chloe's turn to cry - so she did.

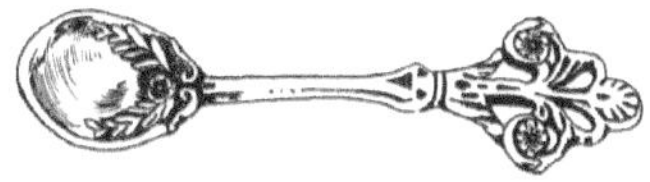

EPILOGUE

Scotland - October 1993

Marta

MARTA STOOD OVER her mother's grave three years after she had passed. Margaret Shirley Ingles would have rolled over the moment the dirt hit the casket if she knew she'd been buried under Scottish soil. And to this day, Marta still couldn't forgive herself for denying her mother's last wish. Even though her father, Lionel, had awaited Maggie's arrival beside him for seven years, it hadn't deterred Maggie of hope that someday she'd return home.

Not only had Marta failed her mother in death, but now it appeared she had also failed her in life too. Her mother's final words, penned in ink, evidenced a lie of unspeakable proportions. Marta couldn't believe it. She wouldn't.

Her father wasn't really her father at all. It said so in a letter she'd just found this morning in her mother's journal.

Her mother's deception was intolerable. How could she accept it, let alone prove it was a falsehood. Ever since leaving New Zealand Marta had done everything she could to prove herself worthy of love. That her parentage was above reproach and the mistakes of her youth had been pardoned and atoned for. To have everything now in question seemed as ludicrous as a pair of bloomers on a goat.

She scrunched the paper hard in her coat pocket and turned her attention to her father's gravestone.

He'd known apparently, Mum said so in the letter. Dad agreed to remain married on one condition. That she never say a word - to anyone.

Her father could be cruel, mean even. But this? This was something else.

He didn't love her at all. How could he? She wasn't even his own child.

Masterton - December 2017

Marta

STANDING AT THE open farm gate to her old family home, the memory hit her again. She raised her hand and flattened it against her cheek. She was not his flesh and blood. She'd buried that truth many years ago along with her past in Masterton. Why had she wanted to return here? The idea seemed foolish now. But keeping her promise, Marta agreed to take the trip and show her children where she grew up.

The hills hadn't shifted, but the dirt track leading to the house had and now it was gravel. The property's towering trees, now full grown, provided unthinkable shade, and she marvelled at the life the current owners must now enjoy.

She couldn't move. Recollecting every step she'd taken along the driveway to catch the bus, and every sunset and frost that had made it's presence felt on the land.

"Are you all right, Ma?" Max placed a hand on her shoulder and gazed out across the grass fields with her.

"Aye, I'll be all right."

"Would you like to go see it? Inside I mean. We could go and knock if you like."

"No. I don't think so, Max."

"Och, come on, Ma. You've come all this way. Don't you want to see it? I do."

"Please, Ma. We want to see where you grew up," said Vera.

Marta nodded and re-entered the car. Max pulled along the driveway slowly all the while eying her sideways as if to capture her response.

With the house now in full view Marta leaned forward and ran her eyes from the corrugated tin roof, down the weatherboards, and to the front door. It needed painting. It always needed painting. The house had seen new colour but even that now looked tired of the weather.

Someone split a net curtain from the kitchen window. Whose curious eye watched them?

Thanks to Max, animated introductions were made with the owner, and Marta entered her old home for the first time in fifty-six years. A few walls had been removed and the small kitchen was now open to the rest of the living area. A huge timber deck extended far beyond where the old one had, and a new sliding door opening onto it let in a glorious view of the farms beyond.

Marta nodded, shuffling her eyes about the foreign fixtures and furniture. It wasn't anything like how she remembered and it somehow felt bigger than the tiny house she had lived in.

"May I use your bathroom?" Marta inquired of the owner.

"It's down the hall…"

"And to the right. I remember," said Marta.

The woman smiled.

She took her time making her way there, gathering particles of memories as she went. To her left was where Jimmy had landed on the floor and split his head open on her bedroom door jam. Then the room opposite the toilet on the right was Jimmy's. Inside is where she had her first kiss. Should she tell anyone? What did it matter now? Marta's breath shuddered inward. She let it go when her eyes swelled with sadness. She entered the toilet and locked the door.

What could she say or do now that her memories had surfaced. Should she tell Vera and Max. Was it really necessary? A gentle knock on the door sounded.

"Are you okay, Ma?" said Vera.

"Aye. I will be."

Marta returned, thanked the owner, and insisted they leave.

"Is there nothing here that you want to tell us about, Ma?" Max tried.

"No, Max. Let's go. I have something more important to tell you and the answers aren't here."

Both Vera and Max swapped glances.

Marta directed them into town and told Max to stop outside the Library. He did as she instructed. She had one goal, and that was to find Suzy Thomas. Her old high school was gone, according to Danielle, but her granddaughter had given her further information about how they'd come to find her. Suzy Thomas had all but admitted her mother was partially to blame for the gossip they spread about her family, and Marta was determined to find out what else she might know.

After a few inquiries she had an address for a retirement village not far from where the old high school once stood.

On arriving, Suzy invited them in and seemed oddly thrilled by her visitors.

Marta took a seat promptly. "I won't beat around the bush, Suzy. I only want to know one thing. Why did your mother dislike mine so much?"

Suzy clutched her hands in her lap and looked at a painting on the wall before speaking.

"You know, Marta, it was a terrible time for you all then. And what's done is done. Are you sure you want to know the answer to your question?"

Vera turned to look at her, her forehead crinkling.

"Aye. I do. I already know the truth. I just want to know who else did."

"Well in that case. My mother did not like your mother because… she had an affair with my father."

Marta's eyes bulged. "She what?!" Suzy realised then this news was not what Marta had expected to hear at all. "Are you sure?"

"Yes. I'm very sure."

"But how?"

"Well. Perhaps you don't know as much as you thought. It was a few years after I got married that Mum told me about Maggie. Apparently she had seduced Dad because your father, Lionel, was sterile - because of his injuries from the war. Maggie was desperate to give him a son after you. She'd tried but couldn't conceive. She told my father that she feared Lionel would leave her because…"

"Yes?"

"Because, you were not his child either. Your mother was so desperate, and very attractive I might add. It's no wonder my father took pity on her and gave her what she wanted."

Vera and Max were at a loss for words.

"So Harry and Jimmy? They're not…you mean to say they're *your* half-brothers too?"

"Yes." Suzy frowned. "Well I can't be a hundred percent sure about Jimmy, but Harry is definitely Dad's child."

"Oh good heavens!" Marta cried. "Who else knew about this?"

"Just my parents and yours, and possibly Mrs Heslop. I'm sad to say that when you fell into disgrace my mother made a plan to rid our family of yours for good. I don't think she did it out of hate, I think she only meant to hurt Maggie the way she'd been hurt by my father."

"I don't blame her." Marta stared into the wall as if she could see right through it.

Suzy cleared her throat. "So you knew then, that you weren't Lionel's?"

"Yes. I guess deep down I knew. I didn't want to believe it, so I left the memory behind when we left here. But Mum left me a letter explaining things after she died. But still, if what you said is true, that still leaves me with questions. If Lionel wasn't my father, and I certainly wasn't a child of your father's, then who was my father?"

Suzy cleared her throat again and dipped her eyes. "Well I do recall some chatter amongst the mothers. It was said that Maggie might have been pregnant before Lionel returned from the war. That usually only meant one thing, you were a war baby. If that's true then your father was likely an American solider here on leave."

"Really, you think so?"

"I can't be certain. But if I were you I'd request a verified copy of my birth certificate from the registries office. Most of the restrictions on old births certificates have been lifted. But if that leads nowhere, then I'm afraid your trail will end. It would be nigh on impossible to track down a US soldier on not much more than a few dates and hearsay."

"I'm sure you're right."

"But, Ma," said Max, "wouldn't you like to at least try?"

"I would. But based on how little time Lizzy had to find me. I don't hold out much hope I'll find anything."

"Well. That's why you have us." Max smiled. "Jess and Ella are going to love this!"

Vera didn't look one bit excited by the prospect at all.

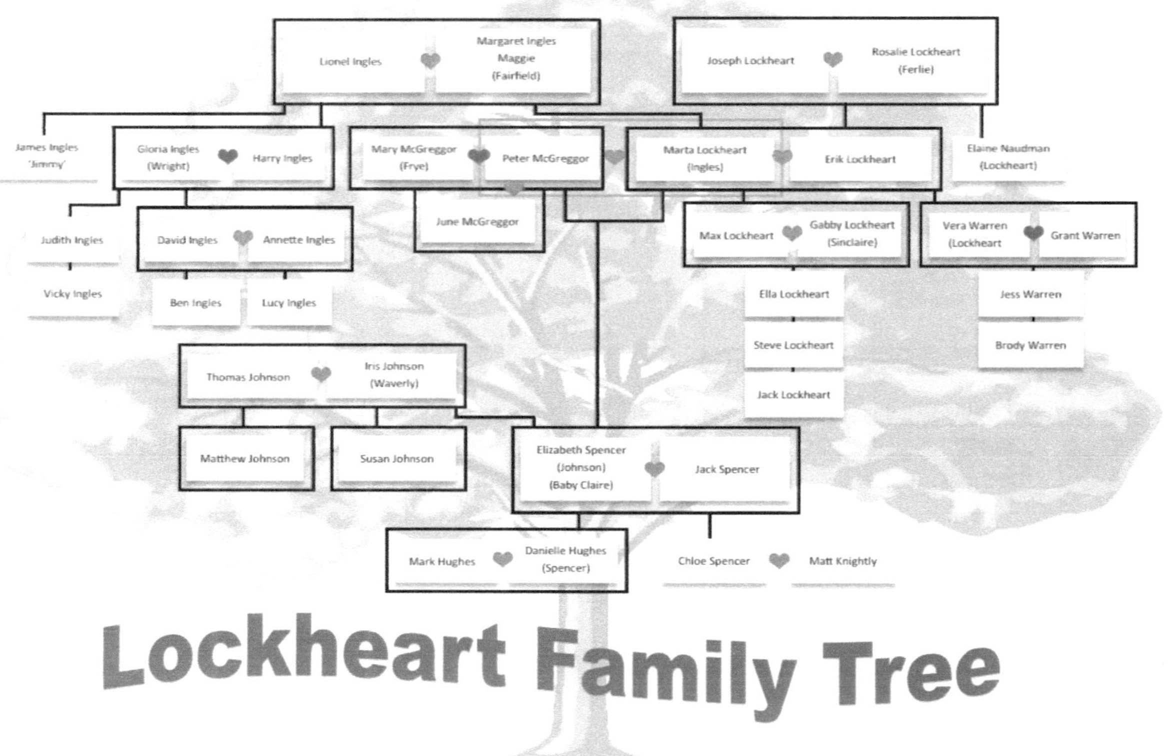

Lionel Ingles
Margaret Ingles Maggie (Fairfield)
Joseph Lockheart
Rosalie Lockheart (Ferlie)
James Ingles 'Jimmy'
Gloria Ingles (Wright)
Harry Ingles
Mary McGreggor (Frye)
Peter McGreggor
Marta Lockheart (Ingles)
Erik Lockheart
Elaine Naudman (Lockheart)
Judith Ingles
David Ingles
Annette Ingles
June McGreggor
Max Lockheart
Gabby Lockheart (Sinclaire)
Vera Warren (Lockheart)
Grant Warren
Vicky Ingles
Ben Ingles
Lucy Ingles
Ella Lockheart
Jess Warren
Steve Lockheart
Brody Warren
Jack Lockheart
Thomas Johnson
Iris Johnson (Waverly)
Matthew Johnson
Susan Johnson
Elizabeth Spencer (Johnson) (Baby Claire)
Jack Spencer
Mark Hughes
Danielle Hughes (Spencer)
Chloe Spencer
Matt Knightly
Lockheart Family Tree

Note from the Author

My sincerest thanks for reading my book. It is because of readers like you that I continue to write this series. Your feedback and encouragement make it all worth the effort.

I hope you enjoyed the second instalment in my Lockheart Mysteries series, and I trust you'll be eager to read the next one too.

It has been a rip-roaring dash to complete my second novel. I began writing *Locked in Lies*, way back in early 2017. The story came to me while I was finishing up book 1, *Locked & Found*. Marta had been quietly waiting in the side-lines for her turn. She was desperate to further come clean about all the secrets she'd been hiding away.

I made very little progress on it until, November 2017, when I was able to get away to a little bach at Ohope beach to continue writing it during NanoWriMo (National Novel Writing Month). Thanks to my mother taking over all housekeeping responsibilities, over four days I was able to write almost half of the book. But as life goes, returning home brought all kinds of distractions and other commitments. So in a bid to make any kind of progress I turned my attention back to editing book 1 and set the goal of releasing *Locked & Found* later in 2018 - A goal I actually achieved!

I now had much more motivation to return to book 2 and give it the push it needed. A new target was set. I still had at least a third of it to write and only two months to get it done! This was to be no easy feat and took every one of my wits to succeed, but the proof is in your hands!

Once again I must thank my wonderful writers group. The Central Coast to Coast chapter of RWNZ. They never cease to be an amazing source of support. I am most sincerely grateful to them all.

Also, a big thanks to my family for their love and support and to my mother, Janette, who has been a wonderful source of dinners, guidance, and motivation.

A final shout-out also goes to my wonderful Beta-readers who have helped nudge me in the right direction.

I am glad to know that I still have at least one, possibly two, more stories to write about the Lockheart family, and I am eager to get the next book out to you as soon as it's complete. Vera's tale and the origins of the Lockheart family will no doubt enrage and excite you as all the pieces of the puzzle come together. I am so incredibly excited for you to read it.

The best way to support me to continue my writing is to post your honest review. It is so helpful when readers like you write a few lines about your experience with one of my books. You can do this at www.goodreads.com, or www.amazon.com

It is my greatest wish that you enjoyed this Tale from the Tea Cup and that it lingers with you in some way.

Until next time,

384

About the Author

Meredith Reece is addicted to tea and spends much of her time crafting her tales over countless cups of the stuff.

Meredith has authored high stakes Young and New Adult Family mystery sagas that'll make you wonder if any such secrets lurk in your own family tree.

While sifting through her grandmother's photographs, for use on a heritage quilt, Meredith became fascinated by the countless generations who had come before her and lived seemingly ordinary lives just like her own. But searching deeper, she found their stories were filled with loves, losses and life's little triumphs. It is these home truths that have become an integral part of her writing and form the life lessons that are woven throughout her tales.

After almost three years of writing and editing, Meredith's debut novel, *Locked & Found*, finally made its way into the world in late 2018.

Locked in Lies, is the second of three in the *Lockheart Mysteries* series and was much tougher to write than the first. The final instalment in the Lockheart Mysteries series, *Locked in Time*, will round out the family saga and delve deeper into Vera's history and the origins of the Lockheart Family. As always - the assortment of adventures, both sweet and savoury, are best enjoyed alongside your favourite beverage - whether that's tea or not!

Writing has become one of Meredith's greatest pleasures and each story that's comes through her fingertips is a wonder - even to herself.

Meredith's past careers include being a fashion designer, a self-taught cake decorator, a Clinical Massage Therapist, a craft business entrepreneur, and a travel blogger.

She has hot air ballooned over the plains of Nevada, skied the slopes of the Remarkables, cycled the Otago rail trail, and during the summer she completes more of New Zealand's Great Walks.

One day, she would like to walk the PCT (from Mexico to Canada).

Her dream is to continue to write family tales, and discover new and exotic blends of tea.

She is mother to one amazingly talented daughter, and wife to a husband who patiently reads everything she writes (Bless him). They live in New Zealand with their cat, Willow, and are often away travelling in their campervan, 'Boots,' during the summer.

To find out more about this author's
upcoming releases and free giveaways,

Sign up for her newsletter and join the community.

Or, come chat with me on Facebook at:
Meredith Reece - Author

You can also visit the loft on my website @

www.meredithreece.com

You can find me on Pinterest @meredithreecewrites
or on Instagram @meredith.reece.writes
Meredith hasn't bothered to sign up for Twitter yet -
but give it time and she'll get around to it eventually

– if she believes she is 'Twitty' enough to do so.
Leave your honest review at
www.goodreads.com or www.amazon.com

LOCKHEART MYSTERIES SERIES
Locked & Found
Locked in Lies
Locked in Time

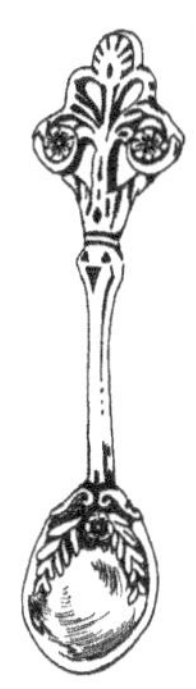